"Clive…Oh, Clive, baby…Oh God I'm so…" She leaned over me. The blood from my shirt soaked her skin, turning it a brownish red. As I looked in her eyes, I could feel her tears, touching my face, as her soft hands used to. Then I realized that I couldn't really feel anything. Because I was dead.

I looked down at me, lying there motionless, and I saw her sobbing over me. Shaking me, trying to will me back to life. But I knew it was too late. I felt this detachment, but at the same time an inexplicable heaviness. Something was pulling me back toward my body, which I didn't really even feel was mine anymore. Something wasn't letting me leave. Suddenly, the room was light, brighter than I've ever seen it. I couldn't see her, or me. Just this blinding light. Whispers from eternity called me, telling me that I had to find out. I had to make peace for peace to come to me.

A DEAD MAN SPEAKS

LISA JONES JOHNSON

Genesis Press, Inc.

Obsidian

An imprint of Genesis Press, Inc.
Publishing Company

Genesis Press, Inc.
P.O. Box 101
Columbus, MS 39703

All characters in this book have no existence outside the imagination of the author and have no relation whatsoever to anyone bearing the same name or names. They are not even distantly inspired by any individual known or unknown to the author and all incidents are pure invention.

ISBN: 1-58571-203-5
Manufactured in the United States of America

First Edition

Visit us at www.genesis-press.com
or call at 1-888-Indigo-1

DEDICATION

I would first like to dedicate this book to my sister Stephanie J. Marioneaux whose enthusiastic response to my earliest manuscript provided me with the impetus to continue on what ultimately proved to be a long and winding road. Along that road I also received invaluable support and encouragement from my parents, William B. Jones and Joanne F. Jones and from my brother Walter C. Jones, to whom this book is also dedicated. Finally, I dedicate this book to the "two Jarones" in my life, first to my husband Jarone Johnson, Jr., without whom I would not have been able to persevere in this endeavor and who is the love of my life and second to our son Jarone III, the light of both of our lives.

ACKNOWLEDGMENTS

I would first like to acknowledge my agent, Lisa Davis. Her unflagging enthusiasm, tireless work and invaluable insight have made this book possible. I truly appreciate her dedication and her ability to persevere, without which, this book may not have been published. I would also like to acknowledge Marie Brown who was the first agent to take a personal interest in my work and who first introduced me to Lisa Davis. I would also like to acknowledge the support that has been given by one of my closest friends, Raphael R. Carty who read the book in its earliest form and has always been an enthusiastic supporter of this project. Finally, I would like to acknowledge the excellent work of all of the editors and staff at Genesis Press in bringing this book to print.

CHAPTER ONE

New York 1987

The acrid smell of burning coke was everywhere. Seeping into the soft, plush furniture, burrowing into the silky carpet and the smooth walls. It stinks, but I didn't mind 'cause there was nothing like it. Opened up the mind, made a man forget himself, and God knows I needed that. *Her hand rubbed my cheek. Tiny, soft hands.*

My mind drifted back over the evening. It had only been a few hours earlier, but now it seemed like an eternity…Wall Street faces flowed past me, my colleagues, my friends…my enemies.

"Congratulations, Clive…great work, stupendous fourth quarter."

My enemies surrounded me, whispering words of praise, silently wishing that I'd fall. I wanted to close my mind on everything and walk away from my life. But I couldn't, one more deal, that's all, just this last one, and I'd be free. For good.

I noticed him watching me, envy creeping around the corners of his eyes. Maneuvering his way over to me as if he'd been holding back, waiting for the moment to drop it. "We need to talk…"

I looked through him, a short dark squirrel of a man, with wide-set eyes and a large nose, his wrinkled, bald head made him look older than his forty years. His body quivered with anxiousness as he sidled closer to me. I wondered for the first time, how I'd ever brought him in, why I'd ever trusted him. "Not now…"

"But Clive…"

"We'll talk tomorrow…"

"Tomorrow may be too late…"

"Why?…"

"It's just that…well I got a call, from…" And he lowered his voice.

"Not here." I interrupted. My enemies surrounded me. I couldn't afford even one slip, one minor indiscretion. Now I hissed angrily, more at myself for ever making myself vulnerable to his manipulation. "I told you we'd talk tomorrow."

"But what about later tonight..."

"I'm leaving the city, I won't have time."

He rocked back on the sides of his shoes, the way he always did when he was angry, but knew better than to say anything, pleading, almost begging me to listen to him, to give him the dignity he thought he deserved. "But they want to increase their position, and we'd have to make the trade tomorrow morning—"

"So then just do it." I turned my back on him, leaving a trail of whispers behind me.

I slipped into my car, the creamy leather seats enfolding me as I whizzed down the expressway...the smell of the ocean filled the car...an aphrodisiac, teasing my senses. I thought about her waiting for me...opening the door...And then I saw her face, the light green eyes clouded against her golden, taffy-colored skin, the thick mop of dark, curly hair framing her face. How often had I held her, how often had I seen her lips part in that same half-teasing, half-defiant smile...

"Hi..."

I grabbed her, wanting to make love to her before I told her. But she smiled playfully, pushing me away. "Look what I got."

She pulled out a gram of icy, white coke, licking the edge of the paper hungrily. "To celebrate." Would she still want to celebrate when I told her that I'm leaving, but not with her? All the years between us, but I still can't do it; I still can't surrender my soul to her. Would she understand this time, too?

"Here, Clive. It's good..." A sucking noise. The dull light glinted against the pipe, trembling ever so slightly. *She must really be fucked up.*

"Almost as good as the first time...remember..."

That's what she always said. Sssssssssssss, a nice long one. My eyes shut tightly, letting the *feeling* curl over me like a woman's touch, soft, seductive, and always so deadly.

"I'm gonna get some champagne." She leaned down over me, kissing me slowly. I could taste the coke on her lips. Her hand rubbed my cheek. *Tiny, soft hands.*

My eyes followed her small body weaving out of the room, down the hallway, and into the kitchen. I closed my eyes again, going over every detail of my plan in my mind for the hundredth or maybe thousandth time; I'd lost track now. Every step sharpened by time and urgency. One more week, and I'd have the final payment and my freedom from a life that was no longer mine.

I was finally starting to relax; the blow was starting to kick in. It always took longer when I was tensed up, but now the tingly feeling was rushing through me. A sharp, searing pain was suddenly tearing through my back, ripping the breath out of me. I doubled over. It felt as if someone had taken a thousand knives and exploded them in me. And it was all a blur, except for blood everywhere: on my chest, covering my hands, the white carpet, and the room's empty.

And I realize, I'd been fuckin' shot…somebody's…but now the room was spinning. I knew this was it. The dark curtains were enveloping me and then the light…like the light at home, soft…beckoning…taking me to the place I thought I'd forgotten. And then I smiled, I understood now, all the years, all the money…the lies, but you could never escape, it would always pull you back…

CHAPTER TWO

Hendersonville, Mississippi 1957, Clive: Four Years Old

"How's my little Clive?" Daddy scooped me up as if I were a bundle of soft rags.

I laughed and buried my head in his warm chest, which smelled of tobacco and sweat. He lifted me up so high. Sitting right there on top of his shoulders, I was ten feet tall. I looked into his face, dark brown, and smooth as stone. The kind I'd throw in the muddy puddles of water out back. And when Daddy laughed, it was that big laugh that I knew even God must hear...shaking the sides of the house.

Until we'd hear Ma's voice, always the same. "Lorenzo, put him down! Clive, I tol' you to stop horsin' 'round in the mornin' with your father."

Ma almost never smiled. In fact, I can't remember when she ever smiled, except maybe in church when the preacher got going. But that was only on Sunday. The rest of the days she was just a tall, thin woman with a long, hard line where the smile should be on her face. I don't think she was really sad, maybe just mad. Especially when she'd touch me with her hard, red hands.

Ma worked at a big place in town, sewing buttons on hundreds of dresses. So when she got home at night, usually after it was already dark, she'd bang around in the kitchen making dinner for Daddy and me. She hated doing it. And then she'd eat, without saying a word.

"If he gits sick, I'm the one who's gotta stay home and take care a him, and here you're like to freeze him to death, put him back in the bed."

"But, Ma, I wanna get up..."

"Sarah, the boy's not a baby anymore..."

"And he's not growed yet either." Without saying another word, she'd walk back into the tiny bedroom, muttering something to herself.

Me and Daddy smiled, sharing our private joke. Daddy wrapped me up in a blanket. The big red one that had MILLERS DRY GOODS on it. It had a big hole in the bottom, so Daddy tucked it up under me and carried me over to the leaky furnace. "Ready, partner?"

"Yep!"

"Let's see what we can git outta her."

He rared way back and gave the heater a big kick. The heater made these grunting, gurgling kinds of noises, just before one big wheeze, and then a blast of warm dry air.

"Guess she's in a real good mood today, feels pretty hot."

Daddy took my hands in his huge ones, and we stood over the heater together. The heat was tickling me, running all up under my hands, shoving away the last little bits of cold. And I didn't even care that Ma never smiled at me.

CHAPTER THREE

1962

"Sssshhhh!!!!"

"Aw shut up, Clive. You always bossin'."

"Look, if you don't shut up, somebody'll hear us."

"Well I don't care. Don't think this's such a good idea anyway. What if—"

I shoved Jesse in the ribs to be quiet. Fat Mr. Arbunk was heaving across the street. He stopped for a minute and looked over in our direction, squinting in the early morning sun. I motioned for Andy and Jesse to get closer so he couldn't see us behind the magnolia bushes. Mr. Arbunk scratched his wormy lookin' head, tilted it toward us, then scratched his butt. Andy snickered. I glared at him. We had to keep real quiet. We curled up further under the bush so the only thing you could see was green leaves and big, droopy, white Magnolia flowers.

But I wasn't looking at them; my eyes were fixed on the object of this intense secrecy. Across the street, next to the creaky post office. The gleaming new playground. A slide—the biggest piece of shiny steel I'd ever seen. Just waitin' for me to glide down at a hundred miles an hour. And the swings with the red leather seats, dangling lazily in the wind. Surrounding what had to be the closest thing to heaven I'd ever seen, was a nasty-looking black wire fence with WHITES ONLY stamped on it.

The playground was empty. It was early Saturday morning, so none of the white kids were up yet. Just as I planned it. Post office wasn't even open. And except for Mr. Arbunk who'd disappeared down a narrow alley, the town's main street was completely empty.

Further down the same street was the other playground: the swings completely broken, the slide not even worth lookin' at, much less using. And the dirty, rusted fence that surrounded it had COLORED ONLY plastered across it. The first time I saw their playground, I knew I was gonna use it. I just had to get my troops in line. That's what I called Jesse and Andy when we played war with the Jeffers boys. I was always the general, and Jesse and Andy were my troops, so I guess I just got used to thinkin' of them like that.

I motioned for them to follow me. Finger pressed against my lips telling them to BE QUIET! They were a little chicken. I really had to keep them in line. But this was the best thing we'd done yet. It was worth everything.

I whispered, "Okay, jus' follow me." I looked to the right, then the left. The big clock in the square toned seven times. I froze. Jesse and Andy scurried back to the Magnolia bush. Disgustedly, I motioned for them to get back over here.

They crawled out slowly, looking around. Then, they reluctantly followed me across the street. I don't know how many times I'd thought about this. Climbing over the black fence. Hoisting myself over the top. I was a pirate, capturing the prize ship. "C'mon, last one in's a rotten egg!" I ran over to the slide. And just about jumped up the ten steps to the top. Looking down over the town, I was the *king*.

Whoosh. The wind sung around my ears, whipping across my head. "C'mon, Andy, get your big, fat butt over here. Jesse's got you beat!"

"You worry 'bout yourself. I'm right behind y'all!"

Andy clunked up the steps of the slide, plopping down on the cold steel and flying down after me. Again and again. I don't remember how many times. But every time I did it, I was on top of the world; and nobody, not Ma, not nobody could stop me now.

"Why you little pickanninnies! What the hell you doin' in there?!!!!"

My heart literally jumped outta my stomach into my mouth. I don't think I was ever so scared. Even when Ma went out back and got the switch, and I knew she was gonna lay into me. This was different 'cause this was the white man. Or the Ofay or the bogeyman like

Daddy sometimes called 'em when they weren't listenin. And everybody knew what the bogeyman did to you.

"I said what the hell are you little coloreds doin' there?!"

My mind suddenly started working again. I ran around the slide and in between the swings with Jesse and Andy right behind me. There was another gate in the back—if we could just make it there before the white man got over there.

"Just like a bunch of dumb negras. You really think you kin outrun me!" He heaved over to the fence, blocking the way, but I wasn't giving up.

I kicked him as hard as I could in the knee, yelling to Andy and Jesse, "Run!!!!"

"Why you little…sheet! There's negras in the white playground!" He shouted at the top of his mean squeaky voice. "There's negras in the white playground!"

Andy cried, and Jesse looked like he was about to start.

"I tol' you we shoundna…"

Suddenly, the whole square was filled with angry white men. You'd a thought we'd killed somebody or something.

Slap. A fat, white hand smacked me across my face as I tried to scamper away. Another white man had already nabbed Jesse and Andy.

And the last thing I remember was thinking maybe this wasn't such a good idea after all.

"Look at them little negras, just like little monkeys over there…"

"Yeah throw 'em a chicken bone. You knows how negras likes chicken." A loud, raspy laugh belched out of the dirty sheriff who sat in front of the jail as he whipped a greasy chicken bone through the bars.

Me, Andy, and Jesse were huddled in a corner of the stinking jail. It smelled like piss and vomit. That's 'cause in the corner was this drunk colored man. He must've thrown up in his sleep 'cause little pieces of dried vomit were stuck to his face and to the front of his torn shirt. They'd thrown us in here after they pulled us outta the playground.

Andy and Jesse just kept crying the whole time and asking for their mamas. I don't know why, but I didn't cry. I couldn't. I guess I just knew that somehow we were gonna get outta this. I mean, they couldn't keep us here forever. The colored man in the corner hiccupped and opened one eye, tipping dazedly over in our direction.

Jesse wiped the tears off his cheeks and hissed to me angrily.

"It's all your fault…I tol' you I didn't wanna do it…I tol' you. Now they gonna leave us in here…"

Andy jumped and shoved me. "Yeah, now they'll never let us see our mamas again!"

I knew we'd get out, but I couldn't think of anything to say to Andy and Jesse to convince them. I just hugged my knees against my chest and looked at the fat, drunk man in the corner snoring again.

He sounded like a sick horse. The deputy sheriff pressed his pink face against the bars of the jail and cracked up listening to us. "Well, now I guess that'll teach y'all darkies to stay in your place. Don't you know you can't do like white folks can?"

The other sheriff spat some tobacco in our direction. A big wad of smelly, dark-brown tobacco landed right by my foot. "That's the problem with the negra nowdays. With all them sit-ins and what not, they really startin' to think they is equal to us."

Jingling his keys, the sheriff gnawed on his tobacco some more, waddled over to the jail and stood next to the deputy. His breath smelled like chitlins and sour lemonade. "It'll be a cold day in hell 'fore any of yous ever have what the white man's got. You remember that, stay in yo place and you be all right. But you start thinkin' you can have what's ours and only ours, and well…little negras, I guess you'll just end up right where y'ar now. Under the got damned jailhouse."

Right under the jailhouse alright, for playing in their playground. Or dead. They never did like us to play with their toys. I guess that's why I'm sitting in a pool of blood now. My future, my plans, my life all ebbing out in a bloody mess around me. All for playing in their playground. And now the thoughts are rushing, and I hear the voices, but where is she, how could she leave me? Did she...No, I couldn't believe that. It must be *them*. And the voices in my head that won't stop, the spinning wheels of my past rushing at me like a thousand crazed horses...

*Snort, snort, heee, heee...*The deputy laughed some more, and then turned his skinny butt to us and farted—a big, fat, disgusting one.

And at that moment I knew that I was getting out of Hendersonville, out of the South, out of everything that could ever remind me of this place. And I wasn't scared anymore 'cause I knew that there was a whole lot more out there than this stinking jail, and I knew I was getting far away from there.

"Well lookie who's here. If it ain't yo mamas."

"Maaa!!!!" Andy and Jesse jumped up. The three of us ran to the bars of the jail as Missus Caters and Missus Lewis ran over to the jail. Only Ma wasn't there. I couldn't believe it. I mean, I always thought she didn't like me, but...

"There's my boy!" Daddy's big voice boomed out from the corner.

"Daaaddy!!!!!" I don't know why now, but I cried. I mean really cried. Daddy had come for me. And I just couldn't stop crying.

CHAPTER FOUR

Ma's Revenge

"I tol' you the boy's no good. I'm like to lose my job after this. And then what're we gonna do? You ain't had a paintin' job in months, and winter's comin, who you thinks gonna hire you if Clive's stirrin' up all kinda trouble?"

"Sarah, white folks is always jumpin' up and down 'bout somethin'. I ain't worried. We made it every other time. This ain't no different."

"Yeah it is. You don't know how mad those white folks is. Talking 'bout not letting the white kids use the playground 'cause negras been there. And all cause that boy broke into there. Jus' like a thief he is. I don't raise no thieves in my family. When I git through with him!"

"Sarah, the boy was just havin' fun. It ain't no big deal."

"Ain't no big deal!"

I could hear Ma slam her chair against the wall. I was in the other room with the door tightly shut, but I knew from the way she sounded that her face looked like an ugly steam engine black and belching smoke.

"Yeah, Sarah, it ain't no big deal. It'll blow over, and everythin'll be fine again."

"Look, I hear the crackers talkin' in town, they saying that Clive is the ringleader. That he's dangerous. That he might start some mess with the colored folks."

I could hear Daddy snort, like the way he did when he didn't believe something. "The boy's ten years old. What the hell kinda ringleader can he be? Who in they right mind gonna follow a ten-year-old? That's just crackers talkin' crazy."

"No it ain't. I tell ya, Lorenzo, the boy's gotta go."

Suddenly, it felt like a cold hand went up my spine. I ran out into the other room shouting, "Nooooooooo! I don't wanna go away!"

Daddy walked over to me calmly. He was never upset about nothin'. He put his arm around my shoulder—warm and heavy, as if I could lean on it and count on him. "You ain't goin nowhere boy. Jus' relax. Now go on back in there. Your ma and me's talking."

I looked into Daddy's eyes, and they were the same as always—warm, dark brown with the smile underneath—and, suddenly, I felt better. He gently guided me back into the room and shut the door behind me. I pressed my ear against the door. They were whispering, really hissing, but I could still hear them. "I don't *ever* want to hear you talking about sending the boy away again. He's staying right here."

Silence. Just the sound of Ma banging pots and pans on the stove. She knew better than to say anything.

"Jail bird! Jail bird! Clive's a stinkin' jail bird!"

I glared at the taunting group of kids. My friends, or at least they used to be, were just as bad as the white kids in town. Everywhere I went these days, somebody was teasing me or pointing a finger. I guess it's because the town's so small. That's why I knew I was getting out someday. *When I grow up, I'll never be here again. And all these kids, they'll just wish that they'd been my friend?*

But right now, all I could do was turn my back on them. Sometimes I'd yell back at them, but today I didn't even care. I just wanted to get home and away from them.

I walked down the narrow road alone. Normally, my troops would've been with me, but Andy and Jesse's mamas said they couldn't play with me anymore. And truth is, they were both so mad at me still, I don't think they would've played with me anyway.

It was fall, and the leaves were in high piles along the road. Red, yellow, and the crunchy brown ones. I jumped in, and it felt like a deep, prickly mattress of leaves.

Swishing my arms back and forth in the leaves, I laughed. Sometimes I'd pretend I was rich and I lived in a big house with big, soft mattresses. Not the narrow, stickly ones that I had. And I knew that I'd just lie in bed all day and have people serve me ice cream and sodas. That's what I'd do if I was rich.

Suddenly, a dark cloud moved across the sky. I felt huge, heavy drops of rain on my face. I jumped up and ran the rest of the way home, trying to dodge the raindrops and doing fancy moves around the puddles. When I finally got up to the front steps, I was soaked and panting hard from running. I pushed open the door and then stopped.

Ma was standing there looking at me. Not saying a word. Immediately, I started feeling strange. She was usually still at work this time of day. But that wasn't as strange as the fact that Gramma Deedee, Ma's mother, was also sitting there. She didn't even live in Hendersonville. I'd never actually been to her house. All I knew was that she lived on a farm and that she worked all the time. Or at least that's what Ma always said.

They both had looks on their faces as if they'd been waiting for me. Then I saw it. The battered suitcase next to them.

Ma hissed at me, "Where you been, boy?"

I tried to swallow, but my throat was too dry.

"Well, it don't matter now. We got your things all ready."

"What d'you mean?"

"You're going to live with Gramma Deedee for a while."

Suddenly all the fears that I'd had at the back of my mind rushed forward. "No! Daddy said he'd never send me away!"

"Boy, shut up and get over here."

I tried to bolt for the door. The only thing I was thinking was that I had to get out of there. I had to find Daddy. He'd make everything all right.

Ma had reached a long, calloused hand over to me. She grabbed my collar and pulled my face up to hers. "Now look. I had enough of you. You're going with Ma, and that's it. Your Daddy ain't here, and you're not going to him." She slapped me so hard that I fell down on the floor. My face was burning, but I was determined not to give her the satisfaction of crying.

Gramma Deedee lifted her heavy frame out of the rocking chair and grabbed the suitcase. "C'mon, boy. It's better for everbody. If you stays here, no tellin' what the white folks'd do to you or your mama and daddy."

I turned and looked into Ma's eyes, narrow, and yellow at the edges, and I realized at that moment that I hated my mother.

I stared up at the cracked ceiling. The room was dark and close. Gramma Deedee was breathing heavily in the bed. I didn't even have a bed, just a strip of rag on the dirt floor. I swallowed back a tear. I couldn't believe that Daddy had just forgotten me. It'd been almost a week since Ma had forced me to go with Gramma Deedee. I kept expecting Daddy to come, but everyday would end as it started—out in the fields pulling weeds between the rows of brown, prickly cotton stalks. I felt like a slave.

At night I ate the foul tasting food that Gramma Deedee made. Now I knew why Ma couldn't cook. Everything was boiled in heavy smelly grease. We didn't even have a bathroom in the house. Just a hole out back. But nights were the worse. I hurt all over. There was nothing I could do besides eat and go to bed as soon as it was dark. Gramma Deedee didn't have any electricity, but even if she did, we'd probably still go to bed 'cause she never said anything to me.

She was an old version of Ma: tall, skinny, same color skin and her hair in tight curls around her face except that they were grey instead of black like Ma's. Her hands were also like Ma's: hard and calloused. The kind that gave you goose bumps if they touched you.

I tried to stay awake as long as I could. I was always afraid a field mouse would bite me or that one of the big, black, shiny beetles that crawled around in the corners would run over my face. But this night I just couldn't keep my eyes open, and I fell into a deep, unhappy sleep.

A hand *clamped* over my mouth. I bolted awake, but I couldn't say anything. Then I was being picked up, and I was looking into Daddy's eyes. Relief, happiness, everything good I'd ever felt rushed over me. I looked over toward Gramma Deedee who was snoring and completely unaware that I was escaping finally. Daddy hadn't forgotten me.

CHAPTER FIVE

Daddy and Me

I settled into the stiff seat of the bus. My face pressed against the dirt-speckled window. Trees, bushes, little houses, and colored kids on bicycles all passed by me. I'd never been on a bus before, and I felt free. I knew I was headed someplace where I'd be safe 'cause I was with Daddy.

"Hungry?"

"Uh huh!"

"Well let's see what we got." Daddy opened a greasy brown bag and took out the biggest juiciest piece of fried chicken I'd ever seen. Then he dug down further into the bag and took out a soft, crusty biscuit and the best of all, a big bottle of strawberry soda! Now I knew I was in heaven. Just me and Daddy and the best food I'd ever eaten. In between munches of chicken and big gulps of soda, I listened eagerly to Daddy.

"Now the way I figure, we'll settle in Aiken for a little while. I found a nice place for us to live in. It's small, but it'll do for right now. There's lots a work there, it's kinda a boom town, lots a building going on 'cause of the new factory. So there oughta be plenty of painting work. I figure I'll be able to save up some money and buy a little house in not too long.

"I already moved all my painting gear to the place where we'll be staying. It's the colored boarding house, and the landlady, Missus Foster's her name, real nice lady, anyway she's letting me store all my stuff in the basement."

I couldn't believe this was all real. The week I spent at Gramma Deedee's seemed like a bad dream that I finally had woken from. The best thing was that Ma was nowhere around. It was just us men. Daddy and me. Thinkin' about Ma made me feel funny. I didn't want to, but

I couldn't help it. I was still mad at her for sending me away, but mainly I was confused. I thought that maybe Daddy could help me understand.

"Daddy, why doesn't Ma love me?"

Daddy looked at me with this real sad look in his eyes, which was pretty strange for Daddy, 'cause Daddy usually didn't look sad. He rubbed his hand over the top of my head and kinda played with the collar on my jacket. "She loves you, Clive."

"Then why'd she send me away? Nobody else's ma would send 'em away like that, why don't she like me Daddy, what did I do wrong?"

Daddy took my hands in his and rubbed 'em gently. "Nothin', partner, nothin' at 'tall. Your ma, she just had things kinda rough for a long time. And I think that 'cause a that she don't really know how to show that she loves folks even when she does..." His voice kinda stopped, like he was going to say something else, but he didn't. I didn't want to stop there. I'd always known there was something wrong between me and Ma, but I didn't know what. This was the first time that Daddy and me had ever been alone to talk about it.

"So Ma really loves me, Daddy?"

"Course she does..."

"Like she loves you or her own ma?"

"Sure she does." Then Daddy stopped for a second and hugged me real tight. "By and by, when you get a little older, I'll tell you some things."

"What kinda things?"

"Just some things you oughta know, but not now, when you get a little bigger. In the meantime, you gotta just try and love your ma. Don't hold things against her, even the mean things she done. Just remember she's your ma, and things ain't been easy for her. So just love her, cause she needs to be loved."

But all I could remember was the way she looked when she shoved me out the door to Gramma Deedee's house and the way she slapped me and grabbed me by the collar. "I don't care if I should love her. I don't. I hate her!"

As soon as I said it, I was sorry. I thought sure Daddy'd be mad at me. Instead, he gently rocked me back and forth, saying softly, so I could hardly hear him, "Don't ever hate nobody, Clive. Leastwise not your ma. When you hate somebody, you're the one ends up getting hurt, 'cause all the anger and bad feelings you have just eats up your insides, and 'fore you know it, you're worse off then the person you're hating. Remember you can always love somebody, even if they don't love you. God loves everybody, even when we ain't been good or nice. That's what it says in the good book, and that's how I want you to live, Clive." Daddy looked at me real serious. "Promise me that, Clive. Never hate nobody. Just try, no matter how hard it is to love 'em."

I nodded my head yes, even though I wasn't sure how or why you'd want to try and like somebody, much less love 'em if they didn't like you, but I could tell it meant a lot to Daddy. "I promise, Daddy. I won't hate nobody ever again. Not even Ma."

Daddy gave me another hug and then settled back into his seat. "Now that's my little Clive." The last thing I remember was snuggling up next to Daddy, closing my eyes and being happier than I think I'd ever been.

"Well, hello there. Aren't you a fine-looking young man?"

I sorta smiled, but I didn't quite know what to say. The landlady, held out her hand to me.

Daddy nudged me gently. "Shake Missus Foster's hand, Clive, and tell her thank you for lettin' us stay here."

"Uh...thank you..."

"Oh, it's my pleasure. I'm happy to have you both here."

Missus Foster sounded different than other colored women I'd met in town. Her voice was sweet, and she talked really proper. Maybe it was because of all the books she read. In her living room, all the walls had bookshelves from the floor to the ceiling, and they were all filled with books.

Now I could read. In fact, I could read really good, but I don't think I'd ever seen so many books in one place. Maybe in the library in town there were that many books, but it was for whites only, so I never got to go inside.

There was another way Missus Foster was different from other colored ladies I knew. She always looked kinda like a picture out of a magazine. Her hair was smooth and black, and her skin was a pretty, red-brown color that I'd never seen before, but I guess the most different thing about her was the color of her eyes, light brown. So light that when I looked into them, I could see my reflection, like a mirror.

There was no Mr. Foster, or at least nobody who lived with her. I guess he musta been dead. When I asked Daddy about it once, he just said it wasn't none of our business. So I didn't ask him again. One thing about Daddy, when he had that certain tone, I usually knew better than to ask any more questions.

The months passed nicely at Missus Foster's. Every day me and Daddy would get up early and go down to breakfast. The only other boarder was a really old man named Mr. Beavers. He would come down at 8 A.M. every morning, have a cup of steaming black coffee and a sugar donut, and then he'd go in the living room and read. Missus Foster told us that Mr. Beavers had been a teacher, but he didn't have any family or anything, so now he lived there with her. Seemed that lots of folks who didn't have anywhere to go came in and out of Missus Foster's place.

She was nice to everybody, but I think that she was the nicest to us. For instance, what she'd fix us for breakfast, every day it was something different. One day she fixed eggs in a way I'd never had before. She said it was called an omelet. There was cheese and crisp pieces of bacon and onions and tomatoes all fried in, and then she folded it over. There'd be steaming bowls of hot cereal, but not the lumpy kind that Ma would make. The kind Missus Foster would make was smooth and had a cinnamon flavor to it. Sometimes she'd plop a big raisin or cut up pieces of apple in it. It was always special.

After we had breakfast, I'd go with Daddy to his painting jobs. I couldn't get in the local colored school until the next semester, but I didn't care. I'd rather be with Daddy anyway.

I loved the way paint smelled, not as much as I loved the smell of gasoline, but that was a different kind of smell. Paint was clean, but at the same time not like soap or stuff like that. Every color had a different smell. The white paint was kinda potato-starchy smelling. The bright green paint that Daddy used for the trim of the buildings had a grassy smell to it. The best was the red paint. Daddy didn't get to use red paint much. Most of the houses in town were either white or brick with dark green or black roofs. Once in a while he got to paint a rooftop red. I'd help him get his brushes ready, and then he'd let me stir the paint with a big, long stick that he took along with him.

He'd give me my brush, and I'd paint the bottom parts, while he painted the top. Daddy would never let me paint anything where I had to get on the ladder. Said the ladder wasn't that sturdy. But I didn't care that much 'cause climbing that ladder reminded me too much of the stairs on the slide in the white playground, and right now, I didn't want to think about that too much.

At around noon Daddy would turn to me saying, "Ready to take a break, partner?"

"Yep." And I'd pull out the plastic bag with our lunch in it—usually thick, flavorful sandwiches that Missus Foster made us. Sometimes, leftover pot roast or meatloaf or my favorite, sharp cheddar cheese with mayonnaise and pickles.

At the end of the day, we'd head back to Missus Foster's. She'd have dinner ready. We'd go and sit in her living room. Sometimes she'd take out one of her books and read out loud to us, or other times, Daddy and her would talk or play cards, and I'd take out one of her other books and read it myself. Her furniture was so nice and comfortable that I could just sink in it and disappear with my book.

It was one of those times that I'd jumped in the biggest most comfortable chair, that I heard Daddy and Missus Foster talkin' about Ma. They thought I was asleep 'cause I'd closed my eyes and sunk down real far in the chair. I could hear Daddy settle into the couch. I heard the strike of a match, and I could smell the sweet, woody kinda smell of the tobacco that he put in his pipe. I knew that he was rolling his pipe around in his mouth, making little clicking noises in between his words. Missus Foster was quiet, so I guessed that she was just listenin' real hard to Daddy talk.

"When I picked up my boy and hugged him, I couldn't believe that he'd almost been taken away from me. 'Cause lemme tell ya, when I found out what Sarah had done, I almost hit her. I mean it. I almost knocked all the life outta her. And I'm not that kinda man. My daddy raised me good. 'Always respect women. Don't do nothin' to 'em that you wouldn't want me to do to your mama,' he'd say. But when I saw that she'd stole my boy away, I almost forgot everything that Pa had told me. But anyway, I stopped m'self just in time. That's when I tol' her it was over, 'tween her and me that is, and that I was gettin' my boy back, and I didn't want nothin' more to do with her."

I'd never heard Daddy talk that way before. He sounded mad, madder than I'd ever heard him, but I felt good, 'cause he was mad at Ma.

"What did she do when you told her you were leaving?" Missus Foster's voice broke in, it was real light, almost like she was singing 'stead of talking.

"Oh, she cried and begged me, but I'd already made up my mind. Truth is, I'd stopped lovin' Sarah a long time ago. She had a real nasty mean streak. And worse is that she always seemed to take it out on the boy. He was jus' the cutest thing as a baby, warn't his fault he didn't take to the breast."

I could hear Daddy make a long, sucking noise on his pipe. When he started talking again, his voice was quieter. I almost couldn't hear him, and I had to kinda edge a little closer to the end of the chair to hear him.

"Sarah had a real tough time at the delivery. Doctor said she might die. Afterwards, she was real sick. Couldn't even pick up little Clive. I pretty much took care of the boy on my own 'til he was 'bout a year.

Took her almost that long 'fore she had her strength back real good. Then she got pregnant again. We had a little girl. She was the prettiest, sweetest child you ever seen. Sarah was a different person when she was born. For pretty much the first time I 'member, 'xcept when I first met her, Sarah seemed happy."

Daddy was quiet for a minute. He took a deep breath and said softly, "Well, the baby got sick one day. And then...she...passed away. Took Sarah a long time to get over it. She didn't want no more kids after that."

"And what about you, did you want other children?" I could hear Missus Foster ask in a curious kind of way.

For a minute Daddy didn't say anything. I could hear him stretch back in his chair. "Well, truth is, I'd always wanted to be a Daddy. From the time I was twelve, I grew up pretty much on my own. My folks died in the typhoid epidemic in '32. After that I went to live with my Daddy's sister. She had a baby, cute little thing. He was always gettin' into things. Well, one day he drank something outta one of them medicine bottles. I don't really remember what it was, but after that he was never really right. I sorta became like his Daddy and big brother all in one. Then one day he went to sleep and didn't wake up. Doctor said it was from when he'd been sick b'fore. I felt real bad. Almost like it was my fault 'cause I was supposed to be watchin' him. I thought if only I'd had another chance, if only I'd seen him 'fore he'd drunk that stuff. I think right at that point I promised m'self that if I had another chance to be a real Daddy, I'd do it right. It'd be different.

"Well then things got real bad b'tween my aunt and me. Finally, when I was fifteen I just left, and then I was on my own 'til I met Sarah. When we got married and little Clive came pretty much right away, I'd got what I wanted, a son. Sure it woulda been nice to have had other kids, and if our little girl had...lived...well...it was God's will, I figure. But truth is, for me just being a daddy for Clive was enough."

Daddy stopped for a second, and I thought that I couldn't be any happier, but he kept on talking. "I tol' you that Sarah almost died when she was deliverin' Clive, and when the doctor tol' me that I might have to choose between her or the baby, I didn't even think about it for a minute. I tol' 'em that I wanted the baby."

Now, I felt happy all over. My toes even curled up. This was better than when I'd had a double chocolate ice cream cone on my birthday. I wanted to run over to Daddy and give him a big hug. But I didn't want him to stop talking, 'cause everything he said made me feel happier and happier. Daddy loved me more than Ma, more than anybody! I felt happier than I'd ever been, and I didn't want it to go away, so I just kept listenin', tryin real hard not to make a sound.

"I'll never forgit when I first saw Sarah. I'd gone to visit my cousin Joe Allen. He lived in the same town as Sarah's mama."

Daddy sat up in his chair and turned his head to the side real funny. I almost laughed. Except I couldn't, 'cause then they'd know I wasn't 'sleep, and they'd stop talking, so I just held it in real tight and watched Daddy talk. It was almost as if Ma was right there, but only the way she was then. And he was describing it so good, even everything that him and Ma had been sayin' back then. I could see it right there in front of me the way Pa could and the way it had happened back then…

Eleven Years Earlier, Lorenzo and Sarah through Lorenzo's eyes…

"M'name's Lorenzo."

"Don't b'lieve I was askin." She kinda tipped her head up so the sun covered her face in this yellow brown glow. I looked dead at her and almost had to catch myself from sayin' somethin' stupid. I'd never seen nobody like her. She was tall and pretty in a different kind of way, had her hair tied back in a ponytail with a bright red rag that matched her skirt. She had real high cheekbones. I figured she was part Indian or somethin'. And her body was lean and strong lookin', kinda like them mountain cats up in the hills, with small round breasts that I jus' knowed would fit perfect right in the palm of my hand. Her mouth was wide with lips that curled up like a flower jus' 'fore it was about to open in the sun. And her eyes were dark black and slanted on her face. She didn't say nothin'. She just kind of smiled and looked at me, like she was somebody from someplace else that had jus' come down for a little while to be with us regular folks. I felt kinda stupid. What with her not saying nothin' and me neither, so I cleared my throat and tried again.

"Uh, I didn't catch yo name...Miss..."

"Guess that's 'cause I didn't give it." She flounced that red skirt of hers, turned her back on me and started walking away. Now I wasn't no patsy, in fact I had plenty a girls after me back home, so I wasn't 'bout to just give up easy like that. So I walked faster and caught up with her, which wasn't easy 'cause she had long legs and was pretty tall. In fact, she came up almost to my nose, and I was darn near 6'5 last time I got measured.

"Mind if I walks with you?"

"Ain't no law 'ginst it, I s'ppose."

"I'm new 'round here. I came to visit my cousin. You might knows him, Joe Allen Spencer."

"Can't say I does." She turned real fast and ducked in a little shack that was sellin' lemonades and sweet corn cakes.

I figured this was my chance, so I ducked in after her, and fore she could say no, I plopped some change on the counter in front of the old colored woman dippin' the lemonade out of a big glass pitcher that was full of ice and fresh mint all swimmin' 'round together.

"We'll take two lemonades and uh...two of them corn cakes." The woman just grunted somethin' I didn't quite hear and scooped up my money. She set the lemonades in front of me and wrapped the corn cakes in a coupla pieces of clean newspaper. "Lemonade." I held the glass in front of her.

For a minute I thought she was gonna say no, but then she smiled in that funny way where I couldn't tell if it was a smile or somethin' else that was kinda uppity like she was just toleratin' ev'rybody, 'cept maybe some special ones like her.

"Thank you, Lorenzo."

My heart jumped a little bit. The way she said my name made all kinds of thoughts jumble around in my head. Things I probably shouldn't be thinkin' after only knowin' her 'bout five minutes.

She took a long sip from the glass and bit into the corn cake. Her teeth was straight and white like little soldiers, lined up perfect. As she finished it up, she raised one eyebrow. "You know, Lorenzo, I already got a fella. In fact, we're gonna be married soon's I finish high school next year."

My heart jumped a little bit, and not in a good way, but I wasn't givin up. "Well that's nice, but you ain't married yet, and I don't see your feller here, so no's harm in talking and walking, way I sees it."

"No harm, I guess."

I could tell she was likin' this.

"But I jus' don't want you t'git disappointed or nothin', Lorenzo, seein' how I'm takin. And he ain't from around here neither. His Daddy's got a big farm outside a Greenwood, not sharecroppin' neither. He's goin' to college next year, and he got me a job in the colored doctor's office. I'm gonna work in a office and study to be a nurse. I ain't workin' on no more farms. Nope. My feller wants his wife to be somethin'."

"Well that sounds real nice." I didn't really mean it, but what else could I say. "But the way I sees it, you already is somethin'. You don't need no job or nothin' else to make you somethin' you already is. And likewise, ain't no job or no big farm or nothin' that kin make somebody somethin' when they ain't nothin' to begin with." I don't know quite where that all came from, kinda surprised me, but I guess since she was speakin' her mind, I could speak mine, too.

She raised her eyebrow in that funny way again, and put the glass back on the counter, saying kinda fast, "My feller's waitin' for me. He's got his Daddy's car, you know. I best be goin." She turned and then stopped and walked back over to me and planted a big kiss on my cheek. "Thanks for the lemonade and for bein' real nice."

I knowed I musta been grinning all over the place as I said, "You never tol' me your name."

She hesitated, then looked me dead in the eye. "Sarah, m'name's Sarah Wilcox." Then she ran away. I knowed I musta turned red, even though it's pretty much impossible for me to turn red, given my color and all. Anyway, for just that one minute when she turned and kissed me, I saw somebody else. Somebody who wasn't maybe so sure of herself and wasn't so uppity as she liked folks to believe. "I'll be seein' you around, Sarah."

Missus Foster's voice broke the silence. "What happened to her young man?"

Daddy reached in his shirt pocket and took out the plastic pouch with his tobacco in it. He dipped his pipe in the pouch like it was an ice cream scooper, and then filled it all the way to the top. Shaking his head slow, he lit the pipe and continued.

"We'd see each other by and by that summer, nothin' serious, 'cause her feller would come for her every Saturday and have dinner with her folks on Sundays. I figured I'd just be a good friend, but I guess, truth be told, I was always wishin' that maybe I'd get my chance with her. Well later that summer, I heard that Sarah's feller had left her and went off with somebody else, some college gal that his mama wanted him to marry. An since he was the reasin' Sarah was gonna be movin' to Greenwood an' all an' workin' in that colored doctor's office, all that was done, and so she'd be stayin' where she was. I knew she'd be wantin' to get outta that small town, with all the folks talkin' an' all, so I figured now that she was free, it might be my only chance. I remember standin' there. My hands was sweatin. She was lookin' as pretty as the first day I'd seen her, even with everythin' that'd just happened. I took a deep breath and walked over to her.

"Mind if I come in?"

Sarah didn't say nothin. She just sat on the chair looking out the window. I hadn't seen her for almost a month. As I got a little closer, I could see that she'd lost some of her fight. I went over and sat in the chair next to hers. Real slow, I took her hand. It felt light and almost numb. Like there wasn't no life in it no more.

"Sarah, I wanted to ask you somethin, before you say anything, lemme get it all out. I already talked to yo Daddy and yo mama. And it's okay with them." I took a deep breath. "I wanna marry you, Sarah. I'm almost twenty years old, and I got a trade. I ain't rich, but I'm a real good painter, and I'll be able to keep food on the table and give us a better life than we'd be able to have stayin'in this town."

She looked up at me, and she looked almost confused, and real sad. "Do you really love me or is it jus' 'that you feels sorry for me? 'Cause I don't needs yo pity!" She turned away and wiped a tear from her cheek. I guess it shoulda hurt, her saying that and all, but truth was, even though I liked Sarah a whole lot, I don't know if I really loved her. 'Cause I don't figure I really knew love back then at twenty years old. But I was ready to be a husband, and I guess I cared as much for Sarah as I had for anybody, so I said, "I do love you, Sarah. Mor'n I ever loved anybody."

And then she started crying softly, saying over and over, "I does like you, Lorenzo. I really does. From the beginnin' I did...But all I wanted was to get outta here, get off the farm. I wanted to do somethin' with my life!" She turned back and stared at me real hard. "If you really do loves me, Lorenzo, promise me that you'll let me do somethin' with my life. Promise me I won't end up like Ma and Pa, workin' to the bone from sun up to sundown and never havin' nothin' to show for it. I don't want that. I wanna be a nurse. I wanna work in a office with people that dresses nice when they go to work. Promise me, Lorenzo. Promise me that you'll let me do that!"

I took her in my arms and held her tight. "I promise you, honey, I will."

The clock chimed and Daddy stopped, like he'd needed to take a breath after all that . Everything was quiet for a minute. All I could hear was the sound of the big clock in the corner of the room. Then I heard Missus Foster say, "I'm glad you came here." I couldn't see Missus

Foster but I guessed that she was probably smiling, 'cause her voice had that nice smiling kind of sound.

Daddy was quiet, then he cleared his throat. "It's gettin' kinda late, me and the boy better get to bed." Daddy shook me gently. "Wake up, partner, time for bed."

I had to pretend that I was sleepy even though I was wide awake and ready to burst with happiness. I pretended to yawn really loud and said, "Where am I?" It must've worked, because Missus Foster smiled at me and kissed me goodnight on the forehead. Daddy put his warm, heavy arm around me as we walked up the stairs. That night when I said my prayers, I thanked God for Daddy, for Missus Foster, and for giving me such a perfect life.

I yawned. It was still dark, but for some reason I woke up. I turned over toward Daddy's bed. The covers were thrown back, and it was empty.

I sat up. Through the half-light, I could make out his coat and boots neatly by the door, like always. So he couldn't be far. *Must've gone to the bathroom down the hall.* I plopped back down on the couch. Pulling the thick comforter around my chin.

I don't really remember what I was thinking about. I guess I figured I'd just wait up till Daddy got back from the bathroom. But all of a sudden I got really sleepy, something about the warm spread and the comforting silence.

Creeeeeaaakk. I turned over. *Creeeeaaaakk.* I opened one eye. I realized I must've been asleep awhile because now it was almost dawn. The room had a grey white light to it as the door opened slowly. I jumped awake. "Daddy?"

"Go back to sleep, Clive, jus' had to use the john."

Daddy came over and kissed me on the forehead, then climbed back in his bed.

For the first time in my life, I knew Daddy wasn't telling me the truth. He couldn'tve been in the john all that time. When I woke up the first time it was dark, and now it was almost light. But I felt funny saying anything to Daddy about it, so I decided I'd just try really hard to stay awake the next night and see if he left again.

I scrunched my eyes up really tightly. I wanted Daddy to think that I was asleep. I could hear the springs on his bed as he got up slowly, grabbing his bathrobe. I waited until he'd closed the door behind him, then I tiptoed over to the door and carefully opened it. The hallway was empty. I couldn't tell whether Daddy was in the john or somewhere else.

I crept out into the hall, sliding against the wall toward the john. Opening the door. Empty. My breath started gettin real fast. The last time I felt like that was when I saw Ma and Grandma DeeDee waiting for me. I couldn't think where Daddy could be. Maybe he went downstairs for a drink of water. I walked softly down the stairs. Everything was completely dark. No lights or anything. He couldn't be there. Now I was really scared. Where could he be? I was walking back up the stairs when I heard it. A low moaning was coming from Missus Foster's room. I ran down the hallway.

The door was slightly open, so I looked in. I couldn't believe what I was seeing, Daddy's naked body on top of Missus Foster, and she was naked, too. They were moving together in rhythm and moaning and touching and kissing each other all over. I knew what they were doing. Me, Andy, and Jesse had seen a book about it. But I couldn't believe that Daddy was…My heart fell to my feet.

That's why she'd been so nice to us. She just wanted to get Daddy. I felt sick and betrayed. And Daddy, too. All I could think was what if they got tired of me and sent me back to Ma's. I closed the door softly and went back into our room. Alone.

The next morning Missus Foster placed a big bowl of hot cereal in front of me. It had a juicy piece of apple in it. Normally, I would've attacked it eagerly, but this morning I didn't want to eat anything. Especially nothing *she* fixed.

Daddy looked over at me and frowned. "Eat your food, Clive. We gotta go clear over to the other side of town this morning, and we won't be eatin' agin for a while."

"I'm not hungry."

Missus Foster gave Daddy a puzzled look. "But that's your favorite kind, honey." She smiled at me.

But I turned away, bitterly. *Traitor.*

Daddy pushed his chair back. "I'm goin' upstairs to git my things. When I come back, I 'xpect all that food to be gone. You hear?"

I looked into the cereal, trying to bury my hurt in the steam coming up off the bowl. "Yeah, Daddy." He looked over to Missus Foster, raised his eyebrows, and then walked up the stairs.

A few days later, Daddy asked me to go to the hardware store in town and get him some new paint brushes. Usually it would've taken a while, but today there wasn't hardly anybody in the store, so I bought the brushes and got back in double quick time. Now I almost wished I'd taken longer.

When I got in the house, I looked around for Daddy, but the house was empty. They must've gone out somewhere. I was about to head into the kitchen when I heard voices coming from a little room off the living room. I'd never been in that room before. It was Missus Foster's private room. I don't know what she had in there, maybe pictures of her and her husband, but anyway, the door was always closed and Daddy had told me not to go in there.

So when I heard the voices, I was a little surprised. I was about to call out Daddy's name, but I decided to go on and investigate on my own. The door was open, and if I slid myself against the wall, I could just see in the room without them seeing me. I stuck my neck around the corner, and I could see Daddy and Missus Foster. They were all snuggled up against each other. Daddy's arm was around her waist, and she was stroking Daddy's hair. They were looking at some pictures and laughing. They were so busy looking at each other, they didn't notice me in the shadows.

"So now who's that?" Daddy pointed to a picture.

Missus Foster laughed in that way that she has. "Me. I think I was about ten there. And those are my parents."

"Your pa looks pretty serious. Your ma, too."

"They were, serious that is. Papa taught school and Mama was a big leader in the Negro leagues, fighting for justice for colored people." Missus Foster opened up another album. "That's Mama leading a march to open up the local five and dime to colored people. And that's Papa. See the one over there in the corner."

"An' what about you?"

"Home, by myself, mainly wishing I had a brother or sister to play with. But while Mama and Papa fought the battles of the race, I played alone, I ate alone and I lived alone."

I could see Daddy kiss her in a comforting kind of way. She opened up another book and pointed to a picture. "That's my ex-husband."

"Pretty handsome fella."

"He thought so. Harmon Theodore Foster. The most desirable and sought-after colored man in Philadelphia. A doctor with a booming practice. And he wanted me. Me, Eloise, or Elle as I liked to call myself. It sounded more interesting and mysterious, you know."

"So what happened?"

Missus Foster hesitated for a minute, then she threw her head back and smiled in a way that wasn't really a smile. "Soon after we married, he started staying out late, not drinking, not even with different women. Just one woman, a woman I later found out he'd always loved, but his parents hated her, a poor girl from the wrong side of town. So he married me to appease them. But he never stopped loving her.

"Marriage is funny like that. It only really changes things for a minute, and then after a while, sometimes it's years, sometimes less, but after a while the old selves that had temporarily come together reemerge, and the one becomes two again. Sometimes never to be one again."

Missus Foster sighed. "So I was alone. Again. That's why I got the boarding house. In hindsight, I think it was my own subconscious way of ensuring that I wouldn't be alone anymore. Even if it was the company of passing strangers, at least the empty rooms would be alive with voices, with people."

Daddy took her in his big arms and cradled her gently. Then he started kissing her, almost like he was afraid she'd leave or something. "You don't never have to be alone again, honey. I promise you," he said so softly I could barely hear.

When I thought I couldn't stand to see any more, Missus Foster pushed the door shut, slamming it in my face. Now I was sure Missus Foster was plotting to get rid of me. Just like Ma had, she wanted Daddy all for herself. I could feel tears starting to come. I didn't want to cry. I wasn't a little kid anymore. But I just didn't know what to do. I couldn't let her separate me and Daddy. I know Daddy didn't love her more than me, but I didn't know what to do.

I was thinking all of this as I sat in the chair I normally loved to sink down in and absentmindedly flipping through a book. I wasn't reading, just thinking. I didn't even notice Daddy walk in.

He looked over at me. "Mighty quiet over there, Clive. Cat got yo' tongue?"

I stared hard at the book, refusing to meet Daddy's eyes. "No."

Missus Foster went over to the credenza and took out a shiny new pack of cards. "Do you want to play cards with us? We're gonna start a game of spades." Her voice, which before I had thought was so sweet and perfect, now just grated against me.

"Uh...uh...I'm reading."

Daddy kicked off his shoes and laid his feet up on the hassock. "You sure you feeling all right? Maybe you needs to git in the bed. We been gettin' up real early lately."

I shifted in my chair, wondering if I looked as mad as I felt. *I bet you do want me to go to bed so you can get back in bed with her, just trying to get rid of me.* But of course I couldn't say that to Daddy, so I just closed my book. "G'night."

Missus Foster smiled warmly at me, her light brown eyes reflecting my face. "No kiss goodnight for me?"

I shrugged. "I'm too old for that baby stuff. I'm almost eleven."

Missus Foster looked hurt, and for a minute, but just a minute, I felt kinda bad. Then I remembered what she'd done and that she was probably just plotting to get me out of the way, so I just kicked my foot in the carpet, looking down on the ground.

Daddy turned to me sternly, and for the first time his eyes weren't smiling. "You're never too old t'be polite to a lady. You hear me, boy? Now apologize to Missus Foster, and then you go git in bed."

I swallowed hard. I didn't want to make Daddy mad, then he'd really send me away, but it was hard pretending when I'd been betrayed. "I'm sorry, Missus Foster."

"That's okay, honey. You're right. That is kinda baby, so why don't we just shake hands. How's that?"

What could I say? I did't want to be anywhere near her, much less shake her hand, but Daddy had made it clear he didn't want any mess. I reluctantly shook her hand. "Goodnight."

"Goodnight, honey, sleep tight."

Daddy settled back in his chair. Barely turning to me as I left.

"Night. I'll be up in a bit."

Yeah right. When Daddy got upstairs, I pretended to be asleep. He leaned over me to check if I really was, but I guess I fooled him pretty good. He quietly undressed, put on his robe, and closed the door behind him.

I tried to stay awake. I wanted to see just how long he'd be there. But every time I tried not to fall asleep, I'd do it even faster. This night was no different. The only thing was that I had this dream.

I was walking down this long tunnel and everything was really bright and light. Like the brightest summer day in August. And Daddy was walking next to me. We were talking just like we used to, and then I remember all of these really odd things all around us. Weird animals and different kinds of plants. They weren't really pretty, just different and more than anything distracting, because now I couldn't really concentrate on what Daddy was saying. I was so fascinated by all of these things around me that when I looked up, Daddy was gone.

I looked everywhere, but I couldn't find him. Suddenly, the place where we'd been didn't seem so bright, and I just kept running around shouting Daddy's name. But I couldn't find him. The light got real bright again. It was so bright that I had to put my hands over my eyes. And I saw HIM, Daddy, standing at the end of the tunnel, he was trying to come to me, but he was stuck. He couldn't move, and I tried to move. But then slowly the light started to fade and Daddy was gone.

I woke up from the dream, shaking. I didn't know exactly what it meant, but it seemed to confirm my worse fears that somehow Missus Foster was going to take Daddy away from me. I looked over to Daddy's bed. He was sitting on the spread, pulling on his big boots. He looked over at me and smiled. "Feeling better?"

I smiled weakly. "Yeah, a little."

"Good 'cause we really got our work cut out fo us today. Gonna be paintin' the old McGyver plantation, 'bout five miles from town. It's a big job, but when we finish we oughta have enough saved to get a little place of our own."

My heart almost jumped outta me. Maybe I didn't have to worry about Missus Foster after all.

"Clive, would'ya think about Missus Foster? She sure likes you a lot."

"She's okay, I guess." I looked Daddy directly in the eye. I wanted to see exactly what he was thinking. "What d'you think about her?"

Suddenly, Daddy looked like a big kid. If he wasn't so dark, he probably would've blushed, but he just said in a voice I'd never heard before. "She's really somethin' special."

I got this knot in my throat that just seemed to be growing.

"Fact I was thinkin' that she might make a nice mama for you."

The knot was now so big that I could hardly swallow. I couldn't believe it. I blurted out. "Why do you need her? We're fine, just the two of us!"

Daddy walked over to me and put his arm around me and gave me a big hug. "Course we are, but it would be nice to have a woman around, too. Don't ya think?"

I couldn't even answer him. Daddy looked so desperate. But I couldn't stand the thought that something else might separate us again.

"Hey now, partner. It'll always be you and me. You're my best friend."He hugged me again and kissed me on the top of my forehead. "But you think about it, okay? Missus Foster's a real nice lady, and she really likes you. I know that deep down you really like her, too. An' you know if anything ever happened to me, you'd have another mama to take care of you."

I turned all the way around so I was facing Daddy, and now I felt tears starting to fill up in my eyes. *How could Daddy ever say that?* "Nothin's gonna happen to you, Daddy. I don't want another mama. I just want you. I just want us!!!"

"And that's the way it's gonna be, but someday we'll each have to share with somebody else. You'll meet some gal, and me, well...just think about it." Daddy rubbed his hand over my head. "But don't worry, I'm not goin' nowhere. Just promise me that you'll at least think about Missus Foster, 'cause she'd sure make a nice mama for you."

I didn't say anything. I was just wishing that something would happen to take her away from us.

Daddy was right. The old McGyver plantation was the biggest job we'd ever done. Some rich, old, white man had bought the place, and now he wanted it all painted new again. Daddy had bought these huge buckets of creamy white paint. He handed me the stick to stir it, but I was still too upset to enjoy sloshing the stick around the thick paint the way I normally did.

Since the house was so big, Daddy and me were going to paint the bottom together, and then he'd get up on the ladder and paint the top. I'd hand him the buckets of paint that he'd put on his platform.

We painted in silence for about an hour. My mind was filled with thoughts of how I could convince him that we didn't need Missus Foster. Or maybe I could convince him that we should just leave Aiken. There were lots of small towns around. There was no reason why we had to stay there. Daddy must've been thinking too, because he wasn't saying anything either. Probably because we weren't talking, we were making good progress on the bottom of the house. We finished it in about half the time it normally took. Maybe there was somethin' good to say about silence after all.

When we'd just about done with the bottom, Daddy turned to me.

"Wanna take a break or keep on going and see how far we can get 'fore dark?"

I shrugged my shoulders. I didn't much care either way. Daddy looked tired, but he seemed to wanna keep on. Probably so he could get back to her sooner.

"Ok well, then let's keep on for about another hour, then we'll rest for a bit."

I still wish I had just insisted that we take a break. I could've, but I didn't. Daddy climbed up on the ladder. As always, he got situated, and then I handed him the bucket of paint. But this time, he couldn't seem to get the bucket fixed right on the platform. So he kept moving it a little to the left, a little to the right. You had to get it at just the right place on the platform or else it wouldn't be stable.

Then I don't know what happened. I looked away for a minute, and the next thing I knew the bucket of paint had started to tip.

"Daddy, the paint's falling!"

Daddy tried to grab it. His hands clutched at the air, missing the can, but then he started falling. I looked on in horror as he crashed to the ground.

"Daaaaaddy!" I ran over to him. I still don't remember much. It was like a bad dream that I couldn't stop. He fell hard on the cement driveway. And then he was just still. But there was blood everywhere, pouring out like a dark fountain from his head. His eyes were closed.

I shook him hard, crying and crying. "Daddy, Daddy, don't die, please don't die…" I yelled and cried at the top of my voice. Running around and around. "HELP ME, PLEASE! MY DADDY'S HURT! HELP ME!"

But there was no one around. I threw myself on Daddy, hugging him, sobbing loudly. "Daddy please, please wake up…please!"

But he didn't move. The last thing I remember was it being dark and somebody coming in a big car pulling me off Daddy's lifeless body.

The pain was beginning to be overwhelming. *Fuck.* Someone had taken a jackhammer and was banging on every joint in my body. So this is what it felt like to die. Blood was starting to fill over my eyes. The only thoughts in my mind were *Why* and *Who* would dare kill *me*?

Then it's as if I heard a chorus of laughter—unearthly beings laughing at me, filling the room with their eery noises. Throbbing pulsating waves of sound taunted me. Telling me to look back. That I had the answers. That I knew why. Look back, they said. Look back. The floodgates of my memories opened up wider, wider than ever before, dusting off memories long buried in the sands of delusion.

And just when I felt as if I couldn't stand the pain any longer, I saw *him*—my father—standing at the end of a long tunnel, beckoning to me. But he couldn't come to me. Like in the dream of long ago. Something was holding him back. Then I realized it wasn't him. It was ME. Something was preventing me from going to him. I tried, and I wanted to, but I was frozen. Immobilized by guilt, the lies, the deceit, everything I had done, and I knew I had to look back. I had to go all the way back. The Pandora's box of my past had to be opened even wider.

CHAPTER SIX

Aiken

"Daddy!" I bolted up in the bed, salty tears running in my mouth.

"Sssshhhh, it's okay, honey. I'm here." Missus Foster wiped my forehead with a cloth. Then she kissed me gently on the top of my head and pulled the thick cover up to my chin. Just like I was a baby. I didn't mind anymore. I had such an empty feeling in me I couldn't even move.

I kept seeing Daddy falling off the ladder—like a motion picture that got stuck and kept repeating the same parts. After they found me and took Daddy away, they called Missus Foster. She came right away, but it was too late. Daddy had died before they put him in the ambulance.

Missus Foster cried and cried. And I cried. We cried together. I knew then that she had really loved Daddy, maybe as much as I did. The other thing I knew was that she hadn't been trying to get rid of me, because she told the people at child welfare that she was my aunt, so they'd let me stay with her.

I felt so bad about all the mean things I'd thought about her. I just kept thinking that maybe if I hadn't wanted so much for her and Daddy not to be together and for something to happen that would prevent them from being together, maybe he'd still be here. In a way I had wished what happened, so it was my fault Daddy was dead. And now it was me who suffered. And Missus Foster, too, because now neither of us had Daddy. We were both nobodies, alone.

Missus Foster must've been thinking the same thing because she hugged me tighter than usual. "You know when I met your father, I thought finally God had brought me some happiness."

I know why Daddy loved her. She was kind, nice and sweet, and if I hadn't been so stupid, I would've seen it, and Daddy would still be here. She gently rocked me back and forth. But I didn't deserve the love that was pouring outta her. I was the one that should've been gone, not Daddy.

"Now go back to sleep, honey. It's okay." She stroked the tears away from my cheeks and turned out the light.

This had been happening almost every night since the funeral. I'd finally fall asleep, then I'd have these nightmares. Sometimes I was running down a dark street alone, looking everywhere for Daddy, but he wasn't there. Other times I was just wandering in a big city, feeling so alone, small and scared. I'd wake up crying, but Missus Foster was always there. Those first few weeks she slept in my room on the couch. She let me have Daddy's bed. It felt sad to be there, but in a way I could feel him next to me. Hugging me the way he used to. And it made me feel better to think that maybe somehow he wasn't really gone. I just couldn't see him.

Life without Daddy was empty. That's about the only word I can think of. The mornings, the afternoons, and especially the nights. Missus Foster tried, and she was real nice. She'd take me places and buy me clothes and books. I even started school, and afterwards, she'd always have something nice fixed for me.

After a while, the hurt stopped being with me all the time. Just when I closed my eyes or when I saw another kid my age with his father. Then the knot would start somewhere in my chest, and I'd have to turn away quickly. *Big boys don't cry.* I had to keep telling myself that. *Big boys don't cry.* After all, I was eleven and a half now almost twelve. I don't really remember much about the months that had gone by since Daddy…died. They just kinda passed. But in the back of my mind I knew I was lucky. At least I was far away from Ma.

It was raining real hard. I don't know why, but things, and not good things, always seemed to happen to me when it rained. Anyway, I was up in my room doing my homework when I heard Missus Foster running up the stairs. That was strange, Missus Foster wasn't a running kind of person. But this time she was running. "Clive!"

I didn't like the tone of her voice. It made the hairs on the back of my neck stand up. "C'min."

Her light brown eyes were clouded over. I couldn't see my reflection in them, only pools of doubt and worry. "Someone's downstairs to see you. I could say anything, she said softly, almost so softly that I couldn't hear. "It's your mother."

I felt sick. I mean really sick. Like I wanted to jump out the window or crawl under the bed or run so fast that she couldn't find me ever.

"She said that she has a letter from child welfare. She wants to take you back."

"She's a fuckin' liar!"

It just came out, I never cussed in front of Missus Foster, but I didn't care. "I won't go! I won't!"

Missus Foster started crying really hard. Almost as hard as she had when Daddy died. "Honey, I don't want you to go, but she's your mother. There's nothing I can do." Ma must've known I wouldn't come, 'cause she had two policeman with her, big, ugly, colored men with mutt dog faces.

Before I knew it, they'd grabbed me. "Okay, ya little runaway. You going back with yo mama."

"I hate her. I hate her!!!!"

"Shut up." Ma slapped me. I wanted to slap her back, and kick her and scratch her, but I didn't 'cause I knew Daddy would never do that.

She stood over me with her hands on her bony hips. "What's wrong you think ya, to good for yo mama? Now you living in this fine house 'n' all…"

Ma spit out the words angrily, like she hated Missus Foster for being pretty and nice and living in a better place than she could ever dream about. She whirled around, her words firing out at Missus Foster. "Ya high yellow bitch, wasn't enuf to take my husband, but you wanted my boy, too!"

Missus Foster was too much of a lady to say what she wanted to so she just slammed the door behind her. And then Ma started throwing my things in a dirty yellow suitcase. The policeman held my arms. I was trying to kick him in the balls, but the other one threw me down on the floor.

"How's it feel t'be goin home…huh. Ya know ya cin run, but you can't hide…"

And the bitterness and hate rose in my throat so all I could do was swallow painfully. Just then I thought about Daddy, and I remembered what he'd told me not to hate nobody, especially not Ma. But I knew at that moment that I could never keep my promise to him, that the feelings I had for her weren't goin' away. And if they ate me up inside like Daddy'd said they would, then they just would. Thinking about Daddy made me wanna cry. But I wasn't going to. I wasn't gonna cry. Never again. I was never gonna cry again.

Missus Foster wrote to me, but after a while I just stopped writing back. Didn't see the point. It just reminded me of Daddy and everything I couldn't have again.

I found out after I got back home that the only reason Ma wanted me back was 'cause it was the only way she'd get her grubby hands on the money that Daddy and me had been saving for a house. Since the divorce hadn't gone through when Daddy died, the bank found out about Ma somehow and told her about the money. It was a lot, almost a thousand dollars. I figured out that Missus Foster must not've been charging us much if anything for Daddy to be able to save so much. Anyway, Ma wanted that money. Guess she figured he owed it to her for walking out on her.

A DEAD MAN SPEAKS

If I had it my way, she could've had the money if she had just let me stay with Missus Foster. All I wanted was a little chance to be happy. But that's the way Ma was, she'd do anything she could to spoil things for me.

CHAPTER SEVEN

1969

"Oooh girl, Clive is fine..." Giggles, laughs, and lingering footsteps passed by me slowly.

Things had sure changed over the summer. In three months I'd grown five inches. I was 6'2, big 'fro, and all of a sudden the one they all wanted me. I smiled to myself. *Shit, what a difference a day makes.* I smiled my come get me smile at the curvaceous sister walking up to me. She lowered her eyes, nudged her girlfriend, and gave me that look that let me know it was mine if I wanted it. I felt like I'd died and gone to pig heaven, girls everywhere, all over me. Five inches and a big 'fro. I was a man!

"Yo, man, whas' up?" my boy asked.

"Nuttin'. Jus hangin."

"I hear ya. Catch ya later over at Smalls?"

"Na, man, not tonight. I got somethin' to do."

My partner gave me a look like he knew I was gonna get some coochie. He slapped me high five and grinned, shouting as he walked off. "Later, man, and 'member if you can't be good, be good at it."

I smiled. But I wasn't about to let up what my real plans were. And it wasn't with one of the sisters on my jock either. I thought about that as I rolled over on my bed, staring intently at the book in front of me. SAT PREP. I was almost through all the exercises. I'd been studying my ass off for weeks, but I still couldn't seem to get it. But I was determined if I had to study twenty-four hours a day, I was gettin' through this, cause I knew college was my only ticket outta this hell hole and away from Ma for good. Somewhere so far away that she'd never find me again.

I lay on my bed, staring at the ceiling. The five years I'd been back had resembled something outta one of those Dickens' novels we read in Miss Davenport's English class. Shit, that woman loved those English writers. Seems like that's all we read. If I didn't know better, I'd swear she was English. Except, nobody but a sister could have an ass like hers. She was a real fox alright. Had a soft curly 'fro that hung over her shoulders. Large, greenish-brown eyes and smooth skin the color of tea. And all of it wrapped up in the body of life. Yeah, she definitely had it going on.

Then it hit me in between thinking about Miss Davenport's ass, that's who I could get to help me with my college stuff. She was pretty cool, even for a teacher. She'd even talked to Ma about me and how I was real smart and should be thinking seriously about college. But Ma had just screwed up her face and snorted, telling her that a job in the factory like her no-good brother Abe had was about all I could hope for. Well, fuck her. I was getting the hell outta Hendersonville and to college somewhere. And Miss Davenport would be the one to help me.

Miss Davenport had a sweet smell, like flowers, soap, and shampoo. I couldn't help thinking about that as she leaned over me. "Okay, Clive, let's go over this one more time."

Shit, I was trying to concentrate, but all I could think about was how tiny her hands were and how smooth and soft they felt when I brushed against them. I had a thing about hands. You know some guys are into tits or asses. Now don't get me wrong, I'm into that, too. But even if a sister's got all that, if her hands are whacked, then it's later for her. I think it's probably 'cause Ma's hands were so fucked, bony, and covered with callouses. I never liked her to touch me, even as a little kid.

"You mind if we take a break?" I smiled my most seductive smile, the kind that usually made all the girls give it up. But not Miss Davenport, she'd been there before.

"Now, Clive, if you're serious about doing well on this test, you're gonna just have to buckle down. Otherwise, I'm just wasting my time, right?" She smiled teasingly. She may have known my game, but what she didn't know is that I was serious. Serious about getting to college and about getting her.

That's what I was thinking as I sat in the back of Miss Davenport's English class. Just thinking about the past few weeks working with her after school. Learning lots of useless words I'd probably never say, 'cause after this damn test I'd forget what they meant.

But I kept on going 'cause every time I did a little better on one of those practice tests, I got a little further away from Ma and a little closer to Miss Davenport. I could tell she had a thing for me. The way she edged real close when we studied. Now don't get me wrong, she wasn't real obvious about it. Naw, she was twenty-four years old, a woman. I mean a real woman, not some high-school girl. So I'd just take my time. I wasn't goin nowhere and neither was she.

"Uh…Clive…"

I turned around quickly, but it was just Verna Smith. Cute, but young. The kind who really wanted it, but her pa had put the fear of God in her that if she gave it up before she got married, she'd go to hell or something. So she just kinda teased you but at the end of the day you knew she wasn't givin' nothing up. That's why we called her a dt, 'cause she'd lead you on, but just when you got ready to go down on her, she'd say no.

"You walkin' my way?" She smiled and kinda cocked her head in a way that let me know she wanted me to walk with her.

"Guess that depends on where you goin'." I figured I'd make her beg for it. She took the bait. Bit her bottom lip. She edged closer. I could smell her Afro Sheen, she was so close.

She kinda half opened her mouth, beckoning me. Then looped her arm through mine. "You know I live on the way to your mama's house."

I shrugged my shoulder. "Who said I was goin' to my mama's house?"

"Oh, Clive, stop foolin 'round and walk me home!" She leaned up against the tree. Her mini skirt hiked up a little. I looked around to see if anybody else more interesting was going my way. But everybody else had gone. So coolly, 'cause I was always cool, I draped my arm over her shoulder. I could feel her thrill at my touch. *You ain't seen nothin' baby. If I opened up and really let you have it, you'd drop your drawers so fast, you wouldn't know what hit you.* She leaned her head against my shoulder as we walked through the schoolyard.

"Your 'fro looks soooo good, Clive. You plait it to make it grow like that?" This girl really wasn't too bright. All she ever talked about was hair and usually who had the best lookin' 'fro.

"Clive, Clive, did you hear what I asked chew?"

"Right, my 'fro. No, I don't do nothing to it. It just grows fast, that's all."

"Your mama don't plait it for you?"

Was she crazy? She was an even bigger idiot than I thought. Ma touch my hair? I'd cut it off first. "No, Verna, my ma don't touch my hair. Nobody does."

She opened up a pack of gum. "Want some? I just love Double Mint, but not as much as Juicy Fruit, jus' that the store was out and all, so I had to take Double Mint. Don't that make you mad when the store don't have what you want?"

I took a stick of gum, chewing it absentmindedly. One thing about being with Verna, it was easy to tune her out and think about more important things. The other thing about Verna was that her conversation never made logical sense. She just jumped from one stupid topic to the next.

"I heard you and your ma don't get along too good."

I didn't answer.

"I heard she sent you away or you ran away or something when you was little, and that's when your pa died."

At the mention of Daddy, my whole body chilled over. I dropped my arm from around her. And if looks could kill, Verna would probably be dead now. "Verna, shut up!"

Her mouth dropped slightly. "Uh…I'm sorry, Clive. I just thought that since you and me was you know…getting to know each other, you might want to talk about things with me. "

"I don't, okay? So just drop it!"

For once she was silent.

That's why I hated Hendersonville. I could never just live in peace. Somebody always had to go dredging up the past, stirring up the memories. That's why I was getting out. Away from the wagging tongues and the well-meaning stares. I was getting away to some place where nobody knew jack shit about me, who I was or where I came from and frankly didn't give a damn neither.

We walked on a little more before she started again. I should've just left when she brought up Daddy, but, for some reason, I kept walking with her.

She cleared her throat. "You know what's the end of the month?"

I looked over at her, bored and still a little pissed. "Your period."

She hit me playfully. "Clive, no!"

I knew that would set her off. But hey, payback's a bitch.

"I'm talking about the kickoff for the prom planning committee. The Senior Prom."

"Yeah."

"Well, are you going?"

"To what, the planning committee meeting?"

"Nooooo, the Prom!"

The last thing on my mind was the damn prom. I was concentrating on the SATs this weekend, getting into college and away from there. 'Cause for me, Hendersonville was hell. The narrow streets, some of them still dirt roads even now, a hundred years after the Civil War. The town was caught in a kind of time warp, where all the white people were right and always on top, and all of us were in this ditch that we could never get out of. But I was getting out and leaving the rest of them behind. Hendersonville was never anything but pain and bad memories for me, and come next fall, I was going to college and closing the door on Hendersonville forever. So when Verna asked me about the prom, I could say truthfully, "I hadn't really thought about it."

"So then you haven't asked anybody?"

"No, Verna, I haven't. I hadn't planned on going, besides it's not till April."

"I know but everybody's making all their plans now. Oh, Clive, you gotta go!" She giggled nervously. The way girls do when they want to say something but aren't sure how to. She looked at me real hard, and then blurted out, "Would you like to go with me?"

I don't know why I just didn't say point blank no then, but for some reason, probably 'cause I was preoccupied. I didn't. She stopped, turning her foot over nervously in the dirt. "Well?"

I looked her up and down, thinking for a minute. Maybe I'd get some that night. Hell, why not? "Sure, I'll go with you."

"Oh, Clive!" Her face broke into a wide smile, and she grabbed me and hugged me tightly.

I guess I should've been flattered, but at that exact moment, Miss Davenport passed us by in that cute little red VW bug she drove. She waved at me and kept on going. I wanted to be right there in the seat next to Miss Davenport, not wasting time with Verna Smith.

CHAPTER EIGHT

Miss Davenport

"This looks pretty good, Clive. If you keep up like that on the real thing, you oughta do real well." Miss Davenport handed me my corrected practice test. I noticed how when she smiled she had the cutest little dimples right at each side of her chin.

I smiled, but I didn't want to seem too eager. Wasn't cool. "I guess I did okay."

She looked at me mischievously, that gentle, teasing, I'm-in-control undercurrent in her voice. "Clive, always the cool one, don't want to seem too happy, huh?" She walked around the side of the desk, hopped on top lightly, swinging her legs slowly.

I wanted to push her back on the top of the desk and go down on her right there. I didn't give a damn who came in. But she just kept talking in that playful way of hers. "Wouldn't be right for the image. Clive January, the coolest senior around."

"Can I help it if that's what people think?" Two could play that game. I may be younger than her, but I wasn't stupid. I could hang.

"What do you think?" she asked.

"About what?"

"About whether you're the coolest dude around?"

"I think..." I walked around the desk so that I was standing right in front of her. If I got any closer, I'd probably be on top of her. The smell of her perfume was covering me. But I wasn't gonna let her think she'd gotten over on me, so I just kept on talking, right up in her face.

Smiling, my best, most award-winning smile. "I think that a lot of women wanna be with me, but I'm choosy. I don't have to take whatever's out there."

She just threw back her head and laughed. I mean really cracked up. I've gotta admit, that did kinda throw me for a minute.

"What...what's so funny? Shit, it's true!"

She could barely get the words out. "Oh I'm sure it is. It's just that..." She cracked up some more. "I'm sorry, Clive. You just seem so serious about being cool, that I can't help laughing."

I was pissed, but I really didn't have anything to say. I mean what could I say? I came out with what I thought was the smoothest line, and she was just laughing in my face.

Knock...knock...

Neither of us heard Verna Smith pushing open the classroom door. She walked in and just stopped. I guess it must've looked a little suspicious with Miss Davenport sitting on the desk lauging and me about two inches in front of her. Verna's face turned real red. She had that high yellow color with a huge, reddish-brown 'fro and freckles, so you could always tell if she was embarrassed.

She looked at us and then stammered out quickly. "Uh...I'm sorry to bother you, Miss Davenport, but I uh...came for my grade on the paper."

Miss Davenport quickly pulled herself together. That woman never missed a beat. I liked that. She'd never get caught with her pants down. I, on the other hand, wanted to smack Verna Smith. Seemed as if she was always nosing around in somebody else's business. And this time she'd just snatched the play right out from under me.

Miss Davenport seemed totally unperturbed—one of the SAT words. She just uncrossed her legs, pulled out a big leather binder from under the desk, opened it, and pointed to a page. "It's right here."

Verna Smith, clearly embarrassed, quickly looked at her grade and then with an accusatory stare, turned to me. "You goin' home now, Clive?"

"No, I got some more work to do."

She kind of sniffed, grabbing her coat. "I bet you do."She slammed the door behind her.

Miss Davenport shook her head, and then laughed again. "Poor child. She really has a thing for you, and you're not even thinking about her, are you ?"

What could I say, she read me alright. "No, she's okay. She's just a kid."

"And what are you?"

I closed my book and looked right at her without blinking. "I'm no kid. Believe me." And this time she didn't laugh. She just kept right on looking at me. And I knew I'd finally gotten to her.

After a minute she turned away, clearing her throat. "Well I think you're ready for the SAT's on Saturday."

The SATs came and went. I knew I smoked 'em. The funny thing was when I actually got there and sat down with my number two pencils, I wasn't nervous anymore. I just went for it. I guess studying my ass off must've paid off after all. Even if I didn't remember any of those damn words after the test.

The only bad thing about the SATs being over was that I didn't get to see Miss Davenport anymore. I'd run into her from time to time, but she was always in a rush, so we didn't ever get a chance to pick up where we'd left off.

I was kinda sorry, 'cause if I'd had just a little more time with her, I would've gotten her right where I wanted. But hey, them's the breaks sometimes. I really didn't have time to think about it too much as the months went by, 'cause I was busy thinking about my future away from Hendersonville. I'd gotten all of my college applications out a while ago, and I expected to start hearing back soon. The rest of the time I was working the night shift at the factory in town, so by the time I got home, I was dead tired. But anything beat having to see Ma. This way I left before she did in the morning, and by the time I got home, she was already asleep. So these days it was almost as if we weren't even living in the same house, and that's just the way I liked it.

I was also starting to worry about getting drafted. I wasn't eighteen 'till October, but already some of the other guys had gotten their notices. I knew I had to get in some college somewhere, 'cause I'd be damned if I was going to leave one living hell for another. I was definitely not going to Nam. All the guys who left from here came back in a pine box. And I had big plans for my life that didn't include fighting some war millions of miles away that I could care less about.

I was sitting on the ledge by the school, thinking about my future and everything else when Verna walked up.

"Hi!" She smiled cheerily. She was truly the last person I wanted to see. But she didn't seem to notice that I wasn't exactly enthusiastic.

"So are you excited about Saturday?"

"Saturday?" I honestly didn't have a clue what the hell she was talking about.

She looked hurt. I guess I was supposed to know. "The prom! You said you'd take me."

"Oh right…I forgot. I guess it is April already."

"How could you forget? That's all anybody's talking about!"

I started to say that I had more important things on my mind than the prom, but I figured what's the use, she'd never get it.

"So what about it? You haven't changed your mind, have you?" She looked as if she'd burst into tears if I said that I had. The last thing I needed at this point was a big scene.

"No, I haven't…"

Her face lit up again. "So what time are you picking me up?"

"What time does it start?"

"Eight."

"Okay, then I'll pick you up at eight." I really didn't care, eight, nine, whatever. At this point it was just one of the last chores that I had to get through before I could get out of Hendersonville for good.

I was ready to go, but she just kept talking. "Did you get your dashiki?"

"What do I need a dashiki for?"

She rolled her eyes. "Cliiiiiive…you know all the black students have decided to wear African dress to the prom instead of tuxes and formals. You know, for solidarity and everything."

About the only thing I was feeling solidarity for at this point was getting out of Hendersonville.

"I know you must've heard that Shushumba got this catalogue from New York of all these African clothes, and…"

"Wait! Time out. Who the hell is Shushumba?"

"Clive, sometimes I wonder if you're even at school."

I didn't say that I was working actively on getting out as quickly as possible, but she didn't care about that. I was convinced that Verna just loved to hear herself talk.

"Shushumba is Kathy Joe Leonard. You know she changed her name last year. Anyway, she has this friend in New York who has a mail order business with Africa for African clothes, so she got the catalogue so that everybody could order their prom clothes."

"Well I didn't know about it, so I'm just wearing jeans."

Verna looked disappointed. But I guess she thought about it. Me in jeans was better than going by herself. "Okay, well if that's the way you feel, but anyway, you're still gonna pick me up at eight?"

"Right, sure, I'll be there."

She had an expectant look on her face, so I bent down and gave her a peck on the mouth. Totally uninteresting, but maybe that would get her hyped enough to give it up on Saturday. That way, at least the evening wouldn't be a total waste.

I sat in the mirror admiring myself from all sides. I wasn't the least bit into this prom, but I must admit I did look damn good. I patted my 'fro, which had to be perfectly round, squirted a little more Afro Sheen on the top and adjusted my flyaway collar. Yeah, I was fine.

Just had to grab the car keys. Ma never let me use her car, but she was out, probably gossiping with her bitchy friends. Besides, what was she gonna say? The days that she could tell me what to do were long gone now. I towered over her, and most of the time she just stayed out of my way. Which was better for both of us.

I went into her room, looking around. After she got the money that Daddy had been saving, she sold the other house and bought a bigger one, with two bedrooms, one for me and one for her. I never went in her room, and she never went in mine. Two separate worlds. So I wasn't quite sure where to look for the keys. Usually she left them on the kitchen table, but she must've known I wanted to use the car, so she hid them.

I walked over to her drawer, rummaging through her underwear and blouses. *Nothing.* I tried the bottom drawer where she kept her papers and checkbooks. *Still nothing.* The only other place was the beat up trunk in the corner. I lifted the top, fishing my hands through the assortment of worthless odds and ends she kept in there. *The keys. Got 'em.* I smiled. She thought she was slick, but not too slick for me. I was about to close the trunk when something caught my eye. It was a letter in my handwriting.

I picked it up, and then my face went cold. It was one of my college applications, stamped and ready to go. Except that I'd put it in the mailbox to be mailed months ago! My heart was racing now, I fished some more and grabbed a pile of mail. All mine, the ten college applications that I thought I'd mailed, all here. Ma must've taken 'em outta of our mail box after I put 'em in there. Then I realized that not one, not even one of the applications that I'd slaved over had gotten mailed. She'd fuckin' sabotaged me! My head spun as the reality of what she'd done starting to sink in. I wasn't going anywhere, not to college, nowhere, thanks to Ma!

A tidal wave of rage rose in me. I started turning her shit over. Knocking over the lamp, ripping the covers. *Why didn't I take 'em to the post office myself?* It just kept ringing in my head. *Why did I leave anything to chance?*

I couldn't stand it anymore. I was suffocating. I ran out of the house and jumped into the car. I drove, pumping the gas to the floor.

Hell, I didn't care if I died at this point. I might as well be dead. My life in Hendersonville was about as close to a living hell as I could stand. I realized I'd probably be sent to Nam, too. Without an S-2 deferment, I was up shit's creek. And I don't know how, but I ended up in front of Miss Davenport's house. I'd never been there before, but in a town as small as Hendersonville, everybody knew where everybody else lived. I banged on the door. I had to talk to somebody, and she was the only person who'd understand.

"Miss Davenport, it's me, Clive. Open up, please!"

For some reason I didn't feel like a man anymore. I was ten years old again, and Daddy had just died. I could hear the latch turning, and Miss Davenport stood in front of me with a puzzled, half-amused look on her face.

But when she saw me she realized that this wasn't another game. "Clive, what's wrong?"

In a daze, I stumbled in the room, still clutching my college applications like still born children. I dropped into a chair. My eyes glazed over. I could barely speak. I was still in so much shock. "She…she fucked me…"

"Clive, what are you talking about?"

"This!" I tossed the college applications bitterly on the floor.

She picked them up, turning them over carefully, then looked at me, puzzled. "Well, these are your college applications. I thought you'd sent them in ages ago."

And then I was yelling. Not really at Miss Davenport, or at anybody in particular, more at myself for being so stupid. "I did or I thought I did. I put them in the box for the mailman to pick up, but Ma took 'em out before he could get to them. I found the shit in her room!"

Miss Davenport dropped into the chair. "Why…why would she do that???"

"Cause she fuckin' hates me!" I buried my head in my hands. I wasn't crying. I couldn't cry. After Daddy died, I never cried anymore. But my head was hurting so much, I just couldn't keep it up.

Miss Davenport walked over to me and softly stroked my head. "It's okay, Clive. I understand. I do. I really do."

"How the fuck could you understand? How could anybody understand my life? She hates me. You don't know what it's like!" The hurt was so heavy, I could barely breathe.

She stood there for a minute, then gently pulled me down on the couch next to her. She took my hand and stroked my cheek, turning my face toward her saying firmly, "Trust me. I know what it's like." Her eyes stared through to my soul, massaging me from the inside with kindness and gentleness, everything she was and Ma wasn't.

She started talking softly, never taking her eyes away from me. I was being drawn into her, becoming a part of her, seeing who she really was for the first time.

"I never knew my real mother. I was adopted." She paused as if it was still hard getting it out after all that time. "When I was seventeen, I decided I was going to find her. I'd fantasized about my mother as long as I could remember. It didn't matter to me who she was, if she was rich or poor or beautiful or just ordinary. I was convinced that she had always wanted me the way I had wanted her, and that she had looked for me, and had always regretted giving me up. I had rehearsed our reunion in my head so many times that when the actual day came, when I finally found her, I was so excited I could barely knock on the door."

"Yeah, can I help you?" the skinny white man who opened the door asked. Fortyish and not very pleasant. For a minute I thought of turning away, running back to the bus, leaving my one chance to find out who I really was. But I stopped myself. I wasn't going to run. I was determined to make peace with that voice inside of me. That voice that never stopped asking who, who am I really? So I managed to say more bravely than I felt, "I'm um…looking for Cynthia McNeil."

"Yeah." He sneered and looked me up and down, as if I were some object. He leaned against the doorway, blocking the entrance and he spit out, "Well I'm Jim McNeil, and who are you?"

"I'm…" I swallowed, not sure how he was going to take this, "I'm her daughter."

"Her what?!" He got up in my face, then laughed, but I could tell he didn't really find anything funny. He shouted, "Shit, you're black! Cynthia, get out here! There's some black kid saying you're her mother!" He let the creaking screen door slam as he stalked back in the house.

A middle-aged white woman walked up to the door. Her face was starting to show lines, and her brown hair hung long and straight down her back. Other than the pale skin and grey eyes, it was the same face, the same mouth, as me. She couldn't deny it.

"Is this some kind of joke?" She looked at me as if I was some cancer from her past that she had cut out, excised with shame and bitterness, but only to reappear, full blown in front of her.

"I've been looking for you for two years. It was really hard, they didn't want to give me the records, but I kept at it until finally someone did and I…" The words were tumbling out faster and faster as the reality of the mistake I'd made in contacting her hit me, but it was too late to go back now. "I'm your daughter, and I thought…I guess I thought that, well, that you'd want to know me, the way I wanted to know you!" This dull feeling in my head was traveling down my body, numbing me all over. This wasn't what I'd planned, the reunion, the life-long bond of love, all withering away in front of me.

She got up real close to me, her grey eyes cutting through me, trembling with anger. "Look. I gave you away, because I didn't want you. Can you understand that? I did *not* want you! I didn't want you then. And I damn sure don't want you now. So do me a favor and stay the hell out of my life!"

The door slammed so hard in my face that my ears were ringing. For a minute, I just stood there. Looking at the peeling paint on the door. Then, I realized that what I had wanted and dreamed of ever since I found out the truth about who I was, was gone. I sat down on the sidewalk and cried. Until I couldn't cry anymore. Until I had emptied out every good feeling I'd ever had, and nothing but the pain was left. Somehow, I managed to stumble back to the bus station and go home. I never saw her again. But the hurt never leaves me. It's always there."

Miss Davenport stopped as abruptly as she'd begun, her words suspended in the air. I could hear the crickets outside. She wasn't even looking at me anymore. I didn't know what to say except, "So I guess you do understand."

She looked up, and for the first time I saw another woman behind the confidence. The mask she wore had fallen off. She brushed her hand against my face. "Yes, I do. I really do." She kissed my forehead softly at first, then again. And through the pain, I felt her warmth reaching over my parched body. I felt love radiating out from her, something I'd never had before. A feeling that totally and completely engulfed me.

"I know your pain," she whispered. "We share the same pain…"

She started unbuttoning my shirt, kissing my chest. I turned her over, pressing my body against hers. A wave rolled over me, again and again. The duality of the pleasure of being with her and the pain of my future, all mingling together, pain and pleasure throbbing together.

I was spinning around and around: her lips and mine, her face and mine, her eyes and mine, with the light from her window, wrapping around us. I couldn't stop the feelings, the new sensations. I wanted to cry and laugh all at once.

And then I felt "It." 'cause there's no words for "It." More than love. I looked in her eyes, and I knew that she felt "It," too. And I knew what "It" was… Fear. The fear of losing yourself, of surrendering your soul to a love that just was. And I knew that "It" would always be there between us. This love and fear. She was shaking and trembling all over, and she held me with a strength that blocked out everything. I closed my eyes and cradled her head against my chest. She buried her lips in my skin, until I didn't know her flesh from mine and the love took over again, shoving the fear away.

As I ran my hands over her bare legs and arms, little charges of electricity fed me with jolts of energy that kept getting stronger and stronger. I released a shower of light into her, pumping in harder and harder all the feelings, wanting and longing that I'd had. I was somewhere else. There was no bottom, no sounds, nothing. And just when I thought I couldn't go any higher, something crashed against me, like a fist slamming against wood. And then, I realized we weren't alone.

Knock, knock, knock.

A loud voice boomed out from outside her window. At first I thought it was a dream. My eyes didn't want to open. I was shaking all over.

Knock, knock, knock, knock...

"Miss Davenport, we know you're in there. Open up the door."

Miss Davenport, or Laurel, she'd never be Miss Davenport again for me, sat up dazedly. "Who in the world?"

From outside the door we heard, "Miss Davenport, we suggest you open the door. It's the sheriff."

"Shit." I shook myself alert. Quickly, I grabbed my pants and pulled them on. She threw a shirt over her head and slipped into a skirt, trying to smooth her tangled hair, walking quickly to the door.

I stayed in the other room, scooping up the rest of my things and jamming them under her bed. My heart was still beating as if it wanted to jump outta my chest, and my knees buckled weakly. Laurel opened the door slightly. I could see Sheriff Miller, and, of all people, Verna Smith in her African dress and her pa. Verna's eyes were puffy and red, and her pa looked ready to kill somebody, presumably me.

Shit, the prom. With everything that had happened, I'd completely forgotten about it.

Miss Davenport was trying to be cool, but she couldn't pull it off this time. Her hands trembled slightly as she opened the door wider. "Is there a problem, Sheriff?"

"Well, Miss, there is. I suggest you let us in, we know Clive January's in there. He stole his mama's car. It's parked outside your door."

Shit, that's all I could think, *now I'm really fucked.*

"I don't think you know what you're talking about, Sheriff—"

"Now, Miss, don't make it harder on yourself. We know he's there. He was supposed to take this little lady to the prom. Instead, he stole his mama's car and came over here. We talked to his mama and she tol' us she expressly tol' him he couldn't take her car."

Laurel didn't move. "Sheriff, you don't have a warrant to search my house, and even if Clive January were here, borrowing his mother's car would hardly qualify him as a fugitive from justice."

Verna, who had been sniffling loudly, spit out viciously, "You bitch!"

Before I knew what had happened, Verna Smith had lunged for Laurel. Her pa tried to pull her off, but Verna was kicking and screaming, in between loud angry sobs. "He was supposed to take me to the prom, and he embarrassed me in front of everybody, and it's all your fault!"

At this point I realized that things had gotten a little out of hand, so I walked out. "Okay e-nuf! Shit, Verna, I'm sorry. I know I was supposed to take you to the prom, but..." A pregnant silence as all eyes turned to me. "I forgot." Now what did I go and say that for?

"You forgot!" Her pa looked like he wanted to strangle me with his bare hands, and he was not a small man. In fact, me and my partners used to joke about him behind his back, saying that we never wanted to piss him off 'cause he could probably kill any of us with one hand tied behind his back. He got right up in my face. He was so close that I could smell what he had for dinner .

"Nobody, and especially not some two bit punk like you stands up my little girl!"

"Mr. Smith, I think there's something you should know."

God bless Laurel, she tried. But Mr. Smith turned to her angrily shouting. "And you! Why you're nothing but a—"

"Slut!" Verna finished the sentence for him.

Now I really expected Laurel to say something or do something. She wasn't the type who'd normally put up with anybody's mess, but she didn't. Except for moving aside to dodge Verna's slap, she just stood there not saying anything. Her eyes were glazed over, and she seemed distant, almost as if she'd gone somewhere where she was kind of there, but not really. Almost like she was looking at a play that she wasn't in anymore.

The sheriff must've realized that things were starting to get out of hand because he finally jumped in. "Okay, okay, folks. I think we needs to jus' go on down to the station and figure this whole thing out. Seems as if Clive here not only stood up this young lady, stole his mama's car and..." The sheriff scratched his head as if weighing how he was going to say it. "Well, anyway, never mind. Let's just all go on down there."

And my last night in Hendersonville was strangely symbolic of my whole life in that town. Me against everybody else. Except this time there was no Daddy to bail me out. Laurel tried, but there wasn't really much she could do. I was actually glad it ended like this. It was easier for me to make a clean break. Ma came down to the station. After she took one look at my face, she immediately dropped the car theft charges. Standing up your date wasn't hardly a crime, so other than a lot of icy looks from Verna's pa, there was really nothing they could do.

And the thing with Laurel, we didn't talk much about it afterwards, in fact, really not at all. Although you'd think that after all this, we would've had a lot to say. But I think that we both knew that something had happened between us, something bigger than Verna and her stupid pa finding out or the sheriff or even Ma. And I think maybe it scared us both a little, because it felt so good, almost too good, that we both thought that maybe we didn't deserve to feel that good, so we tried to push it away, even though we really knew it wasn't going to change anything.

'Cause after I left the station, she was there waiting for me. She walked up to me slowly, she was trembling, and I could see "It" pulling at her. She was fighting "It," trying to be the old Laurel, but that person was gone, and this new Laurel was standing in front of me. I could tell she wanted to kiss me, but she didn't. She started to say something. But the words wouldn't come out at first, and then when they did, her voice was low and soft, and I could barely hear her say, "We'll have our time. I know it." I knew that she'd had the same feelings that I had, and it took one hellish night to bring them out. I held her tightly, kissing her hair, and trying to fight the fear that was starting to edge in. A fear that seemed to be getting bigger and bigger with every touch and every kiss, until I almost couldn't breathe. I looked at her and saw "It" in her eyes, too. And then she pulled away, untangling herself from me. The words pulled from somewhere deep in her.

"I love you, Clive January." She kissed my forehead, and then turned quickly and walked into the night.

"Laurel…wait…" I started to go after her, but then I stopped myself. And it was probably the hardest thing I'd ever done, but I did it anyway. I'd made up my mind on the way to the station that I was getting out of Hendersonville that night, and I didn't want anybody, even her, trying to convince me to stay. I knew what she'd say, there's only a few more weeks left, and you'll get your diploma, at least stay until that.

But if I was honest with myself, I knew it was more than that. The truth is I'd never experienced what I'd felt with her before. I mean I'd had women, but this was more, this was a feeling that reached to the bottom of my soul, filling up all the empty places that had been crying out for all those years. And I knew that if I didn't get away from her, I never would.

It would keep me in Hendersonville, trapped like a dog that wants to run away, but he still keeps coming back to the same old place every time. I knew I was hooked as sure as I knew my name, and I had to go cold turkey. I had plans, a future and nobody, not even Laurel, could get in the way.

Later that night, I stuffed my few things in an old army duffle bag. Shirts, jeans, a couple of books. My SAT scores, they'd come that morning. I'd planned to open them on Sunday, I was superstitious, but I chucked them in the bag, unopened. And one other thing, a letter that had come from Missus Foster. I'd opened it, and there was another letter in it, sealed. On the outside it said, open on your eighteenth birthday. In her note to me, she said that Daddy had given it to her about a week before he died, but that he'd made her promise that if anything ever happened to him she wouldn't send it to me until I was eighteen.

She'd got my birthday wrong, it wasn't till October. I'd started to open it right away, but each time, I stopped myself. In a way it seemed that by opening it before Daddy wanted me to, I'd be breaking a promise to him. But now with everything that had happened, the thought that Daddy had wanted me to know something, made me want to know even more. I had to know. I started to rip it open when I heard the door knob turn. I stuffed the letter back into my duffle bag.

"Where you goin', boy?"

I didn't turn. I knew if I did, I'd probably smack her.

"I said, where is you goin?"

"Fuck you, Ma!"

She didn't look scared. It was as if she expected it. She just spit out. "You ain't goin' nowhere, and you ain't gonna be nothin!"

I shoved her down on the bed. I wanted to take her skinny neck and crush it, but I stopped myself. I just stood over her, my heart ready to jump out of my chest.

"Why'd you do it?" Silence. Nothing but the sound of the steady rain beating against the slate roof. "Why'd you take my college applications out of the mailbox?"

She laughed. I was sure my hatred for her at that moment would overwhelm me. Her narrow hard eyes stared up at me. "I did it 'cause you don't deserve to go to college. What makes you thinks you gots the right to git outta here? You ain't got the right. You ain't goin' nowhere, and you ain't gonna be nothin'."

I shouted at the top of my lungs. Yelling over the rain, over her. I wanted everybody to hear. I wanted God to hear me. "You're wrong! I am gonna be something. I'm gonna be rich, and I'm gonna be famous, and I'm gonna be happy, and you're gonna wish that you could say that I was your son, but it'll be too late 'cause from this point on, I don't fuckin' know you!"

I grabbed my duffle bag and ran into the rain. Free for the first time in my life, I kept running. The rain was absolving me, washing away my doubts, my fears. I remembered a secret place that I used to go when I was a kid, on the edge of town, where huge trees twined around each other. Three of those trees had grown up so much on each other that there was a little space in between them. I crawled in the damp place where the trees curled together, and I lay my head down on the ground. And I slept better than I had since the night Daddy took me away from there.

CHAPTER NINE

The Town With No Name

I planned to hitch as far north as I could. I didn't give a shit where I went as long as it was far away from Hendersonville. I got rides with all kinds of people, hippies, traveling salesmen, truck drivers, just about anybody who was brave enough to pick up a black man with a duffle bag, a wild looking Afro, and an even wilder look in his eyes.

When I saw myself in a cracked gas station mirror, I got a sick feeling that started in my gut and reached up to my temples. For the first time I realized how much I resembled Ma. Like some fucked up joke from God for my hating her so much. I'd have to see her face whenever I looked at mine. I'd never get away from her, no matter how much I tried. I stumbled out of the bathroom and leaned against a post, sticking out my thumb, headed wherever the next car would take me.

That's how I ended up in the town with no name. I just kept hitching until I couldn't go any further. Maine. The last ride let me off in the town with no name. Actually, the town had a name, but it was a long Indian name so complicated that everybody just called it the town with no name.

"Hi!"

I whirled around. I had only been in the town a few hours, and I was wandering around wondering where I could find something to eat for fifty cents. I didn't have much extra money, just the cash I'd saved from my factory job. I'd planned to use it for college, and I didn't want to piss it away just on getting by 'cause I was determined that somehow, in spite of Ma, I was getting to some college somewhere. But right now, I'd just have to get a gig somewhere until I figured out how I'd get things back together again.

"You look lost."

I squinted in the sun, surveying a tall kind of moony-looking girl, smiling at me. I smiled back, not sure what else I could do.

"Hey..."

She circled me, with that dippy look on her face. She had a flower in her dark hair and her boobs were bursting out of her tie-dyed vest. She had a handful of wilted daisies stuck in her cleavage. I couldn't really tell if she was black or white. She had light brown skin with straight black hair almost to her waist, and her nose was long and thin. I was thinking that maybe she was an Indian or something. She did have that kinda Pocahontas look, but before I could think anything else, she burst into my thoughts grinning, "My name's Poppy, and you?"

"Clive."

She handed me a daisy. "Well it's really nice to meet you, Clive."

"You too."

"So, Clive, are you running from the law?"

I gulped, did I look that bad. "Fuck, no!"

"Well I mean, why else would anybody come all the way up here, 'cause you're not from here, right?"

Before I could answer what was becoming an increasingly whacked conversation, a voice rung out from across the street.

"Poppy!" A white chick hopped out of a VW van and ran over to us. "Where have you been? Doug's been waiting for you!"

Poppy looked totally unmoved. She just kept tearing off petals from another daisy, tossing them absentmindedly into the street. "Well, if you must know, I was talking to Clive. He said he wants to be our roommate."

I looked at her like she was fuckin' out of her mind, but before I could say anything, the white girl broke into a huge grin and looped her arm through mine. "Far out!"

I knew I needed to nip this in the bud before it got totally out of hand. "Whoaaaa, ladies. I'm not looking to be your roommate. I'm just passing through."

Poppy looked up at me with the most childlike brown eyes I'd ever seen. "Now, Clive, really, where are you going, Canada?" Cause I mean that's about the only place else to go from here. You know you need a place to stay, and..." she had picked up my duffle bag and was tooling lazily toward the VW van, "we've got the perfect place."

"But wait. I don't have any money to share a place!" I started to protest more, but, the truth is, she was right. Other than what I'd saved for college, I didn't have jack shit to my name and not a clue where I was going next.

The white chick tossed her long, stringy, red hair back, wrinkling her nose in that broad smile. "Oh, that's not a problem, neither do we. We stay upstairs at the no name café. We all work there. They need another waiter, so you can work there, too."

That's how I ended up living on top of the no name café with an Indian chick, a wacky white girl, and this Asian girl named Raisin. The white girl's name was Amber. She had thin red hair, green eyes, and was definitely the most adventurous of the three. Poppy was usually in her own world, and she rarely if ever seemed to come down completely into the one that the rest of us were in.

And Raisin, well, it took a while to figure her out. She didn't say a whole lot, but her small narrow eyes, which actually looked like raisins, were constantly on me, that is until I looked her way. Sometimes I thought I might give her one of my best *Looks*, but frankly, I don't think the chick could've handled it. Maybe she'd never been around a brother. Who the fuck knew? I wasn't gonna trip about it. I was just glad to have found someplace to hang for the moment.

The place was big, more like a huge loft with two small rooms and a large living dining area with an alcove where I slept. The whole place looked as if it had been decorated by somebody on a bad acid trip. Everything was tie-dyed prints and psychedelic colors. It reminded me of pictures I'd seen of the hippie scene in San Francisco. But hey, it was clean. I had a bed, or sort of one, at least it wasn't somebody's doorway or a smelly bus station. It was kind of peaceful, with the trees and everything, definitely made a man forget what he was running from.

Amber strolled into the living room as I was flipping through an old magazine. She grinned and then tossed something in my lap. "Ever smoke pot?"

I picked up the joint, turning it over in my fingers. I wondered what new world it could open up for me. I took out a match, put the joint between my teeth and lit it. "Nope." I took a long drag. It was harsh, harsher than a cigarette. I almost gagged, but I caught myself. The insides of my nose burned. "I'm always willing..." my eyes teared up, and I barely choked out the words, "to try something new."

Amber smiled mischievously, her green eyes lighting up. "Far out, man." One thing about Amber, she usually didn't say a whole lot more than that. But sometimes, you didn't really need to. She plopped next to me on the bean bag hassock, deftly rolling another joint while she sucked on one already in her mouth. "Ever wonder why we're here...on earth I mean?"

I tried another toke of the joint. This time it went down a little easier. I coughed, letting out a roll of smoke. A glass of water would've done pretty damn good now, but I didn't ask, wouldn't be cool. Other than my scratchy throat and burning eyes, I didn't notice any difference yet, but I figured it would come. "Naw, not really...never really thought about it."

"Well see, I read this book that was talking about reincarnation and stuff. It was saying that we were all on this earth for a certain purpose. You know, like to fulfill some divine plan or something." Pot definitely made Amber talkative. "And I wondered what my purpose is. I mean, like maybe I'm supposed to invent somethin' or be a great world leader. You know, something really wild like that."

"Yeah...right, maybe..." I couldn't really think of much else to say. If the chick wanted to think she had some divine destiny or whatever, what could I say?

"Or then other times I think, well maybe my destiny is just here in no name, living in a commune or something with Doug."

Doug. All three of these women seemed to have a thing for Doug. He was the owner of the no name café. A real hippie spiritual leader type. Long, white hair, he must've been at least fifty, but had a twenty-year-old's body. Seriously pumped up. And he wore all this hippie shit, too: headbands, sandals, and walked around with this holier than thou look on his face. I usually tried to stay away from him. Something about him made my skin crawl. My first day on the job at no name, he handed me the apron, and his hand lingered a little too long.

Then, he just gave me this spooky look and asked, "How old are you?"

"Eighteen. Why?" Actually, I was only seventeen. I'd be eighteen in October, but he'd never know.

"Hmmmm."And then he just looked at me almost hungrily.

I figured it was time to end this conversation, so I jumped in quickly. "So, which tables are mine?" I wanted to get away from his stare.

"Oh, how about tables 5, 6, and 7. Those three. Yes." He paused. "Three's a nice number, don't you think?"

Three's a nice number? Well so was two, or four, shit. What is his trip? But whatever it was, I knew I wasn't gonna get too deep into it. Just do my job, save some money, and get the hell out of there.

But he just kept on going. His eyes measured me. "Yes, I really do like three. The unbalance, yet balance to it. Three is a holy number, the trinity, you know."

I grabbed some silverware. "Hey, man, I think I better set my tables."

He grabbed my arm with a strong hand. "Do you ever think about spiritual things?"

Now I knew he'd gone ape shit. I shook my head no.

"We should talk sometimes. I could teach you a lot."

The hell you will. But I couldn't say that. I needed this job and the place to crash. "Yeah, I'll check it out."

He smiled that weird moony smile of his.

"Clive!"

I realized that I'd totally spaced. Amber was waving her hand in front of my face. "Wow, man, I thought I'd lost you for a minute."

"Sorry, I spaced…"

She giggled. "Then it's working."She kinda danced around me, twirling a scarf around my face. "You're officially fucked up."

CHAPTER TEN

Girls Just Wanna Have Fun

The nights in no name were quiet. A different kind of quiet than Hendersonville. There you always had night sounds, crickets, and shit. But here, it was just, quiet. Sometimes at night, I'd see her face—Laurel. I'd see her eyes. One time it seemed so real that I just knew that she was here, next to me. It started happening so much, this feeling of her being there, that one day I decided to call her. I had to know what she was doing, if she was thinking about me as much as I was thinking about her, or if I was just going plain crazy. So I called her. I don't really know what I expected to say or what I expected her to say, but I sure didn't expect what I got.

"This number is no longer in service." I hung up. *Shit, she's moved on.* Right then I decided no more thoughts of her. Whatever it was that happened that night would stay there in Hendersonville, buried in the past. A past that I was determined was not gonna fuck up my future. So whenever thoughts of her would try to creep in, I'd push 'em away and think about the reason I left.

I'd been here two months now, and I was starting to save a little cash. I'd also found out that there was a college not far away, Whitmore. I figured I'd hang here for a few more months, save some more dough, and then see about getting into Whitmore or anyplace else for the winter semester. I hadn't forgotten my goal. The way I looked at it, no name was just a temporary stopping place before I got into the real shit. College and the rest of my life.

These thoughts were tumbling through my head, as they did most nights, so I didn't hear the soft approach of footsteps. I opened my eyes and was looking into Raisin's dark black holes of eyes. She didn't say anything at first, she just stared, the way she always did. Then she let her robe drop to the ground. She was totally naked. I smiled. "Well hello." *Now this was live.*

She smiled shyly. Not a bad body. Small, compact, but serviceable. She sat on the edge of my bed, and then crawled in. Burrowing next to me, kissing me all over. For a woman who'd barely said two words to me, she was all in my shit.

"I want you." And that's all she said. She just went for it.

And so did I. The last time had been that last night in Hendersonville, so I was ready for some. And she was more than ready to give it up. She was so small and light that she could do all sorts of acrobatic shit. But the weird thing was that she didn't make a sound. No moans, or groans, just silence.

And when we finished, she got up as quietly as she'd gotten in, draped her robe around her small warm body and whispered, "Don't tell Amber and Poppy."

"No problem." I slept real good that night.

The next morning, Raisin looked like nothing had happened. She stared at me as usual, and then looked away quickly. But one time, just once I caught a glimpse of something else. Then it was gone. The ultimate zipless sex, I supposed.

I closed the bathroom door behind me. I liked to get in early before the girls got in and steamed it all up. But today I figured I didn't really have to worry. They'd all been out late with Doug, some poetry reading or something. They'd asked me to come, but I got out of it. The less time I spent with Doug the better, and eight hours a day at the no name was plenty for me.

I turned on the water nice and hot and stepped in. Letting the warm water run over me. Felt good, sensual. I grabbed the bar of soap and started lathering up when I became aware of somebody's hands on my back, massaging it with a bar of soap. I smiled, thinking it must be Raisin, back for some more. That chick never got enough. But when I turned around, I met the clear brown eyes of Poppy. Wet and nude. Shit, this whole thing was starting to have a déjà vu feel to it. I smiled, not quite sure how to react. I was usually good on my feet, but I gotta admit, this had kinda thrown me for a loop.

"No daisies?" That's about all I could think of to say. Cause it was the first time I'd seen her without a bunch of half dead daisies stuck between her boobs. This time, there were no daisies, nothing. Just bare flesh, brown and damp from the steam of the shower.

She smiled, that half-dazed smile of hers. "I can get some if you like, and tickle your you know what." She giggled again.

I couldn't believe this, thinking about the dry spells I'd had in Hendersonville, this shit was unbelievable. "No, I think we can manage without them."

She let the bar of soap slip out of her hands to the floor. I pulled her in and closed the curtain.

When we finished, she pressed her wet body against mine, twirling her hands in my hair and whispered, "This is our secret, right?"

I was beginning to get it. "Sure." But I wanted to say I'm starting to have the same secret with everybody around here. I thought about all of that as I bussed the tables at no name and carted the dirty dishes to the tiny kitchen in the back. Doug had been gone all day, so I could relax a little more than usual. When he was around, I always had to watch my back. Literally. He was just a little too friendly for my tastes. But I figured I could take his weepy stares a few months more, just 'til I could save up enough to get to a college somewhere.

"Hey, watch out!"

I ran right smack into Dobey, the lanky white guy who bussed the other tables. "Shit." He spilled the bottle of ketchup he'd been carrying all over the front of my white shirt. "Fuck!"

"Wow, man, I'm sorry, I guess I wasn't looking."

"Damn." I sucked my teeth in disgust. The last thing I felt like doing was having to change my clothes. The place was packed with the lunch time rush, and I couldn't afford to lose those tips. But it wasn't all his fault either. I hadn't exactly been concentrating on where I was going, so I figured why trip. "Don't sweat it. I'll just run up and change. Cover for me, okay?"

"Yeah sure. No problem."

I stuffed my tips in my pocket and bolted up the rickety stairs to our upstairs apartment. The minute I opened the door, I knew something was up. Call it sixth sense or whatever, but I knew I wasn't alone. I walked quietly down the hallway into the living room, half expecting to jump on somebody trying to rob the place, when I stopped dead in my tracks.

I couldn't believe what I was seeing. Doug and Amber getting into it. I mean really into it, but on *my bed*! "What the fuck are y'all doin'?" I musta scared the shit outta them, because they jumped up as if there'd been a fire alarm or something. The funny thing was that Doug didn't look surprised. In fact, he looked pleased.

He threw the covers back exposing his nude body. I turned away. The last thing I wanted to see was his naked ass. He got out of the bed, parading around like some damn stud horse. "Want to join us, Clive? I can assure you it would be like nothing you've ever experienced."

I think I was too shocked to say anything. The thought of being in bed with a naked pervert was about all I could take. My stomach turned over. Amber wasn't saying anything, but truth is she didn't look too upset to see me either. I think I was the only one who gave a damn. Doug turned to Amber, waving his hand toward me dramatically. "Amber, darling, make Clive feel welcome."

She grinned. "Right on!" She hopped out of the bed, her plump breasts flapping against her chest as she jumped over to me and started trying to unbutton my pants. "Wanna get high first?"

Doug gurgled with satisfaction at the mention of pot. He stayed half-high most of the time anyway. "Oh yes, let's do," he cooed, sounding like some drunk pigeon.

"Naw! Get the fuck outta my bed!"

Doug turned to me coolly as he took a long toke from the joint that Amber had just rolled. "Whose bed did you say this was? I do believe that I still own this place." He stopped, letting the smoke curl into his nostrils. "And everything in it."

He turned to me, the smile gone from his face. The look in his eyes, demented and far away, made me stop short. "Amber, I think that Clive has a rather nasty attitude for someone in the family, and that won't do. You see, Clive, we are family here, and as family, we share...everything. And everyone."

Amber, suddenly, looked scared. She whispered, almost pleaded with me. "Just do what he wants, okay. It'll be fun..."

But I didn't see fun in her eyes, just pure naked fear. That's when I knew I was getting the hell out of there before something went down that I didn't want to be a part of. "This shit's too crazy for me!"

I bolted for the door. Amber tried to run after me, but he held her back as she shouted. "Wait, Clive...come back...please...please!"

Doug leaned back on the bed, his eyes following me out of the room. "Oh, let him go. He'll be back. Where else has he got to go?"

But I didn't go back. I'd had enough of no name and women who fucked you without saying a word, and then acted as if nothing had happened. I was getting away. That night I slept in the woods. The next morning I waited until they'd all gone. I knew they had their regular Saturday morning meditation thing with Doug at his place, so I went back in and gathered up my stuff in double quick time. I thought about leaving a note. The girls had actually been nice, and not bad lays either, but I figured I'd better just make a clean break.

Thinking about the whole situation, I just couldn't erase from my mind the fear I saw in Amber's eyes. And the more I thought, the more the whole thing made sense, Poppy's detachment, Raisin's queer silence and especially the way they latched onto me. As if I were some kind of savior or protector. Then it hit me. That's exactly what I was supposed to have been. Their protector from Doug. But I didn't quite go along with their plans.

Now, the question in my mind was what were my plans? I had no job, no place to live, and just a little more saved than when I'd left Hendersonville. Maybe enough to cover college for a semester, maybe two. I'd always counted on getting some kind of scholarship or financial aid to fill the gap. I sat at the base of the tree. And for some reason, I thought about Missus Foster. I hadn't thought about her since I got her letter right before I left Hendersonville. The sadness was still there, because I couldn't think about her without thinking about Daddy, too, and how different things would've been if he'd still been here.

I pulled Daddy's letter out of my duffle bag. I turned it over in my hand, holding the sealed envelope up to the moonlight, trying to see inside. It's almost as if everything that Daddy ever was, was inside that envelope. A couple of times I'd almost opened it. But I'd decided that I'd keep the promise to Daddy, and I wouldn't open it 'til my eighteenth birthday, a month from now. I could wait a month. For, Daddy. I could wait. I put the envelope carefully back into the corner of my bag, ramming it way in the back so there'd be no way it could fall out.

As I stuffed it in the bag, I looked at my few things crumpled up inside, and I saw my SAT scores, still unopened. *Hell, I might as well open 'em now, what do I have to lose.* I was too tired and stressed at this point to even be scared at how I did. For a minute I saw Laurel in her classroom the way it used to be, helping me, and that sweet smell of soap, shampoo, and flowers she always had. Then I shoved the memory away. I swallowed hard and tore open the envelope.

I smiled. I did ok. Shit. I did real well. I was going to college. Somewhere. I promised myself that. And I wasn't letting myself down.

New York

"Clive...Oh, Clive, baby...Oh God I'm so..." She leaned over me. The blood from my shirt soaked her skin, turning it a brownish red. As I looked in her eyes, I could feel her tears, touching my face, as her soft hands used to. Then I realized that I couldn't really feel anything. Because I was dead.

I looked down at me, lying there motionless, and I saw her sobbing over me. Shaking me, trying to will me back to life. But I knew it was too late. I felt this detachment, but at the same time an inexplicable heaviness. Something was pulling me back toward my body, which I didn't really even feel was mine anymore. Something wasn't letting me leave. Suddenly, the room was light, brighter than I've ever seen it. I couldn't see her, or me. Just this blinding light. Whispers from eternity called me, telling me that I had to find out. I had to make peace for peace to come to me.

I had to know. Who would do this to me? I heard a rushing noise pulling me backwards in time. I saw my wife and my office, and then they faded away as I went back further. Something was guiding me. I knew that something was my father. He was here but not here. Talking to me. It was his voice whispering to me. I knew that he knew, but that I would never be able to come to him unless I knew, too.

Where did it begin? Where did the change start? I knew when. And then I was back there, looking at those faces. Being there again, like I'd never left and become someone new.

CHAPTER ELEVEN

College Boy

"Tell me your name again."

"Clive January."

"Uh…huh…and tell me again, Clive, how you got here, to Whitmore, I mean. It seems like a long way to go from Atlanta."

I met his steady gaze without flinching. I knew that I couldn't blink, 'cause if I did it was all over. "Well, my father was in the military. He was killed in Nam, and so I lived with my grandmother in Atlanta. She was sick, and then when she died, well, I didn't have any other folks or anything."

"What about your mother?"

I didn't move a muscle. "She was killed in a car accident when I was five."

His face softened for a moment. "So you're completely alone in the world?"

"Yes, sir, completely."

He leaned back in his chair, wrinkling his brow. The leather creaked as he settled in. I looked around the room. There were diplomas on the wall and a large bookcase in the corner stuffed with books that looked like a million students had opened and closed their covers, with each one wearing the spines thinner and thinner until wide spider web cracks covered the books.

"Well, this is a most unusual situation. You don't have your high school transcripts, but I must admit that these are exceptional SATs, and you would…" He cleared his throat apologetically. "Uh add to the…diversity of the student body at Whitmore."

He glanced over at the white woman sitting in the corner. She was probably in her thirties, but her faded brown skirt and slightly rumpled blouse made her look older. The sunlight from the window in back of her formed a hazy circle around her, giving her and the room an almost surreal look. She and the dean seemed to exchange a secret glance. "So what I'm proposing is that we give you the freshman qualifying exams. If you pass, well then I think that we could invite you to be a part of the freshman class here at Whitmore."

That was four years ago. I sipped on my pina colada and thumped my fingers to the strains of Disco Inferno. I smiled to myself, the room was starting to have that nice wavy feel to it. I almost laughed. What a scam.

And now I had my degree and my passport to the world, and all because a little college in Maine needed a few more black folks to qualify for their federal money. I found out later that's why they jumped on me when I showed up with my orphan story. The funny thing is, I'd felt like an orphan since Daddy died, so in a way it was true. Even if it weren't true, at this point I'd said it so many times that I had actually started believing it. Hendersonville and that whole period of my life was something that had happened to someone else. I shuddered, realizing how true that really was.

I found out just how true when I turned eighteen. I'd just started at Whitmore. I remember wandering over to a far end of the campus. The trees looked like bright blotches of reds and yellows against the cool blue sky. It was October, and it had just started to get cold, but that's not why I was shivering. I was about to find out what Daddy had wanted me to know so much that he'd put it down in a letter and had it sent to me all these years later.

Dear Clive,

I want you to know that there's never been nobody in my whole life, not even my folks, who I loves like you. You're my son, my boy. You always was, and you always will be. I'm 'bout to tell you something so's you hear it from me and not somebody who don't love you.

As I read further, my heart sank lower and lower. Some black thing was covering me up, choking me, forcing this bitter taste up from my gut. I couldn't stop myself from wrenching forward and vomiting in the grass. Daddy's handwriting was big and awkward on the yellowed paper, screaming out what I'd asked to know, but now wish I never had. I knelt next to the tree, wishing that tears would come out. I threw up repeatedly, wishing that *I'd* fallen off the ladder, not Daddy, because nothing else seemed to matter anymore. My life was a lie, everything about me was a lie. The last words of the letter stung my eyes.

...Now maybe you can understands your ma a little better. Why she been the way she is. I know she done some mean things to you, but you gotta try and forgive her. Try for me. You'll always be my little Clive. I love you.

Daddy.

The letter I'd been waiting for, for so long felt like a knife that had been jabbed in me. Not deep enough for me to die right away, just enough for my life that had been to trickle out of me in a slow stream. The letter fell from my hands. I felt Daddy there on that cool fall day, sitting next to me, trying to make it all right. I could almost feel his heavy arm around me, just like the day he took me from Gramma Deedee's. Making the hurt go away. 'Cause the truth hurt so much.

I lay there for a long time that day. Until the blue sky had turned to black and the cool breeze was a cold wind cutting through me. A strange silence settled over me. After a while, I could hear the dawn starting to come, the birds and the wind and the sounds of the town below me. I think that's when the change happened. Because from that moment, I decided that I wouldn't be hurt by the truth ever again. From that point on, the only truth would be what I decided it was gonna be. So now I was somebody new. Hendersonville with its foul secrets and unhappiness weren't a part of my truth anymore. It was dead. More dead than Daddy, more dead than the little boy who died with him.

I was now Clive January, from Atlanta, GA, only son of a decorated Vietnam vet. Hell, Daddy could've kicked ass in Nam if he'd had to. So I didn't feel bad. And it gave me a whole new feeling as if I'd shed the old skin and become someone new. And I wasn't looking back. I squeezed the last drops of my drink out of the glass as I heard a loud voice behind me.

"Congratulations big guy. We made it!" Red slapped me on the back, sloshing beer on the table as he lowered himself into the chair. Red was one big white boy. He got that nickname 'cause of the color of his skin, bright red with blondish red hair. When I first met him, I thought he was just another cracker only from up North instead of the South.

But as I got to know him, I realized that he wasn't all that different from me, except that he was white and I was black. Red was running from something, too. He didn't talk much about his family or his past, and I didn't ask him. He didn't ask me much about myself either. I guess that's why we became friends. Neither of us talked about the past. Just the future. And we both had the same dream. Money. Shitloads of money. So much money that we could say "fuck you" to anybody and mean it.

Red leaned over to me as he took a huge gulp of beer. "You know partner, I got this feeling in my bones that we're gonna make it real big in New York. You ever been to New York?"

I shook my head no.

"Me neither, but a buddy of mine used to go there every summer. He's the one that told me that New York is the place to go to make the serious money."

I smiled. I got a little thrill every time I thought about New York. Almost like the city was a woman. Waiting to be conquered. And I was ready. I grabbed a pretzel, biting down into the salty part. I kicked back in my chair. "Why else do you think we're going there? Not to fuck around, that's for damn sure."

Red cracked up. "I hear you, buddy."

I turned to the bartender. "I'll take another one of these." I held up my empty glass. "And he'll..." But before I could finish my sentence, I saw her. Through the film of my glass. Like a dream coming to me, only it wasn't a dream. She was walking slowly toward me, with this come hither smile on her face.

"It's been a long time, Clive."

I put the glass down quickly. I didn't want her to see my hand trembling. Instead, I gave her a peck on the cheek, hoping that I wasn't breathing too hard. "Yeah, it has. You look good."

And she did. She hadn't changed at all: same smile, same small hands and round ass.

Red nudged me. "Introduce me, buddy."

I turned around quickly. "Oh sorry…Red this is Miss Dav…I mean Laurel."

She smiled coyly at Red, holding out her hand to him.

"It's a pleasure."

The deejay threw on another tune, Marvin Gaye's "Let's Get it On." Laurel grabbed my hand."Well aren't you going to ask me to dance or do I have to ask you?" She smiled. I could tell that the old Laurel was back. Whatever had changed after that night in Hendersonville had faded away, and she was back in control. Never betraying her real feelings.

But I wasn't a kid anymore, even though at this point, I felt like one. Laurel seemed to have that effect on me. Like I'd always be her student. But I figured I'd play it off. I led her onto the middle of the dance floor, draping my arms around her. I'd forgotten how tiny she was. I was more than a full head taller than she was. She could almost fit her entire body in the space between my shoulders and my waist.

All these thoughts were galloping through my brain so fast that I couldn't really make much sense out of them: the last night that I'd seen her, the police station, the pain of my college applications, and her touch.

I remembered her touch, and now I was feeling it again as she whispered in my ear. "I love this song."

I held her closer. I was almost afraid. Afraid that I wouldn't be able to let her go. That she'd take back part of my soul. She leaned her head into my chest. I could feel her heart. Beating steadily. Not like mine that felt like it would explode through my chest. I wanted to say something, but I couldn't. So I just let myself go, surrendering to the music.

"Ok, now, Laurel, tell me about, Clive. You said you knew him way back…in Atlanta?"

Laurel looked right through me. But she didn't miss a beat. The old Laurel was definitely back. Always cool.

"Yes, I guess it was in Atlanta. Our families lived next door." She turned to me defiantly."Isn't that how we know each other, Clive?"

A thin film of sweat beaded up on my forehead. In the four years since I'd left Hendersonville, she's the first person who knew me, the real me.

"Uh right, yeah…neighbors…" I was hoping that Red would just cool it at this point, but he kept up. Beer always did make him curious.

"So tell me about my buddy. What was he like and all?"

I could tell that Laurel was enjoying this. "Well, let's see. All the girls wanted him, but he always said that he was saving himself."

Red slapped down his beer, laughing until his face was so red that you couldn't tell where his forehead ended and his hair began.

"This guy…save himself…shit, things sure did change at college. He was with so many chicks…damn I couldn't even keep up, and that was saying something, believe me."

Laurel just smiled mysteriously. "Well you know people do change."

"Right," I jumped in. "So Red, I think we're gonna split. It's been a while since Laurel and me have had a chance to talk."

Red winked at me. "Sure thing, buddy. I'll check you in the morning. The bus for the Big Apple leaves at eight. I'll see you on it."

"Later, man."

He disappeared through the crowd.

It was just me and her. Staring at each other.

"Why do you lie about your past?" she asked.

My head throbbed. But I wouldn't let her know that. I turned back to her, unsmiling. "It's not a lie."

"Oh really, neighbor."

"It's the truth. My truth."

Suddenly, she understood what it meant to hate who you were because the only person who'd ever loved you was dead. She stroked my cheek, the way she'd done that night so long ago at her house. She kissed my hand.

For a minute I saw the look she had in her eyes that night in Hendersonville. "It's okay, Clive January, I love you no matter who you are." She got up and walked away.

I wanted to run after her, but my limbs were frozen. My voice was frozen. Then something snapped, and I bolted up. I ran past the crowds to find her. This time, I wasn't letting her disappear into the night, only to see her face, and feel her touch, but know that she's not there. I dashed into the street. Nothing. She was nowhere. Only a cat scratching itself against the lamp post. She couldn't have gotten away that quickly. I ran down an alley. Nothing. All of the emotions of the past four years and the aching loneliness I tried to deny rushed over me. I collapsed against the wall, and tears streamed down. I hadn't cried since Daddy died. But now I couldn't stop. All the times I'd held it in were coming out now.

I don't know how long I was there, crying alone. When I opened my eyes, I saw a man staring at me. He was far away. I couldn't really make out his features. Except that he was just still, very still. He reached out his hand.

"Who are you?" I yelled at him, my voice echoed back against the empty walls. He just stood there watching at me. Then his face became very light. Blotting out his features completely. Only his outstretched hand was clearly visible.

"Who the fuck are you? I don't know you!" I ran toward him, but as I got there, he disappeared in a flash of light, and I saw her. Laurel.

"Clive." I could see that she'd been crying. "Oh, Clive, I'm so sorry." She buried her face in my chest. We stood there holding each other, drawing strength from each other. I knew it was right. I knew she was right for me. But I couldn't. Not yet. I couldn't.

"Let's sit down." She gently pulled me down onto a damp park bench. I didn't want to let her go. She whispered to me. "I knew I'd see you again."

For the first time in years, I could let go. I lay my head in her lap. She kissed my forehead, softly.

"When did you leave, Hendersonville?" I hadn't actually spoken that name in so long, it still stuck in my throat. All the tortured memories, Ma, everything I'd shoved away.

She smiled, brushing my fingers lightly against her mouth. "Right after you did. I was bored with teaching. I was only twenty-four, with the whole wide world waiting for me. Hendersonville was just a way station. I needed a break. I had begun to feel like a top that had spun out of control. Hendersonville had centered me. For a minute. After you left, I knew it was time for me, too. So I packed up and stayed with about every friend I knew. When I'd stretched my pennies almost to the point of non-existence, I'd take a short-term teaching job. Substitute teaching usually. Something where I didn't have to go in every day. The rest of the time, I'd read, and think. and try to figure out why I was here. Was there something I was supposed to be doing other than exploring life's possibilities? But maybe that was enough. More than most people ever do."

She cradled my head in her hands, propping me up from her lap so that her eyes bore into mine. "Do you believe in fate?"

"I don't know. I don't know what I believe in."

"Well, I do, I believe in star-crossed love. And I believe that we're part of some larger romantic scheme where we'll always be in each other's lives. But not completely. Like the perennial ships that pass in the night. To touch briefly, but always passing. Why else would I have walked into that little club? I knew that I'd see you. I just knew it."

"But how did you know it? I figured I'd never see you again."

She smiled. "Well, truthfully, I knew you were at Whitmore."

I sat up, shocked. "How?"

"Your freshman year I got a call from the registrar's office there, somehow they had tracked your high school down to Hendersonville High. They got my name since I'd been your faculty advisor. Whitmore wanted to verify that you had graduated, and you were who you said you were. The school sent your transcripts and pictures, but Whitmore still wanted to talk to me to make sure that you'd actually done the work in the classes."

I looked away from her. I couldn't believe that Whitmore knew all those years, and here I'd really thought I was slick. I was just stupid, that's all, and lucky. Damn lucky they didn't boot my ass out after they found out. I shook my head, realizing how close I'd come to blowing everything.

She kissed me softly on the forehead. "I'd left a forwarding number at the school with Ralph Warner."

Ralph Warner, I remembered him. A big line backer type guy who was my high school principal. He seemed to know exactly what I was thinking, especially when it came to Laurel. I remembered the day he'd taken me aside and said seriously, "Boy, remember you're a student in this school, and we don't allow any crossing that line between students and teachers. Miss Davenport is your *teacher*. You remember that now, hear?" I smiled remembering how I'd just shrugged him off, frankly not giving a damn what he or anybody else in that hell hole of a school thought.

"He knew I had a thing for you. And he didn't like it."

Laurel sat up and looked at me. "Ralph Warner, no…I don't believe that."

I drew her closer to me and whispered teasingly, "Well believe it 'cause it's true. He knew I wanted you."

"Well it was mutual then." She snuggled closer to me. "Right from the first time I saw you outside of town in front of those trees that had all grown together…remember?" She laughed a light, sparkly laugh that I'd almost forgotten, but which still sent little shivers across my back.

I played with her small hands, remembering again her touch. "So why didn't you ever call me? I tried you, but you'd left."

"I almost did, a couple of times, but I knew you needed to be free to make yourself what you wanted to be without me or anybody else pulling you back to a past you so obviously hated." She was quiet for a minute, and then she said softly, "So mostly, I just thought about you…a lot, and hoped that you were thinking of me…at least sometimes." She looked up and I could see that her eyes had changed; they were clear and seemed to be pulling me into her so fast that I couldn't turn back.

I drew her closer to me. I didn't want to let her go this time. "Oh God Laurel, I was. So much…I had to stop myself."

She looked away from me, but her words tumbled out even faster. "I almost came to your graduation. I got to Whitmore and went there the morning of commencement. Then I got cold feet, so I turned back. I knew I still wanted to see you, and knew that somehow I would."

I pulled her into my arms, feeling her against me, needing her to know that it was the same for me, the same feelings, the same wanting.

She burrowed closer to me, saying, but looking away from me, "When I was eleven, I had this dream…about someone who was a part of me in a way I couldn't really explain, but we were linked by something outside of us. For a long time I didn't remember the dream, I think because it happened on one of the worst days of my life."

She paused a minute. "And the funny thing is, the day started like just about every other day in Cleveland. I walked to school passing other kids who all seemed to have some best friend or somebody to share a laugh with. But I was alone. It didn't really bother me anymore. I had my routine. I'd run through the back playground and try to get to school before the other kids so I could take out my books and read before class. But this day when I got to my locker, Linda and Celia, two girls I didn't really like, were waiting for me. Linda stood in front of my locker and looked at me defiantly."

Laurel Age 11:

"Guess what I heard?" Linda asked to no one in particular.

I ignored her and kept stuffing books in my locker.

Celia chimed in, "What did you hear, tell me. In fact…" she raised her voice a couple of notches so that anyone passing by could hear clearly, "Tell *everybody*, what did you hear, Linda?"

Linda looked over in my direction smugly, then said loudly so that all the kids streaming into homeroom could hear, "Well I heard that Laurel has a secret, and it's so secret, that even *she* doesn't know what it is!"

Hearing my name, I whirled around abruptly. "What are you talking about?"

They smirked at me. By now other kids had started gathering around to hear my big secret that I didn't even know.

I glared at Linda saying coolly, "Whatever it is, I'm not interested!"

Unperturbed, Linda blurted out, "Well I'd sure be interested to know if I found out that I was *adopted*!"

You could almost hear a pin drop. Everybody looked at me. The blood rushed to my head, and the word "adopted" jumbled around inside of me I felt sick and light-headed. I couldn't breathe, but I had to get away from the taunting stares, whispers, and giggles. So I just ran all the way back home, bolting into the room, with tears choking my throat so I could barely shout out at my mother.

"Is it true? Is it true that I'm adopted?"

Silence. My mother just sank onto the couch, and I knew. She didn't have to tell me that it was. I knew it was true. And everything that I'd ever been or thought I was had been a lie. And it hit me that I had no real family. That I had no one.

That night I prayed, "Please God, show me that I'm not alone, that there is someone for me." I don't know if I was dreaming or awake, because I all of a sudden felt this light and warmth all around me, like someone who loved me was close. I closed my eyes and saw a face, faintly at first, just his eyes, then his smile, and then he began taking shape. I sensed something or someone say, "He will love you and you him because you're the same."

Laurel's eyes were half closed, and her breathing was shallow. I held her closely to me until she started speaking again.

"And when I woke up, I felt this peace." Laurel turned to me and said almost sadly, "The eyes were yours, the face was yours. I never told you before, because I thought you'd be afraid, so I didn't say anything. But I wanted you to know."

I could feel a tear against my face. Her tear. And I don't know why, but her words shot through me like little pellets, leaving pin pricks. Tiny holes for my soul to seep out through. There was so much I wanted to ask her, to tell her, but for some reason I didn't or couldn't say anything. I kissed her, slowly at first, then more and more until my head was spinning again, and I was throwing aside her jacket and blouse and my coat and shirt. I could feel the hardness of the park bench jabbing against me and the softness of her under me, the hard edges and the soft touch. The fear and the love mingled together, fighting each other, filling me up, and at the same time emptying out every other thought or feeling I'd ever had.

As I pressed my body into hers, I felt the love rushing out from me to her and back to me, trying to eat away at the fear, but not quite. It was still there. I kissed her and held her and ran my fingers over her face, trying to memorize every curve because I knew that the fear was winning. And then I slept, with the cold bench and her warm body against me.

When I woke up, it was snowing that thick, mushy snow when it's really too warm to snow but for some reason it does anyway.Laurel was twirling around in the street, laughing like a little girl. "Clive, look. It's snowing in June!"

I sat up on my elbows, looking around at the thin blanket of white that had covered everything. Laurel looked like the snow queen, dancing around to the music in her head. "C'mon get up. It's beautiful."

"You are outta your mind!"

"I know, but isn't it wonderful!"

I don't know why, but I laughed. Maybe it was catching, whatever it was. This spark Laurel had. 'cause for some reason this woman could make me go through the weirdest mood shifts from sadness to fear to love to this feeling that everything was cool. Cooler than it'd ever been and cooler than it would ever be. I ran out to her, picked her up and held her up in the air like Daddy used to do to me. We both laughed as the snow licked our faces and clung to our clothes like crystals from God. I was out of breath from laughing and twirling her around in the air. When I finally sank down on the bench exhausted with her in my arms, I asked the question that had been burning into me since last night.

"So what about us? I'm going to New York. I've got a job. I don't know what your plans are, but…"

She pressed her fingers against my lips. "Shhhh, don't worry. You do what you need to do. Right now it's not the right time." She paused. "For either of us. But it will be, and then…well then we'll just have to find each other again. I'm not worried."

She kissed me and the last thing I remember her saying was, "It's good luck, snow in June. It's good luck for us."

CHAPTER TWELVE

New York 1974

"Hey, buddy, whatcha thinkin' about?" Red nudged me, and suddenly I was on the bus again, speeding past the New England scenery headed for the Big Apple.

"Nothin' jus thinkin'..."

"Shit, man, you can't fool me. You're thinking about her aren't you?"

I had to smile. Red did know me. Hell, we were like brothers. We'd roomed together since freshman year, and when you live with somebody that long you get to know their thoughts and their moods without them saying a thing.

The truth is, I was thinking about Laurel. I hadn't stopped thinking about her since we said goodbye. She'd gone with me to the bus station. And she'd smiled that old smile of hers, the confident, I'm-in-control smile. Only behind the smile, I knew she was just as scared as me. Scared of the feelings we had that seemed to lead us to places where we'd never been and that nobody else could touch. She didn't have an address to give me because she said she was just moving around for a while, and I didn't know where I'd be in New York. So in the end, we just sorta held each other until the bus driver started closing the door. I scrambled on, barely making it. I pressed my face against the greasy window and watched her smile blending into the trees and the telephone poles and the grey sky to a speck no bigger than the birds to nothing.

I'd meant to ask her other things, but somehow there just wasn't time. We both knew without having to say it that this wasn't it for us. That in a way it was more like a beginning. 'cause there was this connection between us. No matter what happened, we'd always be together. Even when it seemed like we weren't we would be. That's what I was thinking as my eyes roamed past the white New England houses and the brown green trees.

Red nudged me again. "She was a cutie." His blue eyes sparkled. "Did you get some?"

I started to tell the truth, I started to say that what I got from her I couldn't ever get from anybody else. That it was more than a lay. That it was a part of my soul. "Naw, man, we just talked."

A big shit eating I-don't-believe-you-for-a-minute grin spread across his face "Sure." He settled back in his seat with a chuckle.

"NEW YORK CITY PORT AUTHORITY LAST STOP!"

I bolted awake.

"We're heeeeere!" Red jumped up excitedly, grabbing his bag from the rack.

Truth is, I was still a little dazed. I think the last thing I remember was passing by Boston, and I'd been knocked out since then.

Everybody else on the bus was jostling and pushing as if there were some prize for being the first off the bus or something.

"C'mon, man, let's go!" I followed Red off the bus, down the steps, through the madness of the station. Then I stopped on the sidewalk. I'd never seen anything like it. The buildings rose up from the sidewalk like giant steeples. Tall, taller than anything I'd ever seen. People were everywhere: on the sidewalks, in the streets, laughing, talking, selling shit, a sea of movement.

My face broke out in this huge grin. I knew I was where I belonged. All those small towns in the backwaters of life were jails that I'd escaped from. I'd been doing time all my life. Finally, I was free.

I don't know how the hell we ended up at the Pier at Coney Island. Must be a white boy thing. Red had insisted that we go out there in the middle of the night. We'd been hanging out in bars for most of the evening, when all of a sudden he turned to me and said let's go to the pier. I didn't know what the hell he was talking about, and I don't think he did either, really. But his friend, the one who'd told him to come to New York to begin with, had told him some shit about having to come to the Pier at Coney Island. I wasn't that hyped about going, but I didn't want to hear him tell me I was chicken shit, so I went.

I must admit, it was pretty wild. It was a ghost town, especially at that time of night. Most of the old amusement park had closed down in bits and pieces and now all that was left was a rickety Ferris wheel, a rusted merry-go-round, and empty vendors booths. And the pier. A huge, rickety wooden pier, jutting out into the black waters.

Red waived his arms out wide and ran to the end of the pier, shouting like the drunken fool he was. "This shit's fantastic! Whoooooaaa." He whooped like an Indian, doing some lame dance at the end of the pier.

"Man, chill out. It's just a pier."

"Fuck you, Clive. C'mon out. What's wrong, you scared?"“

"Hell no, I ain't scared."

"Well c'mon then." I heard a huge splash as Red jumped feet first into the dark green waters. "The water's great!" He'd kicked his tennis shoes off first, but other than that, he was splashing around in all his clothes.

"Red…what the…Are you outta your fuckin' mind?!" All I could see was the churning black waters. Red had completely disappeared under the foam. And now my stomach had started to turn over. I didn't want to think the worst, and I sure as hell didn't want to have to go in there after him. Swimming was definitely not my thing.

"Red!"

"Chicken shit, chicken shit!" Red had bobbed up to the surface, his face pink and wet. He dog paddled around the moss-covered pilings. He gulped water and laughed as he taunted me from the water. "Man,

Clive, you are chicken shit. You're scared to jump in. C'mon, it's not cold!"

He somersaulted back under the waves, his water-logged arms flailing around. "I love it. This is better than the Charles in winter."

I shook my head, watching him zooming under the water, laughing. "Man you are one crazy white boy!"

He paddled over to the piling closest to me, his eyes bloodshot and red from the water, or the gallons of beer he'd drunk, I didn't know which. He splashed a handful of water in my direction, grinning. "Yeah and you are a scared ass n—"

"Man, fuck you!" And don't ask me why, but at that moment I saw all the challenges I'd ever faced in my life lining up before me. I knew that I had to do it. Not for Red and his crazy assed self, but for me. In a way, it was 1962 again, and I was in front of their playground with the WHITES ONLY sign. Only this time it was 1974, and I was going in.

I closed my eyes whispering, "Oh shit!"

The icy waters stung my face, drenching my clothes to the skin, crawling inside of me. I gasped. Trash and dirty seaweed wrapped itself around my arms. The only thing I could think was I gotta get air.

As hard as I tried, I couldn't get to the surface. Everything was black around me. I was swallowing water and feeling myself tunneling down. I didn't know where. My lungs ached for air. But there was only water, and murkiness. I knew that I couldn't give up. I couldn't let the water get me. I started pumping my arms, willing myself to the surface. Propelling myself up, up, until I thrust my head into the dark night. I remember seeing stars. And then, I laughed, because I was floating, bobbing on the water next to Red. "I did it! I fuckin' did it!!!"

I got this incredible rush better than anything I'd ever gotten getting high. I could conquer anything. For the first time in my life I knew I was something and I didn't give a damn what anybody else thought. "I am the shit!!!!!"

I dove under the water, my heart still racing. I wanted that feeling again. That feeling of winning, of fighting something and beating it.

When I came back up, I lay on my back, floating on the surface of the water, looking at the pinpoints of light piercing the darkness above. I felt a peace that I don't think I'd ever felt before, covering every part of me with calm.

I don't know how long we stayed there, but when we finally pulled ourselves up, light had started to eat away at the edges of the night.

Red shook himself like a wet dog, slapping his thick hands against his stomach. "Now was that the shit or what, man?"

I grinned. I had to give it him, sometimes crazy white boy mess was okay. "It was..."

He gave me high five. "Now we're officially New Yorkers. We've been baptized."

I shook the water out of my hair, threw back my head and shouted as loud as I could. "Now let's make some *mooooooooonnneeey*!" It was my turn to dance, singing the Ojay tune "Money, money, money!"

Red didn't know the song, but he followed along anyway, rumbling off key as we headed for the train. "Money, money, *moneeee!*"

CHAPTER THIRTEEN

Detective Bob—New York 1987

"What can you say about Clive January?"

The room was deathly silent. The huge white casket in the front of the church, shiny and still.

"He was a man like no other: a good man, a family man, a man loved by all..."

I think I noticed people shuffling in their seats. But the speaker went on. I took out my pad, scratching down notes of what he was saying.

"Especially by me. Clive and I were like brothers: our wives were friends, our children played together and together we built one of the most formidable boutique powerhouse investment banking firms that Wall Street had ever seen. They said we couldn't do it. But we did. Because that's the kind of man that Clive January was: my friend, my partner, my brother."

Someone started crying, a woman in the back. A small, slight black woman. She was so covered in black veils and scarves that you see couldn't much else.

Her cry seemed to come from somewhere deep in her soul. It reminded me of when my uncle died. His mistress, the woman everybody in the family hated, sobbed like that at the funeral. This woman whoever she was had that same kind of cry. Clive's wife was quiet, stone-faced and dry-eyed.

I remember that day at my uncle's funeral. I was about seven. I remember 'cause it was the first time I think I knew that there was something different about me. Something most people wouldn't or didn't want to understand. Something it took me years before I understood. For a minute I blinked and I could almost see my dad's face in front of me, wide and angry—the way it looked as long as I could remember…

"Dad, who's that lady crying?" My dad's red cheeks were redder than ever, and the little bits of thin, blonde hair on his head were plastered down with sweat. I poked him again and whispered louder, thinking maybe he didn't hear me. "Dad, who's that?

"Bobby, please!" It was my mother. She hadn't said anything since we got to my uncle's funeral. She'd just had her lips pursed real hard. My uncle was my dad's only brother. Maybe that's why he was looking so funny. It must be hard to lose your brother. I wouldn't know. I didn't have brothers or sisters.

Now that woman in the back had started crying even louder, people were turning around and giving her the kind of look I get when I've done somethin' bad.

"Why's everybody lookin' at her, Dad?"

"Bobby, your mother told you to be quiet. Now shut your trap!!!!!"

I kicked my feet against the bench. Mad. *Why do I always have to shut up?* I looked back at that lady again. Wondering why nobody seemed to like her. She seemed nice and kinda pretty, too. I looked back at her again and tried to pretend I could get inside her head and figure out what she's thinkin' and what was makin' her cry. It's a game I played by myself sometimes. I was Houdini or one of those fortunetellers on the pier who could read your mind and tell the future. I played this game a lot 'cause most of the time I was by myself. Mama wouldn't let me play much with the other kids in the neighborhood. She said they weren't our kind. I didn't know exactly who that was, our kind that is. All I knew is that it meant that I played by myself most of the time.

I scrunched my eyes real tight, trying to see inside that lady's head again. All of a sudden, I felt sick to my stomach. *I'm gonna throw up.* My head was hurting. I reached over and grabbed Mama's hand. I closed my eyes tighter, but couldn't stop the pictures from coming into my head. Cramming out all the other thoughts. I couldn't control the pictures. They rushed into my head so fast, I couldn't really make out what they were. My head felt hot, and I was breathin' so hard and fast folks would have thought I'd run around the block ten times without stopping. Then the pictures started to make shapes. I could see my uncle clear like he was still alive. He was waiting for someone. He kept lookin' at his watch. Then I saw her. That lady. The one who was crying. Only she wasn't crying. She was running across the street, smiling at my uncle. My uncle came up to her, and then...he...yuck. He kissed her! And not on the cheek. This was a movie star kiss, all big and slobbery.

I popped open my eyes, trying to make the pictures go away. Mama put her arm around me. I was shaking and my hands were sweating. I wanted to cry. I somehow knew something that I wasn't supposed to, and it had made me dirty. I was afraid to close my eyes, afraid the pictures would come back again. So I just stared ahead and held Mama's hand even tighter.

The woman choked, bringing me back to Clive's funeral abruptly. Shaking off the past, I turned back toward the woman and caught her out of the corner of my eye as she gathered her coat and ran out of the church. Heads turned, eyes lowered, and significant glances were cast. I wondered again who she was. I made a note in my pad. Find the woman in black.

The man at the podium looked rich. Everything about him said money: the suit, the finely manicured look. Everyone in the church had the same look. Money. But black money. Before this case, I didn't even know these kind existed. Hell, growing up in Brooklyn, the only blacks I ever saw were as poor as we were. Playing stickball in the street just like we did, no fancy playgrounds like the kids in Manhattan, just the streets and the sun curling up the pavement in August.

"Bobby!!!!"

I turned around and saw my dad behind the wheel of the city bus he drove. He looked mad. But then my dad always looked mad. I think he was mad at life and everybody in it, especially himself.

"Bobby, get over here, now!!!!"

Turning to Howie, I whispered desperately, "Don't go away. I'll be right back." My stomach was tight and my legs were cramping up. I could tell I was in for a whipping. Dad's face was bright red, and his big fat fingers were thumping the steering wheel of the bus. I started to climb the steps of the bus. Before I could get to the top, he grabbed me by the collar and yanked me up so I could barely breathe.

"How many times I gotta tell ya to stop playing with them blacks? You go find some white kids to hang around. I won't have no son of mine tarred by that brush. 'Fore you know it, you'll end up just like'em, good for nothin' sons of—"

"But, Dad, Howie's different!"

He turned me around and practically spit the words, "They're all alike. You remember that. There's none of 'em different!" Dad threw me on the ground. I could feel the blood filling my mouth where I scraped my lip against the pavement. Out of the corner of my eye I could see Howie, running away.

Dad leaned over to me, his eyes red and moist looking. "I don't wanna see you with no more blacks, you hear me?"

The sound of the organ rolled over the church, knocking me back to now. I wondered what my dad would think. Probably'd roll over in his grave. Me sitting in a church full of blacks—the only people he hated more than himself. My job—to get inside their lives and figure out what had happened to some rich SOB that could probably buy and sell me with his lunch money. Somebody I couldn't give a damn about and who probably deserved the bullet in the back that he got. Dad and me didn't agree on much, but I had to give 'em that. He was right, they were all alike. I used to think that you couldn't lump people in all together, but after the way they'd sold me out, I'd seen the light. The irony of it all was that with this case I needed to prove that I still had it. That I was still Detective Bob, still the shit.

I didn't have time to piss away, thinkin' about ironies or other such bullshit. Right now I needed to close this case out, find out who did it, and in the process, somehow figure out what happened to Detective Bob, the guy I used to be and how to get him back. Looking around here though, I could tell that these people were from a different world, a world I'd never seen. Yet a world that I knew that I'd come to know real good. Whether I wanted to or not.

I turned back to the man on the podium. Funny, for someone who had supposedly just lost his best friend, business partner and the rest of that crap, he didn't look too upset. In fact, nobody in this whole church looked upset, except the woman in black. I put a little star by her name.

"Clive, my brother, we'll miss you."

The organ swelled up from the back of the church as the business partner left the podium. I checked my list of names—Andrew Haven.

My eyes roamed around the church taking in the most non-sad looking group of folks I'd ever seen. Another man walked up to the podium. Cleared his throat. *Must think he's something.* Ten years being a detective you get to know the little signals folks send out. Clearing their throat. Sure sign every time of somebody who thinks they're something.

"Clive was more than a son-in-law to me. He was like the son I never had. He provided a good home for my daughter and my granddaughter, and for that I am thankful." He cleared his throat again and looked over toward the open casket. "May you accomplish in death all of the dreams that you could not in life."

At that point in any other funeral, the wife should've broken down. But not this one. She had that Jackie O look. And everybody knows what a fuck up as a husband JFK was. I put another note in my pad, next to Wife.

The music had started again, my cue to slip out.

"So, didya figure it out, super cop?"

I didn't even have to look up. *Captain.* And his unfunny sense of humor. "Yeah, I figured it out. The wife did it. Isn't it always the wife?"

Captain was the kind of black guy I was used to. He reminded me of the kids I grew up with: a little rough, liked to crack on you, joke around. But basically, a good guy. Least that's what I used to think 'til he turned on me. Him and all the rest of 'em.

I looked around the precinct at the sneers and underhanded looks. For a minute, I froze, back to *then*. When my life changed for good. I heard the question, "Detective Greene, did you see Officer McCarthy shoot the suspect after the suspect had fallen on the ground?"

Trying to be a good cop, a fair cop—the memory still fresh—I hesitated: seeing this black kid who couldn't have been more than eleven or twelve, fall on the ground, crying, begging McCarthy not to shoot him. I could see McCarthy laughing as he took out his gun, walk around the kid, and shot him point blank in the back…and I said, "Yes, sir, I saw him shoot the suspect after the suspect had fallen."

From that point on, I'm a traitor, an enemy in the camp. Worse than a scab. A cop who turns on another cop. I'd be better off dead myself. The ironic shit was that the black cops hated me worse than the white cops, said I shoulda stopped McCarthy, shoulda held him back. Like there was a damn thing I coulda done to stop him. When the black ministers got in the act, they damn near crucified me. You woulda thought I'd killed the kid.

"Greene's a racist cop. Greene's a racist cop!" Sometimes I still hear the chants when I close my eyes. Still see the flashbulbs in my face.

"Detective Greene, do you think that there was anything you could've done to stop your partner from killing Leon Williams?"

"Detective Greene, the court records show that you were aware of your partner's emotional instability."

"Detective Greene, shouldn't you have reported that to Internal Affairs so that he could have been removed from the force before this tragedy occurred?

"Detective Greene, do you have a comment for the black press?"

"Yeah, fuck you! Fuck alla you!" I yelled in the glowing lights of the camera. They bleeped it out on the evening news. But it didn't matter. The next day the headlines screamed, "WHITE COP SAYS FUCK BLACKS!"

Dad was right, you couldn't trust any of 'em. I tried to be fair and do the right thing, and that's the thanks I got. *Well fuck all of you! Black press! Black people! All of you!*

Maybe I should've just resigned. But what else could I do? Where else could I go after twenty years on the force? That was two years ago, and now nobody will lift a finger to help me, all just wishing I'd fall on my ass one time too many and be outta here. So I just keep my distance, joke around like it's still the way it used to be, but Captain knows and I know and every other asshole in that precinct knows that it's never gonna be the way it used to be no more.

I turned back to the Captain, trying to get back to now, trying to sound casual, like the shit was no big deal. "You know what, Captain, you people sure don't get too upset at funerals."

"What the fuck is he talking about? Will somebody tell me what this fool is mouthin' off about?" He threw up his hands. But he wasn't pissed. Captain was always throwing up his hands or cursing somebody out for no particular reason.

"There wasn't a wet eye in the place."

"Don't you mean dry eye, Greene?"

"Not there I don't. Nobody, and I mean no fuckin' body except for this one woman who didn't really look like she belonged there, was cryin'. No sniffles. No wet eyes. Nothin'. Now that ain't normal. With all the funerals I been to since I started at homicide, this is the only one where nobody cried."

"Well, I hear he was a regular son-of-a-bitch anyway."

"Yeah, well tell me somethin' I ain't figured out already."

"So then I repeat my question, Greene, or are you deaf and stupid?"

"Fuck you, Captain."

"Who did it?"

I grabbed the thick file off my desk marked CLIVE JANUARY HOMICIDE and waved it up in the air. "I don't know, but I'll find out. Don't I always?"

"Whoooo, thinks he's hot shit, don't he?"

I smiled defiantly. I liked to fuck with the guys. "Yeah, and what of it?"

The captain got up and started walking into his office. "Just find out, 'cause word on the street is that some heads might roll on this one."

I looked at him curiously. This was getting interesting. I liked my cases interesting. "What do you mean?"

The captain motioned me into his office. I followed him and plopped down in one of the chairs.

"Close the door."

I glided it shut with my foot. "So shoot, what's up on this one. What do I need to know that's not in the file?"

Captain raised his thick eyebrows. His bald head wrinkling up at the same time. "Well, it seems like our man was knee deep in shit. All kinds of shit."

"What, drugs, women?"

"We don't know. He was coked up when he died, but we're just not sure." Captain got up and paced around his desk. I could tell he was thinking. That was his thinking mode. Walking back and forth, wrinkling his bald head. "The other thing was his business. There's some question as to whether he was trying to sell it from under his partner before he was killed, or if somebody with big money was trying to force him out because he knew too much."

"About what?"

"We don't know. That, Detective Bob, is for you to find out. And real quick. We're getting pressure to close this one up neatly." Captain sat down. He didn't seem to want to say the next thing, but he did anyway. "Another piece of advice."

"Yeah."

"Don't dig too deeply on this one. We don't want to upset the apple cart if you know what I mean."

"No, I don't know what you mean."

"Shit, Greene, just play it cool on this one, okay. Don't go off half cocked, 'cause you might be squeezing your own balls if you do."

I wandered back to my desk. Thinking. The captain is a fast one. Must have been something for him to tell me to cool it. He was usually gung ho. On everything. I picked up Clive January's file. January and Associates Annual Report dropped out. Newspaper clippings, copies of school records. A man's life reduced to an 8 x 12 file. I hoped to God when I went, I got more of a send-off than his.

clive

so i'm a son-of-a-bitch now. assholes. all of them. if they only knew, the half. but now i'm dead. not even in heaven or hell. god didn't do me the dignity of kicking me either upstairs or down. i'm just nowhere. floating. pulled by forces that i don't understand. one minute i'm looking at my own body in the casket. dressed up like i'm stepping out. except that i'm not going anywhere. except six feet under.

now i'm in a police station. probably smells like stale cigarette smoke. except that i can't smell anything. and for some reason, i'm drawn to this white guy. this racist cop who's looking through my life, making judgments about me. but i know, i don't know how, but the same force that came to me when i died is telling me through some means that this guy is the key. he'll find out who did it.

questions. nothing but unanswered questions. why him. why this guy. but no answers. if i have to depend on someone to put together the pieces of my life, why not someone like me? someone who's felt the pain that i have, who's lived the hell that i lived. someone who would understand.

it's the same journey. i keep hearing that echoing in my head. the same journey. you have the same journey. you chose him, they're telling me. i look down on him, sitting at his desk going through my life, asking questions about me and i don't see it. nothing. no connection. just a dumpy middle aged white guy who probably thinks he's better than me just because he's white.

they're telling me that he'll help me find peace. because they tell me that if i don't find out i'll never have peace. our lives are locked together. somehow. a pact we made. to find the same thing. what is this thing? this something that will free me from this void.

because god knows no man deserves to be killed like i was. but worse no man deserves to live in this nether existence this world of neither good nor bad, happy or sad. just nothing, loneliness and nothiness.

i have to let him know. i've got to find a way to talk to him. to tell him my story, and then maybe if he knows my story, he'll find out the rest. and i'll know. and the world will know the truth.

Shit!

I woke up in a sweat. I'd been having this dream about him. That dead black guy. Clive January. Don't ask me why. But I kept seeing his face in my dream. He was trying to say something. But no sounds were coming out of his mouth. It was weird as shit. I lay back down, half expecting to feel Margie's warm body. But she'd been gone. How many months now. Five, or maybe six. I'd lost track. After our last big blow up, she'd just left. This time I knew it was for good. Cop's intuition or whatever. We were never married, but it felt like it. When you're with somebody for ten years, you're married. Don't matter whether you got the paper or not.

I turned back over, still kinda spooked me to sleep on her side. 'Cause it'll always be her side, even if she never comes back to claim it. Closing my eyes, I saw his face again. Clive January. Only clearer than before. Shit, if he wasn't dead, I'd swear he was right there in the room with me. Sometimes a case sticks to me like that. 'Till I figure it out, it gets under my skin, and I can't get rid of it until I close it out. Clive January was gonna be one of those cases.

CHAPTER FOURTEEN

"Shit, will you look at this place?" I wandered around the house. It was like nothing I'd ever been in before: ultra modern, slick, windows that reached from the floor to the ceiling, with the ocean covering every inch of glass. Blue water, tan sands. Sailboats in the distance. And everything else high tech. Couches you could sink into and get lost, art work, that expensive-looking abstract mess, long stemmed champagne glasses, a wet bar, and everything white, white. Except for the dark bloodstain on the chair and on the thick, white carpet.

"What did this guy do again?"

The Long Island cop shrugged his shoulders. "Had a company on Wall Street's all I know. Hadn't had the house two years…then boom. Dead." He leaned against the window. Staring at the waves that crashed against the sand. "Some people seem to have all the luck."

I kneeled, looking carefully at the bloodstain on the carpet. "Yeah. if you call getting shot in the back lucky."

"You know what I mean: the money, the house…I wouldn't mind it."

"Not me. I gotta be able to sleep at night."

"And how do you know he couldn't?"

"I don't, but with this much cash and dying the way he did, something wasn't right." I took out my notebook, flipping to the page where I'd written the notes at the funeral… *Wife*…then snapped it shut. "Like I said, I gotta be able to sleep at night."

The Long Island cop wasn't really listening. I figured it was time to get back to business.

"So what'dya guys got for me?"

"On the case?"

"I didn't haul my ass out here from Manhattan to look at seagulls."

"Yeah, well not much." He handed me a plastic bag. "Bullet shell, standard garden variety 45, coulda picked the piece up on any corner. We're doing a test on it now, but my guess is we're not gonna find the owner, 'cause it was probably hot, not registered under anybody's name."

I rolled the shell between my thumb and forefinger.

"We also found a second set of prints in the place. Ran it against the wife's and the maid's, neither of 'em matched up. We sent it to central FBI files, but so far no match."

"Well it looks like you Long Island boys hit the jackpot on this one. Shell, but not a clue whose it could be. Fingerprints from the invisible man. Yeah, I'd say you really did your homework on this one."

He glared at me. I guess he didn't think I was too funny.

"Yeah, well now that the Manhattan DA has taken over, let's see how much you find. 'Cause me personally, I think it was some jealous lover or something. This guy had a rep a mile long. He used to have all kinds of women in here. I think either the wife found out and did it, or one of them mistresses."

"Just like in the movies, huh? The wife did it, or is it the butler?"

The cop just kept looking at the ocean. And I thought I was kinda funny. Nobody ever did appreciate my jokes. I think that's when I knew it was quits between Margie and me. She stopped laughing at my jokes. Just a matter of time, and sure enough, she was gone.

The cop turned back to me, interrupting my thoughts. "So you got everything you need?"

"Just about, but you go on. I want to stick around here for a little while longer."

"Okay. Lock up." He left and I was alone. In another's man's house. I sat down on the couch and closed my eyes. Whenever I had a case that threw me like this one, I'd do this. Close my eyes and try and get in the head of the victim. Try and think his thoughts, live his life, for a minute. Maybe understand why and who did it to him. Same as the game I used to play as a kid. Except that now it wasn't a game no more. I could control it. At least most of the time. Sometimes I felt like it would take over. That my life was becoming the feelings I had about other people's lives, but then I'd pull back and take my own life back.

I'd been doing this as long as I could remember. Having feelings, that is, about things before they happened or being able to see things that nobody else could. When I was a kid, I could yell out the answers before the teacher asked the question. Used to call me a smart ass. But it wasn't like that. I just knew. Didn't know how I knew, but I did.

I think it came from my mother. She'd been in a concentration camp in Poland. She used to tell me how she knew before the Nazis came to get her and her parents that she'd had feelings to get out of Poland. Her father was a famous violinist. She told me people would come from all over to hear him play. He never wanted to believe that people could be so vicious. He used to say it would never happen. But my mother, she knew what was going to happen. She had dreams months before the Nazi's invaded Poland. Her mother had the feelings, too. So my grandmother sold all her jewelry and helped her neighbors escape to Switzerland before the Nazis came. Only thing is, my grandfather wouldn't leave, so when the Nazis came, it was too late for my mother, grandmother, and grandfather to escape.

I remember my mother tellin' me how after the Nazis took all their silver, art and books, they set fire to their beautiful house. She said that her and her parents looked out from the cart they'd been loaded onto as everything they'd had went up in the flames. She told me that she and her mother cried, but that her father had just sat and looked in silence as the cart took them from their home to the concentration camp.

My grandfather died in the concentration camp. They broke all his fingers before they murdered him. See, they knew who he was, Abraham Vlidensky. Everybody knew him. They said his music would heal you, no matter what was wrong. My mother said that people would leave his concerts, and they'd be different, somehow. He was famous, and they hated him because he was Jewish and he was brilliant. They wanted to take away the thing that meant the most to him, his music. His hands had made the music come alive.

So after the war, my mother and grandmother came to New York. She met my father. He wasn't sophisticated with books and everything like her father. He wasn't Jewish either. Dad was Irish, Irish Catholic, but he had a steady job and kept a roof over her head. After everything she'd been through, I'm guessing that's all she really wanted. As a kid, I never really understood him and Mama's relationship. I'd watch other folks' moms and dads, and they'd be laughin' together and sometimes holdin' hands or seeming like they had special jokes together. But not my dad. Sometimes I wondered if he even liked Mama. I remember one day they didn't know I was lookin'. I was in the kitchen, and the door was open into the living room. I could see Mama and Dad in there…

"Callie, how do I look?"

Mama had on a new dress and hat, and she was walking around the living room twirling in front of Dad, only he wasn't paying much attention to her.

"Callie! What'dyou think? It's new. I just got it!"

My dad just kinda grunted the way he usually did and turned back to his newspaper.

"C'mon Callie, say somethin'!"

"Rebecca, you look the same's you always do. No different." Mama looked a little hurt, but she went over to the couch anyway and tried to snuggle up next to Dad. She put her arms around his neck and looked like she wanted to kiss him.

He got up real fast and turned. "Not now. Okay. I'm goin' out." He didn't even look at Mama, all dressed up in her new dress. He just walked out and didn't say another word.

Mama looked like her feelings were so hurt that I rushed in the living room and hugged her real tight. "I love you, Mama!"

Mama started crying, but she didn't want me to see, so she just hugged and rocked me back and forth. I don't think I ever saw my dad kiss Mama, or hold her hand or nothin'. He'd just come home and wouldn't say much, and then he'd go out with his buddies. So Mama, Gramma and me were alone most of the time. Maybe it was because of that that I started having the feelings. Or maybe they were there all the time. I don't know.

Sometimes Mama, me, and Gramma would just sit, the three of us, and we wouldn't have to say anything out loud because we could understand what the others were thinking without talking.

"Okay, Bobby, hold Gramma's hand...Good. Now take my hand...That's right, not too tight...That's my good boy. Just tight enough to feel the beat...Do you feel the heartbeat...?"

"Uh...I think so, Mama..." I wasn't really sure what it was supposed to feel like, except that Gramma's hand was soft and fleshy, almost spongy feeling, and Mama's hand was firmer and thinner. Mama's fingers were long and pretty, and she always wore light pink nail polish on them. It felt good to be in the middle of Mama and Gramma. It made me feel special and important.

"Now concentrate, Bobby."

"Mama, what am I concentrating on?"

"The heartbeat, the heartbeat goin' way up and down your body."

I nodded and squeezed both of their hands a little tighter, determined to find that heartbeat.

"What do you see, Bobby?"

"Just black right now."

"Okay, now close your eyes a little tighter and tell me what you see now."

Shapes swirled around in my head. Mama, Gramma, and me had played this game before, trying to see if we'd all see the same things in our head. It'd never worked all the way for me before, but this time, I was feeling different. My head felt lighter, and for a minute I thought I was going to fall over. I think if I'd been standing up, I probably would've fallen down.

"Breathe, Bobby, don't let the light feeling take over. You've got to control the feelings. You can't let them control you."

I took a deep breath and held it as long as I could, then I let it out real slow. It must've worked, 'cause something was starting to take shape in my head.

"Triangles and circles, triangles with circles inside of them!" I shouted out.

Mama squeezed my hand saying softly, "That's good, Bobby, that's the image we're sending you. Triangles for the three of us, and circles for the unbroken circle of life. Whenever you get scared or you're not sure of something, just concentrate on that image, and it will bring you back."

I was listening, but not really because now I was starting to feel panicky. The triangles and circles were gone, and I had that sick feeling in my stomach. I jumped up and ran into the bathroom. My head was wet with sweat and my knees felt like they couldn't hold me up anymore.

"Mama, I'm gonna be sick."

"No you're not, Bobby. Just think about what I told you. C'mon, you can do it, Bobby. Don't let the feelings control you. You've got to be strong."

I was trying as hard as I could. I grabbed the edge of the toilet seat. As I was about to be sick, I felt this wave of cold air over me. I closed my eyes and let the air brush against my face. In my head I saw Mama and Gramma standing next to me, holding me up. I opened my eyes quickly, and I could see that they were still in the other room. Neither of them had moved. I knew something had happened, something important, like I'd passed some kind of test.

My dad wasn't like that. Like I said, he never said much. We never told him what we were doing. Sometimes I'd try and fight it, these feelings I had, this way of knowing things before they happened. Hell, where I grew up in Brooklyn, you knew what you saw, not some mumbo jumbo kinda shit that didn't make sense half the time, but always seemed to be right.

I remember the first time I decided to try and use the feelings for somethin' good. To help somebody. I was about seventeen. I was gonna help Mrs. Moynihan. Her husband had been one of my dad's drinking buddies. Well, one day he just disappeared. Nobody knew where. The police looked around the neighborhood and asked everybody a load of questions. But no Mr. Moynihan. Every night, Mrs. Moynihan cried and walked up and down her apartment. I knew because she lived on top of us, and her bedroom was right on top of mine. The people in the neighborhood said that he'd run off with another woman. I felt sorry for Mrs. Moynihan because all the talk only made it harder for her.

Now I liked Mrs. M., as I used to call her. She was one of the only people in the neighborhood who was nice to me. When I was a little kid, she'd make me vanilla pudding and give me a big bowl every day after school. Now that I was seventeen, she'd be the one I'd talk to when I couldn't take Dad's yelling no more. She was the one who always understood. So I think because of all of that, I decided I wanted to help her. I don't know how I got it in my head that I could, but somehow I knew I could use these feelings I had. I knew about things that other people didn't to find Mr. Moynihan.

I started every night just before I went to sleep to try and see Mr. Moynihan in my head. I didn't tell nobody what I was doing, not even Mama or Gramma. I wanted to see if I could do it on my own without any help from nobody. First, I'd try and remember exactly the way he looked. Then when I got a clear picture of him, I'd concentrate real hard and try to see what was around him, where he mighta gone. Anything—maybe a sign in the background or some buildings, something that would tell me where he might be. So far all I was gettin' was his face, didn't look happy, almost scared. But that's all I got 'til that one night.

"Bobby!"

I jumped up. It was late, still dark outside. No sounds, but I could swear I heard somebody call my name. I listened hard. Nothin' but the sound of my dad snoring like a frickin' steam engine. Always made me mad to hear him at night. Thinkin' about Mama and what she had to put up with, no wonder the dark circles under her eyes seemed to get darker and deeper every year.

"Bobby, over here!"

Now I knew I wasn't dreaming. I swear the little hairs on the back of my neck were standin' straight up. The sounds in the room seemed to get louder and clearer, as if there were a giant microphone magnifying everything. I couldn't move. I was too damn scared. Then out of the corner of my eye, I saw it, or him. I wasn't sure what. But there was a shadowy figure sitting in the chair next to my window. I tried to say somethin,' but nothin' would come out. Sweat poured down my body. The sheets were soaked. The first thing that popped in my head was one of them ghost movies that I liked to watch on Saturday afternoons. I half expected the thing, whatever it was, to start moaning and groanin' and glasses and shit to start breaking.

Instead, it just hovered over there in the corner. Then I caught it. A feeling of sadness, depression, confusion, all that shit rolled up together, coming from the thing. I wasn't as scared now, so I called out, "Who the hell are you?"

In my head I heard the words, "Petie."

"Petie? I don't know a Petie!" Then I remembered. Shit. Yes I did. Petie was Mr. Moynihan. Hardly anybody called him that, but his mother, one day she was visiting and I heard her call him Petie.

"Mr...uh...Moynihan?" I wasn't quite sure whether to call him that or Petie, but I figured that wherever he was or whatever he was, it was probably better not to get too familiar.

No sounds were coming in my head. But I felt like he was calling me over to him, even though I couldn't hear him saying that. I got up slowly and walked over to the window. I was covered in this feeling of depression and blackness. I couldn't see the rest of my room. It was covered over in this kinda cloudy gauzy thing. The only thing that was clear was the window, almost like a big screen. I looked out and saw Mr. Moynihan walking unsteadily. He was right near the abandoned piers on the lower west side, over near the meat packing companies. Drunk. Drunker than I think I ever seen 'em. He fell down on the ground. I could almost smell the water. The strong fishy briny smell. Then I heard the low rumbling of a truck. Getting louder and louder.

I put my hands over my ears. I couldn't take the noise. It sounded like it was rolling right on top of me. I looked up and saw what he saw—a huge crane hovering right over him. The claw was filled with rocks, trash and dirt. As the claw opened, it dumped the rocks, dirt and trash on him, hitting him in the face and the chest. He tried to scream, but he couldn't. Dirt, garbage, rotten fruit, and spoiled meat pelted him in the face, plugging up his eyes and filling his mouth. Nauseous, I closed my eyes and covered my ears, trying to make the sights and sounds go away.

"Bobby, bring me back home!!!!!"

I heard the words in my head. But when I opened my eyes, he was gone. My room was empty. And quiet. Like nothing had ever happened. I managed to crawl back in my bed. It was a few days before I got the guts to tell anybody. I didn't want 'em to think I was crazy, so I just told them I'd had a dream and that they should look for Mr. Moynihan by the west side piers.

They found his body right where I'd told 'em under a mound of garbage. They figured out that the garbage truck dumped everything in the early morning when it was still dark outside, so the driver never saw him. Mr. Moynihan must've been unconscious, dead drunk when it happened. After that people in the neighborhood were scared of me. They thought I had some kind of powers or something.

Then one day Mrs. M. came down to our apartment looking for me. For a minute she didn't say nothin'. I felt weird and stupid. I started thinkin' that maybe I shoulda just kept my big trap shut, like Dad was always tellin' me, and stay outta other people's business. I was thinkin' all that and feeling weirder and weirder when she walked over to me, takin' my hand and kissing me on the cheek.

"You're a good boy, Bobby, don't listen to what the rest of them is sayin'. You're a good boy. You found him for me, and now I can go on...lay his soul to rest." She hugged me tight, and then whispered, so only I could hear, "You keep on helpin' people like that. Don't mind what other folks say. They's stupid and ignorant. So you don't listen to them. Listen to yourself. What you know is right. 'cause that's the only thing that counts in the end." She hugged me again, and then left. She moved out a few months later, and I never heard any more about her.

But what she said stuck with me. Maybe it was 'cause it was the only time that I didn't feel like I was a total fuck up. Dad had a way of makin' me feel like whatever I did was stupid and that I was just a dumb-ass SOB who could never do nothin' right. But Mrs. M. made me feel like I had done the right thing and that maybe I wasn't so stupid like Dad was always tellin' me. I felt good after that. I was still feeling good when Dad took me aside for one of his talks, or really him yellin' and me listenin'. Only this time he didn't yell. It was almost like he was scared of me or somethin.'

He sat down on the edge of my bed. His hair was almost white now and still sticky and greasy, wound in a few strands at the back of his head. His cheeks, which used to be pink only on Saturday night after one of his binges, were red and veiny now with age.

"Bobby, folks are talking."

I tried to sound nonchalant, even though I knew damn well what he was talking about. "'Bout what?"

He scrunched his bluish red eyes up and looked like he was about to yell, but he stopped himself, and instead said slowly, "About you bein' some type of fortune teller or somethin'!"

I shrugged. "It's not true. It was a lucky guess, about Mr. Moynihan, that's all."

Dad snorted. "You think I'm stupid? You think we's all stupid? Nobody has a lucky guess like that. That just happened to be the exact pier, exactly like you said, in the exact spot...shit. There ain't that many lucky guesses in the world."

Dad leaned forward and looked me up and down. "I didn't raise no circus freak, you hear? So if you have anymore of them 'lucky guesses,' you just keep 'em to yourself."

I was mad, madder than I think I'd ever been. I wanted to get up and sock Dad in the mouth. I was bigger than him now, I coulda flattened him. But I didn't. I just held it in. Only because of Mama. It woulda hurt her if I'd hit him. Even though he never gave a damn about her, but I did and I wouldn't do anything that would cause her any more pain than she'd already had. So I just swallowed hard and tried to push the pissed off feelings as deep down as I could.

"Sure. Whatever," I said.

"Good."

That's when I decided I wouldn't tell nobody anymore. I'd just keep it all in. It was about that time that I stopped having a lot of friends. You know, buddies you'd hang out with, shoot the shit, knock down a couple of beers. But me, everybody thought I was a little crazy, so I stopped trying to convince 'em I wasn't. I just started hangin' by myself. 'Till I met Margie. She was different. She understood. She didn't laugh or call me crazy or nothin'. She just understood.

"Can I buy you a beer?" I'd noticed her the minute I walked into the bar. Hell, you couldn't not notice her. The only chick in there that seemed to have some class, long dark brown hair, wavy and thick, olive skin. She had on this reddish-orange colored knit dress. Not a kind of red that said hey, look at me. Naw, a more subtle color that stayed with you.

I remember the day I took her hands into mine and said, "You're gonna fall in love with me." I don't know why I said that. It just came out. That was ten years ago. She was eighteen and I was twenty-eight. Now I'm damn near forty. She did fall in love with me. Hell, I fell in love with her. But after ten years, she fell out of love with me. I still don't know exactly what happened. Must be the Bob Greene curse. Anybody I get close to ends up leaving at some point. Or dying, like Mama.

Before my mother died, she called me in her room. I still remember the smell in there—death was just around the corner hovering, just waiting. She could hardly talk, but she held my hand real tight.

"You've got a gift, Bobby." That's what she called me. "Use it for good. Use it to help people. Remember our family," she said. "We help people. That's the most important thing." I knew what she was talking about, but all I could do was just nod.

Maybe that's why I joined the force. I was eighteen, right outta high school. Figgered maybe I could find out things that other cops couldn't. Maybe I could help find out who killed the poor slobs that nobody gave a damn about. The ones who ended up in the unsolved pile. 'Cause if I didn't, sure as hell nobody else would. Then they'd never have any peace, like Mr. Moynihan. They'd always be haunting us, crying out for somebody to help 'em, somebody to care.

When I joined the force, I'd know things that weren't in the file or know things that there was no way I coulda known, unless I'd been there when it happened. I had a second set of eyes, eyes that saw what nobody else did. The other cops started calling me Super Cop 'cause I never missed a case, cracked every one of 'em wide open.

'Till that shit with internal affairs blew everything to hell and back. I'd lost my second pair of eyes. All I could see was the black hole of my life. And no matter how hard I tried, I couldn't seem to crawl out. Then Margie left. I guess she'd had enough of my shit. Now this case. Clive January. It could bring me back or push me over the edge. I knew I had to crack this one. I had to get my eyes back.

This time I relaxed right away. Had to be the sound of the waves that did it to me. Rocking and gentle. Right away, I felt a power from somewhere flow through me. I wasn't quite me no more. Something was invading my body, taking over my soul, my thoughts, every bit of who I was. Nausea churned my stomach.

Shit. I'd been doing this for more than ten years now. I was in control. I knew how to make it work for me. That is until now. 'Cause this was different. Whoever this guy was had this will that was stronger than anything I'd ever felt before. It was pushing me aside and taking over. I wanted to run to the bathroom and puke, but it wouldn't let me. This will, this force, that was taking over. I tried to remember what my mother had said years ago.

"Relax," she'd say. "Relax, Bobby. Let it flow through you. Not over you."

But I couldn't. I couldn't control it. I was afraid, but there was nothing I could do. I was feeling things that weren't a part of me, that were his feelings, his thoughts.

Fear. Desperation. I was drowning. Literally. I couldn't breathe. I could feel the water filling my lungs. Images were coming at me now. I was him. I was Clive. Nothing like this had ever happened before. I fought to keep myself, but he was taking over.

I saw black water, swells of waves. It was dark, and I was going under. I saw a hand being held out to me. I tried to grab it, but I started choking. I woke up. I was sitting on his couch again. Looking at the ocean. I touched my brow. It was wet, and my hand was shaking so hard I had to lay it on the table.

Drowning? This guy was shot. I felt myself slowly settling back into my body. Weak kneed. Stomach still churning. I'd probably sweated off about five pounds. Weird as shit. It had never seemed that real before. I knew this case was different. 'Cause in spite of what I'd just been through, I felt a little thrill. I was still scared, but I knew I was onto something.

"Yo, Greene, Haven's here"

I took out my notebook—Andrew Haven, Business Partner.

"Detective Greene." He held out his hand.

"Yeah."

"Andrew Haven."

I looked up into the eyes of a short black man. Funny, he seemed taller at the wake standing at the podium. But now that I was eyeballing him face to face, I could see he couldn't be more than 5'4", maybe 5'5" not more than that. A little guy with little hands and feet, wide face, eyes dark and set into his face. Little knots of hair stuck on the side of his face with nothing in the middle. Nothin' to look at, even for a black man.

"Sit down." I pulled up a chair next to my desk. He looked around the station, his shiny new wing tips squeaking. His suit was dark blue crisp, with a red tie and white shirt that looked like some poor stiff in a Chinese laundry had been sweating over the iron, making sure that every crease lay flat.

"Will this take long?" He glanced at his watch. Rolex. And me with a broken Timex on my dresser. Some people do have all the luck. I pulled out the file, turning my back to him as I flipped through it. This was my party now.

"Why, you got someplace to go?"

"I do run a business, Detective."

"So I hear."

He shifted in his seat again, scraping his heels against the floor. I could tell he was pissed.

"Tell me, Mr. Haven, how long did you know the deceased?"

"Twelve, thirteen years, I don't remember exactly when we met. We'd seen each other in the halls, and then one day he introduced himself."

"This was where now?"

"At Bender & Grace. We both worked there. He was in the training program at the time, and I'd been on the floor for two years at that point."

"On the floor?"

"Trading. I traded municipal bonds at the time."

"What'dya think of him when you first met him?"

He looked away, then turned back to me. "Driven. Absolutely driven." He sighed. "There was no one like Clive."

His eyes kinda half closed like he was re-living every word, and then he started talking without me even prompting. But the funny thing was, it was like he almost forgot I was there, like he'd gone back to some place in time, remembering it more for himself than for me. So I sat back and just let him spill it out.

"Clive was definitely one of a kind. I remember the first time I saw him. I was walking down the hall at Bender. I was late getting somewhere when I heard this voice behind me..."

Now my eyes were opening again. The second set, the ones that could see what no one else could. I was inside of Haven's head, and I was seeing what he was as if it was happening in front of me. Only it was ten years ago.

Through Andrew Haven eyes as he remembers Clive ten years earlier:

"Yo..."

I turned and faced a tall, lanky black man. He was handsome in a very unusual way. His face was chiseled and a light brown color. His black hair was cut neatly, and his large hands were thrust in his pockets. He seemed almost out of place in those halls. Filled with nothing but white people.

"My name's Clive January...I've noticed you, not too many brothers here you know..."

"You've noticed. Five of us out of what three hundred...almost 1/10th of a percent..."

I laughed. He smiled.

"It's good to meet you Clive. I'm Andrew Haven..."

He clasped my hand, the brother shake.

"So what's the deal here, Andy...?"

I flinched. Normally, I hated people calling me that. It always reminded me of being a fat little boy that everyone made fun of. Andy can't do this. Andy can't do that...but for some reason, the way he said it made it sound almost endearing, like a pleasant, familiar nickname instead of a childhood taunt.

"What do you mean...?"

He stopped for a moment, as if he weren't sure whether to take me into his confidence or not, looking around.

"Listen, were you heading home?"

"You wanna grab a beer?"

I almost said no. I had plans. But for some reason, I couldn't say no. I felt somehow as if his will were controlling me.

"Sure…let's go to the Oak Bar, on Wall…" The bar was packed with the Wall Street regulars, old, white guys who'd been on the Street so long they were like a fraternity of college boys except the pranks were worth millions and could make or break a man in seconds. But Clive wasn't looking at any of them. It's like he'd blocked out the bedlam of clinking glasses, the off-color jokes and pale fingers clutching stools to steady themselves, and nails stained with cigar smoke. And as far as you could see, no women, and no blacks.

Clive ordered a whisky and didn't drink a drop. He just talked like he'd been waiting for a sounding board. "How does a brother make it around here? I mean really make it. I'm talking stupid money, all the shit the white boys got."

"You work hard…"

"Aw c'mon, man. You know that's bullshit. You're telling me that every trader on the floor that's pulling down half a mil a year is doing it 'cause he's just working hard. That's total bullshit."

I was a little put off by his intensity. He was like a hot, white fire that was just starting to burn at the edges. "Well, finding a rabbi doesn't hurt either…"

"A rabbi?"

"A mentor, somebody who will pull you up with him."

He twirled the glass around in his hand, still hadn't touched the whisky. "So in other words, the right ass to kiss."

"You could put it that way."

He leaned back in his chair, in deep thought. His eyes sunk into his face. And in the half light of the dark bar, he assumed an almost ghostly air. "Me and this buddy of mine, a white guy I knew in college, are thinking about starting a business."

"Really."

"Yeah, buying and selling stock of small companies that nobody's doing much with."

"Interesting but risky."

He smiled. "Isn't that the only way to make the real money?"

"I suppose so."

He looked at me curiously. "How long have you been at the firm?"

"Two years, almost three."

"And you?"

He leaned back in his chair, a half smile lighting across his face. "Three months." He pushed his whisky away and leaned his elbows on the table. Staring at me, like he was trying to bore a hole in my soul. "So would you like to work with us?"

I probably should've laughed. I mean really. The nerve. I was a second year trader, making probably five times as much as he was, and he had just barely gotten out of the training program. "You're kidding right?"

"No. I'm not. You've got the kind of experience we need and I like you."

"Well thanks for the offer, but…I think I'll stay at Bender…"

He shrugged his shoulders, seemingly nonchalantly. "Hey, you may regret that…'cause we're gonna make it big. Stupid big." He grabbed the check. "My treat."

My eyes were closing. I knew I wouldn't see anymore. So I turned to Haven, cutting him off. "So when did you start working together?"

Haven jumped. "Oh, not for years later—ten years later."

"Did he start that other business, with the white guy?"

"I don't know. I don't think so, something happened to him."

"Who?"

"The white guy. I don't know what. I left Bender a few months later and moved to Chicago. I lost track of Clive until he approached me about being a partner in the business."

I glanced at the clock. *Five-thirty. Shit.* I was supposed to meet Margie. She'd finally agreed to see me.

"Listen, Mr. Haven, I gotta be somewhere in a few. You mind if I stop by your office? I can look around, speak to some of your people, you know the drill."

"No, anytime."

He snapped open a thin silver cardholder and handed me a card. "Just call me and speak to Cindy, my assistant. She'll set everything up."

"Thanks."

I glanced at his card, ANDREW HAVEN, PRESIDENT. *Didn't take long to change the cards, I see.* I pulled out one of Clive January's cards from the file: CLIVE JANUARY. PRESIDENT.

Like I said, didn't take long.

CHAPTER FIFTEEN

Margie looked different—not better or worse, just different—standing on the corner waiting for me with all of New York rushing past her. Her cheeks were tinged red, the way they always were. Her dark hair was stuffed in a huge red wool hat that made her look like one of Santa's elves or something.

She didn't see me just yet, but I spotted her right away, always could. For a minute, I got that little jump in my throat I'd get when I first saw her. Like the first time we went out.

"You look great," I said

"Thanks, you don't look that bad yourself."

She looked more than just great. Shit, she had on a black knit dress that showed off every curve in her body and picked up the little light brown flecks in her eyes. Her thick dark brown hair was done up in some fancy way on top of her head and made her seem even taller and more like some Greek statute. Damn. She looked *good.* But there was something in her eyes—like I'd really fucked up bad and was probably never gonna be able to make it up.

"How're you doing?"

Her smile seemed different, too. Confident, in charge. "Good. In fact really good."

I wished I could say the same, but I'd be lying if I said I was doing anything but just okay.

I got a little closer to her. "So you wanna get a cup of coffee or something?" I really didn't feel much like hanging on a corner. A half-drunk bum staggered past us and collapsed in a heap against the light post. Since this was New York, nobody noticed. Nobody gave a damn. Including me. All I really wanted was to somehow get Margie back, even if it was just for a cup of coffee. Hell, it was better than nothing.

"No, I can't. I've got something to do at six..."

"Oh yeah, what's his name?"

"Fuck you, Bob." She jammed her hands in her coat angrily. "I don't need it today, okay."

"Yeah right, tell me I don't have reason to wonder. You walk out on me after ten years with not so much as a see ya later Bob, and you wonder if I don't wonder if you ain't screwing somebody else."

"You just can't face the truth can you? How many times did I try and talk to you, try and tell you about the things that were bothering me? Then when I finally decide after ten wasted years that I was moving on, you insist on thinking that it's got to be somebody else. It's you, Bob. Just you. You're the reason I left, 'cause you're a selfish shit. And I'm tired of it."

"So why the hell did you want to see me?"

She pulled her hat down lower over her face, the way she always did when she didn't want to say something, or didn't know how to say it. At that moment, I just wished I could grab her and pick her up, and we'd land on my old plaid couch, just the two of us: with a couple of beers, the TV, the sound of kids outside the window and the feel of her next to me. Like nothing else.

"I'm...um...joining the force."

"You're what?"

"I'm gonna be a cop."

"No fuckin' way!"

I knew I was hearing wrong. My ex a cop. Shit. Like they say, be careful what you ask for. I wanted her so bad, now I got her.

Her eyes flashed angrily. "It's a free country, I can do whatever the hell I want to do and be whatever I want to. You don't own NYPD."

I shook my head in disbelief. "You're doing this to mess with me, aren't you? Just admit it. Walking out on me wasn't enough. Now you gotta fuck with me on my job, too." Even though I was damn near yelling, no one noticed. The early evening passersby only knotted their scarves more tightly around their faces and pressed their bodies more determinedly into the icy winds. Nobody wanted to notice a red faced guy getting more agitated by the minute.

Margie continued wearily as if she was tired of having this conversation. "Believe it or not, the world doesn't revolve around you, and I don't make every decision in my life just to spite you. And before you think I was on some vendetta or something, you should know that I didn't want to be in your division."

I couldn't believe there was more.

"I tried to get a transfer but—"

"Shit, Margie!"

I needed a drink, but I was too stunned to move. "You mean to tell me that you can't live with me, you think I'm a selfish shit or whatever, but now you're gonna go and work with me!?"

"It wasn't my choice. I asked to be placed in another precinct, but they put me where there was a vacancy."

"What about your job at Nynex?"

"They were gonna lay me off. I hadn't been there long enough to get any kind of real severance or pension, so I did what I had to. One thing about New York, there will always be criminals, so they'll always need cops."

A mean-assed headache started at the back of my head and moved up to my temples. I had to sit down. I crumpled on the bench.

Margie was silent for a while, then she slung her purse over her shoulder and turned to leave. "I just wanted you to know." And then she left.

Fuck. Goddamnit! Like my job wasn't hard enough already without having to see Margie's face everyday and know that she wasn't mine. That some other knucklehead was going to be screwing her. I massaged my aching head, wondering how I was gonna get through the next few months, before I could get a transfer or something. And that damn January case, still no further along than when I started. I wanted to go home sit in front of the tube with a bottle of Jack and watch cartoons. Forget everything. But I couldn't. I had to keep on going.

what a pitiful shit. and this is who i've got to depend on to find out who killed me. a screwed up cop who can't even control his woman. i knew how to control a woman, never let her get to you, never let her know that you wanted her, or worse that you needed her. there was only one woman who i couldn't control. no matter what i did, i couldn't stop loving her.

and i keep thinking about her. the last time i saw her when she handed me the pipe and disappeared out of the room, and then the gun shots. did she do it? she couldn't have. she loved me. or so i'd thought. but now i wonder was i ever capable of being loved or loving. maybe it was all an illusion. my wife didn't love me. but she had, and i guess that i'm to blame for what happened. monique. sweet monique, turned to bitter bile.

i wonder where she is, what she's doing, does she miss me or is it relief she feels? i want to see her and our daughter, baby ariel, does she miss me or has she been poisoned against me, too? i feel like i'm moving, like i'm going somewhere. now i see. i'm floating over our apartment. i can see monique. i can feel what she's feeling, and think her thoughts…now i'm in her head. i wonder does she know i'm here…

Monique

I looked over at my mother-in-law dozing peacefully in Clive's leather recliner. She had unofficially claimed it as her own since he'd died. My daughter, Ariel, was asleep in her arms. The bond between them was strange. They were almost inseparable from the moment she'd arrived at our doorstep on that rainy April night. And Clive, strong Clive, who taunted the world and everyone in it, for the first time looked like somebody had pulled the rug out from under him when he saw his mother's face.

"Clive, there's um…someone…You just better come here."

He curled the ever present portable phone under his chin, frowning in annoyance. "Monique, I'm on the phone."

"I can see that, but there's a woman who says…" I couldn't keep my eyes off the tall solemn woman standing in the open doorway. Before she told me who she was, I knew already. Because no matter what Clive said, no matter what lie slipped so easily from his mouth, I knew who she was: same tall thin frame, long face, high cheekbones and piercing intense eyes that could cut through you in a glance.

"She says that she's your—" Before I could finish the sentence, Ariel tottered into the room, walking uncertainly almost curiously toward the tall distant stranger.

The woman, my mother-in-law, picked up Ariel, cuddling her into her damp body. "This must be my grandbaby."

Clive bolted into the room and literally snatched our child from his mother. "Noooo! Get your fuckin' hands off her!" He turned to her with a viciousness and hatred that seemed to bubble up from somewhere deep in his soul that I, nor I think anyone else, had ever seen. "You are not my mother!"

Ariel started screaming loudly, a tiny pawn between the woman that she had only met a moment ago, and the father that she'd known her entire short life. And for a moment, just a moment, I felt superior to my husband because this time there was no easy answer. Truth was staring at him plainly in the face.

"You never could lie good." His mother's words sliced him.

Shaking, he shouted. "Get out! I don't know how the fuck you ended up here, but get out. I don't know you!"

My mother-in-law smiled smugly. "My grandbaby knows her grandma, don't you baby?" Ariel stopped crying and smiled hesitantly through her tears at her grandmother.

Clive looked as if everything that he had become had suddenly been snatched away from him in a single moment. And now his voice was low and terse. All of the violent emotion gone. He turned to me, slowly. "Tell this woman that if she ever comes here again, I will call the police and have her immediately removed."

"But, Clive, she's your mother!"

"I will call the police, and I will have her removed." He turned, carrying our daughter out of the room.

His mother's dark cold eyes followed him out of the room. She smiled strangely, as if somehow none of this was a surprise to her. "Don't worry none, Monique. He'll come around. I know my boy." The way she said my name made me shiver. "How do you know my name?"

"Oh, I knows, lots, lots more than he thinks." She wrapped her thin coat around her shoulders. "You kiss my grandbaby for me."

She disappeared into the driving rain without so much as an umbrella, braving the wind and the sheets of chilling April rain, as if it were no more than a mild shower.

Now as I looked over at her gently stroking my daughter's dark curls, I wondered what unspoken secrets lay between her and my dead husband. Never to be talked about. Buried with his soul.

I supposed I'd never know. She and I rarely talked. Except for last night. It was the only time she'd ever revealed any of herself to me. Most of our conversations in the past consisted of the bare necessities. I never felt comfortable around her, as if she were sizing me up, judging me against some standard to which I was doomed to fail. I only allowed her to stay out of guilt. I knew she had nowhere else to go, and despite what I might have thought Clive would have done, I wouldn't be accused of putting his destitute mother out in the street.

Clive would have had no mercy, but I don't know why I couldn't just bring myself to put limits on her, tell her to leave and go back to where she'd come from. It seemed as if every time I got close to taking a stand, asserting my rights over my home after all, I caught a glimpse of someone else under the hardness, and something in me wouldn't allow it.

Last night, I couldn't sleep, so I'd climbed out of bed and headed to the kitchen, thinking that perhaps warm milk would help this ever-present insomnia, when I noticed a light coming from underneath the study door. Clive's study. His prize. The room where he kept all of his first editions like trophies. Books from all of the famous writers, shiny leather covers, dusted lovingly, but never opened. But now as I walked into the room, I saw Clive's mother, doing the sacrosanct. Reading one of Clive's books. Books for show not for use.

"Mother?" She looked up, startled for a moment.

"I was lookin' at all his fancy books. Bet he didn't even read none of 'em."

I didn't answer, torn between defending my dead husband and blurting out the all too obvious truth. She snapped the book shut abruptly and turned so that she was facing me directly. Pulling her faded bathrobe around herself more tightly, she said, "Yo daddy's a doctor, right?"

Surprised by the sudden change in subject, I nodded. "Yes, a surgeon."

"I was supposed t'have worked for a colored doctor, long time ago fore I was married. Was s'pposed to have gone to school and studied to be a nurse, two times. First time, I didn't 'cause I got married, second time…" She sighed and put down the book, her eyes narrowing as she stared ahead not so much at me as through me, as though I was a bothersome impediment to some wisp of memory that was materializing in front of her.

"Clive was 'bout three. I'd been goin' to this school to learn the things I'd need to take the 'xamonation for nursin' school. Things had been real bad for Lorenzo. The white folks was mad 'cause of the things that had been happenin' in the South, boycotts and sit-ins and what not, so they'd made it hard for the colored men in Hendersonville to get work. Lorenzo had been a housepainter, but the crackers had decided they didn't want no more colored men paintin' they houses. So it'd been 'bout three months since he'd worked. Money was tight. What with him not workin' much and me not workin' at all. One day I got home from school. Clive was playin' with some broke down toy and Lorenzo was sitting' there looking' kinda low, when I walked in…"

As I listened to my mother in law, it was as if her life was playing out in front of me, like a tableau vivant. Only I was seeing it as she would. I wondered, was there some force that I was not aware of there in the room that was opening a window into her past for me. It was at once thrilling and unsettling, but I couldn't and didn't want to shake off the feelings.

Perhaps it was him. Clive. I often felt as if he'd never really left, that he was just there close enough for me to touch but then not too close. As he'd been in life—there, but not really. Perhaps I was seeing what Clive could see with the eyes of the dead. Eyes that could peel away the layers of time and make what was yesterday appear as today. For I saw clearly my mother-in-law's life through her eyes as it happened, so many years ago…

Through Sarah's eyes as she remembered…

"Sarah, we needs to talk."

I didn't like the way Lorenzo looked. He'd been lookin' worse and worser every day that he didn't have no work. I kinda sidled over to him and sits next to him on the bed. Afraid of what he was gonna say. He kinda cleared his throat and tooks my hands, rubbin' 'em like he was tryin' to figure out what to say.

"How much more of this school you got 'fore you finish?"

"I don't know exactly, 'pends on how I do on the next tests. The teacher says he thinks if I keeps up like I's doin', I oughta be finished by year end."

"So three mo months."

"Yeah, 'bout."

"Sarah, we ain't got three months. I gotta call from the landlord. We is three months behind on the rent, and he's gonna put us out 'less we pay up this week."

This sick feelin' crept up from my stomach to my head. I knowed what he was gonna say, but I couldn't let him. There had to be some other way. Not what he was gonna make me do.

"I talked to your ol' boss over to the factory. They'll give you your old job back and some money in advance if you'll start—"

I turned around and screamed, "No I ain't doin' it! You promised me I could do this, you promised me when we got married that I wouldn't have t'work, that I could go back to school and do somethin', that I wouldn't end up like Ma and Pa and all the rest of the colored folks in this town!"

Lorenzo looked like I'd hit him in the gut. He tried to gently pull me back on the bed and into his arms, but I wouldn't let him. I hated him. I hated all of 'em. Stealin' my dreams again. First before, now this. This was my one chance, and I warn't givin' up. I started cryin', even though I hates cryin', Mama Joe said never let a man see you cry, then they knows they got you. But I didn't care no more, all I cared 'bout was my chance, my one chance to be somethin' was gettin' snatched away again.

"Can't we holds out a little longer? We got some money saved up, don't we?"

"It's all gone."

"Cain't you do somethin', anythin to make some money?!"

Lorenzo was real quiet. He didn't say nothin' for a minute. Then when he did start talkin' it was low and so soft I couldn't hardly hear it. "Sarah, baby, I'm sorry. I asked yo boss, if I could take yo old job, but he said his boss didn't want no men in the factory, only women. No colored men on the line. Said they caused too much trouble and headaches for the folks. I been tryin' to find work. I even looked in the other towns, but they's nothin, nothin' for colored men." He stared ahead with this sad look on his face. For a minute I felt kinda bad. I knowed Lorenzo warn't the kinda man that'd go back on his word. I knowed that he'd tried, but all I could think about was how close I was to gettin' out to doin' somethin'. I decided right then that I warn't givin' up. Not this time.

'Twas late, must been 'bout two, three in the mornin.' Lorenzo was sleep. I gets up and grabs a paper bag, stuffin' my things in it. I'd decided what I was doin'. I was goin' back home to Ma and Pa, even though I'd swore I'd never go to that town again. But it 'twas my only chance. There was a school there. I'd live with Ma and Pa. I could find some work there at night and send the money back to Lorenzo for him and Clive, and that way I could keep on. I had to keep on. I looked around. I felt kinda sad leavin' Lorenzo and Clive, but they'd understands. I'd sends 'em money. I'd finish school, and then we'd all have plenty a money. They'd see I was doin' the right thing. They'd see.

Late afternoon I was walkin' up the dusty road to Ma and Pa's house. I itched all over from the mosquitoes and gnats. My head ached. I was sticky and tired from walkin' the whole way. Thirty miles. But I didn't care. At least here, I'd have a chance. I opens the door, stickin' my head in.

"Ma…is you there…it's me…Sarah…"

Crash.

The sound of the wind slapping against the window jolted me back to reality. Clive's mother stopped. Startled by the sudden noise, she just sat there, shivering slightly. I was almost afraid to say anything, but I had to know. "What happened after that, were you able to finish?"

She looked at me with aching sadness, as if the answer was all too obvious. "No chile. Ma and Pa made me go back to Lorenzo and Clive. Said a wife's place is with her family. They closed the school in Hendersonville, an' I went back to the factory. And that was that."

She said it with finality that couldn't mask the bitter disappointment of a life forever on hold. So now when I see her with my child, even though I want to grab Ariel from her and hold her, I feel the ghosts of the other person that Clive's mother was, before the sadness settled in, and I can't. I can't tell her to leave now. Maybe in a few weeks. But not now, she's lost too much already.

"She reminds me of my baby." She hugged Ariel tighter against her gaunt frame.

"Clive?"

She didn't look up. She just continued rocking Ariel back and forth, then said softly as if almost to herself, "No…not Clive…his baby sister."

I looked up at her sharply. "Clive never mentioned a sister. I always thought he was an only child."

"He warn't much mor'n a baby when she died. He didn't 'member much 'bout her. Seems like just a little while ago…but it t'wasnt…'twas right after her birthday…same day…"

Her eyes sunk deeper into her face, like her soul was somehow traveling back again to that different self. As she remembered, I saw once again what she was seeing, through her eyes…

Through Sarah's eyes as she remembers…

"C'mon, now. You let yo mama wipe yo face…" I leans down and wiped the little dribbles of yaller birthday cake from her chin. She gots crumbs in her hair, tangled up in the shiny black curls. Indian hair. That's what Mama said when she seen her. Looks just like yo daddy's mama…Mama Jay, pure Indian, a Seminole from Florida. Her husband, Pa's daddy, had been a slave. But Mama Jay growed up in the swamps with her people. Granddaddy had run away an' hid out with Mama Jay's people. An' after the war, they'd left together. Him an' Mama Jay had seven chillun's. My pa was the youngest, an' Mama Jay had lived with us since I could 'member. I 'members her sittin' on that cushion in the corner of the room, wise like. Maybe if she'd been there, things woulda been different for me. Mama Jay always made it alright. Even when Ma and Pa, beat me for somethin' I didn't do, Mama Jay would make it alright. She'd hold me an' tell me I was special. I was diff'rnt, that I'd git out. I'd be somethin'.

"Ma-ma…"

I hugged my baby an' gives her a big kiss on the forehead. My pretty baby. At least I had my pretty baby. Chocolate brown like Lorenzo, but with Mama Jay's Indian hair and big black eyes that follows me evr'where. Clive comes up and tugs at the baby's pink dress. The one I made special for her birthday from the scraps at the dress factory where I worked.

"Wanna play, does baby wanna play?"

I pushed Clive away, saying firmly, "She don't play. Now go on, git. I tol' you not to bother yo sistah." The baby's body trembled, and she coughed. She'd been coughin' like that off an' on since the mornin' before. I held her a little tighter, yelling out, "Lorenzo, she' still be coughin. I thinks you needs to go git the doctor."

Lorenzo bends down and scoops her up real gentle. "How's my little lady, hmmm? How's Daddy's birthday girl?" I dunno know why, but I felt tense. I almost yells, "Go on, Lorenzo, git the doctor, and take Clive with you. I can't handles him with her right now."

Last thing I 'members is the door closing. Later, I was in the bed, holdin' her. She'd been coughin' since Lorenzo left. I didn't wanna sleep, but I's so tired. The baby was quiet now. I held her closer to me. An I must've slept, 'cause now they was shaking me, Lorenzo an the doctor.

"Sarah, Sarah, the baby"

I looked down an' it's like she's sleepin' cept when I touches her, she's cold. I can't believes it, I won't, so I holds her tighter cryin' to Lorenzo.

"Git some blankets, the baby's cold, can't you see, she's cold!" I'm cryin' an' the doctor's tryin' to take her from me.

"Sarah, she's gone…"

"Nooooo! She jus' cold thas' all!"

Lorenzo picks me up and takes the baby outta my arms. But I was cryin' so much an all I can think and say is, "I cin't leaves her. I gots to be there when she wakes up, or she'll be cryin'. I got's to be there!"

Thump.

Something fell to the floor. I jumped. Ariel had awakened and slid off Clive's mother's lap, tottering over to me. I scooped her up, not knowing quite what to say. Clive's mother looked smaller hunched in the chair. The room was quiet. Only the muffled sound of cars outside the long windows. After a moment Clive's mother spoke.

"T'was influenza, she warn't the only baby that died that winter, jus' the first."

"I'm...sorry... ." And I was. I remembered the baby that I'd lost. The pain that never really leaves you. I held Ariel a little tighter. Thinking of the baby that I'd lost, and then the baby that she'd lost, wondering if somehow they were linked, together in the place where they buried the souls of infants. And for the first time, I felt something for this woman in front of me. I reached over and squeezed her hand. She held my hand tightly as if thirsty for human touch. And I saw tears on her face.

I don't know how long we sat there in silence. I must've fallen alseep, because now the shadows were longer. I glanced at my watch. "There's a detective coming in a few minutes."

Clive's mother hummed a nonsensical tune, rocking Ariel in her lap. "Good, they gotta find out who killed my boy."

Her remark struck me as odd. After all, she and Clive were not close. However, I suppose that even a child that you grew distant from as an adult, you would still mourn in death. I shuddered, hoping that I would never know first hand that type of loss. I was still unable to believe Clive was gone. I couldn't convince myself that the police would ever really find out what happened. Clive was into too much, too many people, too many things that were unspoken. Part of me wanted to bury it all with him. Lock it away in an airtight mausoleum with the rest of our life together.

"Mrs. January, Detective Greene is here."

"Thanks, Dolly, tell him I'll be right there. "

I turned to my mother-in-law. As usual, she anticipated my question before I could say it. "You go on, I'll watch my grandbaby."

I lit a cigarette. Why I was nervous, I don't know. I had nothing to hide. I suppose it was just the old adage that has one believing that the wife always did it. Detective Greene looked around my living room, as if he never expected that black people could live like that. I'd gotten so used to it that I'd forgotten how lovely it all was.

Large and sunny, one of those cavernous Central Park West apartments that reeked of old world charm and even older money. Clive would have nothing less. Of course. A broad staircase descended gracefully from the middle of the polished marble halls. The living room was done in pale shades of cream and antique green and had fresh cut flowers. A far cry, I suppose, from what a detective would suppose that "we" could ever afford. Typical of them. Usually, I would have been righteously indignant that he could ever believe that "we" couldn't live like that, unless of course we were athletes or drug dealers, but at this point, I just wanted the whole damn thing to be over with.

"Sit down, please, Detective."

"Thanks." He sat on the edge of my brocade sofa as if he were afraid of breaking something. "Mrs. January, I just got a few questions for you. I might have to come back later and talk to you again, but right now I'm looking for something pretty specific."

"Yes," I said trying to sound more detached than I felt.

"Now don't take offense at what I'm asking, but I gotta know..."

I wanted to scream, "Go on ask the damn question! The one everybody asks!"

"Was your husband seeing another woman?"

I crushed the cigarette slowly out into the blue and white porcelain dish, letting the ash trail slowly around the pale blue figurine. "Another woman? I think you mean women, Detective. My husband never limited himself to just one other woman."

I lit another cigarette, and then looked at him defiantly. "Now is there anything else that you want to know?"

"Did you kill your husband?"

"I wanted to. Many times." I watched out the window as schoolchildren crossed the street, all bright and cheery in their plaid jumpers and crisp blazers. There was something so orderly and comforting about school children. They were like harbingers of another era.

"Mrs. January?" The detective interrupted my thoughts.

"Right, to answer your question. No, I did not kill my husband. Why should I, there were others who could do a much better job than I?"

"Oh yeah, like who in particular?"

"Oh I don't know really. My husband was envied by many people."

"Like maybe his business partner?"

"Andrew…Yes, I'd say he envied my husband."

"Enough to kill him?"

"I don't know. You're the detective, right?"

"And you're the grieving widow, right?"

I smiled, this little verbal cat and mouse was beginning to be amusing. "Well, I am the widow."

He shrugged his shoulders and snapped his notebook shut. "Yeah, that's just about how I figured it." He looked like he was about to leave, then he turned back, raising one eyebrow. "So why didn't you leave him, get one of them quickie divorces, take half his shit and go on about your business?"

Scenes flashed across my mind, Clive standing over me, and I'm shrinking. Shrinking until I don't know who I am or where I am. Is it the hospital? I don't know. The only thing I'm conscious of is his anger. Filling the room like a thick blanket.

"Well, why didn't you?"

I'm back in the now of my life, and I'm angry, angry at myself and at the detective for uncovering what was better left alone. "I don't think that's any of your business, detective."

"I think it is, 'cause I think it might have something to do with your husband's death… maybe something so simple as a big fat insurance policy, or maybe half of a multi-million dollar business, a fancy Central Park apartment, house in the Hamptons and who knows what else? So ya see, Mrs. January, it is my business."

I swallowed hard, about to light another cigarette, but I resist, I'm not going to let his memory push me over the edge. It's bad enough that he tormented me in life. I will not allow him to continue in death. So I turn to the detective, trying to keep a level voice, after all, what if I were a suspect? This jealous weasel of a white man would probably like nothing better than to haul me in on murder charges. "Well if you must know, I couldn't leave Clive January. No one does."

CHAPTER SIXTEEN

Detective Bob

Weird chick. That's all I could think. Real ice queen. But somehow my gut told me that she wasn't the one. Don't ask me why. I just knew she wouldn't do anything to embarrass herself or her family. And one thing a chick like that wasn't about to do was to go to jail for killing somebody that she didn't give a shit about anymore. I looked at the faded newspaper clipping. *New York Times*, June 1980. A picture of Clive January and his blushing bride-to-be. The one I just talked to. Only, she wasn't blushing no more.

I skimmed the short article: "Clive January investment banker and founder of January & Associates will wed Monique Raymond after a whirlwind courtship. The ceremony and reception will be held at the Long Island summer home of the bride's parents, Dr. and Mrs. Steven Raymond. The bride's father is the chief of Pediatric Surgery at St. Johns Hospital in New Rochelle. The bride's mother is an administrator with the New Rochelle school system. The groom's parents are deceased. Over 400 guests will attend the festivities, and the couple will honeymoon in St. Kitts."

Well la di da...so she comes from money, too. Not him, though. From what I'd been able to piece together, he was just a regular guy who married up after he'd made good. The American way.

I glanced again at the picture. He looked young and cocky; and her, innocent, fresh, and totally in love with him. None of that left on her face now. I was about to file the article away, but I couldn't tear my eyes away from it. Something kept drawing me to his eyes. I got that feeling again, of being pulled into the picture, into his world. My stomach turned over as if I were about to lose the stale pastrami sandwich I'd had for lunch. I swallowed, breathing, trying to force myself back. It was a repeat of that day at his beach house when a force stronger than me pulled me back, back into a tunnel of the past. Clive's past. Faces started rushing past me like moving pictures, and then I was seeing through his eyes, hearing through his ears and Bob Greene was gone, lost in his will. I was Clive.

Bright sun blinds my eyes. I am looking down a beach. A narrow strip of white sand. Children, all black children are playing in the sand and diving in and out of the waves of the calm bay. Houses dot the grassy dunes, and everywhere, black people relax, joke, sip drinks, play cards. This is home for them. I've never seen anything like this before.

I'm walking down the beach alone. Everyone seems to know someone but me. I feel like I've stumbled on an exclusive club, only I'm the odd man out. I feel self-conscious. Like I used to when I first got to college, afraid that someone would dig too deeply into my past.

People turn and look at me as I walk, curious glances, raised eyebrows. I'm about to turn back when I hear my name.

"Clive…Is that Clive January?"

I turn and see a short, brown-skinned man, starting to bald slightly. I blink in the sun, not quite sure where I know him from.

"It's me, Andrew Haven, from Bender. I left right after you got there."

"Andy…what's up, man?"

I feel better, a familiar face. I sense my confidence starting to grow again.

"Not a whole lot. I moved to Chicago a couple of years ago, but I'm thinking about moving back. Goldman made me an offer that's looking real good, especially when I think about those cold assed Chicago winters."

I smile, remembering the first time we met, figuring I'll rub it in. "You shoulda taken me up on my offer. I started my own firm two years ago, and we're kickin' ass man. I mean big boo-ty."

"So I hear. Congratulations."

Insincerity. But I don't give a fuck. I'm glad to have somebody to rap with. To make me feel like I belong. I look around at the comfortable black folks, and I know that this is someplace I want to belong.

Andy looks suddenly like he's not sure of what to say next, then blurts out, almost in spite of himself. "Well, maybe I will work with you someday, five or ten years from now..."

He laughs a forced laugh. High pitched, nasal, like the white deputy in that jail years ago. I turn away from him, focusing on the sea eating away at the glaring white beach. "I won't be here in ten years..."

I look into his face, an army of sweat on his round brown forehead, and now I smile saying, "Man, don't you know the good die young..." I skip a shell across the sand. A perfect arc. "And I'm the best there is..."

Andy smiles politely. Envy falling across his face. But what can he say? A soft, almost airy voice comes from behind us. "Andrew, don't be so rude. Introduce me to your friend."

I turn to a pretty light-brown skinned woman. Her wavy black hair is pinned up, and her pale blue swim suit reveals just enough. Something about her eyes remind me of someone, clear and so light brown that you can see your reflection in them.

"Oh sorry Monique,...Monique Raymond, Clive January..."

She smiles warmly. An innocence and vulnerability etched in her face. Again, I think of someone. And now I know who. Mrs. Foster. I feel as if I've stepped back into time to that small Southern town and folded myself up in the warmth and goodness of the first woman who ever loved me. I feel close to this woman, Monique, as if she's always been a part of me. I smile at her, wanting to know more. Suddenly needing to know, who she is, this ghost of my past staring into my present.

"Do you live around here?"

"Uh huh...Over there...at the end of the beach." She points to the biggest house on the bluff, a modern white ranch with a long wrap-around deck. Two middle aged black couples are lounging on the deck, laughing, playing cards.

And I notice that Monique has been staring at me like she knows me, too. And I think of Mrs. Foster and her eyes are the same and she is the same and I want her. Suddenly, I feel like I need her to close the circle of my past to be for her what Daddy wanted to be for Mrs. Foster…

It's night now. The beach is empty. Lights dot the air from the houses perched on the dunes. I'm alone. Occasional conversation floats out. I kneel on the sand, still warm from the day's sun. I take out my wallet. A small photo. The stupid kind you take in the booths in Woolworths. Her face smiles back at me, her voice playing in my mind.

"So, Clive January, will you marry me?" I look over at her smooth body lying next to mine. I cradle my face in the small of her back, her perfectly round brown ass jutting in front of my face like two delicious scoops of chocolate ice cream, melting slowly under my tongue. She turns over and places a small firm breast in front of my face. "Well, will you marry me?"

And suddenly I feel drunk or drugged, like I always do with her. "Laurel, I love you…" She sits up, entwining her small body into mine, so that our hearts drum together. "So marry me then." She's kissing me. Licking my chest, squeezing me. I let myself go, swept away, being totally at one with her.

And I hear myself saying, "Yes, I'll marry you, Laurel. I'll marry you…" A cold wind tugs the photograph out of my hand. I grab it from the sand. The voices have stopped. The memories frozen, filed back in my brain. That was six months ago. I haven't seen her since. She wrote, said she was coming back to marry me. But she didn't come. She wouldn't tell me where she was. Then the letters stopped. She called once, but she wouldn't say where she was or when she was coming back.

I wrote, but the letters came back with no forwarding address. I called, but the number had been changed. And I thought shit, it's happening again, like when I left Hendersonville, I can't get her out of my mind. I think she's there and she's not. But this time, I felt like there was this hole in me that wouldn't close up. Then I realized I was hooked. What I'd fought all along had happened. I'd gotten used to seeing her, used to waking up next to her and her just being there.

We had lost track for about five years after that time I saw her after college, and then one day she'd just reappeared, and almost from the start we'd started living together. Marriage wasn't really my thing, and she hadn't seemed too pressed either until right before she left. Then she disappeared, saying she had to straighten some things out, she'd be back in a few weeks—and now it's been six months.

I look out at the sea stretched in front of me. Calm. Like it is waiting for me to make the next move, I have to decide whether to ripple the waves. And I just stare. Something is pulling me to act, to break loose, get on with it. But I keep feeling her touch, like the wind against me, warm then cool. I kneel down in the sand and draw a circle, like the hole I couldn't seem to close up. But maybe it was better. Maybe this was my chance to take back that part of me that I'd lost to her, for good this time, leaving it and her in the past, where they belonged.

I kick the sand across the circle, and picking up a stone skip it over the smooth surface of the water. And now I've met the woman I'm going to marry. And it's not her. I look at the photo again. And then around me. The homes, the comfort, the quiet. And I let the photo slip from my hands. Carried by the night air, higher, higher, and then resting on the black water, disappearing under the hungry waves. I get up and walk toward the lights.

Shit. I'm in the tunnel again, whizzing forward, passing time. I don't know how much time. I stop. A gentle Long Island evening. The air is heavy with the smells of the sea and flowers and life subdued. I'm looking into Monique's eyes. But now she's in white. It's our wedding. Everyone is smiling. But for some reason I have this sense of foreboding, like nothing this good can last forever.

I'm whirling her around the dance floor. She whispers in my ear, "Clive, I love you so much."

I kiss her gently behind her ear, brushing her hair away from her face. People laugh and titter. Seeing faces in a blur, snatches of "They're so in love…aren't they a beautiful couple?" Again, that feeling, this can't last. I close my eyes. She holds me tightly. The music, the people, the sea air, transporting me away…

Then a voice crashing through my thoughts. Her voice. So near. But different, slurred, like she's been drinking. "No I'm not leaving. I said I want to make a toast to the happy couple."

My eyes shoot open, and I'm staring at Laurel. She's drunk, and for the first time not in control, waving a champagne glass high over her head. All I can think is how did she get here? How did she know?

Monique tugs at my arm. "Clive, who's that woman?"

I meet Laurel's red eyes, from crying or drinking, I don't know which. I turn away, whispering to Monique, "A friend, just a friend."

But Laurel has maneuvered her way between us. "I'd just like to toast your wedding…and your eternal happiness…"

Monique smiles politely, digging her fingers into my arm, never taking her eyes off of Laurel.

"We haven't met…"

"You mean Clive hasn't told you about me…his, let's see, was it 'neighbor,' or was it…lover…I forget now."

Monique has stopped smiling, and the room is suddenly quiet.

Monique's father, Dr. Raymond, raised eyebrows, but cool, always cool, has gently grabbed Laurel's arm. "Now why don't we wait until after the cake is cut for the toasts…Miss uh…"

And before Laurel can protest, he glides her away from us and out on the veranda. That's how these people are. No scenes, no shouts just discretion and a quiet calm to cover over everything.

Monique's clear brown eyes are clouded over, like Mrs. Foster's when I hurt her, too. And I want to hold Monique and make it up to her, but I can't. It's like a part of me got a charge out of seeing Laurel, the old seduction pulling me in. And all I can do is kiss Monique gently on the cheek and say, "I'm sorry..."And I think for the first time how cold her cheek is.

The scenes are changing around me again. I'm in a room, the wedding is over. But I know it's my wedding night. Monique's gown is crumpled on the chair. I'm lying next to her. Trying to let her gentle breathing rock me to sleep. But my mind won't relax. I feel like I'm suffocating under an unknown force. I get up and look down at the beach. I realize that I'm at her parents' home. The beach is empty and quiet, the sea wanting me. I leave quietly, not really dressing, just slinging a shirt over my head and slipping into sweats. And now I feel free, stretching out on the damp sand, closing my eyes.

"I knew you'd come."

And I see her. Taunting me. "Laurel!" I bolt up. Damn. She's standing over me, tiny as she is, she seems to tower over me now. Coolly saying, "You know you're mine. You promised to marry me."

"Fuck, Laurel, what the hell are you still doing here?"

She hasn't moved, still standing over me, back in control. The temporary emotional lapse at the wedding fading away with the champagne. She looks through me calmly, like she can read every emotion on my face, her words rising over the sound of the sea...

"And what the hell are you doing married?"

I spit out, confused, angry, "Don't gimme that shit. You disappeared, and then come back expecting everything to stay the same. Who the fuck do you think you are!?" I try to get up and walk away from her, but I have to know, the question that had been with me for six months..."Where did you go?"

For a minute she doesn't say anything, the sound of the water bubbling up around her feet blanketing out everything. I can barely hear her whisper, "I went to find him."

"You went to find who? And who the hell is *him*?"

"My father! That's who! I've been looking for almost ten years. I had to find him. For me, so that I would know who I was. And I did. I finally did find him. He was sick, in a nursing home, so I spent the last six months with him until he died. I wanted to feel whole like I knew me or at least a big part of me before I could give myself to you. That's why I left. That's why I couldn't come back or even call you until it was over."

Her voice was numb and emotionless like whatever feelings she'd had had been spent months ago with a man she barely knew, but who'd consumed her life for the past ten years. She looks at me without blinking. "But it doesn't matter now, does it, obviously… it's too late."

"You're damn right it's too late!" I turn away from her, not sure of my feelings even as I said it. Everything was coming up, the hole that wouldn't close, wanting her so much, and then shoving it all aside, a new life with my wife. I try to swallow my uncertainty and force the words out … "It's over…it's all over."

But she isn't really listening to me. There were words in her head that I couldn't hear. Only a quiet determination. "Things *are* the same. Nothing will ever change with us, don't you know that by now, Clive January?"

And then she kneels down straddling me, and with more force than I ever thought she could summon up in those slender arms, she yanks my sweats down so that they're twisted around my ankles. And I'm lying there naked from the waist down as she descends on me, cradling her mouth over me, swallowing me. And I can't move. My body is charged with the same electricity that I'd felt the first time we made love, like I was a prisoner to her will, like I was nothing under the strength coiled up in her tiny body.

The sound of the waves split my head, and I push her over, twisting my body around hers, filling her with everything I'd dreamed of while I was making love to my wife…

And now I'm climbing back in bed with Monique. Dawn casting a pale grey haze over the room. Her breathing still regular and gentle. And I think of the other dawn when Daddy crept in the room after being in Mrs. Foster's bed, quietly, almost guiltily. But I wasn't Daddy. Because Daddy had a soul.

The tunnel was closing in on me, faster and faster pushing me back to me. To my life. Clive was gone. I was sitting on my bed clutching his wedding announcement, sweat trailing in my mouth. My heart in the seat of my pants. Weak, I knew if I tried to stand up I'd probably fall over. My hands were starting to shake, and the nausea was starting to creep in again. But I didn't care. I was determined to see this through. Clive's will was strong, but so was mine. Damn it and I don't know why, but I shouted out to the nothingness, "I ain't afraid, Clive January. If you're trying to scare me, to make me blink, it ain't happenin' d'you hear me you black son-of-a-bitch. You hear me. I ain't afraid!"

I was dizzy and weak, yet somehow I got up off the bed, half expecting to see him. But just silence. The only thought in my head was Laurel. She's the one I've got to find. She's the key. He wanted me to know that. I was starting to figure him out now. He wanted to me find out who killed him, because he didn't know. Whoever did it shot him from the back, so he wouldn't see them and maybe cry out their name. I knew he'd keep taking over me, imposing his life on mine until I did.

I shuddered. Shit, I'd wanted my eyes back. I'd wanted to be able to do what I thought I'd lost. Now I was doing it more than I ever had with anybody or any case I'd ever had in all the years I'd been on the force. So then why didn't I feel good? Why did I just feel this heaviness? I didn't really want to see what was out there in the past, Clive's past. Maybe whatever it was, was going to pull me in so deep that I couldn't get out. Somehow I knew that it was already too late. There was no turning back. I'd opened my eyes to him, and I couldn't close them now.

I lay back on my bed, trying to forget, trying to get back to me, but the same face kept coming up before me. This woman Laurel. The woman who screwed him on his wedding night.

CHAPTER SEVENTEEN

"Yo, Bobby Greene, you figerred the shit out yet?"

A white bright light reflected off the Captain's shiny black face. He was chomping on an old cigarette. Guys, cops I'd known for years, glared at me. In the corner of my eye, I could see the hookers being lined up and booked. Petty thieves, yelling for their lawyers as if they had a pot to piss in or a lawyer to call. The phones continually rang. Before you could hang up one, another started.

"Yeah, I'm gettin there, but I need your help on somethin'."

"So what the fuck else is new. Like when didn't you need my help on one of your cases?"

"Fuck you, Captain, just gimme a second."

"Ok, you got five, starting now."

I leaned back in my chair, thinking how I was going to put this to get the least questions from Captain. Him being a stickler for knowing sources and all. "I heard there's somebody he was screwin' named Laurel, don't have a last name, but I heard they knew each other, from way back."

"And who the hell you 'hear' this from? Boogie joe grinder, the sweet spot finder, the blank who sat by the woodpile? I'd fill in the blank, but I don't like to use the 'N' word in front of you white boys."

I rolled my eyes, thinking that for once I wished that the captain could just answer my damn question without the bullshit. "Well I heard it from his wife."

"His wife told you the name of the bitch he was fuckin'! Now that's the kind of wife I need! Knows I'm gettin' some on the side and don't gives a damn. That's a good woman."

"Yeah right, but anyway. I wanted to know if you had this Laurel's name on the list of witnesses the Long Island cops saw before I got on the case."

"Man, do you ever look at the paper work before you get on something, or do you just figure you can ask me all the questions, and then you trot around and do the fun shit, talking to witnesses and going to funerals and shit. 'Cause believe it or not, Greene, this ain't the only case I'm worried about. So go do your own damn work. Go on over there to the file room." He smiled one of those shit eating grins he did when he thought he got you. "I think you know who's working there now."

That knot had started to grow in my stomach. So everybody knew my business. 'cause if the captain was onto it, you can bet that every cop in the place knew my ex who'd dumped me was working in my face every damn day.

"And I want a report from you by the end of the week of exactly where you are on the January case. People have been asking about it, and I intend to have somethin' to tell him. So get your ass in gear." He waddled off, biting down hard on the unlit cigarette.

Shit, the last thing I wanted to do was to have to go back to the file room on this one. The Long Island cops did such a piss poor job of the investigation before I got there, I'd figured or actually hoped that there wouldn't be any reason for me to get any of their crap.

There she was in front of me. Margie. Looking good, I had to admit, in her cop uniform, standing behind the file room desk with her back to me, leaning over, digging through some boxes. That cute butt stuck up in my face. I could almost see the outline of her panties through the thick cop's pants. I wondered what color they were. Margie never wore white panties, always colors, said it made her feel sexy. I got that jump again. Only this time it wasn't in my throat. It'd been months since I'd been with a woman. The last time was a damn joke. I picked up this chick in a bar, got to her place, and then I didn't even feel like it no more. So I just left, while she was yelling and screamin' at me, who the fuck did I think I was…yeah…yeah…blah, blah, blah.

I didn't owe her no explanation. But now seein' Margie again, her cute little bod in that cop's uniform, made me think about that time, the first time...I didn't know it was gonna happen then, I figured I'd have to wait a little longer, but somehow, it just...happened.

She turned and smiled as if she'd been expecting me. "Come for the January file?" Shit I had to shake myself back to the present. It was over, but damn it still seemed so real. I could swear I was probably sweating. I tried to pull myself together and managed to squeak out, "Right, how did you know?"

"C'mon, Bob, I'm not stupid. Even you can't do a murder investigation without eventually pulling all the files on it."

Had to get back in control, couldn't let her know what I'd been thinking, wouldn't give her that satisfaction. "Yeah well I came damn close, didn't I?"

"Not from what I hear."

"Oh yeah, and what does a *rookie cop* who don't know dog shit about being a cop, know what it takes to solve a murder?"

She just pulled out a thin file from under the desk and handed it to me. "Well, aren't we in a good mood today? What's wrong, Bob, can't find anybody to take my place?"

I grabbed the file from her, didn't want her to see my hands shaking. They always shook when she got me. I went back to my desk to find comfort in the bedlam around me. Away from Margie. I had to get Margie's face outta my head. *I have to concentrate on this case. It's over between us.* She'd moved on. I had to.

I pulled out a notebook. But then again, not much was on that list. The maid, the wife, a couple of neighbors, none named Laurel, or even close to it. Laurel...friend, worked with him? Laurel...the best fuck he ever had...the first one...? Laurel...remembering the vision...her words in his head... neighbor...lover?

I picked up the phone. "Yeah, it's Greene, send the police artist up here. I got a description of a suspect in a murder case. I wanna send an APB out on it as soon as it's done...Yeah right away."

If I could remember the vision good enough, I could get a sketch of it. 'cause one thing was for sure, she was in the shit deep. Laurel…somebody…lover…lover. Work? I kept getting back to his work. Somebody would know there. They always know your shit at work. The secretary probably set up the "secret" rendezvous, paid the Amex bills you couldn't send home.

I grabbed a number from the January file and punched it out on the phone.

"January and Associates, good morning."

I leaned back in my chair. "Andrew Haven."

"I'm sorry, but Mr. Haven is away on business until Tuesday. Would you like to leave a message?"

"Naw, I'll call back."

I hung up. *Good. Cause while the cat's away, the mice will play.*

CHAPTER EIGHTEEN

Detective Bob

Black people in suits scurried around the office. Barely two or three white faces were around. I shook my head again. In the ten days I'd been on this case, I'd seen more blacks with money than I had in my whole fuckin' life. *That's why a white man can't get ahead, too many blacks sucking up all the cash with their affirmative action bullshit.* I could almost understand what my dad had meant when he said give 'em an inch, they'll take a mile. We let 'em get ahead in the sixties, and now look, they got the fancy jobs and me, I was still living in a one bedroom in Brooklyn. Go figure. The white man ended up on the bottom of the shit pile.

"May I help you?"

I flashed my badge. "Detective Bob Greene, NYPD, I need to ask Andrew Haven some questions."

The woman suddenly looked scared. "Uh, Mr. Haven's out of town."

I pretended to be surprised. "Okay, then I need to speak to Mr. January's secretary."

She looked away nervously, punching out some numbers. Her voice was low as she whispered something into the headset. After a moment, she looked up again. "I'm sorry, Detective, but she's out to lunch."

"At ten A.M.? Pretty early eater."

"Well, I uh…"

I leaned on the desk in front of her, giving her my best TV Detective look, right down to the Kojak walk. Hell, she didn't know it was all an act.

"Look, lady, I'm here to talk to everybody in this whole got damned office, and if you can't cooperate, then I'll just have to get a subpoena and haul all your asses to the station. Now I know you'd much rather talk to me nicely here, wouldn't you?"

"Yes, I mean, I'm really sorry, Detective. Really, I'm sorry, but I guess I should have told you before. Mr. January's secretary doesn't work here anymore. She left right after he died. It's just that Mr. Haven told us that if anybody asked to say that she'd just stepped away from her desk."

"And why did he tell you to say that?"

"I don't know. I really don't. I'm sorry, Detective, but when Mr. Haven comes back you can talk to him. I'm sure he can be more helpful. I really haven't worked here that long, really, just a few months."

I smiled at her now. She'd been more helpful than she'd known. It was starting to get crystal clear that Andrew Haven, the man who barely waited till his partner's dick was cold to change the business cards, was in the shit. Way into the shit. Greed and envy spilt out from every pore in his body.

"Oh yeah, well how long did Mr. January's secretary work for him before he was killed?"

"I don't know, really, I don't. I mean, I think a long time, but please, Detective, I really don't know anything. Mr. Haven's the one to talk to…I promise I'll have him call you just as soon as he gets back."

I turned away from her, didn't want her to see the slow smile creeping across my face. "You do that okay?"

"Oh yes, sir, I promise."

I pushed open the glass doors, my eyes resting on the name on the door for a moment: JANUARY & ASSOCIATES. *Hmm. No more.* I walked down the escalator, thinking what the next move was, when I heard somebody behind me. I can always tell when somebody's running after me, even when they try to be slick, like this person was trying to be.

So I just slowed up to let 'em catch up with me. I merged into the stream of people leaving the building, turned the corner. I knew they were still behind me. I could see a woman in the store window, trying not to look conspicuous, definitely not a pro at this. She was about to say something. I could feel it. So I made it easy on her. I stopped and turned around. I was facing a youngish looking black woman, short hair, earrings, kinda dumpy but not a bad looking face. I think I scared her stopping like that 'cause she looked like she could barely get the words out.

"Detective?"

"Yeah."

"I'm Yolanda Calloway. I used to work for Mr. January."

Now this was getting interesting. "The receptionist told me you'd quit."

"I had to leave…for personal reasons…"

"Was he that much of an SOB to work for?"

I smiled at my own joke. But she didn't seem to think it funny. In fact, she looked about ready to break down and cry at any moment. I took her by the arm.

"Let's go in there where we can talk." I sat across from this woman, knowing I'm about to get a load dumped on me.

She nervously sipped coffee from the cracked cup. "He knows who did it."

Well that was a change from a reluctant witnesses.

"Who knows?"

She whispered shakily, "Andrew Haven…He knows. I know he knows."

My sentiments exactly. I was starting to like this lady. But I had to play it cool, play into her hands, let her spill as much as she wanted to.

"Now Miss…Calloway, is it? Tell me why you think he knows who killed your boss?"

She leaned back, twisting her napkin around her fingers. "Detective, I'm scared. If I tell you what I know, you won't tell him where you heard it from, promise, please…"

"I promise. It's just between us."

"So you won't use my name?"

"I won't have to, because we both know that's not your real name, is it?"

She let the coffee cup slip out of her hands, luckily it was only half full. A few drops of inky black liquid rolled off the plastic table cloth. "How did you?"

"It don't matter. Just relax, and tell me everything."

Truth is, it was just a lucky guess, but my cop's nose was usually right about these things.

"Well, I worked for Mr. January for almost ten years, right from the beginning when he started his company. Mr. January helped a lot of people. Most people didn't know that because he didn't talk about it like most other folks would've. I remember especially this one young man, Albert was his name. He'd been coming to the office for years, selling candy, you know for field trips and extra money. I think he was around twelve then. He was such a hard worker, always hustling. Mr. January would talk to him a lot and ask him what he wanted to do with his life. That boy had real dreams, but no money, you know. I think he reminded Mr. January of himself when he was young. The young man was so determined to make something of himself."

At this point, she leaned forward seriously. "You know, Mr. January paid for that boy's college. Yep, all four years. I know because I wrote out the checks from Mr. January's special account, and every semester we'd send a check to Miner's College in Pennsylvania where the young man went."

I'd only been half listening to the story about the kid, but when she mentioned writing the checks for his special account, I wondered if she'd written out any checks to Laurel. I made a mental note to myself to go back to that point. But for right now, I'd just let her ramble on, no telling what else she'd spill.

"I saw a lot, lots of people coming and going. Mr. January could be hard to work for, but he had to. He was trying to build something, something that was different than any other firm on the Street. He was trying to show that black folks could really play in the big leagues with the other firms.

"But a lot of people he brought in didn't think like that. They didn't have his dream, so they'd last a few months. Then one day I'd come to work and they'd just be gone. That's how Mr. January was. He didn't take any stuff from anybody. And if you didn't agree with him, he'd just let you go. Most of the time it was because the person didn't work hard enough.

I think that's why he approached Mr. Haven from the beginning. Because he'd heard that he worked hard."

She stopped to take a breath. "Work was Mr. Haven's life. He had nothing else."

"I thought he had a wife and kids, a real family man from everything I've heard."

She sniffed in disapproval. "Family man! Please. It's all a front."

I was about to ask her more, but I didn't have to.

"He's as gay as Christmas."

"Hmm...So Haven has a little cake in his pocket. Didn't surprise me. It's always the straight as an arrow ones. Did anybody else know?"

"No way. He kept it real undercover, with his image and everything, perfect father, perfect husband. It was all a lie. But Mr. January knew. He used to make fun of him, say little things, not so obvious that anybody else would know what he was really saying, but enough so Mr. Haven knew."

She stopped for a minute. Looking around at the other patrons. "He didn't want Mr. January to sell the firm. I know that. I heard him talking."

"What was he saying?"

"Trying to convince Mr. January not to sell. He kept talking about some accounts."

"Client accounts?"

"I think so, but it was some new client. Somebody I hadn't heard of."

"Do you remember the name of the client?"

"No...they never mentioned a name They just said the account."

She was quiet for a moment. I could prod her more, but I figured now would be the right time to change gears on her.

"Did Mr. January know anyone named Laurel?"

She thought for a moment. "Laurel?"

"Yeah." She fidgeted. I knew she knew exactly who I was talking about, but I wasn't sure she was going to spill it. "That woman."

She looked down, avoiding my eyes. Then she took out a small address book. Scribbled down a name and an address. "Go over there. They'll know her."

"Who was she, his lover, girlfriend?"

She hesitated, then softly, slowly said, "She was..." She closed up. Something went over her eyes, and I knew that I wasn't getting anything else out of her. "I...I don't know."

I cursed to myself silently. Shit, just when I was beginning to get it all in place. But I'd been a cop long enough to know when to push a witness and when to just let 'em go and come back another time when they're fresh.

"Miss Calloway, is there someplace I can get a hold of you? I may need to ask you more questions."

"I'm moving, but you can call my brother. I'm staying there until I find a new place." She wrote down a number. And then gave me a look that was so desperate, so sincere, that I wanted to take her into my arms and tell her everything was gonna be all right.

I handed her my card, scribbling my home phone on the back. "Call me if you want to talk, again."

She took the card and carefully tucked it in her purse. "Find out who did it, Detective. He was a good person underneath everything. He didn't deserve to die like that."

I squeezed her hand. I liked this lady. She was honest, in spite of her lying about her name. True blue. The kind of friend I'd like to have. I looked down at the paper where Yolanda had scribbled the address, and I wondered where Laurel was now. One thing I was damn sure of—she was on the run and as far away from this place as she could get.

Laurel

How did my life get so fucked.

"Now this is the nicest unit we have in the building. Sunny and quiet. That is what you wanted. Miss...excuse me, Miss?

"I'm sorry, I didn't hear you." I looked around the small bare apartment: greenish walls, linoleum floors, and a cubbyhole for a bedroom. Nothing like our apartment with the wide sunny windows facing the narrow Manhattan street. No smell of flowers drifting in on summer days and burning leaves in the fall. No little oasis in the middle of the craziness that was New York. Our refuge. Away from the past, shut off from the future, just existing in the now of the moments of our lives. For that point in time, now gone. How did my life fall apart? When did it start, or was it always like that?

"If you'd like the apartment, it'll be first month's rent and last month's as a security deposit."

"How much is the rent again?"

"Five-fifty a month, plus utilities."

I added the numbers in my head quickly, at that rate I could afford three months before I had to move again. My life would never be the same, running now.

"So would you like the apartment?"

My life was fucked. Running, always running. "Yes, I'll take it." New faces, but none of them his. None would ever be his again.

"Have you been in town long?"

Why didn't this woman shut up? Couldn't she see that I just wanted to be alone? "No."

"Where are you coming from?"

My head throbbed now. I kept seeing him. Everywhere. "A lot of places. Everywhere."

"Well I think you'll like it here. We're a small town, but there's things to do. I'd be happy to introduce you to some of the other people in the building. I think you'll find them a real friendly bunch."

I'd never be able to stop running. Never. "No. Thank you. I'll be fine on my own." Thoughts, all tumbling on top of each other, collided and filled my head. The first time Clive made love to me. I remember wondering to myself, why do I feel like this? I'm in control. I'm the one who seduced him. So why do I feel like I'm the one who has been drawn into this abyss of bottomless feelings and sleepless nights of thoughts wrapped around another's face? Why do I feel like this? And I remember clearly thinking. Because I love him.

I knew the first time I saw Clive that he was different. I think it was in his eyes. A look that told me that life had dealt him some blows, but that he'd come out okay. I understood the hunger in his soul. A craving so deep that once unleashed, I knew it would swallow up anyone or anything in its path. I knew that someday the world would know about Clive January.

I used to laugh a lot. people never understood why. Sometimes I didn't understand either. I guess my first reaction was to laugh. Even when perhaps I should've cried. I laughed. So I laughed when I found out that he'd left Hendersonville on that crazy and sad night. I wasn't really surprised, anything as wildly delicious as he was couldn't stay in Hendersonville.

I'd known a lot of Clives in my day. Sure of themselves, but not really; strong, but not really; cold, but not at all. I know that's why I jumped on Clive. He was my other half. The blue of my black. Even then, I knew that our souls would find each other again. Then when I saw him in that small town in Maine, I wondered if I'd changed. To him, I mean. I remember looking in the mirror. Same face, same smile. To me. But to him. I wondered. Pieces of thoughts floated into my mind—his marriage, which should have been our marriage. Maybe if I'd never left, things would have been different, but who would have known that it would have taken so long? Even if I'd called him while it was happening, perhaps then he would have waited...maybe, but then maybe not.

The thoughts stopped as abruptly as they'd began, washing up memories like stones on a beach. Only to be thrust out to sea again. I closed the door behind the woman and walked out into the street. Another anonymous town. Like so many I'd been to before. Only now there was no turning back. No laughter now.

Detective Bob

I checked the address that Yolanda had given me—480 West Twenty-eighth Street. Yeah, this was it. Nice building. Discreet. Modern, but not too new. On one of those quiet, narrow streets in Chelsea. Doorman keeping watch. Perfect to hole up with a mistress in.

I wondered how much I'd get out of the doorman. Didn't look like the talkative kind. I'd use my "we're all from the same clan" talk with him, see how far it'd get me. "Nice day, huh?"

He kinda shrugged.

"Yeah, a day like this makes me wish I was twenty years younger."

He shrugged again.

I knocked a cigarette out of the pack. I had noticed the ashes by the ground. A smoker for sure. "Smoke?"

"Can't on the job."

I lit my cigarette. "Now ain't that a bitch. What's the world coming to, seems like you can't do anything you want anymore."

"Tell me about it."

The first whole sentence I'd gotten out of him.

"A lot of folks move in and outta here?"

"No more than usual."

I tossed the cigarette. "Yeah, I bet this is the type of place where all the rich cats put their girlfriends."

He smiled, but that was all. At least it got a rise outta him. "You could say that."

Bingo. Now I could work it.

But just as I was about to get some more out of him, an overweight, overdressed New York matron type barged in between us. "Henry..."

He perked up to attention.

"I thought I asked you to tell the mailman to have that woman's mail forwarded."

"I did. Twice, in fact."

"Well I don't know why I'm still getting her bills." She dug around in the bottom of her purse and shoved a handful of letters to him.

He rolled his eyes, but not too much, as he took the letters. "I'll take care of it Mrs. Newman."

"Yes, you do that, and tell that mailman that I don't want to see another piece of her mail." The woman harrumphed loudly as she maneuvered her way out of the door. Shit, one look at the doorman and I knew I wasn't getting another thing out of him now. *Son-of-a-bitch.* But I'd try anyway. I didn't want to have to show the badge, you usually got more if they didn't know you were fishing around for information.

"So uh…what were you saying?"

"Look buddy, I really don't have time to chat, I gotta take care of the rounds." He tossed the letters on the bench, muttering to himself, "Overstuffed bitch."

"Yeah, I know you wanted to give her what for."

He smiled. "Listen, do me a favor, toss these for me. I can't leave, and I want to get the shit outta my face."He handed me the bills the woman had given him. *Damn.* Pretty clear this was the end of the conversation.

"Sure, no problem." I dug in my jacket and handed him a cigarette. "For the road."

"Thanks."

Shit. I stuffed the letters in my pocket and walked down the street. Next time I'd have to show the badge. There'd be another doorman later on when this one got off his shift. But this time, I'd have to be direct. This Columbo crap was for the birds.

I shoved the letters in a trashcan. The breeze blew one of them off the top of the pile of trash. And as I was about to pick it up, I froze. LAUREL DAVENPORT, clear as day on the letter. I dove for the rest, LAUREL DAVENPORT, N.Y. Telephone, LAUREL DAVENPORT, CCNY, LAUREL DAVENPORT, addressee unknown.

"Hey, Scoffo, I got a lead on the January case."

"'Bout time, I heard Captain telling Lindsay that your ass was out to lunch on this one."

"Yeah, well fuck Captain, cause I'm getting close, real close."

Scoffo, a big, hairy, red-faced Italian who looked like he never gave a damn about anything, grabbed the letters from me.

"So whatcha got?"

"Letters from his girlfriend's place."

"Which one? Word is that he had a bunch of 'em."

"Yeah maybe, but I think this was the main chick."

"Oh yeah, and how do you know that?"

"I got my sources."

Scoffo shook his head. "You and your got damned sources."

"Just run a check on the phone bill. Every number she called. Get me names and addresses. I wanna record of all her calls for the past six months. Also get me everything you can dig up on her: school records, priors, marriage, parents, kids, everything. I wanna know more about her than she knows about herself. "

"Whoooo, going big time, huh? That'll take a few days."

"Then I guess you better start now."

The laugh track from the *Dick Van Dyke Show* filled up the lonely corners of my bedroom. And I poured myself another drink. Dark brown, Jack Daniels. When I first started drinking, it used to sting my tongue, just a little. But now it went down just right, smooth. Numbing every part of my body, even the voices in my mind.

I turned up the volume. Laura Petrie was on, my girl, she reminded me of Margie, same perkiness, dark hair, cute little bod.

Sometimes I used to think that I could have a life like theirs, a little problem here and there, but by the end of the thirty minutes it was all right. Laura and Rob would be just as much in love as ever. A commercial came on so I turned the volume back down. But I never clicked away from the show, not while Laura was on. Margie…I wondered what she was doing now. Was she fuckin' somebody or was she sitting alone watching our show, like me, trying to remember the good times?

I loved her. But I was afraid to marry her. Maybe afraid, I'd end up like my dad, and she'd end up like Mama, unhappy and alone. The thought of ending up like my dad had been eating away at me a lot these days. Maybe it was 'cause he'd been sick a lot. I couldn't even feel no sympathy for him, even though he was sufferin'. I kept remembering the way he made me suffer when I was a kid. Nothin' I ever did was good enough. So now it was his turn. But I was afraid. Afraid. Was father really like son? Was I like that fat racist bastard who made me miserable and everybody around him, was I him?

I couldn't think no more. I was so tired, tired of the January case and I wasn't half finished with it. Tired of my life. I had to make some changes, but how? I'd been a cop for twenty years. What else could I do?

I closed my eyes, trying to see Margie's face behind the darkness. But I couldn't. I couldn't see or feel anything. Suddenly, the room was quiet. I couldn't hear the TV, or feel my hard bed under my ass. Shit, God damn it. He was doing it again. He was taking over me. But this time I was gonna fight back. Damn you, Clive January, you can't take away my life, my dreams, and impose your own on me…but I couldn't fight him. He was too strong. My eyes were his, my breath his. I was him. Again. But this time it was different than before. When he'd let me in the last time, I felt everything just as he had the first time, the emotions, the people everything happening in real time. Now I could feel him receding. I was a silent eavesdropper as he turned back the pages in his life and remembered as it had been.

Detective Bob looking through Clive's eyes as Clive remembers…

"When did you get here?"

I was looking at her again, Laurel. She was standing in the doorway of the apartment. Our apartment. Every piece of furniture, picture, pillow, candle, all looked familiar. I bought everything: the rich chocolate velvet couches, the Indian silk pillows, the teak side tables, the large brightly colored pieces of art that I'd found in the offbeat Soho galleries. This is where our lives intersected. Nothing else mattered when I was here, but us. The way we'd always been, together yet alone, trapped by a patchwork of the past that always seemed to darken the present.

She leaned down and kissed me. I took out my wallet and knocked two crisp hundred dollar bills onto the table. Then reached into my pocket, and carefully removed a small white envelope. Folding each of the hundred dollar bills in half, and pouring lines of coke in the creased bills.

Laurel looked over my shoulder. "I thought you were going to cool it on that."

I ignored her. My heart felt twisted with pain. I barely looked up as I said softly, "She's back."

"Who?" She nonchalantly threw her coat on a chair.

"Ma."

She turned me around, forcefully, worry in her eyes. "Your mother?! How the hell did she find you after all these years?!"

I couldn't talk. I couldn't do anything. But I had to tell her. She was the only one who'd understand. "I don't know. Yesterday I was on the phone, and Monique opened the door, and she was there…"

I closed my eyes, trying to blot out the memory. Only I couldn't. I could still see Ma's face, the small eyes, harder than I remembered. The thin hands, calloused, holding my child in her hands. I was ready to explode. Laurel was sitting next to me, stroking my head gently.

"What did you say to her?"

"I told her to get the hell out! What did you think? I told her that she wasn't my mother, that I didn't know her!"

"Oh Clive, baby…Clive…"

I'd lost control. The past had taken over my present again. I didn't know what to do anymore, so I lay in her lap, letting her kiss me, trying to make it better.

"You've just got to make sure that she doesn't come around anymore. All she'll do is upset you."

"I know, but I'm not home that much. How do I know what's happening when I'm out?"

"Tell Monique not to let her in. She should at least be able to do that." Even after all these years, she still said Monique's name with bitterness. Anger that Monique had the place by default, which should have been hers. But in reality, she had the place even if no one knew but us.

I couldn't think of anything but Ma holding my child. The same hands that had slapped me down, holding my child.

"I don't know what to do. I told Monique and everyone else that Ma had died years ago, and now she shows up on my doorstep."

I sat up, tilting the coke creased in the hundred dollar bill into my nose. Letting it linger for a second before I inhaled it sharply. *C'mon the feeling's got to come. The feeling of peace, settling over me.* But all I could think about was Ma. Laurel held my hand now.

"That bitch." I got up, roaming around the room. I had to do something. "I'm getting out. I'm selling the business and getting out."

"Clive, what are you talking about, all of this because your mother found you, throwing away everything, because of her!"

I walked over to the window, looking out onto the tree-lined street. Wishing that I could bury myself in the cool green canopy of leaves below me. "It's not just that. It's my whole life. I don't feel like it's going anywhere anymore. I don't love my wife. I barely know my daughter, and now this. I've got to start over somewhere else, as someone else."

"So that's it. Clive's running again. Just like when you left Hendersonville. So what about us? Are you gonna run away from me again? Well, are you?!"

I didn't want to hear this. I didn't want to fight with her anymore. "I'm not running from you. This doesn't have anything to do with us."

She was about to say something, but I cut her off.

"The only reason I'm telling you is that I need to use this address. I need to have some mail sent here that I don't want at the office or at home."

"What are you doing, Clive?"

"Business. Just business." I swallowed. My throat was dry. Parched. Coke did that to me. I needed to drink something. Mellow out the high. "I have some new accounts, and I need to have the paperwork sent here. That's all. Just business."

"And who do you think I am? One of those bimbos you fuck when you think I'm not around? I'm not stupid, Clive. I know what you're talking about doing!"

I turned away from her. It always came up when she was mad. The other women. Like she was supposed to be the only other woman.

"And if it's the same thing that you got into with Red, leave it alone. Isn't it enough that Red died? Do you want the same thing to happen to you!"

"I can handle it now. It was different then. We didn't know what we were doing. We got in over our heads. But things are different now. That was ten years ago."

"But those people never change. You know that. What makes you think that anything has changed? So they went after the white boy that time. How do you know it won't be you this time?"

I didn't want to hear this. The memory of Red and what could have been was still too real. But I had to do it. I had to. I couldn't let my life fall into the spiral of my past again. I had to get out and this was the only way.

"What about Andrew? Is he involved?"

I couldn't let her see my face. She could read too much without me having to say a thing.

"Well, is he? You know you can't trust him."

"Look, just leave the mail out so I can take it when I come over."

"And if I don't?"

She stood in front of me, but my heart was hard. I wasn't changing my mind. Even she couldn't stop me now. I was not getting trapped in a situation that I couldn't get out of anymore. This time I was making the move first.

"Robbbbbb!"

Back in my own place, Laura Petrie sounded exasperated at Rob. Shit, I didn't know how much time had passed. Couldn't have been more than a few seconds, but it seemed longer.

"Damn you, Clive January! Get the hell out of my life!" I clicked off the television. I didn't even care that Laura was still on. I felt like crying. Hell. But I knew it wouldn't do any good. He'd just keep coming. And the thing that scared the shit outta me was that each time I could feel him getting stronger, coming in easier and faster. My right hand shook now. Sometimes I couldn't stop it. And the nausea was getting worse and worse every time. It's like he was suckin' the life outta me, little by little each time he came. Totally knocking *me* out of the way. I had to get to the bottom of this case. Otherwise, I'd lose my life to him just as sure as he did to that killer. "Damn you, Clive January!"

"Damn you, Bob Greene!"

Shit. I heard him in my head, but the room was like nothin' had happened. I ran around the room yelling out "C'mon, show yourself, asshole! You can take over my life, but you won't show yourself. C'mon!" I thought I saw something over in the corner, but when I blinked whatever it was disappeared. *Damn him and his fucked up games.* "What're you afraid of?"

A heavy force sliced through me, throwing me on the floor. I tried to get up, but I couldn't. An invisible hand had pinned me to the ground. My eyes were glazed over, and I could barely speak, but I wasn't afraid. I was over the fear, and now I was just pissed. Pissed at him, pissed at myself for not being in control. Pissed that I needed to solve this case as much as he needed me to.

And I think I saw him out of the corner of my eye. But not quite. Because then he was gone. The weight lifted off me, and I crawled back over to my bed. I wanted to sleep. I wanted to wake up and everything would be different: my life, his life. But knew it wouldn't be. I knew I couldn't close my eyes to it.

why him? why this cop? but they won't answer me. why must our lives be coupled together in some unholy pact? they won't let me leave him. maybe that's my punishment for a life of self absorption. the ultimate sin i suppose. love yourself. just not too much. so now i'm stuck with him. but what if he doesn't find out?

what if I never know? where will I be? where will I go?

CHAPTER NINETEEN

Detective Bob

Playing cards with an invisible opponent. That's what solving a murder case was. This case at least. What the hell did I have? A lover named Laurel, skipped town. I thumbed through her mail—city college, old paycheck, never collected…sent right after the murder. Must be when she left, in a real hurry. I had to get that APB back. I would check on it again. Cops weren't what they used to be. Ten years ago, I'd a had that back in a snap.

Somebody named Red, died…friend partner. Not sure. Accounts…illegal, maybe, probably. Leading right to Andrew Haven's doorstep. A bunch of cards, but, was it a winning hand?

The front of City College was red brick and had ivy snaking along the walls. Students lounged around the campus. I looked down on the letter. OFFICE OF CAREER GUIDANCE.

I walked down the hallway of the building. I never liked colleges, reminded me too much of what I didn't have. Maybe I shoulda gone back and gotten my degree, but hell, when I started on the force, none of the guys had gone to school.

Now, all the detectives got some kinda degree, but me. But I didn't give a damn. I could still run rings around them backwards when it came to cracking a case. All of 'em but this one. I didn't know why. Maybe it was the shit with Margie. I couldn't focus like I usually did, or the stiff feeding me information when I don't want it. I didn't know. All I knew was I had to get it done, so I could move on with my life and figure out what I wanted do, or what I could do.

"Can I help you?" a smallish woman, thin nose, pinched face, asked.

I flashed my badge. I didn't have time for the fun and games today. "Yeah, I'm looking for a Laurel Davenport. She works here."

The woman sniffed disapprovingly. "You mean *worked* here. She hasn't shown up in over a month. Never was that reliable, even when she was here."

"Oh yeah? Well I need to talk to somebody about her. See her office and things. We think that she may be involved in a murder case."

The woman sniffed again. "Well if you'll wait a moment, Detective, I'll call her supervisor."

"I got nothin' but time." I leaned against the wall, looking at the steady stream of students weaving in and out of the classrooms. After about ten minutes, a forty-ish looking black guy walked over to me. "You wanted some information on Laurel Davenport, Detective? I'm Harry Moss, Ms. Davenport's supervisor."

"Yeah, like I was telling her. We think that Ms. Davenport may be involved in a murder case."

"I see. Would you come in my office, Detective?"

I followed him into a cramped dark hole of an office stuffed with books and papers. "Sit down, please. Laurel, worked next door. I can show you her office in a moment, but first, Detective, tell me what this is all about. Laurel was somewhat of a free spirit, but I wouldn't consider her the type to get involved in anything like murder."

"Well you never know about these things, Mr. Moss. I've been doing this a long time, and it's usually what you least expect is what ends up being the case."

"I see."

He didn't seem to know what to say next, so I filled in for him.

"How long did she work here?"

"Two years, or at least, it would have been two years, next month…if she'd stayed."

"Do you have any idea why she'd leave so suddenly?"

"No, except…Well, she seemed troubled for at least about the last six months before she left."

"Did she ever talk to you about what was on her mind?"

"No, we didn't have that kind of relationship"

"What kind of relationship did you have with her, Mr. Moss?"

If he hadn't been so dark, he probably would've turned red. "Business, strictly business. She was my employee, and that was the extent of it."

But by his reaction, it was pretty clear that there might've been more, or at least, that he might have wanted more.

"So what exactly did she do here?"

"She was a guidance counselor. She advised the students on career opportunities."

I scribbled down some notes while he talked. It was always good not to seem too interested in what they were saying. Let 'em talk more. "I'd like to talk to some of the students that she advised."

"That won't be a problem, but I don't think that's really going to tell you much. I mean, they were just her students."

Something was going on here that he didn't want me to know about. I was definitely talking to those kids. "Well you know, Mr. Moss, we gotta cover all the bases."

Silence again. Maybe he figured if he said too much he'd spill what was really on his mind. "Did she have a boyfriend, somebody she was seeing?"

"I told you, Detective, that we didn't have that kind of relationship. She might have. In fact, I'm sure that she probably did, but I wouldn't know about it."

"Who would know?"

"I don't know, Detective. We were not friends. I don't know how much more bluntly I can put it. We had no personal relationship at all."

"Right, I forgot. Well, did she have any friends, since you weren't one of them?"

"I couldn't really say. She pretty much kept to herself. She didn't go to lunch with the other girls...I mean ladies that work here, and she usually didn't have much to say to anyone but her students."

"Like I said, Mr. Moss, I definitely want to talk to some of those students."

"I'll arrange that for you this afternoon."

"Do you have any pictures of her? Official, of course."

He glared at me, but then stiffly reached for a yearbook from his shelf. Thumbing through the pages, he stopped on one. "There she is."

Bingo. The face...from the visions. Her, clear as a bell. Small face, attractive...but more...now that I was seeing her like this, I knew I'd seen those eyes before. But I didn't know where. Shit. "Not a bad looking chick."

He ignored the comment.

"I'll need to take this yearbook, if you don't mind."

"No, Detective." He handed it to me crisply. "Take it. I can get another copy."

I looked at her face again and without looking up, asked, "So tell me, Mr. Moss, what was she like? I know she wasn't your friend, but after working with someone for almost two years, you gotta have some impression of her."

He leaned forward, and for a moment, looked like he was going to break down. "She had this...incredible...sadness about her." He cleared his throat. "Almost like she'd lost something and had never been able to find it again." He settled back in his chair. "I don't know if it was a child, or a husband, someone close to her. She'd been married before, but it was over before she came here."

"How do you know that?"

"She listed herself as divorced on her personnel records. It was no secret, Detective."

Interesting. "Did she ever mention the marriage, or her husband?"

He pursed his lips. "Never."

"Well, I'll definitely need to see those records and any other files you have on her. You know, personnel evaluations, that kind of thing."

"I'll have my secretary pull everything on her." He leaned forward and almost whispered, "You don't think, Detective...I mean she could-n'tve...?"

I finished the sentence for him matter of factly. "Killed somebody?"

He swallowed hard. But I just smiled, the way I do when something's not really funny, but I smile anyway. "I never say never, Mr. Moss."

"Okay, I want you to get the prints from everywhere, desk top, chair, windows. The whole nine yards." I was in Laurel's office. It was pretty much what I expected. Neat, orderly, like somebody wanted to make sure that there was nothin' ever out of place. No clues to what was really going on. My antennae always went up when something was too neat.

The cop glared at me. "Believe it or not, Greene, this ain't the first time we done this."

"Well, you know boys, you just can't make no assumptions nowadays. They're not recruiting the way they used to."

"Fuck off, Greene." The other cop put his hand over his mouth. He was a rookie, and he probably figured it wouldn't look to good to be laughing at me right off the bat and all. But his partner didn't have no problem with it, kinda hissed under his breath, "Yeah, and what wouldya know about recruitin' anyway, you're too busy rattin' on your partners."

"Whooo…rat, dirty rat…bang, bang he's dead…" The rookie cracked up again.

It took everything I had not to slam him and his partner on the ground and shove my foot up their asses, but why give 'em the satisfaction for hauling me on for assaultin' fellow officers. Naw, this time I wouldn't bite. So I held it in, turning my back on them saying, "Just get the prints." The shit never seemed to end. Even after two years, they just wouldn't let it rest.

"Detective." I looked up and saw the thin woman who worked for Moss staring at me. "I've got the files you wanted."

I took them nonchalantly, but really, I couldn't wait to dig in.

"And, Detective…the students you wanted to talk to…"

I pretended I didn't know what the hell she was talking about.

"They're waiting outside Mr. Moss's office. I had to pull some of them out of class, but Mr. Moss said it was urgent, so I did."

I smiled at her for the first time, and funny thing is, I think this made her more uncomfortable than me being a hard ass with her. "Well, you done good."

She just nodded and walked quickly out of the room.

I yelled over my shoulder to the cops behind me. "Call me when you're done. I wanna get a rush on those prints."

"Yeah right…soon's we're done…Detective." The snide one, kinda spit out the last word, and the rookie, looked away from me, like he didn't want to get caught laughing in my face.

Like I said, they just couldn't let it rest.

CHAPTER TWENTY

"So tell me about your teacher." I pressed the "ON" button on my tape recorder and turned to a heavy set kid perched on the edge of his chair. I was in a classroom, and all of 'em were looking at me like something was about to go down.

"She wasn't a teacher." He kinda smirked.

"Oh yeah, so what was she?"

"To me personally or to everybody else?"

One of the other kids snickered. I'd figured I'd see a bunch of 'em together first, get a feel for the dynamics, and then grill 'em one by one afterwards.

Ten of them, eight men, and two women. The guys looked like jocks. Big beefy types. They were all smirking except for this one black kid. He looked mad, but he didn't say anything.

I turned to him. "So what was the deal on Miss Davenport?"

He stared me straight in the eye. "No deal. She was the counselor. That's all."

One of the white jocks, gave his friend high five, then catcalled. "Aw c'mon, Jackson, tell the detective about 'Mrs. Robinson.'"

One of the women, a tall blonde who looked too good to be true, swiveled around to the guy who'd cat called. "You are *soooo* disgusting. I think she was nice."

The jock gave her a sappy look, and then fired out at me. "So did she kill somebody, Detective?"

Before I knew it, the black kid jumped across the room and collared the white kid. "Shut the fuck up, Kowalski!!"

"Hey…hey…break it up." I threw the black kid on the ground. Shit, he started it. I felt like gettin' out my cuffs and hauling him in on

GP, but I figured I'd get more outta him if I just let this thing play out. Another jock called out to the first kid.

"Yeah, Kowalski, you're just pissed 'cause you didn't get nothin."

The black kid tried to get free from me and lunge at the new guy. "Fuck all y'all…assholes."

"Calvin, I don't know why you're getting mad at everybody. I was defending her. I think Kowalski's a dick, too!"

"Looks like Ms. Davenport had some real fans around here."

"Yeah ask Jackson. He knows all about her."

Before Jackson could yell out something else, I clapped my hand over his mouth. Unprofessional, but it worked. I turned to the group. "Okay…now I'm gonna ask everybody here to tell me in their own words something about Ms. Davenport."

"What is this, Detective, kindergarten?"

His buddy catcalled, "Or better yet, show and tell."

Loud whooos went through the room. This was turning out better than I thought. I was pretty sure I'd get something pretty juicy out of this.

I eyeballed the loud jock. "Okay, you first…Kowalski, right?"

"That's me. With a 'K.'"

"Okay, Mr. Special K, tell me about her."

"Well, I'd say she was helpful…to certain, people that is…like Jackson."

Jackson glared but managed to keep his mouth shut. I turned to the tall blonde. "What about you? First tell me your name."

"Sally Gonzalez…"

Gonzalez, okay. Didn't look like a PR to me, but who knows these days. "Sally, tell me about her, especially the last six months. Did she seem upset, or troubled about anything when you talked to her?"

"No, not at all. In fact she was always very helpful to me. Whenever I had a career problem or something, she was always ready to talk."

"And you?" I turned to the other woman. She'd been noticeably quiet.

"Pretty much the same, Detective. Except that I do remember one day I came into her office, and it looked like she'd been crying. When I asked her if she was okay, she just said that it was her contacts." The woman shrugged. "So I guess it didn't really mean anything."

"What about the rest of you? Anything pop in your head when you thought about her?" The rest just shrugged. After the initial flare up, everybody seemed pretty much subdued. "Okay, so when was the last time any of you remember seeing her on campus?"

"Couple of months ago."

"No it was longer ago than that."

"I don't really remember."

Jackson had been quiet the whole time, so I guessed it was time to talk to him again. "And what about you, Jackson?"

The room became real quiet now.

"When was the last time you saw her?"

"I don't remember."

"Now, sure you do."

He stared at me with crystal clear dark eyes that didn't blink.

"No I don't, Detective."

I got up and walked around the room. Time for Colombo again.

"You know, I don't think that you kids understand that this is a murder investigation. And anything that you don't tell me now voluntarily, you'll just have to tell me later at the station. And anything you don't tell me there…well, you'll just have to tell the whole world in court."

I looked straight at Jackson. "So I think that you better tell me when you saw her last."

"It was about six months ago. I came to her office, I think it was maybe around five or six, just about everybody was gone. I'd had an appointment for earlier, but I had to cancel it 'cause of a midterm, so anyway she was on the phone, talking to somebody. I don't know who.

All I remember is that she was really pissed. She slammed down the phone. Then she asked me if we could talk later, and I said okay."

I looked him over carefully, wanted to make sure he was telling the truth. I'd let everybody else go, I knew he wouldn't talk as long as the rest of them were there. "Okay, so then you saw her, what…the next day, week, when?"

The kid looked me straight in the eye again, unlike most kids.

"I saw her that night."

This was getting interesting. "Kind of late for office hours, don't you think?"

"Detective, just let me tell you the whole thing from beginning to end, and then…well…you just figure it out, 'cause I'm tired of thinking about it. She was…well…" And he started telling me, fast like he wanted to get it out of his soul so it would stop polluting his heart.

"I was home studying. Kowalski, who was my roommate then, was gone over to his girlfriend's, when somebody knocked on the door. I thought it was kinda weird because it was so late." He hesitated before he continued. "When I opened the door, she was standing there…"

Suddenly it was like I could see it as he was telling me, right in front of my eyes, the whole scene playing out like a movie. Just as it had when Andrew told me about when he and Clive first met. And I could see everything, just like I was there…

"Can I come in?"

"Ms. Davenport?"

"The very same…" She walked past him nonchalantly and leaned against the wall, as if she were waiting for something. "Since I was so, unfortunately, tied up when you came by this afternoon, I thought we could talk now. Because we certainly wouldn't want you to miss out on any job opportunities."

He swallowed hard. "It's really kinda late, maybe we should just talk tomorrow. I can come back to your office in the afternoon. No problem."

"It's no problem at all. I'm free right now. Well, aren't you going to take my coat?"

"Yeah,...sure...sit down."

When she took off her coat, she was wearing a white dress, but not just any white dress, it looked almost like a wedding gown: lace and pearls sewn in the neck, and long and sweeping to the floor. The kid looked like he was gonna jump outta his pants.

"Were you...uh...coming from something?"

"No, why?"

"I mean, your dress. It looks like...well, it's so formal...and everything."

She sat down. "Do you have any wine?"

"No. I don't drink."

"Well aren't you something? Is that because of sports? You are an athlete, right?"

"Track and field."

"Uh...huh...so is that because of track, or," she leaned back on the couch and closed her eyes for a moment, "is it because you don't want the girls to take advantage of you?"

"I just don't like the taste of alcohol, that's all."

"Well that really is novel these days." She opened her eyes again and looked straight at him. "I wish I could say the same, but I have to admit that I love my champagne, but only the good stuff, Cristal, Dom. Nothing cheap for me. I'd rather drink water than even inhale cheap champagne."

"Uh, Miss Davenport, it's really late, and I should get back to studying. Maybe we can talk tomorrow."

Her face broke into a smile. "You know, Calvin, you remind me of someone." She leaned forward and almost whispered, "We were supposed to be married, seven years ago today. It's our anniversary. Unfortunately, my husband-to-be took a wrong turn."

Calvin was quiet with a slightly stunned look on his face.

She kept on talking as if she didn't care whether he listened. "With someone else. But he'll come back to me. It's inevitable." She smoothed out her dress, softly stroking the lace and running her fingers across the smooth pearls. "Do you believe in fate, Calvin?"

"Maybe, I'm not sure."

"Well, I definitely do. That's why I know I'll have him someday. It's fated. Really it is."

"I believe you…but…"

"No buts, Calvin. Let's just enjoy the time that we have together, celebrating my anniversary." She got up and walked over to him, leaned over and then kissed him gently on the forehead.

Calvin stiffened. He looked pained.

Playfully, she said, "Don't worry, I don't bite." She sat next to him on the couch. "Do you have a kiss for an old married lady?"

"Ms. Davenport, this is really not right. I mean. I'm sorry about your boyfriend and everything…but this isn't right."

She fiddled with a ring on her finger, a beautiful ruby, only it wasn't on the wedding finger. "We still see each other, you know. We have an apartment, a very nice place, in Chelsea, but it's not the same. Because he's not mine all the time. But that will change. I know it will."

She snuggled closer to Calvin on the couch, and looked at him with the saddest eyes… as if all the pain she'd ever known in her life was reflected in them.

"I'll go," she said slowly. "I don't want to make you uncomfortable…"

But just as she was about to get up, the door swung open, and that loud-assed jock Kowalski walked in the room. His eyes pop out of his big head. "Well…hello…Miss Davenport. Didn't expect to see you here."

"I'm leaving." She got up as abruptly as she'd come, slinging her coat over her shoulders and brushing past Kowalski, without looking back.

The kid had stopped talking, but I could still see the outlines of their figures in front of me, like ghosts leaving a faint trail.

He cleared his throat, and looked me dead in the eye again. "So that's it. That was the last time I saw her."

"Pretty interesting."

"No. Just sad. She was very sad."

"And so my guess is that Kowalski then spread it all around campus."

Calvin nodded grimly. "Yep. It got back to the dean, and they were going to fire her, but I wouldn't talk. I felt sorry for her. She was obviously hurting badly. I didn't want her to be out of a job, too. I mean, she didn't hurt me or anything, so I just let it go."

I wished sometimes I could be that philosophical about shit. "You just let it go..."

"Yes..."

"Do you know who she was talking about? The guy she was supposed to marry?"

"No. I don't know. She didn't mention his name." He screwed up his face.

"What?"

"Well, there was one other thing. When she was leaving, really fast and everything, when Kowalski barged in...she said goodbye, Clive, to me. I figured she'd just forgotten my name. I didn't really know her that well and Clive, Calvin, they're kind of similar."

Not really, especially if you know the deal like I did. But no need to clue him in on it.

"Well, Calvin, you've been real helpful...and I want to ask you one more thing."

"Yeah."

"If she ever contacts you or you hear from anybody where she is, you tell me right away, okay? There's a dead man that we believe she was involved with, and she may know who did it."

Normally you would've thought if you told a kid something like that he'd be a little uncomfortable, but not this one, he just stared me straight in the eye without blinking. "Sure thing, Detective. I'll call you."

CHAPTER TWENTY-ONE

Detective Bob

Laurel Marie Davenport. Her whole life was spread out in front of me. For once. the boys in blue had been able to haul ass. Now if they could just find her. I got it all: personnel records, school records, parents, the whole thing.

Forty-two, married once to a Lani Hillgrove in 1972… I made a note to myself, track down this guy…talk to him…divorced…1980…Same year Clive was married. No children.

She was adopted. Records sealed by court order. That's how they did it back then. Adopted parents deceased. Raised in Cleveland, Ohio, no siblings. A loner in college, not in any organizations. From school records, she didn't seem to have many friends, asked to live alone each year. Taught school for a year in Hendersonville, Mississippi, then a series of odd jobs until she came to New York in 1980. No job records from 1980 until '85 when she started at city college. Permanent address, Clive's place in Chelsea under her name from 1980, until she disappeared.

So they took up right away. Right after he married his wife. Damn, he took care of her, too. The rent on the place that I saw couldn'tve been cheap. And for somebody who didn't have a steady job for almost five years, there's no way she coulda hung there without Clive stoking the checks.

So what next. Find her. Talk to her. Maybe book her. Talk to the ex. I was writing all this down, minding my own business when I felt somebody looking over my shoulder.

"You look like you need a cup of coffee."

I looked up and met Margie's eyes. Before I could say anything, she handed me a Styrofoam cup of coffee, light cream, heavy sugar—she still remembered.

"Thanks." It had gotten kind of quiet around me. Every cop in the place's eyes were on me. Probably taking bets on what I was gonna do next. But I wasn't gonna play into their hands. I was gonna stay cool. "Sit down."

Margie looked a little surprised that I was so pleasant. I guess she half expected me to bite her head off. "How's the case going?"

"It's going."

"Do you have any good leads?"

"A couple, an ex-girlfriend, maybe a business partner who knows something. I'm making progress."

"Good. I'm glad to hear that." She didn't sound like she believed me.

"Well." She bit on her bottom lip.

"Well."

"So how's the apartment?"

"Mrs. Cooper's still playing that opera shit at eight in the morning on Sundays, and the Fein kids are still running around on top of us at all hours of the day and night, but other than that, I guess everything's the same."

She smiled. It had been a long time since I'd seen her smile.

"What about you, did you get your own place yet?"

She shook her head no as she sipped her coffee. "Not yet, but I did move out from my parents. They got a little hard to take after a while."

Trying not to sound too curious, I asked, "So where are you living then?"

"With my sister in Flatbush."

I tried to sound nonchalant. "You can do better than that, Margie. You could move back with me. I got plenty of room."

She smiled again, but firmly. "I appreciate the offer. But I think we should just leave well enough alone."

"That's not what you said ten years ago."

She pressed the lid onto her coffee cup. "Ten years ago I was eighteen. Now I'm closer to thirty than twenty. So things change."

"Margie…I…"

She leaned over and said softly, "I still love you, Bob, but I can't live with you."

What could I say to that? That I still loved her and wished she'd come back, that we could work out whatever needed to be worked out. But I wasn't about to bare my soul in front of a room full of cops. I wondered when it had been really over. I mean, we'd had fights and all for a while. But the day it was really finished. The day I knew there was no turning back. The day of Dad's funeral...the smell of death...ironic...

"C'mon Bob, we should go."

Margie tried to lead me away. I looked at Dad's fat, pudgy face, one more time. They'd cleaned him up for the funeral. My dad lying there, even in death, it seemed like they couldn't get the scowl off his face.

I swished the coffee around in my cup. It's later now. We'd been in this diner for about an hour not saying much. I don't know what it is about funerals, but it seems like you never want to talk much after they're over, and this time was no different.

"So are you okay?"

Margie looked over at me. I shrugged. "Sure, why not, knew it was coming. B'sides, my dad and me wasn't exactly best buddies."

"Maybe, but he was your father. There had to be some good times."

"With him, shit, what good times? It was a living hell as long as I could remember."

"Bob, at least try and forgive him for it. 'Cause I bet he suffered as much as you did."

"Yeah right."

"I'm serious. You've got to try and make peace with your feelings. I'm just sorry you two couldn't talk and come to some understanding before he died."

I looked the other way, not really wanting to have this discussion.

"Bob, a part of you is him, whether you like it or not. When you hate him, you're hating yourself. You've gotta get outta this. You've gotta move on with your life." Silence. "We've got to move on with our lives."

I knew what she was talking about: marriage, kids, always the same.

"Margie can't we lay off the marriage shit for one damn day? Please!" I regretted my words as they were coming out of my mouth, but it was too late.

She threw the napkin down on the table, looking at me without blinking. "You know what, Bob, this isn't about marriage anymore. It's about you not liking you. Because of your father, or whatever, I don't know. All I know is I can't be here 'til you figure it out. You're always talking about you don't want to be like your dad. Well, guess what? You are! You're emotionally distant, angry and hate everybody and everything, but especially yourself. How can I love you if you don't even *like* yourself?" She pushed away from the table, slowly grabbed her purse, and walked out without giving me a second glance.

A few weeks later, her shit was piled up on the sidewalk. And now she's a cop. In my precinct. In my damn face. Every day.

"Bob, you've got to stop being mad, at me, at Internal Affairs, at everything."

I turned back around, shaking off the past and exploding with all the anger and hurt I'd kept in since that day she'd left me. "Don't start that shit again. What have I got to be pissed about, right?" I tried to laugh it off, but she just changed the subject.

"That's not why I wanted to talk to you."

"Well that's good to know. I'm kinda tired of hearing about what's wrong with me all the time."

She ignored my temper tantrum. "Bob I wanted you to know that if you need any help on this case, I'm here for you. I know I'm a rookie, but I'm still your friend, despite everything that's happened."

"Look, I don't need any help."

She took my hand and said softly, "The guys around here talk. They're saying you're over your head on this one. That you've lost your touch." Her words were cutting through me, but I was really too stunned to say anything. "I know it's probably because of what you've been going through, or we've been going through the past few months. It's been hard on me, too. I just wanted you to know that I'm here."

She squeezed my hand. "I can't stand to hear them talk about you that way. I know you're the best. You're better than any of the guys around here it's just…"

I don't know what happened, but I couldn't stand anymore of her pity. I'm Bob Greene, I don't need her fuckin' sympathy…I don't need it!

I swept my hand over my desk and knocked over the cup of hot coffee, over everything, like a river of blackness, covering my notes. "God damn it. Look what you made me do!"

A loud applause sounded from behind me. All the guys making fun of me. "Way to go, Greene." Laughter. Sarcasm.

Somebody in a fake falsetto said, "Yo…you think he'll snitch on her?"

Somebody else imitated the Captain, "Better call Internal Affairs. Looks like this shit might get ugly!"

Callahan, that fat Irishman from Queens, turned to Margie, cutting his eyes at me and saying, "Better watch out, little lady, hangin' with him could be dangerous to your health. You could end up behind bars, like his partner."

"Ex-partner!" somebody shouted out.

"Sorry, his *ex*-partner."

I could feel the hatred swirling all around me. Like the stench of a dead body, getting into the walls, the floor. 'Cause once a corpse's been in a room for a coupla days, you never really get the smell out. That's how this was, seemed like no matter how much time passed, this hatred they all had for me was always around, just circulating, never really gone. My head was splitting. I couldn't move.

Margie turned red, saying quickly. "Wait, I'll get a towel."

I wanted to tell her to forget it, you've done enough. But I couldn't say anything.

That night, I'm lying in bed thinking about my life. Wondering how it got to be so screwed up. I didn't even feel like any Jack. I just wanted to sleep and never wake up. I closed my eyes, wishing that if I had to wake up, everything would be different. I started drifting into sleep. Thank God for sleep. I began dreaming. Images were floating past me. My apartment, only it was filled with this warm light, which was strange 'cause my place was usually so dark, being on the back of the building. I was walking around and everything looked familiar but different.

I realized it was because she was back. Margie. I didn't see her, but I sensed her near me. I was pissed. She was right about that. I don't know why. I'm thinking, why did it take her so long? Why didn't she come back when I wanted her to? Then I saw her in front of me, but far away, holding out her hands. I was so happy I ran to her, but as I got closer, her face changed, and she was gone.

It was him. Clive. His hands were folded like he didn't approve. I wanted to cry out *Margie!* But I can't, no sounds are coming out of me. But my eyes are opened again. The other eyes. It's like the first time that Clive came through me. I've lost myself and I've become him. I'm seeing what he sees and feeling what he feels as it happens playing out through him. His life is rewinding like an old tape that won't stop. Just as it happened back then.

Through Bob's eyes as Bob experiences Clive's life in real time.

He yanks my arm, pulling me after him. I try to resist, trying to find Margie, but the harder I fight, the more he pulls me. I feel like he's gonna yank my arm out of the socket, he's pulling so hard. We're passing by streets, dark, narrow alleyways, places that look familiar, but I don't know why. Then I realize I'm in Brooklyn, the seamy underside of Brooklyn, way out where the cops don't like to go. We're in a little bar, a dive. He's pulling me to a table. Two men are sitting there. One's in his early twenties, red hair, big guy with a pinkish red face. The other man looks like a typical wiseguy if I ever saw one. Looking all around, intense. They're arguing. I'm trying to hear what they're saying. Clive pulls me closer to their table. Now I can hear and see everything clearly.

The red-haired guy looks like he's trying to threaten the other guy. Not smart. You don't talk like that to this kind of guy, if he's who I think he is.

"We don't have the money now, but you'll get it, ok, just lay off of me..."

The wise guy leans forward. "That wasn't our deal. We get the money when you promised, or we take the gig. It's real simple."

The red-haired guy looks like he's about to go ballistic now, shouting, "Do you know who my father is...well do you?!"

And now the wiseguy type takes the other guy by the collar saying real low, but like he means serious business..."You ain't your father, remember that, asshole. If it weren't for who your old man was you wouldn'tve gotten shit from us. It's outta respect to him that we even talk to punks like you."

And then the red-haired guy gets up and pushes his chair back angrily. Gettin' all up in the other guy's face. Like I said, not too smart, and saying, "Fuck you...you'll get the money when we got it."

The other guy just watches him, without saying a word as the red-haired guy storms outta there. One thing I know being a cop as long as I have, it's better when the wiseguys say something. It's when they're quiet that you better run for cover.

Now Clive is pulling on me again. We're passing the streets of Brooklyn again, going over the bridge into Manhattan. We're in a run down kind of building, in the Wall Street area, but a little off the beaten path. I pass a sign on the door: CALLAHAN & JANUARY CAPITAL CORP. Fancy title for a shitty office. No receptionist, just a seedy lobby, holes in the carpet and a small room with a couple of computers. Then I see Clive, or Clive how he must've looked fifteen years or so ago. And the red-haired guy is there. Trying to look cocky, but I can tell he's scared. Clive looks scared, too. He's talking real quiet to the other guy.

"So, Red, what did he say about an extension on the loan?"

"He didn't exactly agree to it, but don't worry. I told him we'd give him the money when we had it."

Clive doesn't look too convinced. "And he was okay with that?"

"What could he say? I mean, we don't have the money."

Clive gets up and paces the room nervously. "If we hadn't lost our shirts on that Bilco stock, we would've had it."

"I know, but that's the business. You can't make money on every trade, otherwise everybody'd be rich. Right?"

Clive doesn't look convinced. He straddles the side of the desk, knitting his brow. "I don't like owing those guys…"

"What choice do we have?" Red walks over to the window, looking out for a minute, then closing the blinds. "If we hadn't taken their money, we never would've been able to buy this business, and we'd both still be stuck knocking our asses out for somebody else in the training program at Bender."

Red turns back around and grins in an odd way, like it's the only thing that he can think of doing at that moment. "We wanna be millionaires by thirty, right? Nobody else was coming up with the cash, so what other choice did we have?"

Clive doesn't say anything. He's turning everything over in his mind, then quietly, quieter than I've ever heard him say before, "Yeah I guess you're right…"

The guy Red jumps up. He's gotten real excited about something all of a sudden. "You know what we should do?"

"What?"

"Go to the pier!"

Clive shakes his head no. "Naw, man, not today…I'm just not into it."

"C'mon, Clive, what better time? We had a blast before. It'll take our minds off all this shit…"

And then Red grabs his coat, motioning eagerly to Clive, "C'mon!"

I can smell the sea air now, and my skin feels clammy and damp, I've been transported to the old pier on Coney Island. Clive and Red are standing in front of me. Then everything's in slow motion as they both jump feet first into the swirling black waters. Now I feel like I'm underwater. I feel a heavy pressure against my lungs. I need air. And I remember when I had this feeling before—the first time I was at Clive's place in the Hamptons, I distinctly remember feeling like this, like I was drowning.

I'm trying to pump my way to the top of the water. But my arms feel heavy and useless. I realize that I'm feeling what Clive is feeling, that my arms are his, my thoughts his. All I can think of is I gotta breathe. I gotta get to the top. But I can't. And now I feel myself sinking further and further into the depths of the muddy dark water. I'm not aware of much anymore. Except falling.

The next thing I feel is something pulling me to the surface. I can feel Red's thick arm dragging me up. He grabs my head and forces it out of the water, towing me to the piling.

"Grab it…shit…man…grab it…"

I don't really know what happened next, I just remember ending back up on the pier, with Red thumping on my chest and screaming, almost crying.

"Breathe, damn it BREATHE, CLIVE, BREATHE!!!!!!" And then I see his soaking face looking puffy and wrinkled, his hair like stringy red seaweed plastered to the side of his face.

"I'm…I'm okay…shit…I'm okay…" I manage to prop myself up on my elbow, weakly. Now we're walking through the deserted streets of Brooklyn. My clothes are still soaked, and my legs feel like jelly. Neither of us is saying anything.

Red turns to me, like there's something he's been wanting to say. "I guess that was pretty stupid…jumping off the pier, I mean."

I'm cold and damp, my teeth are chattering, as I turn to him. "It was, but…" And I stop, looking into his bloodshot eyes.

"You saved my life. Thanks…"

Red just nodded. He doesn't say anything right away, then after a long pause…"It's the least I could do…it's not like you wanted to go…"

I don't want to make him feel any worse than he already did, so I slap him on the back saying weakly, "Hey we're brothers…so don't trip…it's okay…"

But he turns away, hiding his face from the light. "Clive, I'm scared."

I stop, looking dead at him. "What did that guy really say?"

He hesitates, avoiding my eyes. Taking a deep breath, then blurting out quickly…"That it was either the business or the money."

"Shit…did he say when, did he give any kind of deadline or anything!"

Red just shakes his head numbly. "No."

"Then you need to talk to your father. Now! Red. Right now! Those guys don't play…they can fuck us both up, and nobody would know a thing!"

"I know…I just didn't want to. I wanted to do it on my own for once…I'm so tired of having to go to him…" Red sinks down on the sidewalk, holding his head, like he wants to cry, saying, almost wailing, "Always my father, always having to run to him, Sean Callhan, the enforcer, the tough guy. I just wanted to handle it on my own for once."

I get this feeling in my gut that it wasn't going to be all right, that we have to do something fast. I turn Red around, facing him squarely, shaking him hard. "Look, now's not the time to play hero. Talk to your father, Red. Talk to him!"

But I can't hear what Red's saying, because suddenly there was a screech of brakes, and a car careens around the corner, tilting on its wheels crazily. A long thin tip of a gun is pointed out the window, and I don't hear anything, but a POP. A silencer. And Red crumples on the ground in front of me. "RED!"

The car has disappeared. Red is on the ground, a hole the size of a crater in his head, with blood flowing out. I see him, but I don't, I can't. I kneel down, holding him in my arms…"Red…Red…don't die…Don't…don…God…Nooooo!" I'm crying because I know it is already too late.

Clive is sitting in his office alone. Boxes packed up around him. Someone is taking the name off the door: CALLAHAN & JANUARY CAPITAL CORP. The workman sticks his head in the door, asking,

"You want this, mister?" He holds up the sign. Clive looks at it, and then slowly takes it out of the workman's hand.

Without saying anything, he numbly walks back into his office, still clutching the sign, then carefully he lays it on his desk. Running his hands across the letters, saying softly, "Red, why, you too, why? You were my brother. *Why are you gone, too?*" And he lays his head on the sign, bitter tears falling silently on the cold steel letters. Then I notice a kid standing in the doorway watching Clive's shoulders shake with sobs.

The kid kinda tentatively walks over to Clive, saying like he was real concerned, "Uh, mister, are you okay?"

Clive looks up, his eyes red and swollen. Disoriented, like he wasn't quite sure where he was.

The kid asks him again, "Are you okay…Is there anything…?"

Now Clive cuts him off. "Who are you?"

The kid looks surprised, like that wasn't what he expected to hear, but recovering quickly says, "Albert Wilkins, sir. The other guy who was here, Mr. Callahan, asked me to come back today. He said he'd buy a case of candy from me." The kid points to a cardboard box filled with candy.

Clive looks like he's about to break. Voice real soft, he says, "Red said he'd buy this from you…" Before the boy can answer, Clive reaches in his pocket and takes out some cash, stuffing it in the boy's hand. The boy looks down at the bill, and then his eyes open wide in amazement, "Wow, mister, this is a hundred dollars. The whole case is only twenty-five…Thanks!"

Clive looks down at the sign, saying sadly, like his heart is going to break in a million pieces. "It's for him, for Red. He would've done it."

Clouds. Clouds of time, passing quickly. I'm back in the apartment he shares with Laurel. The same night I saw before. Like he picked up the same thread of memory. Laurel is angry, angrier than before. "Always a plan, some scheme, like the one with Red. Is that what you want, to end up like Red…shot dead on some street corner?"

"These aren't the same people. It's different, I tell you. It's totally different!"

"But they're the same kind of people...Clive, please...please don't do this. You can't trust Andy...I know it and you know it. At least don't bring him in on it."

I felt a hard bump on my head, then woke in my own bed. The dream evaporated in the darkness. Haunted, I couldn't get it out of my head. Red. *Sean Callahan,* I quickly wrote down the names before I forgot them, *Andy Haven*, him again.

Tomorrow, I'd be on his ass like white on rice. I was beginning to feel the downward spiral of Clive's life. And the funny thing is that it felt like my own. Maybe that's why he could come through me the way he did, 'cause I was drowning in the same kind of frustration and hopelessness that he'd been in. And it killed him. Suddenly, I heard inside my head...

"We're the same you and I. Bob Greene."

I jumped up 'cause I wasn't dreamin' no more. I heard his words in my head clear as if he was right in front of me.

"How do you know me?" I shouted in my head. In front of me I could see his eyes. Dark, unblinking. Just staring ahead. Nothin' else, just his eyes. And I knew he was with me.

"I know you, 'cause you're me. And I'm you. I see the same hole in you that's in me. You can't see it. But you feel it, Bob. Every day of your life you feel it. Just like I did."

I was confused. I didn't know what to say, but I didn't have to because my thoughts were words, and he was answering them.

"Think back to the first time you felt it, Bob."

Shit. I began cryin'. Not sobbin' or nothin', but I could see my life from the time I was four years old...

"Dad..." I ran over to him and tried to take his hand.

"Not now. I ain't got time, Bobby. I got things to do." He pushed me away and walked over to the table and picked up his glass.

"Clive, how do you know what...?" But all I could see were his eyes. Unblinking still. But looking away from me now. And I felt the sadness, the pain of dying without knowing why. A heaviness shrouded me. I didn't know if it was his or mine. "Clive!" He closed his eyes and was gone.

I shuddered and reached for the bottle of Jack. But as I raised it to my lips, I suddenly didn't want it anymore. It couldn't cure what was eating away at me. Only I could do that by looking in.

CHAPTER TWENTY-TWO

"Detective, I think that I have the right to see your subpoena for these records."

I looked over at Haven, his pudgy brown face looked like a rotten plum ready to burst. His hands shook and his entire compact body quivered as he watched police officers load files into large boxes marked EVIDENCE.

"Detective, do you hear me? You just can't come into my office and start ordering my staff to remove files. This is a place of business!"

I was gonna let him rattle on a little longer, but I was getting damn sick of hearing his mouth at this point. I took out the subpoena and waved it in his face. "This, Mr. Haven, gives me the authority to take the files and any other shit I think might be evidence in this murder investigation. So if you'll just move out the way so my boys can work, it'll make it a whole lot easier on all of us. Yourself included."

He glared at me, yelling out to his assistant, "Cindy, get Bill Carter on the phone. Now!"

Her face flushed red, and she fumbled with the phone, whispering loudly, "But, Mr. Haven, he's out of town, remember you said—"

He turned and shouted so that anybody within ten miles coulda heard him. "Well then get one of the other lawyers at the firm! He's not the only one that works there. Damn it! Are you stupid or just incompetent? Do it now!"

He turned like he was gonna light into me, hissing, "Detective, I don't care what kind of God damned subpoena you have. Nobody comes into my office and just takes files. Who the hell do you think you are?"

I smirked and got right up in his face, calmly saying, "Your dedicated public servant. The one *your* tax dollars pays for every God damn mother fuckin' month. Any more questions?" I turned my back on him. I truly think that if he'd had a gun, he probably would've shot me dead right there. I just laughed to myself. I had him just where I wanted him. He'd probably spill his guts as mad as he was without even thinking.

"Oh, I almost forgot. I'm gonna need to ask you some more questions, Mr. Haven, if you got a few minutes now." With the vibe he was sending my way, if looks could kill, I'd be dead right now.

"I will not talk to you or to any other person without my lawyer."

"No problem, just bring him with you to the station, 'cause I need to talk to you today." I figured I'd done enough to ruffle his feathers for the moment. I wandered down the hall. The carpet was red, that money looking Wall Street red, not the cracked linoleum I was used to at the station. At the end of the hall was a double door, closed tightly. By the looks of the light spot on the paint on the wall, I could see that somebody's name had been there. I figured it was probably Clive's.

I pushed open the door and clicked on the light. In front of a picture window so big you could almost see to the tip of Manhattan, was a semi-circular desk, polished wood, or at least used to be polished. Right now, there was about an inch of dust on it. Dark green leather couches faced each other with a glass table in between. More dust on the table covered a bunch of crystal paperweights on it.

I picked up one of 'em to get a better look at the writing on the side: "January & Associates, A&L Securities, Initial Public Offering $20,000,000, March 18, 1985." All of 'em had the same kinda stuff on it, names of companies with big numbers written on it. I wondered how much of a cut Clive got outta all this. No wonder he could live like he did. And me in a one bedroom in Brooklyn. But at least I was alive.

Something told me to check out the desk again. Sometimes there were hidden drawers, even though I figured that Haven would've already taken out anything incriminating. Just two sets of drawers. Empty, like I guessed. I was about to check out the rest of the room when my eye caught the bottom of the desk. Nothing special, except that the wood in one rectangular spot was discolored. I got a little closer. Two small nail holes were on the side of the discolored spot under the desk. One of them was jagged like the nail had been ripped out real fast. Now I could see that something had been there, probably bolted to the bottom of the desk where it couldn't be seen from the front of the desk and behind a drawer slot so that you couldn't see it from the back either, unless you knew where to look.

I pushed Clive's chair back and sat in it. *Three inches by four inches*...My mind wasn't working for some reason. *C'mon, c'mon.* Normally a hundred possibilities would've sprung in my head. But for some reason, I was just blank. Digging in my pocket, I grabbed a cigarette. The one I kept for times like this. *Shit, no ashtrays.* I lit up. First time since I tried to get that doorman at Laurel's place to talk, and then I wasn't really smoking, just trying to get him to spill his guts. I think the nicotine was starting to clear my head, relax me a little.

"Excuse me, Detective?"

I swiveled around quickly and met the scared eyes of the secretary Haven had just chewed out. "I'm sorry to bother you, but Mr. Haven doesn't allow smoking at the firm. I'm really sorry, and I know you're working but..."

I looked at her, middle-aged white woman, faded brown hair, eyes ringed, probably younger than she looked. Hell, working for an asshole like Haven would age anybody. I felt kinda sorry for her, so instead of giving her what for, I just smashed the cigarette out on a piece of paper. "No problem. I was leaving anyway." For the moment that is, cause I'd be back.

"We can go in here." I motioned Haven and his lawyer into the interrogation room, pulling back two metal chairs for them. I never sat when I questioned witnesses. It put 'em more off center if I could just meander around the room. That way they never knew where I was coming from. "So, Mr. Haven, did Clive January ever mention any new accounts that were, shall we say, a little out of the ordinary?"

Haven stiffened and looked sidelong at his lawyer, who nodded for him to answer. "What do you mean by out of the ordinary?"

"Oh, I don't know. Why don't you tell me what ordinary is?"

"Any institutional clients with the assets to trade large volume of stock. Our clients run the gamut from insurance companies, pension funds, and occasionally high net worth individuals."

"So then if I came to you and wanted to buy some stock, what would you say?"

"You're obviously not a high net worth individual, so we wouldn't even be having this conversation."

"Ok, so then regular guys like myself, would not be 'ordinary' type of clients."

"Yes, that's right."

"So what other kind of clients do you have?"

"I really don't know what you're getting at, Detective. I think I've fully explained what type of clients we have. There's really nothing else to say."

"Oh, I think there is."

He quickly glanced away.

"Did your firm, that is your and Mr. January's firm, ever have any client accounts that could've been risky? The kind you wouldn't necessarily want anybody to know you had?"

Haven remained silent. His lawyer looked straight ahead.

"Mr. Haven?"

"Detective, Mr. January and I divided up the firm responsibilities in a way so that he was responsible for overseeing the trades and getting new business. I ran the firm's own portfolio and oversaw the day to day operations."

I slowed down, cocking my head in his direction. "In other words, you're saying that you wouldn't know if there were any of these questionable kind of accounts 'cause that's what January handled."

"That's correct, Detective."

Like hell, I thought, *this cat would know what side of the bed Clive January got up on in the morning. Nothing, and I mean nothing, would pass him by.* "So you'd like me to believe that you and Mr. January never discussed new firm business, or what you were doing for who? Seems like a kinda odd way to run a partnership."

He didn't flinch. "It worked."

"So how about now? Since January's dead and all, who runs the part of the business that he took care of, all the stuff that you, of course, didn't know nothing about before?"

"I do. I run everything."

"Seems like a lotta work for one man."

"I manage." *That bitchiness is coming out. I see why Clive liked to fuck with him.*

"Well you really are something, Mr. Haven. And you mean that you've been able to come up to speed on all the shit that January handled in just a month?"

"I do have an organization behind me, Detective. It's not like I'm doing everything myself."

I wandered around the room, and then stopped, looking him dead in the eye. "But you just said that you do…do everything yourself, that is."

He fidgeted. "I meant that I oversee everything. It would be impossible to be hands on with everything."

"Yeah, I guess so." I sat on the edge of the table. "Well I guess that's all for now."

Visibly relieved, Haven readied to leave.

"Oh, one more thing. Did January ever talk to you about selling the business?" If I had kicked him in the gut, he probably wouldn'tve looked more pained.

"No, never," he said tightly. "The firm was an institution, the only one of its kind on the street. He'd never sell it." He stopped for a second. "We'd never sell it."

I decided to ignore the last statement and continue with my train of thought. "But if he had sold it, you would've just cashed out your stock and gone about your business…I assume…or is that not the right assumption, Mr. Haven?"

His lawyer raised his eyebrows, then nodded for Haven to go ahead and answer the question.

"It would be a little more complicated than that, but basically, that's what would have happened."

"I see…Well, so no matter what Mr. January had decided to do with the firm, you woulda been fine, 'cause of your having stock in the company and everything."

Something kept telling me to hammer away at that point of who really owned the company. Not that I couldn't find out myself, but I just wanted to see Haven's reaction. I knew sorta instinctively that this was gonna hit a raw nerve with Haven.

"Damn it, Detective. I don't know if this is what you call effective police work, but I call it harassment. I've answered the same question three times now. How many—"

His lawyer jumped in. I think he could see that this whole thing was heading south for his client. "Andrew, why don't you just answer the detective's question one more time?"

Haven sucked in his breath, spitting the words out angrily. "If he sold the firm, I would've been fine, Detective. Just fine."

"Well that's all I wanted to know."

I leaned over tying my shoe. "I guess I'm done now, Mr. Haven."

Haven was still shaking, glaring at me. "When will you be returning my files? I can't exactly run a business with all of my records at the police station."

I turned my back on him. I got this sick pleasure with fucking with this pompous asshole. Yeah, I could definitely see why Clive liked to fuck with him. "When I'm finished, Mr. Haven. When I'm good and finished. And not until."

Boxes, boxes. Shit, by the look of things I'd never be finished going through all of this. And the worst thing was that I really didn't have a clue what I was looking for. Accounts, some kind of illegal accounts, but how would I tell the difference between what was legal and illegal? I didn't know shit about the securities business. My head was starting to ache, and I was beginning to feel that urge to go in the bottom drawer in my desk and pull out my stash of Jack that I kept in the iced tea bottle.

Maybe if I wasn't on such fucked-up terms with all the other cops in the force I'd been able to ask somebody for some help. But those days were long gone now. At this point it was just me, and this big room full of boxes that I had to go through without the faintest idea of what I was really looking for.

I pulled out the First Pacific Securities file. Sounded legal to me. I put it in the "okay" pile. Conway Capital Corp—legal. Hell, who was I fooling? These could all be fronts, and I wouldn't know the difference.

I shook myself awake. I don't know how long it had been since I dozed off. I'd shut the door so nobody would come in, but as I opened one eye painfully, trying to scrape the sleep off from my eyelids, I saw Margie. She was sitting cross-legged on the floor with a pile of files on one side of her and a large grey book open on her lap.

Without looking up, she said, "Things were slow in the file room, so I asked the Captain if I could help you in here. He said he didn't give a damn, so I guessed that meant yes."

I tried to pull myself together quickly and say something, but she just kept talking.

"I have a copy of Gray's pension fund and insurance company lists. I remember using it when I worked for Larry Stein at Merrill. I figured that any clients that January's firm would be trading stocks for would have to be either insurance companies or pension funds. They might also be rich investors, but I thought I'd start with the obvious things first."

I was really too stunned to say much, but she kept talking anyway, so it didn't matter.

"So far I've gone through about five boxes. I've separated all the files into the ones on Gray's list and the ones not on Gray's list."

I looked over in amazement at the two neat piles in front of her. One about twice as high as the other one.

"Which pile is which?"

"The tall are the accounts on the list, the shorter are the ones not on the list."

"Shit." That's all I could think of to say 'cause the truth is, I don't know what I would've done if Margie hadn't shown up. "Margie."

She looked up with the sweetest and cutest Laura Petrie smile. Fresh, just like the first time that we met. I wanted to run over and hug and kiss her. "Thanks."

She smiled.

"Well that's it…all the boxes."

I looked at the two neat piles. "So how many are not on that Gray's list?"

She quickly counted the files on the smaller list. "Twenty."

"So that means we got twenty possibilities."

"Yes, except that some of them may be S&Ls or rich investors so we can still probably narrow it down…"

"My guess is that one of those rich guys might be the account we're looking for."

"Well you're the detective, and I'm just the rookie cop. So whatever you think is probably right." I could tell when she was teasing, but for some reason it didn't bother me. I think I was just so grateful for her help that I could put up with about anything.

I sat down in front of the piles. My eyes scanned the names…L&M securities, Red Dog investments, that sounded like a code word…but who knew.

"You know the sick thing is that what we're looking for is probably not even in these files. They probably had that account on the computer and Haven erased it right after January died, or if he didn't do it then, he probably has now that he realizes I'm sniffing around for it."

I sat on the floor wearily. My head began aching again. The high I'd felt a minute ago started to seep away with the realization that all this work was probably meaningless. "The one person who probably knows everything, the assholes around here can't even find. You'd think she's a pro the way she's been able to slip away."

"Who's that?"

"January's girlfriend. She's the key. The mail for these accounts came to her place."

Margie could still sense my moods 'cause she came up behind me and started massaging my shoulders like she used to do. It felt good. I wanted her to keep on going.

Just as I was really starting to get into the rhythm, she stopped. "I better go."

I turned to her a little surprised. "You don't have to. We could grab some dinner. I'm buying."

She looked away, not meeting my gaze and then quickly picked up her purse. "I can't tonight. I've got to be somewhere."

"Oh." That's really all I could say. But the funny thing is that I wasn't mad like I'd normally be. I think I was starting to understand things a little better. "Well, have a good time."

She smiled at me as she left. I knew that she understood how hard it had been for me not to say anything else. Maybe I needed to be more like that kid at CCNY and just let things go instead of breaking bad in everybody's face all the time.

Before I had time to really let these new thoughts sink in, the door burst open and a cop stuck his head in the door. "Yo, Greene, that guy you wanted us to track down…Lani Hillgrove, he lives in Queens." The cop handed me a sheet of paper with all the info on Hillgrove. He was a supervisor in the post office, home address, phone number. Bayside Queens. I knew the area real well. It was my first beat as a cop.

I stuck the paper in my pocket. "You sure this is the right guy?"

"Married to a Laurel Davenport in 1972, divorced 1980. How many Lani Hillgrove's fit that description? Give us a little credit, okay, Greene?"

For once I felt like I was being the asshole instead of them, but no need of letting him know that. I just smiled kinda sheepishly. "Yeah sure... Thanks."

CHAPTER TWENTY-THREE

Neat houses, paint peeling a little, postage stamp-sized lawns, people who worked hard and led largely uneventful lives. I checked the address. It matched a pale, yellow-frame house. The grass was neatly cut, and there was one of those black jockey statues at the end of the cracked brick walkway leading to the door.

I was about to knock when the door swung open. A big, light-skinned black man stood in front of me. Or at least I think he was black. His eyes were blue, and his hair was as straight as mine, but his lips were so full and broad it made me think he must be black. I didn't have time to think much else before he blurted out. "Can I help you?"

I took out my badge and opened it in his face. "Detective Greene, NYPD. I'm looking for a Lani Hillgrove."

He didn't move. "What's your business?"

"Are you Lani Hillgrove?"

"Like I said, what's your business?"

"I'm investigating a murder, and I think that your ex-wife may be involved."

"And who says I'm Lani Hillgrove, Detective?"

The contemptuous way he said my name made me think of the guys at the station. "You do, 'cause I'm pretty damn sure that if you weren't him you'd a told me that to begin with."

Hillgrove looked at me suspiciously, but didn't say anything for a moment. I was gonna let him talk first. I figured he'd say something or do something that I could use. "Okay, Detective, what do you want to know?"

"More than we can talk about out here."

He looked like he was about to say something, but then he caught himself and stepped aside, letting me walk through the door. Inside the place was dark, almost oppressive. I could see why Laurel split from this guy. Everything around him seemed heavy and burdened down with some unspeakable secrets.

He sat down heavily on the brown plaid couch. He was a big guy, must've weighed at least 250, thick arms and wide legs. I wondered again why she'd ever marry somebody like this. He cut through my thoughts again. "What did you mean when you said Laurel was involved in some murder?"

"Does that surprise you?"

He cracked his knuckles and frowned. "I don't know."

"What don't you know?"

"If it surprises me. That's what you wanted to know wasn't it?"

I shrugged my shoulders. If he wasn't gonna be cooperative, I wasn't coming up off anything either. I took out my notebook and flipped to a blank page. "So, Mr. Hillgrove, how did you meet your ex-wife?"

"In a shopping mall outside Greensboro. She was working at the information booth, and I came to ask her a question. She was kinda cute, so we just kept talking. Before I knew it, we'd made plans to get together for coffee after she left work."

"Sounds like it moved pretty fast."

"That was her way," he said matter-of-factly.

"So go on. You dated for a while. How long exactly?

"About three months, then one day she just upped and said she wanted to get married."

"So you did?"

"Yeah, I guess I was ready. I'd been to Nam, done my tour and was back pretty much okay. I finished up school, had a pretty good job with the state, so I figured…hey why not?"

"What kind of wedding was it? I mean did she have her family, close friends?"

"No, that was kind of the odd thing. She didn't have anybody there. I wanted to meet her people, but she said they had died, and she didn't have any close friends. We just went to the Justice of the Peace one Saturday and did it."

"After you got married, how was she?"

He leaned back on the couch. "She was...like... the perfect wife...cooked dinner every night, washed my clothes...did everything right, but it was almost too perfect. Sometimes I felt kinda like she was trying to convince herself that she could do it. Sort of like she was practicing for the real thing."

"The real thing?"

"Yeah, sometimes I felt like I was a dry run." He reached over to a little dish and took a piece of butterscotch candy out, unwrapped it and started sucking on it noisily.

"What made you think that?"

"A lot of little things, but mainly something that happened one day. We'd been married a couple of years and things were going okay, or at least I thought so." The sofa squeaked as he shifted his large frame. "I got home kinda early one day, and she was home. She'd quit her job, said she wanted to have more time to be a good wife...but anyway, she didn't hear me when I came in, and she was cutting out things from a magazine. Well when I asked her what it was, she tried to hide it, but I'd already seen."

"What was it?"

"All kinds of articles from those *Brides* magazines, pictures of wedding dresses, where to go on your honeymoon, all that kind of thing."

"Well maybe it was for you?"

He opened another piece of candy and stuffed it in his mouth. "We'd been married two or three years then, so I know it wasn't for us. Plus when she saw I'd snuck up on her, she tried to hide everything and pretend like she was doing it for a friend."

I took all of it down. "Did you divorce right after that?"

"No, it was a few years later. We'd been separated, until one day she just showed up on my doorstep saying she wanted a divorce, and she needed it right away."

I was thinking that must've been when she disappeared, and then showed up again too late to marry Clive. "Did you ask her why she needed it so quick?"

He sighed like he'd rather forget the whole thing. "By that time, I didn't give a damn anymore. I was ready to be finished with her. Only thing is that I wanted to make sure that it was legal. I didn't want any problems. She wanted to go to Vegas and do it there, but I insisted on getting a lawyer and doing it right. She wasn't happy about it because it took a lot longer than she thought it would."

"How long did it take?"

"Musta been about six months. But at least I knew it would stick."

"So you were married, what three, four years before you separated. Did you ever think about kids?"

"I wanted kids, but I don't think she really did. She had this little dog, a cute little Irish terrier. His name was Randy. That dog was pretty much all the kid she ever wanted. She just doted on him."

"What happened to him?"

He shook his head. "It was the strangest thing. She loved that dog more than anything, but the apartment we were in didn't allow pets. First the landlord was okay about it, but some of the neighbors started complaining about him barking, so the landlord told us we had to move. But we couldn't move because we'd lose our security deposit, and since she wasn't working then, we just couldn't afford it. So the dog had to go."

He cracked his knuckles again, coughing nervously. "I thought she'd just give the dog away. One of my friends wanted him, and she'd said okay. I thought that's what she'd done, but then I found out that..." he shifted in his seat again, "she'd had the dog put to sleep. "

"Why?"

"When I asked her, she just got real cold and said that she did it because nobody else could've loved him the way she did."

Back at the station, I knew now, more than ever that I had to find Laurel. And for once I think that somebody upstairs must've heard me, 'cause the minute I got to my desk, a cop called out, "I think we found that chick you've been looking for…Davenport, Laurel Davenport. She's in a little town outside Woodstock, under an alias."

CHAPTER TWENTY-FOUR

Laurel

Music, music in my mind. Pretty music. Reminding me of when I still laughed at everything. What happened to those days? I was so tired of asking myself the same simplistic questions over and over. I knew better than anyone exactly what happened. I made it happen by my insistent nature, that flyaway part of me that could never be grounded. That's what Clive would say.

He was so pretty, so wonderfully pretty and handsome and strong. And he was mine. I know that he was. No man makes love to you on his wedding night without really being yours. *A tear.* I hated crying. But lately that's all done in that barren room, far from our beautiful apartment where I could see trees and people and life, to here where I had nothing. Not even my own name. I couldn't help looking at his face, but for some reason on this day, it hurt more than usual. The anger at what could have been and what I could have done stared me in the face. I took a long drag from my cigarette. Blowing smoke rings the way that I used to do as a teenager growing up in Cleveland.

I don't miss those days. Being the only child of parents who you never really felt were like you. And when I found out that there was a reason for this lingering malaise that I'd had as long as I could remember, this malaise that was born of being of alien blood, not the same as the people who claimed to be of me…then I understood.

But understanding didn't make the malaise go away. My brief marriage had been my attempt at practicing what it might be like to have a family that you chose. Practicing for the family I thought I'd someday have with him. Clive. But I knew that Clive wasn't ready yet. He had his mountains to climb, and at that point I would've just been excess baggage. The marriage taught me about living with someone else, learning to bend your needs and desires in ways that fit with someone else's. But it didn't teach me about myself. It didn't fill the hole that wouldn't go away.

That's why I had to find my father, even if it meant turning away from Clive for a moment, or what I thought would be a moment. My father was the key to putting together the jagged pieces of my life. A white mother who hated the thought of the black child she'd spawned. Had the hate always been there, I wondered, had there ever been love or had I been conceived in a well of distrust or worse? Even if the truth ripped through me, I had to know. I wandered from town to town for ten years, from the time I left Hendersonville. Something about that night with Clive when we first made love opened up the old wounds, the old questions of who I was. So I followed the trail of a man I knew only as Father. From tiny hamlets to backwater towns, piecing together a life of simplicity. Until the day I got the call. He wasn't dead as I had feared, but alive, though barely, in a VA hospital outside Gary, Indiana.

As I opened the door to the hospital room, I remembered my mother. I wondered if I'd see the same hatred or merely indifference to a life quickly given and then forgotten. I walked through the door and was struck by the smell of urine, as if bedpans that hadn't been emptied for so long that the stench had become a part of the walls. I gazed into the eyes of my father, glazed over with cataracts, a thick shock of white, stubbly hair clinging to his small brown face, and I said, "Hello."

He looked up absentmindedly from his pillow and smiled. "Well, hello."

Before I could lose my nerve, I blurted out quickly, "I hate to bother you, sir, but…um…are you…Armand Davis?"

"Yes, last time I checked." He kind of chuckled, and then coughed as if the effort of speaking had taxed him more than his weak frame could take.

"Please, don't take this wrong, sir…but I've been looking for you for a long time and I…I'd just like to talk to you for a few minutes, if you have some time."

"Well, young lady, I think you can pretty much tell by the look of things that I'm not going anywhere, and I don't get much company these days, so I guess I've got a few minutes to chat if you'd like."

I swallowed and smiled gratefully. At least I hadn't been booted out summarily. Yet. He still didn't know why I was here. I pulled up the rickety metal chair and sat closer to him.

"Do I look familiar to you?"

He peered at me. "No, should you?"

I didn't know how to say this tactfully. "Well I thought that maybe, well maybe I might remind you of someone…like…" I hesitated. "Well, like your daughter."

He sat up stiffly, and then said gruffly, "I don't have a daughter, at least not one I know." He sank back into the pillows and closed his eyes. "I did have a daughter. But that was a long time ago. I never knew her."

I don't know why but I took his hand. "I'm her. I'm the daughter you didn't know."

His eyes opened wider, and he sat up and intensely studied my face, then after a long moment that seemed like hours, he smiled very slightly. "Yes, I guess you would be. You look just like her," he said, voice cracking.

"My mother?" I could barely say the word, still remembering the hatred in the eyes of the one who had carried me for nine months, and then dumped me like baggage that she couldn't wait to rid herself of.

He nodded, settling himself on his pillows, his hand fidgeting with the faded sheets. "I wanted to marry her…when I found out she was expecting. We hadn't known each other long, 'bout six months, we'd had a good time. Hadn't expected anything to come of it…so when she got pregnant, well I think it kinda threw both of us for a loop."

He went silent for a moment. "Well anyway, she wouldn't hear of it. 'Twas okay to hang out with a colored fella, 'specially one coming back from the War. All the gals was after us then…but to marry one…in Chicago. No. Wasn't happening. So we…decided it would be best to give you up, give you a chance to be raised by a couple who could do it right, give you things, a nice life."

I wanted to shout out, but they could never give me your love, only you could do that. But I didn't. I just listened.

"I thought about you a lot, especially the first few years. But I didn't want to spoil things for you. So after a while I think I almost convinced myself that it never happened. That you never really happened."

I didn't know what to say. Somehow the pain we both felt bound us together. So I just sat by his bed, holding his hand tightly.

He propped himself up on one elbow, studying me again, then asking hesitantly, "Were they good people…your folks that raised you?"

Memories of them. My adopted parents, hardworking, well meaning but distant, never really understanding their impulsive daughter. "They were good and kind to me. But…I always felt like…" I remembered opening the drawer finding the faded picture, the inscription on the back read: Laurel age 3 mos. "Well, like I was a substitute for another child. Then around the time that I found out that I was adopted, I also found out that there had been another child, their own child who'd died when she was an infant." I was flooded with memories of the christening gown carefully folded in the drawer…of the faded yellow rose, the birth announcement…a single shoe… "Her name was Laurel. Just like mine. Only she was first. And she was theirs. I found out they'd adopted me about a year after she died."

A breeze rattled the metal blinds, and my father squeezed my hand tighter. I had never told anyone, not even Clive about that, and it felt like I had finally released a dark part of me. The secret that I now finally admitted to couldn't hurt me anymore. And now questions, all the questions that had peppered my thoughts for years wanted to come out, to shout out. Things I had to know.

"Father, do you mind if I call you that?" There was a hesitation that seemed like an eternity. I so needed him to say yes.

"No not at all." He smiled. "In fact, I'd like that."

A weight had been lifted from me. The rejection of my mother was somehow being made up for by the love of my father. I looked down, not wanting to pry, but I needed to know. "Father, did you have other children?"

He adjusted himself on his pillows carefully before answering. "No. I never married. I almost did once, but it didn't work out."

"Do you wish you had?"

"Oh sure, who doesn't wish sometimes to be with someone?" He sighed slightly, then brushed his small, knotted hands across his hair, almost self consciously. "But I didn't want to be a burden to anyone. I had this injury, from the war. I was in a bunker that exploded, and a little piece of shrapnel got stuck, right here." He motioned to a slight bump behind his ear. "Go on, touch it."

Gingerly, I touched his scalp and the tough protrusion. "Does it hurt?"

He shrugged. "A lot of times, but mostly I've had these headaches. Sometimes for weeks I could hardly get up the pain was so bad. Went to see lots of doctors through the years. Some better than others. But nobody could ever really help me. That's how I ended up here. It's gotten worse over the years, so now all I can do most of the time is rest."

The plodding sound of nurses feet against the cheap linoleum floors approached. The door creaked as it was opened, revealing a shiny faced Filipino nurse. "Visiting hours are over, Miss. I'll have to ask you to leave now."

Panic took over me. There was so much more I wanted to ask, to know. My father must have noticed because he nodded and said softly but firmly, "She'll be going in a minute." Apparently satisfied, the nurse shut the door.

I got up hesitantly, my head was spinning, and I was trying to get myself together. "Thank you for talking to me…I…" I tried to get out the rest, but for some reason, tears started filling my eyes. My body was shaking with all of the emotion and pain that I'd held in for so long.

My father gingerly pulled himself up and put his arm around me, hugging me tightly and rocking me back and forth. "It's okay, Laurel. It's okay to cry…" His tears mixed with mine.

And so it started. Me hungry for knowledge of who I was, and him happy to share a life and a past of seeming little consequence to anyone else. He showed me pictures of my grandparents, my aunts and uncles, cousins, places he'd grown up. He shared family stories, and slowly I started feeling like the outlines of what had been my life was finally being given flesh and that I was finally being made whole.

The months passed almost without either of us noticing that time, always the silent enemy was coming for its marker. I did part time receptionist work at the hospital to be nearer to him and to pay my few bills. A friend lived nearby, so I slept on her couch and rode the bus in every day. I thought of Clive, but I couldn't call him until this emptiness within me was filled. Then one day it ended almost as it had begun.

My father sat up, coughed a little, and then sipped water from the paper cup by his bed. Neatly he dabbed a few errant drops of water from the bottom of his chin. A fastidious man, careful about his appearance even in these circumstances. "You know, Laurel…I've been wondering."

I looked up not sure what to expect.

"I've been wondering about you, and your life. You've spent so much time with me these past months, a pretty girl like you, must've left somebody behind."

I didn't know what to say. I'd never told him directly about Clive, but somehow he'd guessed.

He patted the side of the bed and motioned for me to sit next to him, then tenderly and with so much kindness, he tilted my chin up like I was a little girl. "You know you can't leave things for too long 'cause before you know it they get restless and move on."

A tight knot starting to form. I knew he was right, but I guess I never really squarely faced up to how long it had been and the possible consequences. Clive and I had always been apart for long periods of time, and then when we'd gotten back together it had been as if we'd never been separated. Tears started to sting my eyes. I tried to hold them back, but I couldn't.

"Darlin', all I'm sayin is that you've got a life, and I want you to live it. If I've helped you understand more about who you are, then I've done more for you then I ever thought I could. But you've got to go back to what you left behind."

"But, Daddy, I don't want to leave you. Not like this. There's nobody to take care of you!"

"That's what the hospital's for. They've been doing a fine job, so don't you worry about me."

I started to say something, but he just smiled and kissed me on the cheek as he always did. But this time it seemed different. He lingered for a moment, and then said quietly, "You know I love you. Daughter." I hugged him and kissed him gently on his thin cheeks. He held me, running his hands over my head. "Now go on. We'll talk tomorrow."

We never did talk again. He died that night as quietly and as unobtrusively as he had lived. They found him in the morning with the sheets tucked neatly under his chin and his hands folded simply on the covers. Sometimes I wonder if he knew he was going and if he was trying to say goodbye to me. To let me go. But it was hard, so hard saying goodbye to him.

That's all long gone now. I'd always been able to hide the pain with laughter. To make someone up who could be loved. That's what I did. I made myself up. The way I would've liked to have been if I'd had any choice in the matter. And the person that I made up pleased Clive. He loved me. And he'd wanted me. He'd been a part of me. But no more.

I feel the pain coming back, it's starting in my chest the way it always does, the way it has since that night when I knelt in blood. His blood. And I cried because I hated myself for what had happened.

The glowing tip of my cigarette reminded me of a magic sword in a fantasy film, possessing supernatural powers. And I took this magic sword and thrust it forward into his face. His pretty, wonderful handsome face, blotting it out from the picture. I couldn't look at it anymore and know that it wasn't mine. So I ended it. Just like that.

Tears. Again. How I hated tears. I heard voices, but not the ones in my head. They were outside my window. Pulling back the sash, I saw policemen talking to the building manager who was pointing up to my window. I knew they were looking for me. Grabbing my purse and the little bit of money that I had hidden away in the corner, I crept out of the room. *The backstairs, the only way. Maybe, just maybe I can get away. But I will. I have to. I have to save myself now. There's nothing else.*

I was running through the woods. My hands were bleeding from skirting around the sides of trees. If I could just get to the highway. The low hanging trees were blocking my path. I brushed back branches and scrambled over scarred rocks that jutted up like giant pock marks in the earth. I could hear the cars speeding by. But I couldn't see where to go. Around me was dense underbrush. Black green slick leaves crept up the side of my legs. The sound of feet, animal or man, I don't know which, grew closer. Then a screech as wings brushed past me.

My heart poked through my chest. Dirt ate into my eyes as I ran faster and faster not knowing where. I searched for an open space out of the green brown maze of trees and decaying moss. Without thinking clearly, I ran out waving my arms and almost stepped head-on into a truck.

Brrrrroooooonk blared the horn. *Screeeeech* went the breaks. The truck stopped dead in front of me.

"Are you fuckin' outta your mind, lady!?" The door snapped open and this woman, a large woman with a cap of pale blonde hair smashed on her face, jumped out. "You gotta death wish or something. I almost killed you!"

I was so tired and scared that my words just tumbled out. "I…I'm so sorry…I…could you please just give me a ride? Anywhere, wherever you're going."

The lady truck driver squinted at me. I knew she was going to say no.

She tossed her head back. "Okay, get in."

Detective Bob

"This is all we found." The cop tossed some beat up photographs onto my desk. What looked like cigarette burns had blotted out one of the faces.

"What d'you mean this is all you found? I thought you said you had her?"

"We did, but she musta slipped away right before our guy went upstairs. The manager told us that she was there. But when he went up, she'd split. In a hurry, too. Didn't take any clothes or nothing."

"Then how the hell do you know that she's gone? Maybe she just stepped out for a minute. Did you assholes ever think of that?"

"Fuck off, Greene. We got somebody stationed outside of there in case she comes back, but if you ask me, she's split. So just live with it."

"You know you guys are really too much. You come within five feet of a murder suspect, and you let her slip out of your hands. You'd think she was some damn pro at this. She's nothing but a fuckin' school teacher. And you can't even get her!"

I was about to really go off, so much for my new attitude, when the captain stuck his head out of his office. "Greene, in here. Now."

I walked into the captain's office still steaming. "Did you hear that? They let her get away. She's the key to the whole fuckin' case, and they let her get away. I don't get it. I just don't get it. Are these guys cops or just excuses for cops?"

Captain let me finish, which is unusual. That should've been the first hint that something was up. "Greene, there's a lot of talk of how you aren't making the mark on this one."

"That's bullshit, Captain. I'm making progress. I got two possibles and—"

"And a whole lot of maybes."

He sat down in his chair and swiveled around to me. "I don't have time to get into some long harangue with you, Greene. I got other things to do, but I'm telling you, and I won't be telling you again, you got one month to bring in a real suspect on this one. Otherwise, you're off this case."

He drummed his swollen fingers on his desk impatiently. "People want this case wrapped up, and you're not moving fast enough for them."

I couldn't believe what he was saying. Take me off a case? Never in the entire twenty years that I'd been on the force had this ever happened. "What people?"

"People, just people." He walked over to the door and opened it, signaling that this was the end of this conversation. "One month, and you're off."

My hands shook as I walked back to my desk. Every eye in the place was on me. Bearing into the back of my head. *Off the case.* The words still echoed around me. Who are these "people?" What shit was Clive really into that somebody's puttin' this much pressure on the captain to get the thing done with?

I had two choices. I could quit and maybe get some peace of mind by just being away from this place, or I could stick it out try and slug away for the next month and crack it. Right now, all I could think of was how alone I felt.

I sat down at my desk and opened the file. Feeling like somebody was knocking at the space between my eyebrows with a jagged rock. I closed my eyes, thinking it might ease the pain. But when I opened them, everything was light around me. I could see the room with the cops talking, bullshitting as usual, but it was all in slow motion with no sound. I was a casual observer in somebody else's movie.

Then I saw Clive, clear as day, sitting on my desk, his long legs swinging over the side.

"You've gotta do this for me, Bob Greene," he said.

I answered, except my lips weren't moving. The sounds were coming from inside my head. "Why…tell me why the hell should I?"

He smiled sadly, an expression full of regret, saying wearily, "Because I need peace." He began fading out. The noises in the background were starting to come back, but I could hear him coming through, words that shot into me…"Because you need peace."

The sounds exploded back around me. The noise, the cursing, laughing, typewriters, and Clive was gone.

His words stuck to me, and I knew that he was right. Somehow we were linked, Clive and me, and if his soul could rest, then maybe mine could, too. So I couldn't quit, not until we knew.

The question was how to find out what I needed with my key witness gone AWOL and a bunch of files that I couldn't really decipher. *The wife. I'll talk to her again. She probably knows more than she was saying.* They always did.

CHAPTER TWENTY-FIVE

Detective Bob

"I"ll tell her you're here, Detective." The maid, Dolly, showed me into the living room. I was prepared for all the richness, and it didn't even bother me anymore, because I knew that behind the money and all the shit that he'd gotten, Clive January was a whole lot like me. A guy drowning in his own fuckin' world.

As I was thinking this, a tall, graying black woman walked in the room holding the hand of a toddler. When I looked at the woman's face, I saw Clive. I knew it must be his mother. And the child, his kid.

"You here to see my daughter-in-law?" Her words grated against me for some reason.

"Yeah."

I figured I'd let her do the talking. She looked like the curious type.

"So do you know who killed my baby yet?"

I looked her in the eye, trying to figure her out. All I could see was somebody who had a wall so thick in front of her, that it wasn't coming down any time soon, if at all. "No, not yet. Got any ideas?"

She glanced at me sideways, almost snorting. "Now how would an old woman like me know something like that?"

"You might have heard things, or seen things. Do you ever remember your son seeming upset at something or at somebody?"

"No more than usual. That was his way, you see, to always fly off at people. He done it to me more than once."

"But I guess you still loved him, in spite of it?"

She held on to the child's hand a little tighter, her eyes looking completely different when she looked at her granddaughter, softer, almost gentle. "Yeah, that's right," she said quietly.

"Mother, I'll take her now." Monique had come into the room without either one of us noticing. She looked pretty good for a grieving widow. Hair done up, expensive dress, no tear lines on her face.

She leaned down to scoop up her child, and for a moment her mother-in-law wouldn't let go, holding the child closer to her saying in a cajoling, manipulating kind of voice. "Now you wanna stay with Nanna don't you, baby?"

The kid looked up and smiled at her grandmother. "Uh huh…Nanna, I waana be with Nanna."

Clive's mother had this real funny look on her face, a mixture of love for the kid and pride, like somehow having this kid asking to be with her was all she really wanted. I actually felt kinda sorry for Monique. She'd lost her husband, and now, at least from what I could see, she was losing her child, too.

"Mother. She needs to take her nap. She's tired, so why don't you just let Dolly take her upstairs?" Monique sounded pissed and at the end of her rope. She pulled the kid away from her mother in-law. The kid, of course, starts yelling bloody murder.

"I don't wanna go upstairs. I waaana stay with Nana!"

Clive's mother brushed Ariel's hair back, cooing, "C'mon now, baby. Yo mama wants you to take a nap, but if you goone upstairs, Nana'll read you a story, how's that?"

Ariel immediately calmed down. "Promise, Nana, promise to read me a story?"

"I promises."

Monique turned away from Clive's mother angrily, and then gently picked up Ariel, holding her tightly as if to reassert her dominance. "C'mon, honey, let's go upstairs." She marched out of the room, yelling back over her shoulder, "I'll be right back, Detective."

Clive's mother had the strangest expression on her face. Like I said, she had a brick wall in front of her, so I didn't have a clue what she was really thinking. Before I could figure out what might be really going on in her head, she turned her back on me and walked out of the room.

I was alone, so I took the time to look around the room, open some drawers, do a little police work. I was drawn to a funny little desk in the corner. I opened the drawer. Empty. I was about to close it when I noticed a folded piece of paper jammed in the corner. A date on the paper said: January 6, 1986. A year ago. The paper was on the letterhead of BENDER, GRACE & CO. The place where Clive used to work years ago. *Wonder why he'd have something from them now.*

I folded the paper carefully and thrust it in my pocket.

"Found anything interesting, Detective?" Damn that woman could sneak up on you. I looked over at Monique leaning against the doorway. I didn't turn around, wasn't gonna give her the satisfaction of knowing she busted me.

"So how's the kid? She sounded pretty upset."

"She's three, Detective. That's how she sounds most of the time, or at least whenever she doesn't get her way."

"I wouldn't know, no kids myself."

She sat down on the couch, facing me with a no-nonsense look on her face. "So what did you want to ask me, Detective?"

I leaned back in the chair, patting the paper that I had in my pocket. "Not much really. I just wanted to see any files or work that your husband might've kept at home."

"He usually didn't bring work home. He wasn't here that much, but whatever he has is upstairs in the den." She took a cigarette out of a silver case on the table in front of her, offering me one. I wanted one, God did I want one, but I figured I'd held out this long.

"I'm trying to quit, but I keep fallin' off the wagon, if you know what I mean."

"Well, keep trying." She lit the cigarette quickly, almost nervously. "I wish I could say the same."

"Does your husband's mother live here?"

She frowned slightly, but then turned back coolly. "For the moment." Getting up quickly, she motioned for me to follow her. "His den is upstairs, this way."

She left me alone, pretty cooperative. I was about to start rummaging through the drawers when I noticed a calendar in the corner. I flipped through it. January 6, 1986. Circled. I glanced at the paper I'd taken from the living room desk. Same date.

I grabbed the calendar and put it in my bag. I looked around the rest of the room, opening drawers, looking under cabinets. Not much here. She was right. He didn't seem to do much work at home. Except for that calendar.

"Find what you were looking for, Detective?" She'd crept up on me again.

But this time maybe she could be some help. "A few things."

"I told you that he didn't work at home much. He rarely even came into this room." She stopped as if in deep thought, then sighed.I took out the calendar, showing her the circled date. "Was January sixth some kind of important date for your husband, or for you…anniversary, birthday, you know that kind of thing?"

She shook her head. "Not as far as I know, but in my husband's business it could've meant anything."

"Mrs. January, did your husband ever talk about any new accounts that he was getting?"

"He never talked about his work with me."

"Not even casually, like at dinner or something?"

"Detective, when we ate together, which wasn't often, he usually didn't have a lot to say."

"Well, what about any phone calls you might've overheard, meetings at the house, anything that seemed out of the unusual?"

"No nothing."

I brought out my TV Detective act again. "Look, Mrs. January, I'm trying my damndest to find out who killed your husband, and I can't seem to get any help from any fuckin' body, excuse my French. You don't know nothin', my main suspect slipped away, so all I'm coming up with is a big fat zero, and if I don't crack this case in a month, my ass is off and they'll stick some pansy on who probably cares even less than you do about finding out who killed your husband."

I took a deep breath. That was a lot to say at one time and sound convincing. It was all true, and I'd made a silent promise to Clive that I would find out who did it. His salvation and mine were both hanging in the balance, and it wasn't clear where the whole thing would end up.

For once, I think I cracked the surface on her. She actually looked like she might cry for the first time. She sat down on the small couch, turning away from me and saying softly, "I do care who killed my husband, Detective. I do care. "

She started crying, but not really crying, 'cause she was trying hard to hold it in. I could tell she was the kind who'd never cry around strangers, never let down her guard. But something I said hit a chord, and now it all just started coming out. My guess is that even an ice queen like her had to let go at some point.

She kinda choked out the words. "My husband and I hadn't been…we had not really had much of a marriage for years, since before our daughter was born. I wasn't in his life, and he wasn't in mine. We were merely roommates, financial partners." She stiffened, continuing quietly, so quietly that I could barely hear her. "But I did still love him." She closed her eyes, talking more to herself it seemed than to me.

"Even though I told myself I didn't, and that it didn't hurt any more. It still did. Clive was like that. Once you loved him, you could never stop. He was like a drug, because when he loved you he was so completely yours and so completely involved in you that you couldn't get enough, you lost yourself in him. So when he inevitably moved on, you couldn't. You kept wanting that high again of knowing that someone completely loved you."

Now I was quiet, seeing where she'd go next.

"I don't know that I'll get over his death."

Suddenly, I felt sorry for this lady. I knew what it felt like for your love to come back unreturned. But I couldn't think about that now. Hell this might have been all an act. 'cause even though one part of me believed her, my cop's intuition told me never say never when you're on a murder case. She still might be holding something back. "Mrs. January, were you and your husband thinking about a divorce?"

She clammed up on me again. The little bit of progress I'd made, shot to the wind. Pulling herself together real quick. Tears gone, eyes open, no more sad memories and choked up voice. She looked at me directly, without blinking. "Doesn't every couple think about it at one time or another, Detective?"

"I wouldn't know. I've never been married."

"Well, Detective, I have been for seven years, and trust me, most couples do. It's the nature of living in close quarters with someone for extended periods of time."

Back to the ice queen. I could see that I wasn't gonna get a whole lot more outta her today, so I figured time to wrap. "I'm gonna send a cop down here, if you don't mind, to cart off the rest of these files...I don't have time to go over them carefully now, but they might have something in them."

Before she could say anything, Dolly came into the room. A real weird look on her face. "Mrs. January, your father's downstairs...with Mr. and Mrs. Lanier."

Monique looked surprised, but then I think she remembered that I was in the room. "Tell them I'll meet them in the car."

Dolly looked like she didn't approve, or that something was up, I couldn't tell. I made a mental note to question Dolly again. I'd talked to her right after the murder, but she hadn't really been that much help.

As I walked outside, I noticed an older black man seated in the driver's seat of a steel grey Mercedes, the kind I'd drool over in the magazines and that him a black man was drivin'. I recognized him as her father from Clive's funeral. Next to him was a white man, Lanier, I guessed. Tall good lookin' greyin' with that I-got-money look. In the back seat was one of them rich bitch types. Loaded with jewelry and bad attitude. Figured it must be Lanier's wife. They didn't notice me. But something about them showin' up like that had changed the deck, stacked the cards in another direction. And I was beginning to feel that my cop's intuition was right. That Monique knew more than what she was saying, and Dolly had a clue of what it was.

CHAPTER TWENTY-SIX

Laurel

"Stick of gum?" The lady truck driver offered me a pack of gum. Gratefully, I took a stick. This would be my lunch. I hadn't eaten anything all day.

I'd been riding for almost three days now. The truck driver, her name was Jan, was a decent person. She let me sleep in the cab at night when she checked into a motel. I think she knew that I didn't have any money.

During the day, she didn't say much. We just rode past miles and miles of desolate landscape. The dreary South in winter, leafless trees, miles of emptiness. We rarely talked, but for some reason, today she seemed to want to open up. "You running from a man?"

I wondered where that came from, but I tried to sound calm. "No…not at all…"

She looked at me like she didn't believe a word I was saying. "I was where you are, once, 'bout five years ago. My boyfriend, we were living together then, had started to get this bad habit of drinking and then coming home and knocking me around." I thought that her boyfriend must've been huge because she was no small woman.

"Finally, I got sick of it. So I left." She snapped her gum. "I thought that would be it, but then he came after me. Found me and came trying to beat down my door." She leaned back in the seat, stretching her legs. "Now in those days I used to carry a gun, so I was ready to blow the shit outta him. If he got in the door, I didn't care if I rotted under the damn jail, I wasn't letting him touch me again."

She took out another piece of gum and stuffed it in her mouth. "So anyways, he knocked the door down, and I had my gun pointed ready to pull the trigger, when all of a sudden, he grabbed his heart. He dropped down in front of me in pain. He couldn't breathe or nothing."

"Was he having a heart attack?"

"Yep, right there in front of me. And then I felt bad 'cause I didn't really want him to die like that, so I leaned down and I tried to help him, but it was too late."

Her words stung me. I knew her feelings, but I wasn't ready for her next question.

"Ever seen someone die before, somebody you loved?"

My eyes clouded over. Trying to block the memory...Clive lying there, the blood, the tears..."No."

She slowed down abruptly, pulling the truck over and stopping it. "Sure you have."

She pulled out a crumpled piece of paper from her jacket. It was my picture...a police drawing: LAUREL DAVENPORT MURDER SUPSECT.

Pain resonated in my chest, but this time it was followed by a sharp searing in my legs. "How...what...?"

"I got it at the motel last night. The minute I saw it I knew it was you." She leaned over me and opened my door, looking at me with unfeeling eyes. "So, sister, this is the end of the road for you and me."

What could I say? Nothing. So numbly, I got out of the truck. I was a fugitive. Without any idea of where I was, or where I was going. I was still holding the police photo of me. But why was I surprised? I'd known since I saw the police outside my window that they were looking for me. But to see it in print in black and white...I was about to close the cab door when Jan called out to me, "Hey...good luck."

I nodded, because I really couldn't think of anything else to say.

"Yo, Greene, we just got a call. Somebody saw your suspect in western Alabama, coupla hours outside of Mobile. She'd hitched a ride with a truck driver when they dumped her out there."

I had already jumped up and strapped my gun on my holster. This time I wasn't taking any chances. I was getting her myself.

"And one more thing. Her prints, the ones we got from her office, matched the second set of prints at January's place. She was definitely at the murder scene that night."

I rubbed my hands together, charging myself up. I was beginning to feel like a cop again. "Bingo! Now I got a case. Call the local cops down there. Get 'em to nab her. I'm leaving on the next plane."

On the plane, looking out over the clouds, made me think about when I was a kid. I used to look up in the sky and pretend that I was seeing faces in the clouds. Sometimes it was like I had a whole 'nother world up there. Pretty funny, then at least. So I was looking out seeing the faces. Only this time, they seemed more real than ever. Probably just tired and stressed from the past few days. But the faces weren't going away, and I knew that Clive was pulling me into his world again.

Only this time I wasn't gonna resist. I could feel him starting to come through me 'cause my stomach was starting to churn. My right hand was shakin' worse than ever. But I didn't care. I'd just relax and go along for the ride. Hell I needed his help if I was ever gonna figure the shit out. So I closed my eyes and let him materialize his past before my eyes.

I heard the sound of drumming, like some kind of African drumming. And I felt the sensation of being on a beach somewhere. The sand was hot, it was burning my feet. And the drumming just kept up, getting louder and louder as I walked down the beach.

I realized I was following a woman, a beautiful tanned woman wearing one of those skimpy g-string kind of bathing suits. She knew that I was following her, but she didn't look back. Then I realized that she was actually leading me somewhere. We passed through small knots of people on the beach. I didn't know anyone. Except for this woman, but for some reason, I had to pretend like I didn't know her.

She ducked into one of those grass huts on the beach. I was hot as hell and thirsty. But I knew that I had to wait there outside until she came out. The ocean was light blue, crystal clear. Not grey and churning like the Atlantic, but pearly blue. She came back out and motioned for me to follow her in. The place was small but smelled sweet, like tropical flowers. A thin athletic middle-aged guy was propped up against the wall. The woman left us alone. I knew this man. I'd known him for a long time.

"Sit down, Clive."

"Thanks."

"So are you enjoying your vacation?"

I shrugged. "It's been fine. Quiet."

"Is your wife here?"

"Yeah."

"Well that's why it's been quiet."

I wiped the sweat from my brow. It was hotter in here than on the beach. I just wanted to get this over with, small talk was meaningless to me. But he kept on talking. "The next time you come to Jamaica, come alone. I know people. Janie has friends."

I wanted to say I could get my own fuck if I wanted it, but I just smiled. "I'll have to do that."

He sipped on his drink, and then put it down. "When you told me you were going to be down here, I thought that it would be the perfect opportunity to talk away from New York and all the curious ears there."

"I'm always willing to talk, Jack."

"I've heard, shall we say on the street, not to coin a bad joke, but I've heard that you might be looking for some new business. In particular, business that's willing to go into some of the high-risk securities that pay so very well."

I didn't say anything. I'd learned years ago it was better not to affirm or deny with him.

"I have some clients who are looking for a small shop like yours to execute some trades for them. We'd do it at Bender, but they prefer the anonymity of a smaller place like yours."

"What kind of clients?"

"International."

"Businessmen?"

He drained his drink, then smiled. "You could say that."

"So I assume that these aren't the kind of clients that I can put on my open list."

"You do as you like. But if I were you, I'd keep these accounts confidential. On a need-to-know basis only."

"What kind of commissions are we talking about?"

"You pick a number that you think is fair, and they'll pay it."

This was beginning to sound better and better. "Any number?"

"Any number."

"So what if I were to say…oh thirty percent…would that be fair?" A smile was beginning to play at the corners of my mouth. I knew the game that he was playing.

"For the type of returns that they're looking for, it might be."

My throat was so dry I could barely swallow. I don't know if it was the heat or the prospect of the money that I could potentially make, but I needed a drink badly. "Do you have any more of that?" I pointed to his empty glass of rum.

He nodded. "So you want to talk a little longer?"

"Jack, you know I always enjoy talking to you…especially when it's about making money."

He untangled himself from the cushion where he was seated and ambled over to the doorway. "Janie, darling…get my friend a rum." He turned to me. "Straight on the rocks?"

"You remember my drink."

Janie appeared almost instantly with my drink, bending over me so closely that I could literally see her heart beating under her enormous breasts. Making me think of how one of her friends might not be all that bad after all.

Jack interrupted my thoughts. "So we were talking about making money."

"Right." I knocked back the rum gratefully, like liquid gold going down. "My favorite subject."

"That's why I like you, Clive. I could see the potential even when you were still in the training program at Bender."

I put down my drink. Suddenly, I wasn't thirsty anymore. Remembering those days. The first day of the training program, going with Red. A wave of sadness hit me every time I thought of him. His face was still clear as a bell in my mind.

Knock, knock.

"You ready?" I could hear Red's voice outside the door.

"Hold on, man." I yanked opened the door to my tiny apartment. Red was clean: suit, tie, hair cut, slicked back.

Seeing me half dressed, he threw up his hands. "You're not even ready, man. We're gonna be late. First day at Bender we gotta be on it, man."

"Don't you think I know? I can't get this damn thing tied."

"Is that all...here." He walked over to me and expertly tied the tie.

I looked at him in amazement. "Where'd you learn to do that so fast?"

He grinned in a weird kind of way. "Lots of funerals...my dad's business."

"Well it looks good." I checked myself out in the mirror. Not bad for somebody who never wore suits. "Ready to roll?"

He buttoned his jacket. "Bender & Grace, watch the hell out!"

I cradled my drink in my hand, feeling Red's presence drain away from my memory.

"How's your drink?" Jack knocked me back to the present.

The heat...the drums, I could still hear them in the distance. I swallowed the rest quickly. "Good. I always did like Island rum."

"So am I to assume that you're interested in pursuing these clients?"

"Yes, in theory, but you still haven't told me who they are."

He took out a small note pad and wrote something on it. He handed me the paper. I looked at it. "JANUARY 6, 1986" was written on it. "Call me on that date, not before, and not after, and I'll fill you in on the rest of the details."

I folded the paper in half and stuffed it in my shirt pocket. I was about to get up. I needed the sea air after an hour in that close hot bungalow, but he stopped me.

"Oh there is one more thing."

"Yes."

"My fee."

I should have known that Jack did nothing for free.

"What were you thinking about?"

"My standard cut for business referral."

"And that is?"

"Fifty percent."

I swallowed hard, but I knew with Jack it was better to never let him know what you're thinking. "Seems a little high."

"Not for this kind of business."

I knew he wanted an answer now, but I was determined to string him along as long as possible. "I'll let you know on January 6th."

He wasn't smiling as he said tersely, "No, Clive, that's not how it works. You'll let me know now, or we can just forget that we ran into each other down here."

The air was close and a fly was buzzing around my head. I wanted to scream, fuck you bastard…but I knew and Jack knew that I needed the business, and if I said no, he'd just go someplace else. There were plenty of small boutiques like mine on Wall Street ready to suck up the business if I so much as sneezed the wrong way. "It's a deal. Fifty percent."

He smiled the way he always did when he'd won a major coup. "Good, then I'll talk to you on the sixth." He stuck his hand out to shake my hand.

I nodded as I walked out the door, leaving him standing there. "I'll see you on the sixth. "

The clouds parted and the faces disappeared. I felt tired and weak, the way I always did after Clive had come through me, but this time I was getting key information I needed to piece the crazy jigsaw puzzle of this case together.

I took out my pen, smiling. January 6, 1986. Now I knew what that meant. But I still didn't know exactly who these mysterious clients were. I jotted down all the information that I did have...International...European? Arab? Asian? could be just about anybody who didn't want their money traced, arms dealers, drug kingpins, smuggling, high tech pirating, shit the list was so long of likely criminal types I could be writing from now to kingdom come...Jack...a top cat at Bender & Grace, somebody Clive had worked for. That should be easy enough to trace. I pulled out the plane phone in front of me, slipped in my credit card and dialed.

"Yeah...it's Greene, put Scoffo on...Scoffo...yeah I'm on the plane...right anyway I don't have time to chat...but I got another lead in the January case...find out everything you can on a guy named Jack, a partner or some kind of bigwig at Bender & Grace. Yeah, I should be back tomorrow if everything goes as planned." I was about to hang up when I thought of something else. "Did you ever find out the deal on that guy Sean Callahan?"

I heard him on the other end shuffling some papers. "Yeah I did...Gimme a sec...Okay here it is...Sean Callahan... He was the mob's bag guy in Boston for years. Died about fifteen years ago, a couple of months after his only son got killed on the street in '75, case was never solved, but by all indications it was a mob hit. And get this, the only witness to the hit was your boy...Clive January."

I nodded my head, remembering the vision...Red's comment about his father's business made sense now. "Thanks, Scoffo...I'll talk to you tomorrow." I settled back in my seat, reviewing all the information in my head. This Jack guy at Bender & Grace, Andy Haven, Laurel Davenport, still some question about the wife. The list was starting to shape up, and as far as I was concerned, I was anything but sure of how it was going to turn out, or even if I'd have enough concrete suspects to show the captain before he shuttled me off the case.

But one thing was sure, I couldn't let Laurel slip out of my hands again. This time she was going back with me.

CHAPTER TWENTY-SEVEN

Laurel

Everything on my body ached: my legs, my arms, my back, but most of all my soul. A dark pit where my soul had been and now it was empty. I was running, but I didn't know where or for how long I could keep it up. Trees were around me. Safety was in the woods; no inquisitive faces, matching mine with the bad photocopy floating around the entire country it seemed.

For some reason I was heading south as far down as I could go. In my heart I knew that I was trying to get to Hendersonville. In some sad sort of way, I felt that if I could get back to where it started, I could erase the inevitability of what had happened.

I was stumbling forward toward a light, hoping that whomever lived out this far wouldn't know my face, wouldn't be able to send me back. I walked hesitantly up to the small trailer. I could hear a television blaring through the tin walls. Inside an old man was eating out of a rusty can of beans. Hunger collapsed my stomach, even the hard moldy beans looked tempting.

Standing at the slimy window of a broken down trailer, envying an old man eating out of a can of beans, I knew that I had truly fallen, and any vestiges of dignity that I had at one time, had seeped away like Clive's dark blood.

A dog came racing out of the woods toward me, yipping furiously.

"Who's that?" The old man turned down the TV and put his can down suspiciously and grabbed a shotgun.

I tried to run, but I was paralyzed by fright, or with hunger. I just stood there as the dog snapped at my worn shoes.

The door swung open, and the old man shoved a shotgun in my face.

I wished that he'd pull the trigger and relieve me from this misery.

"Who the hell is you?"

No sounds would come out of me, and I just dropped down at his feet, all the life gone from my body.

Detective Bob

"Okay, where did you last see her?"

The good old boy, 'cause I'll be damned if that's not just what he looked like, something out of *Smokey and the Bandit*, anyway, he answered in that broad drawl, "My deputy said somebody saw a black woman meeting your description heading over by Yawling's end."

"How far is that?"

"Oh not too far."

"Well what exactly is not too far?"

The cop took off his glasses, blew off a speck of dust and put them back on. "Oh, not too far…'bout two or three miles."

I couldn't believe we were sitting here talking when my prime suspect was only two miles away. These guys were as bad as the cops in New York. "Well let's go!"

"Now wait just a minute. It's more than a notion to go knocking around in those woods. I think we better get the dogs. Otherwise, we'd split up and never find her."

"Well fine, then get the dogs if that's what you need."

He took out his walkie-talkie. "Yeah…Jim. It's the sheriff…Get the dogs out by Yawling's end. I'll meet you there in about ten minutes…Right, ten-four."

"Will he be able to get there in time?"

He got in the car, calling back over his shoulder, "Now why would I have told him to meet me there in ten minutes if I didn't think that he could get there?"

What could I say? Maybe he just sounded dumb.

Laurel

The man shoved the gun barrel in my face. Hissing angrily. "You get away from here. I don't know who you is, or why you is here...but get away from my place." He nudged me with the tip of the gun. "Go on. I ain't got all day. Go on!"

And I ran and ran...stumbling over twigs and leaves. Something was guiding me in a crazy quilt kind of pattern through the trees. I heard voices and I kept running. I could hear water rushing, maybe a stream, in the distance. Jagged rocks were pushing through the paper thin soles of my shoes, and I knew that my feet must be bleeding, but I had to keep running. Something was pushing me, whispering in my ear an invisible chorus...*Run, run...Faster. Run!*

Detective Bob

"Okay, let the dogs out here."

I watched as two bloodhounds bounded out of the truck, howling and slobbering in anticipation. Reminded me of some old movie about the South where angry dogs pursued some fugitive from justice through the woods, and then tore him to shreds.

"They won't hurt her, will they?"

The sheriff looked at me like I was totally fuckin' crazy. "Not these dogs. Naw, they's trained to track, that's all. Once they pick up the scent and find her, they'll pin her in and howl 'til we get there." He tossed a piece of trash on the ground. "They only attack if they're provoked. You know what I mean? You got that scarf of hers?"

I nodded and tossed him a light blue silk scarf that the local police had picked up at the last place where she was living. He grabbed the scarf, and then ducked back in the truck real fast, picking up the walkie talkie. "Yeah this is the sheriff. We're letting the dogs out now…Yeah I'll let you know when we get her…ten-four." He turned back to the dogs waving the scarf under their noses. They sniffed it eagerly, straining at their leashes. "Okay, now Gooone!" Free from their restraints, they blazed out into the woods.

Laurel

I could hear dogs now, sending vicious sounds into the air. My heart was beating so hard I thought that it would explode in my ears. And it seemed that no matter how fast I ran, the sound of the dogs got closer and closer. I could hear the crunching of leaves and dirt being pounded under by their feet. Closer…Closer…I wanted to cry and scream and yell, but I couldn't. I could only run.

Detective Bob

"Should we go out there?" I was anxious, this was taking longer than I thought it would, but the sheriff didn't seem to be the least bit bothered.

"Jus' relax okay. We'll know when they find her. We'll—"

A shrieking sound from the woods cut him off. The sheriff grabbed his gun. "C'mon, they found her!"

We ran through the woods, dodging trees, fallen logs, following the sounds coming from the dogs. Then, out of nowhere, the sounds stopped and there was only a whimpering.

Laurel

I knew that they were going to lunge at me, sucking the flesh from my bones, with mouths dripping with dirty foam and bloody teeth. A sweeping of wind came between the trees and a vague vapor descended around me. Through the mist I saw his eyes: dark, searching, protecting. The dogs had stopped yelping. They saw him, too. Now they backed away from me…whimpering, whining as he got closer to them, covering me in his strength.

Rivers of tears bathed my face, and I could feel his kiss, covering my lips. The wind swept around us, whipping up leaves and branches and sticks and pushing the dogs further and further away. Clive stood between me and them like a shield of love that nothing could penetrate. As he got closer to me the wind became stronger until it felt like the Furies had been unleashed, eating away at the dogs, lashing them with rocks and sticks until they ran shooting back into the woods.

Detective Bob

The dogs dashed back to us, trembling, whimpering. The sheriff looked stunned. "What the hell?" The dogs circled around his feet, panting tongues hanging out.

"What happened?" I asked.

"I don't know. They musta picked up her scent, 'cause we heard 'em but…Shit, I don't know."

He knelt down and tried to pull the leader back toward the woods. "C'mon, Zeus. Let's go." The dog howled, planting his feet firmly in the dirt and refusing to budge. The sheriff scratched his head in amazement.

"Now ain't that the damndest. I never in all my years seen dogs acting like that."

I couldn't believe what I was hearing. "What the fuck are you saying? They lost her!"

He turned back to me pissed. "I don't know what the hell happened in there. All I know is that they ain't going back in those woods!"

"So then radio back. Get a chopper or something. She's in there, on foot. She can't be far!"

I paced around angrily. I couldn't believe this was happening. So close, and then slipping away again.

The sheriff pulled his walkie talkie out of his belt quickly. "Yeah…something happened. I don't know what, but get a bird over here fast. She's disappeared again…yeah, I don't know what the hell happened with the dogs."

Laurel

He was guiding me deeper into the woods. I could hear rushing waters. A stream ran past me. He pushed me toward the water, and I knew that he wanted me to cross the stream. I was afraid of deep holes, of being swept down to a hell worse than what I was in now, but I also knew that he was there and that he'd protect me. I waded in up to my waist. Then to my shoulders. Then I couldn't feel the bottom anymore. He was lifting me up, carrying me across the water. I started choking. Water was seeping into my nose and my mouth, but he kept pushing me closer and closer to the other side.

I fell on the bank and crawled my way up to the other side. Then I saw why he'd been pushing me. An abandoned trailer. I yanked open the rusted door and fell on the floor. Above me I heard the sound of a helicopter, clipping low-hanging trees. I froze.

Detective Bob

I was trying to shout over the sound of the chopper. "What about over there, the other side of that stream? Looks like some kind of trailer or something over there."

The sheriff took out his binoculars. "I don't see nothin' in there."

I grabbed the binoculars from him, squinting hard to see if I could see anything moving through the craters of blown out windows in the trailer.

The sheriff nudged the pilot. "Try to the south of here, over by the bend. My guess is that's where she'd be, trying to get to the highway."

"I think we should go down over there by that trailer!" I shouted.

"We can't get down there. It's not flat enough. Besides, she'd a had to go across that stream, and believe me, there's no way in hell she'd get across there. The current woulda pulled her under. That's real treacherous. Looks easy, but every year we lose a coupla people to those waters. Especially 'round this time of year. They get pulled under in the holes and never come up."

He nudged the pilot again. "Go on over there…south."

Laurel

The sound of the helicopter was fading away in the distance. Slowly, I was beginning to breathe again. I was cold and soaked I noticed a filthy blanket in the corner. I crawled over and shook it out and wrapped it around myself. I couldn't keep my eyes open. I felt like Clive was gently closing my eyes, whispering *sleep* to me.

Detective Bob

"God Damn it!" I paced around the small room, every muscle tensed in anger. "I don't fuckin' believe this. She's within a couple of miles of you, you got dogs, helicopters, cars and she gets away *on foot!*"

The sheriff was quiet, letting me blow off steam, then he cleared his throat interjecting. "You know what I think? I think she's headed somewhere specific. It don't look like she's just running in general. Where's she from? Does she know anybody down in this area? 'Cause my guess is that if she does, that's where we'll find her. I've been doing this for a long time, and nobody gets away like that on foot, away from dogs, choppers and what not unless they been here before, or somebody's helping 'em that we don't know about."

Pissed off as I was, I had to admit that what he was saying did make sense. I sat down wearily, rummaging through my brain, trying to remember if there was anything in her past that would lead back to this place. All I could think of was that she was from Cleveland, and that she had knocked around for a while until she came to New York and basically started shacking up with Clive. But I wasn't gonna give that country hick the satisfaction of thinking that he might have hit on something.

"Just do me a favor and put road blocks up everywhere," I said. "Send her picture to every gas station, restaurant, police station, hotel, motel and any place else where she might be able to hide out within a hundred mile radius. I'll handle the theorizing."

"You sure you don't wanna stick around here for a few more days? With the kind of net we're throwing out, we oughta be able to get her with no problem."

"Like you did today?" I picked up my things and headed toward the door, turning back around saying, "I got other leads I gotta follow in New York, so just call me if you find her. "

The sheriff shrugged. All I could think about was how stupid I was gonna look when I went back empty handed after rushing off like the damn cavalry. I looked down at my pocket calendar, and crossed off another day. *Twenty-eight days and counting. Shit. I better focus on Andy Haven and that crowd before I really ended up with nothing.*

Laurel

The hot Alabama sun was drying out the last bits of dampness from my clothes. I was on a back road; almost no cars had passed me since I started out. Every time a car did pass me by, I turned my head and skirted as close to the woods as I could without looking too obvious. Afraid that one glance would give me away again.

When I awoke, I could still feel Clive's presence there, around me like a protective blanket. I wanted to talk to him, to ask his forgiveness, to thank him for saving my life, but I couldn't seem to get through. Every time I tried to penetrate the cloud, I would meet resistance. Until finally he was just gone.

But I wasn't sad, because I knew that his invisible presence was still guiding me. I looked down the road and saw a sign: HENDERSONVILLE, MISSISSIPPI, TWENTY MILES. I knew now where he was leading me. The same place I knew in my heart that I had to go to resolve the rest of my life. Where it started for us was where he and I could find the answers to the tragedy that was binding us together.

CHAPTER TWENTY-EIGHT

Detective Bob

Usually the midday hum of the New York charged me up. But today it seemed loud and overpowering, a clanging of noises all competing with each other to be heard. That's how I was feeling about this case. There were all these different voices trying to tell me different stories. Which ones were right? Which ones were wrong?

A loud *clap* threw me off for a second. It sounded too much like this morning when I walked in to claps and jeers, celebrating my fuck up. Something that cops do all the time, go after a suspect and lose 'em. No big deal, except if you're Bob Greene.

"Well lookie who's here, Greene, back from vacation?" The captain bit down on his unlit cigarette and glared at me, his narrow eyes gettin' yellow at the corners.

Scoffo jumped in, chuckling loudly. "Looks like he got a tan down there."

"I hope so, 'cause he sure didn't get his suspect!" Callahan chimed in like the red faced asshole he was.

But today for some reason it didn't bother me the way it usually would. The captain's sarcastic mouth, loud assed Scoffo and the rest: I just didn't care anymore. I was on a mission to put my own soul to rest, and after that, I didn't give a fuck, because I would've proved something to myself. That I was still a good cop and nobody could take that away from me.

The first thing that I was gonna do was dig a little more up on Laurel. 'cause much as I hated to admit it, that hick-assed sheriff was probably right about her being headed somewhere specific. I didn't remember her ever having lived in Alabama, maybe on one of those short term teaching jobs she'd had. I rummaged through her file again.

Adopted. Parents dead killed in a car crash in '77, taught for a while in Mississippi, South Carolina, Greensboro and some other little town, musta been when she met Hillgrove.

She did a stint in Atlanta and then up North to Boston, and then Queens where she lived with Hillgrove. But nothin' in Alabama. Classic profile of a drifter. No friends, no ties to anyone or anybody. Except Clive, in her case. The one constant in it all.

Except maybe there was someone she trusted, in one of these little shithole towns. Probably a man, 'cause from what I remember of her, she was a looker, the kind that made women hate her and men wanna jump through hoops just to get a piece. Maybe a neighbor…or maybe somebody she worked with, somebody she saw every day, who'd secretly had the hots for her. Or maybe not so secretly.

Made me think about a case I'd had 'bout ten years ago. It had stumped everybody. Then I cracked it, with a yearbook. The murderer had known the victim in high school, had written a dedication to her way back then, that had unlocked the whole thing. I made a note to have Scoffo dig up any of the yearbooks for each year that she was in any of the places teaching, and any school newspapers during that time. You never knew where a clue might show up.

I was thinking all of this as I walked through the doors at Bender & Grace. Everything was quiet, like people were walking around afraid to breathe too loud. Even the receptionist whispered as she sat stiffly behind a polished kidney shaped table. "Can I help you, sir?"

I said in my loudest voice, mainly to get a rise out of the sallow-faced assholes scurrying around me, "Yeah, I'm Detective Greene, NYPD to see Jack Simmons."

She raised her eyebrows in disapproval, and then whispered loudly as if to underline that *nobody* raised their voice above a whisper at Bender & Grace. "I'll see if he's available."

Jack Simmons looked pretty much the way he had in the vision, without the swimming trunks and the tan. But I'd never forget the narrow green eyes or the muscular face. He looked like he had to be at least sixty, but probably in better shape than I was ten years ago. He was gracious. In fact, he oozed it, like before you could become a partner in a place like this you had to be able to bullshit the shine off the walls.

The insincere fuck leaned back in his chair. "If there is anything, and I mean it, Detective, anything that I can do to help you in this case, you let me know. Clive January was one of my favorite people, and the thought that he had to go in that way still..." He stopped and looked in the distance. "Well, I just can't believe it."

I figured, okay. Now to take him for a little bit of a ride. "Actually, Mr. Simmons, there is something that you can do to help me."

"Name it, Detective...just name it."

Tell me the name of the clients that you referred to Clive. The ones that you were taking your fifty percent off the top from. I knew he wouldn't answer my real questions. "Were there any deals that you and Mr. January had worked on together in the past year or so, or any clients that you had referred to him...in say the same time period?"

He didn't miss a beat. I might as well have asked him what time it was. He pushed his intercom saying, "Sandy, bring me in the Wolco account work." Then turned back to me. "Yes as a matter of fact Mr. January's firm and Bender worked on a muni bond offering together. We were lead underwriter, and they were co-underwriter. It was a complicated deal, but I must say Clive handled it particularly well."

His secretary slipped in, handing him the file. "Thanks, Sandy. The case received quite a lot of press. In fact, it was heralded as one of the better examples of a majority and minority firm working together." He handed me the file. "These are some of the press clippings. Feel free to take them. I've got other copies."

He was slick, but I wasn't finished yet. "So this Wolco, that's the name right?"

"That's right."

"Well this Wolco, was it a US company or foreign?"

"Actually, they were a joint venture between an American company and an Arab venture. They were building a public works facility in Dallas. "

"Tell me exactly how a deal like this was put together. I guess what I mean is how did you divvy up the money, between you and Mr. January?"

A smile crept around the corners of his mouth as he casually played with a pencil. "Mr. January and I didn't 'divvy' anything up personally. All of the fees were paid directly to our respective firms."

"So you're telling me that you didn't get any money out of it personally?" I figured I'd play dumb, make him explain himself more, maybe trip on some of the facts.

"Of course we both made money on the deal. That is after all why we're in this business. I can't tell you how Mr. January's firm paid fees out, but my money was lumped in as part of my general compensation package."

"I see, so what if you had brought in a deal on your own where you were just doing something, on the side, not really as part of the firm, then I guess you'd get your fee directly?"

"In theory, yes, but in practice, I didn't have any deals that would fall in that category."

I looked at him real hard, trying to make him flinch, but like I said graciousness and total calm, that didn't crack.

"Did you do much work with international clients, Mr. Simmons?"

"Almost never, except for the Wolco deal that I just told you about. Since my specialty is bond work, I rarely deal with international companies."

I was about to jump in with another question, but he stopped me before I could. "Detective, excuse my rudeness. I should have offered you something to drink, can I get you some coffee or tea?"

"No, nothin' I'm fine."

He smiled, pushing his intercom. "Well I think I will have some tea...Sandy, could you bring me in a cup of mint tea? Thank you."He turned back to me. "Was there anything else I could help you with, Detective? As I said, I'd known Clive since he worked here in the training program. I had a lot of respect for that young man."

Sandy walked in and handed him the tea, quietly. I couldn't help thinking of that woman on the beach in the g-string bikini handing him the rum. A man that liked to be catered to. And then I hit it. His weakness. "There was one other thing, Mr. Simmons. This really doesn't have anything to do with Mr. January's case. It's something I was wondering on my own. I've got some of the top guys in from Washington, and the captain asked me to set up some entertainment for them. If you know what I mean. Something a little different from what they'd be able to get in DC…so I was wondering if you might know of some places. The kind that you might take real important clients to."

He smiled, almost conspiratorially. I finally seemed to have broken through. "Well actually, Detective, there are a number of places like that, but one of my favorites is this one." He quickly wrote down a name on a piece of paper…same kind of paper he'd written the date down on for Clive. He handed me the paper.

I looked at it: THE SAMURAI CLUB. He'd also jotted the address.

"They'll take care of you. It's very popular with some of the firm's Japanese clients, but believe me, they don't discriminate when it comes to making you feel welcome." He smiled that same smile that I'd seen in the vision, cruel, tinged with lust.

I folded the paper carefully and put it in my pocket. "Well thanks a lot, Mr. Simmons. I know the captain'll appreciate this."

"My pleasure."

He got up like he expected me to leave, but I wasn't finished with him yet. I still hadn't knocked him off balance. "I'm not finished yet, Mr. Simmons."

He leaned back in his chair, easily saying, "I wasn't assuming you had."

"I wondered if you had any personnel files or anything like that from when Mr. January worked here?"

"We should have his reviews. It was more than ten years ago that he was here, so they might have been thrown away. I'll have Sandy check on it." As if on cue, his intercom buzzed and his secretary came over on the line. "Mr. Simmons, your 3:00 is waiting."

"Thank you Sandy. Tell him I'll be there in a moment."

He swiveled back around to me. "Detective, I really have to go, but we can continue this a little later if you'd like."

"I'll call you if I need something else."

Outside of his office, I kept getting this feeling that there was more I could find out from him, something was telling me to go back up there...surprise them. The receptionist was as icy as ever as I leaned on her desk.

"Yes, Detective?"

"I left my notes in Mr. Simmons office. It'll just take a minute."

"You know the way."

"Yeah." I wandered down the hallway, looking carefully into the small cubicle like offices, trying to see beyond the obvious.

I turned the corner to Simmons' office. His secretary's back was to me and just as I was about to open my mouth, she stuck her head in Simmons' office saying, "Okay, Mr. Simmons, I've got Andy Haven on for you."

That's all I needed to hear. She shut the door. Before she could see me, I ducked back around the corner. I half expected Clive to whisper something in my ear, give me a clue, telling me where to go next, but he was quiet, not letting up off a thing.

"Did you get your notes?" The receptionist called out after me. I'd almost forgotten why I'd told her I'd gone back there.

"Yeah...right, I got 'em." But all I was thinking was what was Jack Simmons saying to Andy Haven not even five minutes after I'd left his office.

I was glad I'd busted the captain's ass about that tap on Haven's phone. At first he'd said flat out no. Said there was no way a judge would approve it. But I kept at him, 'til he got a lawyer in the DA's office to file the motion for me and now, bingo, I was about to sit down to what I hoped would be the evidence I needed to link Andy and possibly Jack directly to the murder.

I put on the headphones to listen to the tape of the afternoon's conversation. I fast forwarded through a bunch of bullshit, 'til I got to the point...Simmons' secretary on the line saying, "Hold on just a moment, Mr. Haven. He'll be right with you. "

A pause, I could hear Haven pacing in the background. He was on the speaker, but my guess is that he'd get off real quick once Simmons got on the line. "Andrew..."

"Jack...how are you?"

Just like I thought, I could hear Haven taking the speaker phone off as Simmons replied, "We need to wrap up a few things. Just some odds and ends."

Silence on the other end. I could hear Haven breathing hard, but he wasn't saying anything.

"Did you hear what I said?"

"Sorry, Jack, of course, right away...but—"

Simmons cut him off, he wasn't about to let Haven spill anything else. "I'll see you tomorrow. We can talk then." Again silence, from Haven. *Click*. Simmons had hung up.

Not exactly a road map, but it definitely confirmed that Haven and Simmons were in on something together. And my guess was that it had to do with those mystery accounts. Now if I could just figure the hell out what they were.

I looked down at the paper Simmons had given me. Samurai Club, 504 Oak. Definitely a beginning.

CHAPTER TWENTY-NINE

Detective Bob

Soft Japanese music was playing in the background. The place was dark. I could barely make out the outlines of Japanese businessmen sitting on cushions on the floor with tiny Geisha girl types hovering over them.

I wandered in and settled on a barstool.

"Can I help you?"

"Jack Daniels on the rocks, thanks."

Normally, I wouldn't drink on the job, but I needed a drink after the week I'd had.

The bartender sat the drink in front of me. "Here you are. Anything else?"

I took a sip. Sticking my forefinger in the glass licking off the Jack and pretended like I didn't hear his question. "Mainly Japanese come to this place?"

"No…well…yeah actually I guess most of our clients are Japanese, but we see a lot of American businessmen, too."

He fiddled with the bottles behind the bar. I continued talking in between slow gulps of my Jack. "I was just wondering, 'cause a friend of mine told me about this place. He said he used to come here a lot."

"Is he Japanese?"

"No…a black guy. Works around here. He used to tell me all kinds of things about this place."

The bartender broke into a grin. "Tall guy…right. Always dressed well. He'd usually come in with an older white gentleman. I remember. He always gave good tips. His name was something kind of different…"

"January."

"Yeah, that was it January." He dried some glasses. "I haven't seen him in a while."

"Yeah, he moved…great guy." I put my glass down coolly, trying not to look like I was digging for info. "I was supposed to have come with him, about a year ago. There was gonna be a group of us, some clients of his and the older guy and me. But I couldn't make it. "

I expected him to keep on talking easily, but just as he was about to answer me, someone from the back motioned him over. He ducked away quickly saying. "Be right back."

I drained the rest of my Jack, the place had started to get a little more crowded. I noticed that small groups of men were disappearing with one or more of the women into a back room. I smiled to myself. Those Geishas were your basic call girls with a few more clothes on.

"You were looking for someone?"

Startled, I turned around to the most expressionless face I'd ever seen: a thin Japanese man, dressed completely in black, with his dark hair slicked back.

"Yeah…a friend told me to come here."

"Well if you'd like an appointment with one of our ladies, I can make that for you. Otherwise, we don't encourage single gentleman alone at the bar. We're not that kind of place." The man kept staring at me. Still no expression on his face. "So if you don't mind leaving."

I was pissed that he'd blown what looked like a good lead. "Yeah, as a matter of fact, I do mind. I pulled out my badge, flashing it in his stony face.

He didn't flinch, just continued in a measured controlled voice. "Detective, if you have official business here, you can make an appointment to talk to the owner Mr. Sato in the morning. Otherwise, as I said, I'd appreciate it if you left."

I felt like blasting his head wide open, damn fuckin' foreigners. "Look, I don't know who the hell you are, but—"

Outta nowhere these two sumo wrestler looking types appeared and were about to grab me when the Japanese guy called 'em off, saying some garbage in Japanese.

I got right up in that guy's face. "I don't know how the hell they do it in Japan, but here, what you almost did was called assaulting a police officer. Something you and these overweight assholes can go to jail for."

"Detective, I apologize, but as I suggested, it would be better if you came back tomorrow."

"After I finish, talking to your bartender."

"He's gone for the day."

I looked around quickly, and sure enough he'd disappeared and my guess was probably not to be seen anytime soon.

"Feel free to look around, but I can guarantee you that he's left."

Shit. I cursed at myself. I fished in my pocket for a ten. Without looking at the guy I threw the cash on the bar saying. "For the drink." The night air felt good, I needed to clear my head. I couldn't remember when I'd blown a set up that completely. Losing my cool, showing my badge, practically broadcasting to the guy and everybody in there…hey I'm looking for something, you're under suspicion, better hide everything. Shit.

I was losing it. Every time I thought I'd made a little progress, back to square one again. About the only good thing to come out of that little fiasco was that I knew now that Clive had gone to the place with Simmons. And that more than likely the foreign clients were Japanese. That narrowed it down to about a million companies now. I took out my calendar. Twenty-six days left and still nothing. One suspect AWOL, another lead probably blown because I couldn't just be cool. Andy Haven…still a live one…but I had to make sure before I went off half-cocked at him that I knew what I was looking for, and I just didn't. I just didn't know shit.

The rumble of the train blotted out my thoughts. Sometimes the intensity of the noise was good. I couldn't talk. I couldn't think. I just sit while every jolt brought me closer to my bed.

I tossed some change to the drunk on the corner of my street. Normally I'da looked the other way. If I gave change to every bum in New York, I'd be broke in a day. But 'cause I was feeling sorry for myself, I was feeling sorry for him, too, so I tossed him a dollar.

Walking closer to my place, I noticed somebody sitting on the stoop. I couldn't see that well in the half-light, so it was a minute before I realized that it was her. Margie. "What are you doing here?"

She didn't move, just kinda smiled that half-smile of hers. "What happened to hello?"

I took out my key, avoiding her eyes. "Look, if you've come to tell me what a fuck up I am and how everybody thinks I'm blowing the case, I don't need it. 'Cause I already know, okay?"

I opened the door. I didn't close it behind me. I guess I was half hoping that she'd follow me in.

"Maybe, I should just leave."

I shrugged. I wasn't in the mood to beg today. "Do what you gotta do."

"Bob." She followed me into my apartment saying in a matter of fact voice, "Do you want to talk?"

I looked in the liquor cabinet. *Shit no more Jack.* "Not really."

"Okay, then I'll talk."She opened her bag and took out some papers. "I was doing some more looking at those files that weren't on Gray's list."

I think she expected me to respond. When I didn't, she just kept on. "I found one that seemed suspicious. Not because of what it did have, but what it didn't." She didn't wait for me to ask what she was talking about. She just pulled out a file.

"Like look at this one. It has the name of the client, the stock that was traded, the dates, the brokers' names, commissions, everything. This is pretty much what all of them had…except for this one."She opened another file. "See this one has code numbers under each of the headings…name of client—504, stock traded—504, broker's name—504. Same numbers as the name of client. Now I'm not an expert on the stock market, but I do know from when I worked at Merrill that clients don't trade their own accounts. I mean if they were going to do that why come to a firm like January's and pay their commission?"

I didn't want to concede right away that she might be onto something. "Maybe it's just a new filing system?"

"Well then why wouldn't more than one of the files be listed like this?"

I was quiet for a minute. "Lemme see that again?" I looked at the number. 504. Why did it seem familiar? "You know what?"

"What?"

"I think I'm gonna check this out first thing tomorrow."

She smiled triumphantly. I put the file down on the table, turning to her saying, "One more thing."

"Yes…"

"You know you're not supposed to remove evidence from the station."She circled around me, whispering in my ear, "It's a copy."

Laughing, I shook my head, thinking of Margie sneaking the file out making a copy, and then sticking it in that suitcase of hers that she called a purse. "That's my girl."

"So I did good, Detective?"

I wanted to pull her to me, but I stopped myself, swallowing hard. "Yeah, you did real good. In fact, this is the second time you've pulled my ass out on this case." I sat down, staring at the spot on the rug where we spilled the bottle of wine that night years ago.

"So why are you doing all of this for me?"

She was silent. I got up and pulled her next to me on the couch. "Why don't you spend the night?"

She kinda edged away from me. "Bob…I don't…"she whispered.

"I'll sleep on the couch. You can have the bed."

I took her hand, wanting to kiss each of her perfect fingers, but I didn't. "It'd just be nice to have the company…you know…that's all."

The last thing I remember was her kissing me on the forehead as I closed my eyes on that lumpy-assed couch. Faces began coming to me. Clive's face and voices. I could hear someone talking to him, telling him that he couldn't do it anymore. He couldn't help me anymore. In my head I saw myself a few weeks ago. Sitting there naked from the waist up, lookin' at the doctor. Him asking me…

"Bob, how long have you had the stomach problems?"

"Oh I dunno. About a couple of weeks, maybe a month." The doctor raised one eyebrow. I glanced over at him, my ass aching on the cold table I was sitting on. I hated doctors and hospitals and everything about 'em. Didn't have any use for 'em. But it'd gotten so the nausea was almost all the time, even after Clive left me, so I finally broke down and went in.

"And the hand tremors, when did they start?"

I lied. What could I say, ever since Clive January started takin' over my life my hand hadn't stopped shaking. "'Bout the same time, a month ago maybe."

"I see...well we better run some tests."

After I got the call to come back in, I was sittin' on that cold assed hard table again.

"Bob, we don't know exactly what's wrong. It's almost like your system is shutting down, your blood count is low, your lung capacity is compromised. What exactly is going on in your life?"

"Nothin', doc, just the usual stress of being a cop."

I don't think he bought it, but he gave me some pills. "Slow down, Bob, because whatever you're doing is eating you up inside."

Then the voices, Clive's voice, but I couldn't make out what he was saying, only somebody else saying, "He's on his own...he has to be...it's got to be that way now."

I woke up in a cold sweat. The room was empty. I could hear Margie turning over in the bedroom. The bed squeaked as she shifted position. The voices still rung in my head. Saying you can't help him. I had felt like the last time Clive had come in that somehow he wasn't as strong as he'd been. Something was pulling him away from me. He was fighting, fighting to come through me, to guide me, but a force stronger than his will was blocking him. I shivered, pulling the blanket around my shoulders. Something or somebody was trying to save me, the tremors, the nausea, what the doctor said was happening to me. But knowing the truth was the only thing that could really save both of us.

Margie was gone by the time I got up. I rolled off the couch, aching everywhere, still trying to make sense of the dream I'd had. I stumbled into the kitchen. She'd left me a pot of hot coffee and a note…WAKE UP SLEEPY HEAD, MARGIE…and two little hearts. I smiled, but my mind was on Clive. I poured a mug for myself and stared out the window.

Clive

bob greene!!!!!!!!! i know i'm shouting…before my words would have blasted through your head…but now…only silence…the god awful silence i've been in since i was pushed here to this place, this netherworld. i feel like i'm tunneling deeper into the darkness. i'm fighting it. i can still see shooting rays of light, but with every breath they're getting further and further away.

so this is hell.

why won't they let me help you. i can see you. i'm around you, but you don't see or hear me anymore. the voices again…telling me that my time is up…you have to do it now, and if you don't, the force that i'm fighting will pull me all the way down, and i'll never have peace. but neither will you, bob greene. bob greene!

I jumped. For a minute, I thought I heard somebody calling my name. I looked into the coffee cup, half expecting to see Clive's face smiling up at me. But only dank, slightly cold coffee. I sighed, scratching my day-old stubble and walking into the bathroom.

CHAPTER THIRTY

Laurel

This was Hendersonville. I couldn't believe what I was seeing. Track homes and malls. The sleepy little town of the sixties was gone, completely gone. Even the street names were different. I wanted to stop and ask someone what had happened to the place where it all started for me. But I was afraid: afraid my face would be known again, afraid of running through woods and icy cold waters, afraid of everything because I knew that he wasn't here anymore. It's as if Clive put his protective covering around me long enough for me to arrive in Hendersonville, and then just as quickly as he came, withdrew. I was aware of it when his energy started leaving me, and now I knew that he was gone completely.

I looked around the unfamiliar town. Why was I here, to complete the shame and disgrace by being apprehended where I had first seduced him? I didn't know. I pulled a handful of bills from my pocket. I was now officially a thief as well as a fugitive. I'd slipped into a gas station bathroom on the way and helped myself to the money in the woman's purse that she'd left on the sink while she was in the stall. But at least now I could eat.

I devoured the muffin I'd surreptitiously bought at the drugstore and gulped down the milk. I was about to inhale the bag of Fritos when I heard, "Laurel…Laurel Davenport?"

I looked up guiltily into the smiling eyes of Ralph Warner, my old boss. Before I could say anything, he lifted me up in the biggest and most suffocating bear hug I'd had in years. His chestnut brown face broke into ridges of smiles. His stomach, which toppled over the front of his worn leather belt, squeezed into my chest. He laughed like he'd just found his long lost best friend. "I can't believe it. After all these years…what brings you back here?"

I couldn't exactly say that I was wanted for the murder of one of his students. I smiled. "I wanted to see the old town."

He grinned. "Pretty different huh?"

"Completely."

"Hurricane Betty pretty much destroyed everything in 1981. I'm surprised you didn't hear about it; we were on Ted Koppel."

I couldn't even remember 1981. I was in New York, with Clive, but that's all I remembered.

"The federal disaster relief rebuilt the whole thing from the ground up." He beamed as if he'd personally laid every new brick. He put his arm around my shoulder. "Now I'm just gonna insist that you come on over for dinner…that is if you're not leaving right away?"

"No…no…not at all." Out of the corner of my eye I could see a police car heading up the street. I quickly lowered my head, hoping that they wouldn't see me. The car stopped for a minute. I couldn't tell if the policeman was looking at me or not, but then it rolled back up the street.

"We can walk. It's not far. So tell me what you been doing with yourself?"

I couldn't speak, because there in front of me was the place I'd first seen Clive. Peeling away the years, leaning against that tree. Even with the new homes and the unfamiliar streets, I'd never forget that place. Three trees that had grown up so much against each other that there was a small space, between them. He's sitting there and now I don't know if it's now or then, but I see him just the way I first saw him.

"You're new here?" Startled I looked up into dark eyes, the kind of eyes that revealed no secrets. He was tall and fine, dark hair, medium brown skin, wispy mustache, maybe Hendersonville would be more fun than I thought.

He smiled at me, a kind of sexy inviting smile. I caught the look, and smiled back. "Yes, as a matter of fact, I am. I just got in town a week ago."

He got up and leaned toward me. "I'm Clive."

"Well, hello. I'm Laurel. "

"Where are you from, Laurel?" His words were light and teasing, but his eyes betrayed nothing.

"Oh here and there." I could tell he was the type that didn't like things too easy.

"Okay, Miss here and there, where're you headed now?"

I smiled teasingly. "To English class…"

"Well so am I. I got the new teacher, Davenport."

I leaned against the tree. I was tempted to see how far he'd go, but this was my first week here, so I should at least try and start out on the right foot. "Now that really is a coincidence, because I *am* Miss Davenport."

"Well here we are."

Ralph Warner's voice jolted me back to reality. And, suddenly, Clive was gone. The past was the past and I was standing in front of a large white suburban kind of house, wishing more than anything that I could be Miss Davenport again and Clive would just…be here.

CHAPTER THIRTY-ONE

Detective Bob

"Someone took it, I'm telling you, Bob, somebody took it."

I looked at Margie like she'd fuckin' lost it. "Margie, nobody comes in a police file room and takes a file. That's in the movies. This is real life, okay. If you put it back, then it's got to be there."

"I did. I came in, took the file, made a copy, and then put it back. So if I could take it like that, then somebody else could, too."

Margie was sitting in the room, surrounded by the files from Clive's firm. She had that stubborn look on her face that made me know that there was no way she was changing her mind.

"Look, it probably just got put in another one of these piles."

She stood up, hands on her hip, and raised one brow. "Bob, I have looked through every file in this room. It is just not here. That means that somebody took it."

I threw up my hands and paced around the room, thinking how could a file just disappear? Who would take it? This had to be a coincidence. Had to be. "Well, you've got the copy, right?"

She pulled it out of her purse and handed it to me.

"Let's not worry about it anymore." I took the copy and sat down, flipping through it. Just like she said, numbers where names should have been, and the same numbers—504. Numbers that meant something.

"So what do you think?"

I shrugged my shoulders. "I don't know. It's some kind of code, but I don't have a clue for what."I kept thinking that if I thought hard enough, Clive would float in my brain, merging his thoughts into mine, but nothing. I knew that the voices had been right. Something was preventing him from breaking through. *Shit. Just when I really needed him.*

I stuck my hands in my pocket angrily. My fingers scraped against a piece of paper. I crumpled it up and was about to toss it when something caught my eye. 50...I uncrumpled it and smoothed it out...SAMURAI CLUB 504 Oak Street...

"Oh shit! I was there."

Margie looked up.

"I was there. I was at 504!"

"What are you talking about?"

"That Geisha club that Simmons sent me to—that's 504!!"

My legs were tingling. They always felt like that when I was about to crack a big one. I was gonna pin that owner down and squeeze every bit of information out of him, no matter what it took. This was the first live lead I'd had since Laurel slipped outta my hands. The picture was starting to crystallize in my head. Simmons and January probably met at the Samurai Club to set their deal up, and the clients were whoever was behind the Samurai Club. From what I saw the other day, I'd guess that they were probably laundering the money from their prostitution ring there and dabbling in the stock market. But why kill Clive? What did he know that landed him dead??

Those thoughts were tumbling around in my head as I pulled up in front of the club. Suddenly, I saw cops everywhere, swarming the place. Somebody had just plastered a big sign on the door: CLOSED.

I ran up to a cop, yelling, "Detective Greene, NYPD. What's going on here?"

He barely gave me a glance as he said, "Vice is closing the place down."

"Vice!"

I couldn't believe what I was hearing.

"Why now?"

He spit across the street nonchalantly. "Hell if I know."

"Fuck! Did they take the owner out?"

"Everybody'd split by the time we got here. Somebody must've tipped em off, 'cause the place was dead empty when we got here."

I wandered away from the scene in a daze. But now new thoughts were starting to intrude on my mind. I knew that this was no coincidence, the missing file, and now the place that was probably the key to this case, closed down like this. I knew damn well that vice had known about this shit hole before. *Why now*...I kept asking myself, and the same answer kept coming back. *It's no coincidence*. Then I knew almost instinctively that my little visit to the place is probably what had started the whole ball rolling. It was after that that the file disappeared, and not twenty-four hours later that the damn thing was closed down and the owner conveniently skipped town.

Somebody high up didn't want me to get to the bottom of this.

The captain's voice looped around my brain. "People...want this case wrapped up and you're not moving fast enough for them"

"What people?"

"People...Just people..."

People...what people...people high up enough to make sure that certain things didn't get solved...damn those people. Damn them.

I was still running over the day's events in my mind as I collapsed on my couch. For a hot second, I'd thought about going back into the station, but I was too pissed and drained to deal with those assholes. The light on my answering machine blinked. I pushed play.

"Well it looks like you galloped off into the sunset again. Call me when you resurface. You know who it is."

Shit. Margie. I'd basically left her hanging, and her gut had been better than mine on this thing. I leaned back on my couch and tried to relax. But my mind kept racing back and forth: in the chopper, back at the station, Clive's office, Andy Haven. It was all starting to blur. And on top of it, I noticed that the roof musta been leaking while I was away, cause there was a dark brown spot on the ceiling where the water had dried. *Shit, I gotta get outta this dump.* But how long had I been saying that? Just another broken promise to myself. How many of those did I have?

For some reason I couldn't take my eyes off that spot. It reminded me of something. Something I'd seen before. It was almost square, and about three by four inches. That spot underneath Clive's desk, that discolored spot, was about the same size. Then I knew what it was. And I knew who else would know, too. *Shit, why didn't I think of this sooner?* I scrounged through my pockets and found the number and dialed quickly. *Shit, be home, be home.*

"Hello."

It was her. I knew that voice. "I want the tapes, Yolanda. This is Detective Greene." Silence. "Yolanda, I know you've got 'em, so don't bullshit me okay. A man is dead, and I want those tapes. Now!"

I could hear her breathing heavily on the other end of the line, probably wondering how she'd get out of it—lie or come clean. I was betting that she'd come clean. She had to. *Click.*

Fuck! I slammed the phone down. She'd hung up on me. I pushed re-dial. The line rang busy. *Damn her!* I knew my hunch had been right. That discolored spot under the desk, just the size of a micro-cassette recorder, the nail holes for the brackets holding it in place. And Yolanda Calloway, Clive's secretary, the one who'd thought Andy Haven had done it to begin with. Yolanda, the one who kept Clive's secrets, the one in charge of it all. All the conversations, taped, and I bet filed neatly and labeled for the day that he'd need them, except that now he was dead, and I needed those tapes or my ass was dead in the water on this case.

I was about to pick up the receiver and call her back when the phone rang. I picked it up. "Yeah."

"It's Yolanda Calloway."

Be cool. Just be cool. You can't afford to lose her.

"Detective, I need to see you…I'll meet you by the deli on the corner of Fulton, right by the number two train stop, at six." *Click.* She'd hung up again.

I glanced at my watch. 5:45. *Shit!* I had to make it back to Wall Street from Brooklyn in fifteen minutes. *Damn!* I raced out to the car. Digging under the seat and sticking the siren on the hood, flying over the bridge and through the streets—6:05. I was late, but I was hoping she'd wait. She had to wait. I zipped down the street, dodging pedestrians and street vendors, my stomach was turning over, acid seeping into the corners of my gut. Sometimes I wished that everybody in Manhattan could just stay home for once.

A potbellied delivery truck suddenly stopped in front of me, the driver hopping out for no apparent reason. I stuck my head out the door. "Hey! What the fuck is your problem? Get the hell out of the way!"

He scratched his head and wandered back to the truck. I slammed my hand down on the steering wheel. I was only a few blocks away and now this shit. The truck driver slowly started his truck. The engine wasn't turning over. I couldn't believe it.

"Start the damn thing!"

"I'm trying!" he yelled back.

I revved up my motor and skirted across the sidewalk, my wheels careening over the side. Then I saw her. She was heading for the subway, looking at her watch. I slammed on the brakes and left the car in the middle of the street, the siren still blasting. "Yolanda!"

She'd already disappeared down the stairs. I jumped down the steps. The place was thick with people. I could see her smashed up against a group of suits. In the distance I could hear the subway screeching forward. She was being propelled forward by the crowd.

"Yolanda!"

She looked back, but she didn't see me. Somehow I managed to worm my way forward knocking over people. The subway doors snapped open. She was pushing forward. I reached out and grabbed her coat. "Yolanda, wait!" I snatched her back to me just as the crowd spilled into the train.

I was panting, being badly out of shape definitely didn't help. "Why didn't you wait?"

She looked scared as she backed away from me. "I…I did…but I thought…" She thrust a large stiff manila envelope in my hand, motioning me over away from the crowd. "The last three months or so, Mr. January started taping all of the conversations in his office. He asked me to keep them for him. So that if anything happened. "Her eyes had dark circles under them.

I screamed over the noise of the approaching train. "Did anybody else know about this?" The deafening noise of the train blotted out her answer, and then she just started running, pushing her way through the crowd and wiggling into the open doors. I tried to follow her, but it was like the crowd was conspiring against me, closing behind her. The train pulled off, and the last thing I remember seeing was her face pressed against the graffiti-streaked glass.

I ripped open the top of the envelope. There were ten tapes, each neatly labeled: CLIVE JANUARY PERSONAL FILE, and dates. Whoever was upstairs pulling the strings on this whole thing had finally tossed me a "gimme." At least I hoped 'cause time was running out for me and Clive.

I closed the blinds to my apartment. Shutting out the pale street-lights. After the weird shit that was happening at the station with missing files and key witnesses disappearing, I figured that I'd listen to these tapes at home, where at least I knew nobody would get them. I pushed the tape on.

"Andy, I don't think you understand. This is my business, and I can do whatever the fuck I want to with it. So if I want to liquidate, and I'm not saying that I plan to, you ain't got shit to say. You don't own *one share* of stock, so I don't even know why we're having this discussion!"

I stopped the tape for a minute, taking out my notes, flipping quickly to the day that I questioned Haven. When I'd asked him if January ever thought about selling the business, he'd answered "No…Never."

When I'd asked if January had sold the company if he could have just cashed out his stock, he'd answered, "Yes…basically."

Basically my ass! From what I'd just heard, there was no stock. That's why Haven was so hyped about him not selling the business. He woulda been out on his ass. I pushed the tape back on.

Haven's whiny voice filled my room. "I'm a part of this organization. I have a right to know what your plans are. This is my future you're talking about!"

I could hear Clive pushing a chair against the desk. I could imagine him looking at Andy with that half amused, half taunting look."Well you know what? I never promised you anything when I asked you to come work for me."

The tape ran out. I grabbed the last one. A few weeks later by the date. I jammed it in the machine. Haven's voice again. "Are you sure we should do this, Clive?"

"You're suggesting that I say no to potential commissions like these? Are you outta your fuckin' mind?"

"No it's just that with Jack we wouldn't want to disappoint him if we couldn't really service the accounts like he wanted them and…"

"And what?"

"Well, if they want to accumulate a position in those companies, confidentially and quickly, I don't know if we've got the manpower to execute that many trades."

"Since when do you get cold feet about making money?"

"I'm not. It's just that it's risky. If the SEC traces the trades…I just think that I should be compensated for the risk. I'm the one making the trades. It's me they'll go after. I think that my compensation package should change." I heard Haven shifting in his chair.

"I think that I should have some ownership in the company."

"Oh you do?"

"Yes. I do."

"And how long have you been working here Andy, two years? Where the *hell* were you ten years ago when I was working out of a shit hole office, barely making it…huh? You were sitting up at Morgan pulling down half a mil. Now that I've made something, you want a piece of *my* business! I don't think so."

"Well then I'm resigning."

I heard Clive's laugh, deep and guttural, filling the room. "Go right ahead. If you can find someplace that'll take you. You've been to every shop worth anything on the street. They all took you and they all let you go. So where are you gonna find someplace that'll pay you what I'm paying you? But if you can, go for it. Don't let me stop you."

I could sense Haven's anger through the silence. The tape stopped. I sat back thinking. It was all here…Haven afraid of losing his job…his frustration and anger at Clive—that could make a man kill. It wouldn't be the first time. Haven wasn't the type to do his own work.

He'd have to get somebody else to take the fall with him. Jack? Too smart…maybe these mystery clients…make them think it was in their best interest to do it. But just so Haven could keep his job. Had to be something else. A piece, and a big piece, was missing. I knew I couldn't let anybody else at the station know I was nosing around trying to find out. And the only person who knew was Laurel. I had to find out. I just had to.

I leaned back in the chair. Trying to see Clive's face in my mind. He knew where she was. *Damn it, Clive if you want me to find out…tell me…We've got ten days.* That's all ten days. I tried to relax, but I couldn't. Maybe it was the noise outside. I could hear teenagers, cursing, drinking beer.

Normally, I would've just turned up the TV, but shit, enough was enough…a man needed some peace in his own home, so I stuck my head out the window yelling, "Shut the hell up!"

"Yeah right, asshole!"

"It's a free country, old man!"

Something snapped in me. I grabbed my badge and stuck my gun in my pants. I was taking those punks in. They'd see who was the old man. As I galloped down the stairs, all I could think was how pissed and frustrated I was at everything. I pushed open the front door, grabbing my .45. I was about to yell out when something stopped me.

I don't know what it was, but I know heard a voice whisper, "Don't do it, Bob." Suddenly, I saw my life right in front of me.

I saw myself rushing out the door toward those kids, flashing my badge and them laughing. I saw one of 'em grabbing something, another one shoving me. I felt the rage in me as I saw myself reach for my gun and then shoot, blood running out from one of the kids' chest. I saw the kid turn and curse at me and try and stumble away, with his back to me. I saw myself shoot him again and again, until the kid was nothing but a bloody heap in front of me. I remembered my partner and internal affairs, only this time I was the shooter. This time I was the one they'd be glad to lock up and throw away the key—for good.

The rest of my life ran in front of me. Everything that had been, and everything that could be, the good things and the bad, and how I'd hit brick wall after brick wall and this one thing, one stupid assed thing could have been the final one. My hands were wet and shaking, and my heart was beating fast as I shoved my gun back in my pants. I knew I'd come just this close to blowing those kids away and blowing whatever was left of my future away with them. I leaned against the wall, sweat was pouring off me. Shit, is this what I'd come to? Ready to fuck up everything for a bunch of high school kids?

I stumbled back up to my apartment. I didn't even hear their voices cursing and laughing at me, 'cause all I could think was how I'd almost thrown it all away for a bunch of punk kids. I wondered who or what it was that'd stopped me. Was it Clive? Somehow, I didn't think so, 'cause it seemed like whatever was keeping him from me was too strong for him to break through.

For just a second I saw a face, then it was gone. But it wasn't Clive's face. I knew who it was. A face I'd never seen, but I knew just the same.

Who'd never seen me, but who knew me just the same. I knew it was my grandfather, the man who'd died with his principles. He'd stopped me. I tried to say something, to thank him, but he was gone. Just like that.

Slumping in a chair, I tried to get my breathing back to normal. My legs felt weak. Thoughts of Clive and the case started to creep back in my head. I thought of Laurel dodging cops like a pro all over the country, nothin' but a schoolteacher making New York's finest look like shit.

Nothin' but a schoolteacher—then I remembered the yearbooks. Nothin' but a schoolteacher, but maybe she'd gone back to one of those places where she'd been, off the beaten path, someplace obscure and safe. I propped myself up. Things were starting to come together in my head.

I rummaged around in the pile of shit that I'd brought from the station. I didn't trust anybody now, so I'd started carting everything home with me. I hadn't looked at half the stuff, including the yearbooks 'cause I'd been too busy trying to chase after other clues.

Now maybe, just maybe...There was a bunch of 'em. She damn sure couldn't keep a job. Fayettville High, I flipped through. She wasn't even in this one. Probably hadn't been there long enough. I cracked open a couple of others. Again, she wasn't in either of 'em. Then I saw it, Hendersonville High, where had I seen that name before—Hendersonville. I opened the book and scooted through the pages.

I almost closed it, when I saw it. Her face staring out just as clear as day—Miss Laurel Davenport and her English class. Then I saw the other face. I could barely recognize it underneath all the hair, but I knew those eyes. My finger raced to the names at the bottom of the page. There it was—Clive January, high school senior. I smiled.

She was going back there. They always go back to where it started, twenty years as a cop, and I never saw it fail. They always go back. There was probably somebody still down there, some old friend, probably somebody she worked with that she figured she could hole up with for a few days 'til she decided where to go next. I pulled out my atlas. Hendersonville —about twenty miles from where I'd lost her.

I picked up the phone and dialed quickly. "Yeah, it's Greene…fax a picture of Laurel Davenport to the cops in Hendersonville, Mississippi. Tell 'em she's there and to pick her up and hold her. Also see if any teachers, or anybody that worked at Hendersonville High in 1969 is still there. If there is, have the cops bring 'em in for questioning. Tell 'em I'm on my way down on the next plane."

CHAPTER THIRTY-TWO

Laurel

Ralph Warner hadn't stopped talking since I got there. And I hadn't stopped thinking of Clive. It was as if his presence was hovering just beyond where I could find him, trapped in some dark pocket of eternity, fighting to get out and move beyond where he was now. For some reason I knew that I had the key to his freedom.

"Have some more roast beef."

I jumped, almost knocking over my water glass. Ralph was holding out a plate layered with thick slabs of brown grey meat, dribbling with pale pink blood.

"Oh...thank you. It's delicious." I guiltily took a slice, wondering how he'd feel when he found out that he was hiding a fugitive. I couldn't think about that now. He chatted on in between stuffing forkfuls of food in his mouth.

"You know I've just been running off at the mouth since you got here, and you haven't been able to get a word in edgewise. I guess that since my wife died, I'm so used to being alone in this big place that when I get a visitor, I just don't know what to do. But I'm gonna shut up now and let you tell me all the great things I know you've been doing since you left here."

He helped himself to another generous spoonful of mashed potatoes. "One thing's for sure though...you haven't changed a bit. I mean not a bit, I would've known you anywhere."

Something in the way he said that made me uncomfortable, just for a moment. As if I knew that he wanted me and had always wanted me and perhaps this was his chance at last. As if he'd read my thoughts, he asked, "So where were you planning on staying tonight?"

I smiled weakly, sipping my iced tea nervously. "I hadn't planned to spend the night. I was just passing through for the day."

A big grin broke across his face. "Well you know you can stay here and get an early start in the morning. The next bus isn't out 'til tomorrow anyway."

I thought of lying in a bed in Ralph Warner's empty house, with his huge hands groping over me, roaming over my flesh hungrily, trying to satiate his loneliness. Then I thought of running through the woods chased by dogs and helicopters and policemen with loud-speakers, and bleeding and hungry and huddling in damp trailers covered by vermin infested blankets.

If I had to fight Ralph Warner off, it was better than all of that.

Detective Bob

"Hendersonville..."

The cab driver looked at me wordlessly and slowly started the car. I leaned up to the front. "About how long will it take to get there?"

He lit a cigarette and threw the match out the window. "Two hours, mebbe two and a half... 'pending on the weather."

I looked up in the sky, clouds were traveling quickly, and the last few rays of the setting sun were lighting up the road. "It looks fine to me."

"Oh yeah, well, it's supposed to rain, and this is hurricane season, so it's like to blow up real bad once it gits started."

Shit. It would just be my luck to have a fuckin hurricane blow in. I leaned back against the cracked leather seats. *Shit.* If the weather was going to fuck with me what could I do.

Different kind of country down here. I'd never traveled much out of New York, and I was starting to realize that there was a whole lot out there that I'd never seen or even wanted to see. Maybe when this was all over I could. But right now I had to focus on this case. I was getting down to the wire, but if I could just get Laurel, she either did it, or knew who did it. Either way she was the answer.

Laurel

"You can stay in here." Ralph opened the door to a plain room, furnished in brown and blue plaids, a neat bed, a chair, and some poster art on the wall. He lingered in the doorway, as if waiting for me to officially invite him in. "The TV works, too."

He went over to a small black and white television and turned it on. Someone singing about laundry detergent blared out. "I don't know if you like to sit up in bed and watch TV. Sometimes I do. Keeps me company…The trouble is this darn thing doesn't come in too clear sometimes…" He was fiddling with the TV, trying to get the grainy black and white to take some kind of coherent shape.

Sounds were coming out, but the picture kept jumping around. I wasn't really paying much attention to him. My mind kept racing ahead to the next step. What after this? Where would I go? I just didn't know.

"There, I think I got it now." The picture was light, but I could make out a local newscast. "And now the latest…this woman…"

Suddenly, my face was plastered over the screen. I wanted to melt away into the wall, but I couldn't. I barely remember anything except the woman's voice.

"…is being sought by the New York City Police Department in connection with a murder. Anyone having information as to her whereabouts is asked to contact this station immediately."

Ralph hadn't said anything. He was just staring at me, and then at the television. Still without saying anything, he turned the television off. His back to me, saying softly. "So you're running?"

"I…yes…"

"Why?"

"I don't know anymore…"

"Who is he?"

I couldn't make myself say his name. I tried but I couldn't.

"Damn it, Laurel. I could go to jail for having you here. I think you owe me some kinda explanation."

"You knew him."

He turned around sharply. Looking at me for the first time. "Who?"

"Clive January."

He looked at me blankly for a moment, then a wave of recognition and disbelief came over his face. "That kid?! The one that you…and then he left and you left…" He sat down heavily on the bed. "You just couldn't leave him alone, could you?"

He sounded almost bitter, as if he had wanted to be in Clive's place, but knew he never would. He kept shaking his head. "You had everything…everything."

Neither of us spoke for a minute.

"I oughta call that station right now…shouldn't I?"

A sharp pain descended from my temples to the tips of my fingers, but no sounds would come out.

"Did you do it Laurel? Did you kill him?"

Before I could say anything, before I could shout out the truth, he pressed his fingers against my lips. "No, don't tell me. I don't want to know. I don't want to think of you except, how I always have…Laurel Davenport, the prettiest teacher at the school. The one everybody wanted and you threw it all away for a kid."

He got up from the bed and stood so close to me that I could feel his breath against my skin. "What did he have that would make you love him that hard all these years?" I knew that he wanted to hold me, touch me and grab me in his arms, but he didn't. Instead, he stepped back a few steps.

Walking up to him slowly, I unbuttoned his shirt. Little droplets of sweat were beading up on his chest. He didn't move. I unbuttoned it all the way.

Stepping back, he said gruffly. "You don't have to bribe me…I won't say anything."

"I'm not trying to bribe you…I just want…to be held."

"That's all you want?"

I nodded yes. I felt raw inside, all the running and the tears, the agony of the past few months. I had nothing more inside of me. What had been there had been eaten up by the unforgiving months of time and sadness.

He stroked my face with his rough hands. But I didn't recoil. It was a touch, that was all, a touch that was filled with good intention and love.

He lightly brushed his lips over mine. "Tell me if you want me to stop…'cause I will, I don't force myself on anybody."

I didn't tell him to stop. And as he pushed me gently onto the bed, peeling off my clothes, I shut my eyes, letting him run his body over mine. Inside my head, it wasn't dark. There was a flash of light, and his touch, which had been rough and clumsy, suddenly felt familiar…Like someone who knew every ridge of my body, every core of my being. I knew that it was Clive. I opened my eyes, and Ralph was still there, but superimposed on him was Clive.

His eyes filled with agony as he said, "I love you, Laurel. I love you. Tell me you love me…Tell me!"

"Clive, I do. I always have."

"Say it. I need you to say it, or they won't let me go. You have to say it!"

"I love you, Clive. I love you."

"I wasn't going to marry you…Laurel. I was going to leave without you. I wasn't strong enough to take you with me. I was still afraid. I lied to you, Laurel. I lied to you. I wasn't going to marry you…Now do you still love me?"

Anger surged forward in me. How could he have lied to me again? All I could feel was anger, bitter anger. Suddenly, I could sense Clive pulling back from me, and I realized that my anger was pushing him away. I tried to bury the feelings of hurt and betrayal…Love…I must think Love…only Love…soaking my mind in the love that I had for him, I could feel his presence gaining strength, wrapping itself around me again.

Knowing now why he'd led me here, I let myself love him, releasing everything that I'd held back in anger or hurt. Realizing so clearly that he could only come to me when there was love, and through someone who loved me. That's why he'd led me to Ralph. His feelings for me were a channel for Clive to come in. I had to keep loving Clive, my anger and not forgiving pushed him away…back to that place that he was trying to run from.

My unconditional love for him, for what he was and what he had become was what Clive needed from me. It was the only thing that could free his soul from the pit that had sucked him in. Everything I'd ever felt for him and everything that he'd ever been to me rose up in me, and I made peace with the past and let all the hurts fade away.

"I love you, Clive. I love you. It's okay…It's okay…I forgive you, and I love you. I'll always love you…always!" For the first time since we'd been together, I felt no fear. It was gone. Dissolved finally and I understood. That the fear I'd had first of losing myself to him and then of losing him altogether had been that invisible barrier between us, always tweaking at the edges, always making me run, making him run, until finally there was no place to go.

Lights were in my head, flashing again, more brightly than ever. I was feeling Clive stronger than before, and I knew that this was the last time that we'd be like this. Pushing myself into him, not wanting him to leave, I whispered, "I love you…I love you,"… feeling him covering me, making the feelings all right, making everything all right for the first time since we'd met that day so long ago.

Our life together flashed before me…Hendersonville…New York, the beginning, the end…but for the first time, it didn't hurt, nothing hurt anymore. I just felt joy and this tremendous peace as if finally we were truly together, and that we would be together again. He whispered in my ear, and I knew what I had to do.

Detective Bob

"This is as far as I can go, Mister. I can't see a damn thing. I'm pulling over."

"Can't you go a little further? We can't be that far from there now!"

"We're not, but I don't plan on getting there in a body bag neither."

The driver pulled over to the side of the road. The heavy rain rocked the car back and forth. I couldn't believe it. We couldn't have been more than five miles from the airport when the rains started coming down like liquid bricks.

"What you in such a hurry for anyway?"

"I'm trying to get a murder suspect."

I pulled out a photo of Laurel and showed it to him.

"Ever seen her before?"

"Nope."

I put the photo back in my pocket. It was worth a try. He leaned back in the seat, saying lazily, "One thing's for sure, there's no way she'll get away in this weather. Wherever she is, she's stuck there now."

I'd heard that before, and I was still out here chasing her down. I closed my eyes, thinking what else could I do and tried and catch some Z's, 'cause we sure as hell weren't going anywhere.

I woke up with a start. My neck had a mean crick in it, and I didn't know where I was. Then I remembered, in a cab somewhere outside Hendersonville, Mississippi, in the middle of a hurricane. The cab driver was slumped over the wheel snoring loudly. It was still raining, but lightly, not like before. I shook the cab driver. "Hey…wake up. We need to get going."

He jolted up, waiving his hands wildly. "Who…what the hell? Hey don't wake me up like that no mo'. Next time I might reach for my gun."

"Yeah, well I got one, too." I pulled out my .45. "So let's go. The rain's let up."

He glared at me as he started the car, maneuvering it around deep puddles of water and red brown mud. As we turned down the main street of Hendersonville, my gut told me that I'd missed her again. I don't know why, but I knew that she'd been here and was gone. I almost didn't even feel like going into the police station. It felt like a useless exercise in disappointment, but I had to. Captain would really have my ass in a sling if I flew all the way down here on the department's dime and didn't even check in with the local cops. I paid the cab driver and walked up to the station.

One of the cops reported, "Katlin O'Neil, the chemistry teacher, Ralph Warner, the principal, and Zebediah Franks, the football coach, those are the three who were working at Hendersonville High in '69 and are still there. We got a tip that she'd been seen with Ralph Warner, but when we got there, he said that he'd had dinner with her and that she'd left right after that, just before the storm started, said he didn't know where she was going.

"Said they'd just talked about old times. Said he didn't know nothin' about her being a murder suspect. Nobody saw her after that. Right now, all our extra manpower is on emergency call 'cause of the hurricane, evacuating folks from places that flooded out. No we don't have nobody extra that could look for her. No…don't know when we will. Sorry, just one of them things I guess. There's nothin' you can do when the weather gets bad down here."

The cop's words were clanging in my head as I climbed onto the plane back to New York. I'd gone over and talked to Warner myself, figured I couldn't trust the cops down there to really grill him. But he stuck to his story, signed a statement to that effect.

The other two who'd been at Hendersonville High in '69 claimed they hadn't seen her since she left back then. My gut had been right, she'd come back here to where it started, had stayed with somebody she knew, and then like all the other times, slipped away before I could get her. Another fuck up. This time the damn weather. How was I gonna explain this one to the captain?

CHAPTER THIRTY-THREE

Detective Bob

The phones ringing around me were fucking with my head. I gulped down some coffee and turned back to my notes. For once, nobody had said anything to me when I got in the station. No rude stares, no snide remarks, they just ignored me. I'd gone by the file room looking for Margie, but she was gone for the day. She hadn't returned any of my messages. So I guessed it was pretty safe to assume that she was pissed off at me, too.

The hot coffee scorched the sides of my mouth. I wanted like hell to cool it down with some Jack, but I figured that now was probably not the time to pull my stash out. I'd decided that I had to let up off Laurel for a minute and concentrate on Haven and that crowd. It was my only real lead at this point.

I was starting to write down my list: (1) Samurai Club, find out owners, (2) Do a check on who might really be behind them, (3) Do a check on Jack Simmons...I dug my pen down into the paper. Shit ,all things I should've done days ago, but no...I wasted time trying to find Laurel Davenport. Now Haven and Simmons probably had more than enough time to cover any tracks they might have left earlier. My stomach was starting to churn again, the prospect of another failed lead was more than I could take.

"Greene, Captain wants to see you in his office."

I rolled my eyes. *Shit, probably wants to lay on my ass about what happened with Laurel Davenport.* I closed my notebook and went into his office. I was not looking forward to this.

"Sit down, Greene." The captain was chewing on an unlit cigar, the spit was rolling off the tip as he twirled it in his mouth. "I hear that you been harassing club owners..."

"You mean criminals that I shoulda brought in on pandering charges?"

"Since when did you join vice, Greene?"

I was silent. I knew better than to say anything.

"Greene, you were going off half-cocked, as usual. Whether the club was running girls or not, isn't your jurisdiction. You're supposed to be investigating a murder case! God damn, you're a hard headed SOB I told you from the beginning that this case was very sensitive, and you weren't to go snooping around in things that weren't relevant to finding out who killed Clive January!"

"But, Captain, it was relevant. He'd been seen there. He mighta consummated a business deal there with whoever is behind the place. I think that that deal is what ultimately led to him being killed."

The captain shook his head in frustration. "Just because somebody had a drink there, doesn't mean that it had a damn thing to do with who killed him. Shit, Greene, we'd be shutting down half the bars in Manhattan if that was the way we operated."

"Yeah well I also don't think that it was any coincidence that the club was closed down by vice the day after I was there and in time for the owner to conveniently skip town."

"So now I suppose somebody here at the precinct is trying to cover something up? You're gettin' in real dangerous territory, Greene. It's not enough that every cop in the place hates your guts 'cause they think you squealed on one of them, but now you have the nerve to accuse me, 'cause let's face it that's what you're doing. You're accusing my precinct of trying to cover something up!"

"Yeah, well, Captain, who are these mysterious 'people' that you told me are so determined to get this case closed quickly? What am I supposed to think?"

The captain didn't answer me. He just leaned forward and stared at me, real hard. "Greene, I don't want to hear any more of your grand conspiracy theory. I just want you to answer one question. Do you have a suspect? Did you get that woman Laurel Davenport that you been chasing all around the country for, pissing away taxpayers' dollars?" What could I say, he already knew the answer.

"That's what I thought, you're off the case."

"You said I had a month. I got a week more!"

"Well, I changed my mind. You're off the fuckin' case now!"

I was about to say something when the door swung open, Scoffo stuck his head in the door. "Sorry, Captain, but I thought you'd want me to interrupt you. That woman Greene's been looking for...Laurel Davenport..."

"Yeah...what about her?"

"She's here, at the station, said she wants to see Greene."

The captain looked as stunned as I was, but he recovered quickly, yanking the cigar out of his mouth and turning to me coldly, "Book her...and no bullshit. She's our shooter."

I was finally looking into the eyes of the woman that I'd been chasing since Clive's funeral. Face to face with her, I realized that she was the woman in black, the woman who didn't fit in. The only person who cried at his funeral. Laurel Davenport, maybe the woman who murdered him for love. But for some reason I didn't think so anymore.

"You've been looking for me, Detective." Her voice was rich and silky, soft and sexier than I'd imagined it would be and almost too much for such a tiny woman. Her dark hair framed her face like a soft curly halo. I couldn't pull myself away from her eyes, light green, digging into me. I was being dragged into her soul. I saw what Clive musta felt, and why he could never leave her. She had some power that grabbed you and held you and wouldn't let you go.

Remembering the captain's words, I said, "You have the right to remain silent. You have the right to an attorney. If you cannot afford one, one will be appointed for you by the court..."

"I didn't do it, Detective."

"I expected you to say as much."

She looked unmoved, crossing her legs and saying softly, "But I think I know who did."

We were alone in the interrogation room. I didn't want any of the other cops to be around, because I knew what I had to ask her. "Who were the clients that Clive didn't want anybody to know about?"

"Are you still going to book me if I tell you everything I know?"

"It depends on what you know...and what you tell me."

She looked into my eyes, and I thought of all the things that I knew about her: Clive's wedding night, the obsessive love, the things that no one else should know. But I did.

She cleared her throat and started speaking. "Have you ever heard of the Yakuzi?"

"Yeah, the Japanese mob. They're all over the place in Japan. They run a lot of the so called 'legitimate businesses,' and I hear that in some cases they operate pretty much openly without anybody bothering them."

"Well they're not just in Japan. They wanted to establish a presence in some key American companies by buying up large blocks of stock. But they had to do it discreetly through shell corporations and by having smaller firms execute the trades. Firms that the SEC were less likely to monitor. Firms like Clive's."

She looked away from me. "I didn't want Clive to get involved in it. Jack Simmons convinced him to do it. He knew Clive needed the money. The last year had been tough on his firm. They'd lost some big accounts. People on the street talk, so Jack knew that Clive was vulnerable.

"At first it was going well. Clive would do the trades, make the commissions, kick back Jack Simmons his part, and it was fine...Then the Japanese started wanting more trades and more and more of Clive's time, so he brought Andy Haven in on it. I told him he couldn't trust him. I didn't want Haven knowing about it, but Clive always thought that he could control him."

"But he couldn't?"

"Not once Haven found out that Clive was going to shut the business down."

"So how did Haven know about that?

"I honestly don't know, but he always had his nose in something. He might've found out from Clive's lawyers. I don't know, but I know he did because he confronted Clive. Clive denied it, but Haven's no fool. I think he tipped off Simmons and the Japanese, and they realized that their front was about to be taken from them, so they had him killed. Knowing that Haven would end up running the firm because he was next in line. And with him there they could continue with business as usual."

"What was the name of this Japanese client?"

"I don't know the real name. Clive wouldn't tell me. They used a code to refer to it."

"What was the code name?"

"Samurai."

I was quiet for a moment. It all fit together. All of the clues that I'd had…but it was still all theory, still no concrete proof. I turned to her. "Tell me one thing, Clive had this business, making from what you tell me and from everything I can see a shitload of money, so why was he gonna close the whole thing down? It just doesn't make sense."

"It was all getting to be too much, the pressure. These Japanese clients always wanting more and more. All his money was tied up in the business, and the only way he could get it out was to liquidate his stock and take the money. He wanted to get away from New York and start over somewhere else."

"And what about you? Were you going with him?"

She looked as if I'd stuck a knife in her as she struggled to get the words out. "Yes, that was what we'd planned."

"And his wife, did she know about your plans?"

"She knew he was getting out of the business."

"Did she know about you? That is about you and her husband leaving together?"

"He was supposed to have told her that night, before we…saw each other…We were celebrating starting a new life together…when he …died…" She stopped, swallowing hard, reaching for the composure that she'd had earlier. "I'm sorry, Detective…"

I let her get herself together before I asked, "And if for some reason Clive had changed his mind and decided not to go away with you and to stay with his wife what would you have done?"

She was quiet for a moment, then she looked directly at me with this incredible calm saying, "I still would have loved him. I could never have killed him."

"So then why did you run after he was killed? Why didn't you just go about your business and get on with your life?"

"You really don't get it, Detective, do you? Clive was my life. He's the reason I came to New York. There was nothing else. "

"You didn't answer my question."

She folded her hands in her lap, avoiding my eyes. "I ran because I just didn't know what else to do. When I realized that the police were after me, it was too late to stop running. So I didn't."

"Then why did you come here to turn yourself in?"

"I didn't come to turn myself in. I came to help you find out who really did it."

I knew without asking her that Clive had brought her to me. He had told her to come. So she did. Getting up and walking away from the desk, tapping a pen against the wall, I said, "You were there when he was killed…right?"

"Yes…but I'd gone in the kitchen. When I heard the gun shot…I ran back in the living room but no one was there."

"So do you have any proof of your theory? I mean any indication that Haven talked to Simmons and these clients and that they presumably I guess, sent some kind of hit man or whatever out there to knock off Clive? Why didn't they kill you, too? People like that don't like to leave witnesses."

She stammered, "I…I don't know, but I'm telling you the truth. That's all I know."

For a moment, I looked hard at her, trying to see what was really behind her, but then I looked away, opening the door and shouting out, "Hey, I need a female officer in here. I got a suspect to be booked."

Laurel's eyes filled with horror as she realized what was happening. "Detective…you can't. I didn't do it. Are you listening to me? I told you everything I know. I didn't kill him!" But I turned away. The captain had his shooter.

Laurel

Why would I have thought that he would believe me? Why would I have ever thought that by giving myself up to the cop who'd been looking for me for months that I wouldn't have been booked? Because he told me to come here. *Clive, why? Why did you tell me to come here? Do you think that I killed you? I didn't. Don't you know that? I didn't!*

Maybe because it had all seemed too easy. Ralph helping me get away, posing as Mrs. Ralph Warner, dressed in his dead wife's clothes, wearing her tangled wig and glasses, buying a ticket with her credit card. Boarding the plane. Nobody noticing, and then walking into the station. It had all been too easy. Why would I have thought that the rest would be as easy? Bob Greene, the bastard. After I tell him everything he needs to know to find the real killers—Andy Haven, Jack Simmons—he turns on me and throws me in here. A smelly, dark holding cell filled with prostitutes and junkies and me. Laurel Davenport, wanted for the murder of the only man that she ever loved.

Thinking about Clive made me feel what I felt the last time, when Ralph Warner melted away and Clive stepped in. Remembering that calmed me, the thoughts forming a protective barrier around me, like he'd done before, and I knew that this wasn't it. Something else was happening beyond these walls. Something else that would free Clive and me forever.

CHAPTER THIRTY-FOUR

Detective Bob

Laurel Davenport's pitiful voice kept playing back in my head. *I didn't do it. I didn't do it.* I knew she didn't; I'd known for a while. I had to lock her up, hopefully it wouldn't be for long. It was the only way to get the captain off my ass so I could find out who really did it.

I was thinking all this when the door opened and a short guy in a rumpled blue suit walked in the office. Actually, in his own office. I'd been waiting for him to get out of a meeting and in the meantime turning the details of the case over in my mind. Things were beginning to add up, and if I could verify what Laurel had told me, I might stand a chance of blowing this one wide open.

Alan Burns coughed nervously. A typical lawyer: kinda pale, anal, more concerned with saying it right than what it really meant. I leaned forward in my chair. I had to play this one real easy. "Mr. Burns, I just have to ask you a coupla questions. It won't take long, but it could really help clear up some things about Mr. January's death."

He squinted and played with a paper clip on his desk. "Of course, Detective. I'm happy to help out in any away."

"Good." I flipped open my notebook. "You were Mr. January's lawyer?"

"Yes that's right…for about five years now. Since I came to the firm."

"I see. So did Mr. January ever have you draw up any papers to uh…close down his business?"

"You mean liquidate the concern?"

"Yeah, close down his business."

"Yes, he did. In fact, the liquidation would have been completed the day after his death."

"Uh huh…so what does that really mean, in non-legalese? I mean this liquidation?"

"Well, it was a complicated transaction because of the way Mr. January's firm was capitalized. Essentially, what it would have meant if Mr. January had lived and the transaction had been completed as planned, is that Mr. January would have cashed out his stock in the corporation. Since he was the only shareholder, the business would have ceased to exist."

"So what did that mean for all the employees, people like Mr. Haven, for instance?"

"Mr. Haven had a standard employee contract that was automatically terminated if the business was liquidated."

"So in other words, he would've been out."

"Yes."

"Was there anything that Mr. Haven could have done…legally that is, to stop the liquidation."

The lawyer shook his head. "Not a thing. He didn't own any stock, and he wasn't a director of the corporation. Mr. January was the sole shareholder and the only director. Nobody else had any interest in his business."

"So how much would Mr. January have gotten by liquidating?"

"Roughly ten million dollars. All of the assets of the corporation would have been sold to buy back Mr. January's stock. Once those assets were sold, the corporation would have been essentially bankrupt. Mr. January would have walked away with about ten million dollars."

So Clive was going to pull a fast one on all of them, cash out his stock, close the business, and get out with ten million dollars. My guess was that once Haven told Simmons what was up, Simmons hit the roof. He wasn't about to let his cash cow to the tune of fifty percent of everything that Clive was taking in from the Japanese, go down the drain. I bet that those clients wouldn'tve been too happy with Simmons if all of a sudden they had to find a new front to deal with.

"Tell me, Mr. Burns, who owns the business now that Mr. January is dead?"

"I don't know all of the details of his will. I don't handle T&E matters...but it's my understanding that he left everything to his daughter."

"The three-year-old?"

"Yes."

"So how does that work?"

"Well, I would assume that her mother is the guardian, but with something like this a bank is also involved as a co-trustee of the estate, so it would be very difficult to sell or liquidate the business without a sound business reason...and right now, there really isn't one."

"So Haven is in to stay."

"At least until his contract is up."

"And when is that?"

"I believe he has five more years to go."

Five more years to rape the business, get rich, and then move on. I closed my notebook. "Thank you, Mr. Burns. You've been a big help." Well, everything that Laurel had said, checked out. But I had to find a link, a paper trail connecting Haven and Simmons to the Japanese clients, and then connect the clients to Clive's death. And in a week, there was no way. I had to get more time.

"So she said she didn't do it!" The captain leaned back in his chair, which squeaked under his weight. "Since when did somebody cooling their heels in jail ever admit that they did do it!"

"Look, Captain, I know you think that I'm outta my mind, but I need more time. I've got some other leads that..."

"Like what, more of your conspiracy theory that somebody here is trying to cover up the case? 'cause if that's it, forget it, Greene. I don't have time for that kinda mess." The captain got up from his chair and circled around his desk. "You chased half way around the damn country looking for this woman, and then she walks right in and gives herself up, and now you say you don't think she did it. You're right, I do think that you're outta your fuckin' mind!"

He sat on the edge of his desk, pressing his fingers against the side in frustration. "Look, Greene, do yourself a favor. Let it go. Okay. It's over. You got the shooter. The DA's already drawing up the papers. You solved the case. She was there the night of the murder. Her prints were everywhere. She had a motive, jealous mistress, tired of not having him all to herself, so she figured if she couldn't have him, then nobody would. She was on the run from the day he was killed, so if you ask me...she looks pretty guilty. So why don't you just go on home, fix yourself a drink, and congratulate yourself on a job well done?"

He turned his back on me saying coldly, "Now I got work to do, so if you don't mind."

I started to say something, to beg the captain one more time to reconsider, but I knew it was a waste of breath

Back at my desk, my head was spinning. I was about to send an innocent woman away for a crime that I was even more convinced than ever that she didn't do. All because I didn't have time to get the real killers. *Shit.* I was starting to get one of those mean headaches, the kind that would be with me for half the night. *Clive where are you, you know she didn't do it. Lead me to what I need to find.*

"Congratulations." Margie walked in front of me. She wasn't smiling. "I heard you got your killer."

"Yeah...right."

"Well you should be happy. At least you're vindicated as a cop. That is what this was all about wasn't it, proving that you still had it?"

I didn't need this now. "Margie, I'm sorry I ran out without saying anything...I know I should've called you before...but right now I really can't deal with it...okay? Please."

She looked like she was about to say something, but instead, she just bent down and kissed me on the cheek, whispering, "Just call me when you're ready."

CHAPTER THIRTY-FIVE

Detective Bob

I was turning and tossing. The headache wouldn't go away, and I couldn't sleep. For once it was quiet outside, but that wasn't helping 'cause the noises in my head just wouldn't let up. I climbed out of bed, walked over to the window, and tapped nervously on the glass. I glanced over at my clock—2 A.M. Four more hours till I had to get up, and I hadn't gotten a second of rest since I turned in. My clothes were lying on the chair where I'd tossed them.

I don't know exactly why I decided to go in the station at two o' clock in the morning, except that it had been so easy to pick up my shirt, pull it over my head, step into the pants, and just leave. I looked around at the empty desks. The night duty sergeant was sipping some coffee. A couple of other cops milled around; but, thankfully, nobody who knew me. Maybe I could get my head together and look around, see if something popped out at me, without every eye in the place on me.

I didn't give a shit what the captain said, I was determined to find the real shooter. I owed myself that much. And I owed Clive more. I knew deep down that he didn't send me the woman he loved so I could put her behind bars.

Somebody had tossed a newspaper on my desk. I picked it up casually. The usual murder and mayhem on the front page. I flipped through it, skimming the articles. A big picture of the governor, that asshole, smiling. I stopped and looked closer at the picture. A Japanese businessman and next to him with his arm around the guy's shoulder was—*Holy Shit!*—Jack Simmons.

I jumped down to the article reading: "Jack Simmons, managing director at Bender & Grace and long time friend and supporter of the

Governor, has just formed an international business council to promote ties between the U.S. and Japanese business communities. In his speech to the newly formed commission, Simmons said, 'The future of American business lies in working with our friends and neighbors in the Japanese financial community. I firmly believe that by identifying our common interests and goals, we will all prosper.' The Governor cited the importance of the international business community for the continued growth of New York State and pledged his full support to the new commission."

So those were "the people" the captain had been talking about who wanted everything settled so fast! Simmons and the Japanese were in bed with the Governor, so if Clive, the designated bag man, decided he didn't want to play their game anymore, you just get rid of him quickly. Andy Haven slides in at the top making it business as usual.

Find a convenient suspect to pin the rap on, who better than the jealous mistress, then case closed and everybody goes home with nobody upsetting the real apple cart. And I played right into their hands. No wonder the captain had let me go on the wild goose chase for Laurel. He'd been told to do it. I bet he didn't even know how deep this thing really went. My guess was that he had his orders to get the case closed quickly, and he was smart enough not to get too curious. *Shit.* And Laurel Davenport served up to them, no questions asked.

And no peace for Clive or me. My hands had started to shake. The newspaper fell to the ground. I tried to pick it up, but I couldn't. My hands were shaking too much. The room was closing in on me. All the noise had stopped, and everything had gotten black.

I was floating in this thick murky darkness: no sound, no touch, just darkness and this feeling of oppression and hopelessness. I knew that I was feeling the place where Clive was, the desperation that he was feeling, like he'd never get out, never know the truth, or see light again. Fear crept around the edges of my mind. Subtly at first, then overwhelming me. Paralyzing my thoughts. I tried to speak. But nothing. I tried to reason my way out of this place, but received fear and a feeling of losing myself slowly. The essence of me drained out of my body until...

"Yo, Greene!" Somebody shook me hard, and the brightness of day flooded into me. "You okay, buddy?"

I looked up into Scoffo's eyes. Silently thanking God for pulling me back from that place of darkness. Disoriented, I realized that a lot of time must've passed because it was light outside. Glancing at my watch, I could barely read the dial—7:30. Scoffo shoved a cup of coffee in my hand.

"What'd you fall asleep here all night or something?"

"Yeah, I must've...I don't remember when..."

He slapped me on the back saying, "What'd you tie one on, and then come here to sleep it off?" Grinning, he just shook his head. I smiled weakly. Why disagree with him? I sure as hell couldn't tell him the truth.

"Yeah, you caught me. That's what happened."

"You're too old for that, Greene!" He chuckled and wandered off.

At my feet was the newspaper, right where it had dropped last night. I reached to pick it up.

"Greene, somebody here to see you."

"At 7:30 in the morning?"

"She said it's important."

Damn. I ran my fingers through my hair, trying to pull myself together, wondering who the hell it could be. Maybe Yolanda Calloway with more info. But as I looked up and saw the woman walking hesitantly toward me, I realized I recognized her face, but it wasn't Yolanda.

She edged into the chair, nervously clutching a large handbag saying, "Do you remember me, Detective?"

"Yeah...but tell me anyway."

"I'm Dolly Hernandez. I work for Mrs. January."

"Right...right. I knew that. So what's up, Miss Hernandez? How can I help you?"

She stopped and took a deep breath. "Did you find out who killed Mr. January yet?"

"Why...do you have some ideas?"

Outta nowhere, she just broke down and started crying. Luckily there weren't too many people in the place, 'cause I never woulda heard the end of it otherwise.

"Hey...hey...what's wrong???"

She turned away from me, her face red and bloated. "I...I'm sorry...but yesterday I was cleaning up in Mrs. January's room, I fixing her clothes. You know, ironing and putting the winter clothes in a trunk and taking out the summer ones like she always ask me to do, and...and..." She reached into her purse and took out a gun. Laying it gingerly on the table. "Do you think she killed him?"

I looked at it, garden variety .45. I picked it up with a cloth, turning it over, no distinguishing marks. Two bullets still left in the chamber. "Where did you find this again?"

"In her closet, way in the back, underneath some clothes."

"So it was hidden?" She nodded solemnly.

"What makes you think that Mrs. January killed her husband with this? A lot of people have guns these days."

Her eyes got narrower, and she lowered her voice. "Because she said she wanted him dead. I heard her myself..."

I took out my notebook. "Tell me about it. When did you hear her say that?"

"It was last year. Her and Mr. January and the baby and me was in Jamaica. Her and Mr. January had a big fight and that's what she said. I remember 'cause I heard her say to him, 'I wish you were dead.'"

"Wait, back up a little bit. How did the argument start? Tell me from the beginning." I could tell she was nervous, and it looked like her eyes were beginning to tear up again. "You want some water first?"

"No...thas' okay..." She rocked back and forth in her seat as she talked, knotting her hands together. "We was in Jamaica. They brought me to take care of the baby. I could tell from the start they wasn't gettin' long, Mr. and Mrs. January. They never really did. But this time it was real bad. Mr. January would leave in the morning, and then he wouldn't usually come back 'til late at night. It wouldn't have been so bad, except that Mrs. January, she was expecting a baby."

"Mrs. January was pregnant?"

"Yes, sir. She was about three months then. I don't really know how Mr. January felt about it 'cause he jus' wasn't around that much. Anyway, this day Mrs. January wasn't feeling real good. And then she started gettin' sick. I called the hotel and they sent a doctor. Everybody was lookin' for Mr. January, but they couldn't find him. They finally took her to the hospital." She stopped and slowed down for a minute.

"So what happened at the hospital?"

"They finally found Mr. January and he came to the hospital, but it was too late. She'd lost the baby...and it was there. I was standing outside her door. Mrs. January was crying, and she said to Mr. January that he was nothin'. She said he'd been out with some other woman while she was there. While their baby was dying. She told him. She said she hated him, and that she wished he was dead. I think she really wanted that baby, and she was real mad at Mr. January that she lost it."

"Was it his fault?"

She shook her head. "It wasn't nobody's fault. Them things happen sometimes, but Mrs. January blamed Mr. January. After that, she stopped really having anything to do with him."

"Do you really think that Mrs. January could have killed her husband?"

Dolly looked away for a moment, timidly saying, "I think she really hated him. I don't know..."

"Dolly, was Mrs. January seeing anyone?"

"You mean a man on the side?"

"Yeah...somebody that Mr. January maybe didn't know about?"

"She got somebody. I don't know exactly who, but he calls up to the house. I think he called one of the days you was over." I remembered the phone call: Mrs. January quickly telling Dolly that she'd call him back, the odd look on Dolly's face.

"He calls a lot, especially since Mr. January died. She always takes his calls in private, closes the door…I know she got somebody…I ain't no fool."

"So why didn't you tell me all this when I first questioned you right after Mr. January's death?"

"Cause of the baby, just 'cause Mrs. January got somebody on the side, don't mean she killed her husband. I didn't want nothin' to happen to that baby. She already lost her daddy. She needs her mama."

"But now you've changed your mind?"

"Yeah…That was before I found the gun. I jus' knew I couldn't sleep at night if she was the one who did it, and I didn't say nothin'."

My eyes followed Dolly Hernandez out of the room. I had told her not to say anything to Mrs. January. I'd send the gun down to ballistics to see if it matched the murder weapon. Until then I was just gonna have to sit tight.

CHAPTER THIRTY-SIX

Monique

The last wave of the rainstorm that had ravaged the city hours before was finally beginning to subside. I turned over, looking at his side of the bed. Untouched, just like when he was here. I should have felt relieved. The nightmare that was my marriage was finally over and without the drawn out recriminations and bitterness of a divorce. Just over, in one night, one minute and he was gone.

But was he really gone? Sometimes I felt as if he's watching me, waiting for me to slip up, as if he knows the secret that I'm harboring. Damn him, always controlling, everyone else just a player in his world. But no more. I was going to live now and be free. I was going to cherish this freedom, these stolen fruits that were mine.

"Mommy, I'm scared…"

I looked up and saw my daughter standing hesitantly in the doorway. As if propelled by jet fuel, she ran into the room and jumped into my bed. I drew her close to me, kissing her baby face. "Don't worry. Mommy's here. Nobody's gonna hurt you."

She burrowed further into my lap as I stroked her hair. "Tell me a story, Mommy."

I smiled. "Okay…Well…once upon a time there was a beautiful princess who lived in a huge castle high on the hill. Everyone thought that she was happy because she lived in such a beautiful place and had anything that her heart desired, but she was really very sad because the one thing that she really wanted, she didn't have…"

Looking over at my daughter, I saw that she was sleeping soundly, the deep trusting sleep of a child. I drew her next to me and closed my eyes, wishing for that same sleep to capture and transport me to that world far away where wishes were reality.

Ring, ring, ring, ring... I jumped up. Ariel was still sleeping. I looked at the clock—8 A.M. Damn, who was coming over at this time of morning on a Sunday? I gently untangled myself from Ariel.

She rolled over and sleepily opened one eye. "Where you going, Mommy?"

"Go back to sleep, honey. Somebody's at the door. I'll be right back." Annoyed, I pulled on my robe and stumbled out of the bedroom, down the stairs. What was the use of having a doorman if people could just come in and bother you whenever they wanted? I looked out through the peephole and stopped. Two policeman were standing there. I opened the door. Detective Greene was with them.

"Monique Raymond January?"

"Yes...you know who I am, Detective. What do you want?"

"We have a warrant for your arrest for the murder of your husband Clive January..."

The blood rushed from my fingers to my head. I felt like I couldn't stand up. I tried to speak, "Are you...crazy?"

The policemen were taking out handcuffs. I backed away from the door, but they were coming closer to me. "Mrs. January, you have the right to remain silent. Anything you say can and will be used against you in a court of law. You have the right to an attorney. If..." One of them grabbed my arm, shoving a handcuff over it.

I cried out, "Get the hell away from me!"

A scream, more chilling than I'd ever heard, cut through me as my child tottered forward, clinging to the bottom of my robe, sobbing, "Let go of my mommy!"

It was too late. They were thrusting me out of the door. Someone grabbed Ariel, and I don't remember anything else.

"Tell me again where you were the night of the murder, Mrs. January?"

I looked into Detective Greene's eyes, and I hated him. I hated everything that he stood for. Suspicion and jealousy. I knew that was why I was here. He was jealous of me and everything that I had. I'd known it from the beginning. He'd been dying to throw me in jail. He hated the fact that I had money and more than he could ever dream of.

"You know, Mrs. January. You're not making it any easier on yourself by not saying anything."

"Monique, just answer the question." My lawyer touched my arm gently.

I looked at him, wondering if he was secretly in league with this detective. "I told you when you asked me months ago. I went to the movies with some friends, and then I decided to go for a drive. I came back in around midnight."

The detective circled around me, shoving his fat hands into his pockets. "Yes that is what you told us on…" he flipped through a notebook, "…March 12, but what you didn't tell us was that this drive that you went on was out to the Hamptons. In fact, you told us that you'd just driven around Manhattan because you couldn't sleep. But we've since found out that you stopped in a gas station on the LIE around 10:30 P.M. Now the doorman is saying that he doesn't really remember when he saw you come in. Your husband's time of death was between 11 P.M. and midnight, so tell me again, Mrs. January, where you were at that time?"

I was silent. How much longer could I continue this? They'd find out sooner or later. I couldn't do this. I couldn't subject my child to the humiliation. The detective reached into a file and took out something. He laid it on the table in front of me. "Mrs. January, have you ever seen this gun before?"

"No."

"Our tests have confirmed that it's the murder weapon. And your housekeeper Dolly Hernandez said that she found it in your closet."

"She's lying!" I pounded the table.

"Why would she lie, Mrs. January?"

"I don't know, but she is. I've never seen this gun before. I've never even used a gun!"

The detective looked as if he didn't believe a word that I was saying. I shouted out desperately, "How do you know she didn't do it? Maybe she put the gun there!"

"Sorry, Mrs. January, but we already checked out her alibi. She was with her boyfriend and some other folks in some kind of club all night. About a dozen eyewitnesses confirmed that she was there. Which leads us back to my original question. Where were you on the night of the murder between 11 P.M. and midnight?"

My lawyer tugged at my sleeve, whispering that I shouldn't say anything else. He cleared his throat and turned to the detective. "I've advised my client not to say anything else on the grounds that it may incriminate her."

As they led me away, I saw her, the woman who had taken my husband from me before I even knew him. Trying to avoid my eyes, she looked away. But for one minute, our eyes met, and I felt as if she had done penance for her love for Clive, and now I was doing mine for my hatred of him. And the circle was complete.

CHAPTER THIRTY-SEVEN

John

"Oh my God! John, did you see this?"

I raised an eyebrow warily. My wife was always getting excited about something that more often than not turned out to be of little or no importance.

"John, look at this!" She thrust the newspaper in my face. "It's Monique January, Steve's daughter, they've accused her of killing her husband!"

I felt like my breakfast was about to come up. I grabbed the paper, barely able to read it: "Monique January, wife of well known Wall Street arbitrageur Clive January, has been charged with his murder... The DA's office has filed first-degree murder charges against Mrs. January." Everything was surging forward. The furtive calls, the clandestine meetings, my life of the past year...all starting on that day in Jamaica...

"I'm going home, John. I'm sick to death of this place. All you do is play golf all day with Steve and I'm stuck in this damn hotel room. I told you I didn't want to come back here again."

Sighing heavily, I turned away from her. I didn't really give a damn what she did at this point, having a nagging, unhappy wife around was not exactly how I'd planned to spend my vacation. I knew that I had to at least look like I was making an effort to get her to stay, or I'd never hear the end of it when I got back to New York. "Come on, honey, it's just a few more days. You know how I need the break. Can't you just read or talk to Adelaide or Monique?"

She shot me an icy look. "Adelaide and I ran out of things to talk about years ago, and Monique doesn't do anything but sit in her room and sulk over her obviously unfaithful husband."

My wife had a cruel side to her that I'd learned to accept years ago, but I still didn't like. "That's not very kind of you to say."

"Oh please, John. Everybody knows what's going on. She's a fool to stay with him...and then to go and get pregnant again...I don't know what she's thinking about, frankly. I know I'd be gone if you *ever* carried on the way her husband does." She snapped her suitcase shut, picking up the phone. "Yes, I need a bellboy for room 218...thank you."

She hung up the phone and plopped her hands on her hips. "Well, I'll see you back in New York. Now you can play golf to your heart's content for the next four days without having to worry about me...not that you were anyway...but at least I'll be able to do what I want away from this God awful island. I swear if I see one more strip of sand or one more piña colada, I'll scream. Absolutely scream." Alone in the room, with my wife on her way back to New York and I'm sure heading straight to Bloomingdales to drown her boredom in the latest sale, I felt relieved. At least I could enjoy the rest of my vacation. I stretched out on the couch. Kicking off my shoes, I'd take a quick nap and then head on off to the golf course to get in a few holes before dinner.

Bang, bang, bang! "Mr. Lanier, it's me, Dolly...Mr. Lanier!" I opened one eye.

Bang, bang, bang! "Please, Mr. Lanier...open the door!"

I pulled myself up painfully, feeling every bit of my fifty-one years, and the effects of a week walking around 18 hole golf courses, lugging my own clubs, from now on I'd take the cart. I walked slowly to the door and opened it. "Dolly, what's wrong?"

"It's Mrs. January. She's sick and nobody else is around!"

"Did somebody call the hospital?"

She was crying now, stumbling over her words. "Yes...but the doctor told me to find Mr. Janaury, but I can't, and Mrs. January's parents, they're gone, too...so that's why I come to you. I don't know what to do!" I shoved my shoes on and grabbed my wallet, thinking my God what next.

At the hospital, the doctor hurried toward me. "Are you, Mr. January?"

"No, I'm a family friend, a close friend of her father's."

"Well where is Mr. January? We need his signature on a consent form immediately."

"I…I don't know. I think their housekeeper was trying to find him."

"Well what about her parents? I understand they're here, too."

"Yes, we were traveling together, but they went into Kingston for the weekend. They won't be back until Monday."

The doctor looked worried. "Mrs. January had a miscarriage, but there are some complications. I'd feel better if Mr. January were here in case…well, in case we had to make an emergency decision."

I didn't know what to say. I'd known Monique since Steve and Adlelaide moved in the neighborhood with their cute as a button daughter, Monique. Steve and I were golf partners. Almost twenty years now. Monique was just a child then, eight, maybe ten years old. The same age as my daughter.

The doctor interrupted my thoughts. "I have to go back in there…but if Mr. January comes, send him in immediately." January never did show up until it was too late to make a difference. I left as soon as he got there. I heard that it got nasty, and that's why he decided to take their daughter and go back to New York. The official reason was that Monique needed rest and the doctor felt that it would be better if she were alone. Steve and Adelaide stayed on and so did I. Now I wonder if I'd left then, if things would have been different.

"So you didn't go back after all?" Monique was standing in front of me, looking tired and drawn.

"No…my wife left early, but I decided to stay on for another few days."

She sat next to me on the wall, swinging her legs back and forth like a child. "Well I'm glad you stayed, at least now I'll have somebody to talk to."

"Your parents are here."

"I know, but sometimes it's nice to talk to someone different. We always seem to have the same conversations, and I'm a little tired of it." Her eyes had started to cloud up with tears. I took out a tissue and handed it to her, thinking about years ago when she and my daughter had been playing a particularly raucous game of dodge ball in the street, and Monique had fallen, scraping her knees badly. I remembered picking her up and wiping the tears off her face, just like now.

She tried to smile, taking the tissue from my hands and blowing her nose. "I'm sorry. It just seems like no matter what I think or do these days, I can't stop crying...probably because of the...baby and everything."

"It's normal. You just need to relax, that's all." I remember that she leaned her head against my shoulder crying softly, like she had that day years ago when she was a child. I held her and let her cry out all of her anger and hurt and unhappiness on me. Wishing that I could somehow stop her heart from ripping apart.

That night at dinner with Monique and Steve and Adelaide, I think was the first time that I really looked at Monique and realized that she wasn't a little girl anymore. The experiences etched on her face were those of a woman, a really beautiful woman who had seen and felt the depths of unhappiness and was struggling to pull herself back up.

"Monique...what are you doing out here so late?" I'd noticed her huddled on the beach. She was wrapped in a blanket, sitting in front of the breaking waves.

She looked up without saying anything. I sat on the sand next to her. She took a shell and turned it over in her hands. "I couldn't sleep."

"Neither could I."

She smiled hesitantly, cocking her head to the side as she asked. "So what's your excuse?"

"I don't really have one. I guess I'm just thinking about everything that I have to do when I get back to New York, and I'm not particularly looking forward to it."

She tossed the shell into the waves, saying wistfully, "If it wasn't for my daughter being there, I'd stay here longer."

"Monique, why don't you leave him?"

"You sound like my parents." She turned away from me. "But then, I forget you are almost like my parents."

I got up and walked around her in a circle. "Look, Monique, you're young and attractive. You can find someone else. You don't have to stay in an unhappy marriage."

"You did."

I looked at her hard, wondering how she knew. "I didn't say I don't have my regrets either."

She was quiet for a moment, drawing the blanket around her more tightly. "I told him that I wanted a divorce. He wouldn't give it to me. He said that if I insisted, he'd fight me for our daughter. He'd try and get sole custody."

"No court would take your child away from you."

"Clive January *always* gets what he wants. He'd bribe the judge if he had to…just to prove a point. I can't go through that now. Maybe in a couple of years. That's why I really wanted the baby, to take my mind off the rest of my life. I thought that I could just bury myself in this new little person and forget everything else. I guess it was pretty selfish of me. Maybe that's why God took the baby away from me…I'm being punished."

"Monique…stop. Stop talking like that." I started kissing her, on her face at first, but when she turned her lips up to me, I didn't stop. And neither did she. We didn't make love that night. We both stopped ourselves. I think we realized the implications of what we were doing and drew back. But later in New York after weeks of avoiding each other's eyes at social functions, we finally acknowledged what we both already knew.

I lay there on the slick hotel sheets looking at my naked body. I'd never really cared what it looked like before. My wife certainly didn't care. I couldn't remember the last time we'd made love. But now I cared. I cared how every ripple, every muscle, looked. Pale legs, used to be muscular, from my days as a track star at Yale, class of '66. But now it was 1986, and I was fifty-one, with the stomach of a fifty-one year old, the legs of a fifty-one year old, the graying hair and thinning temples of a fifty-one year old, but the desires of a twenty-one year old.

I also cared what she thought. I heard the water running in the bathroom. I tried to imagine what she must be doing, fixing her hair, putting on perfume in the right places, all for me. A fifty-one year old white guy. I'd never made love to a black woman before. I'd thought about it, but I'd never had the nerve to approach any of them. But Monique was different. She wasn't a black woman to me. She was just Monique, the daughter of my best friend, and now my lover.

The water had stopped. The bathroom light went off. She walked in the room. At that moment, I forgot about being fifty-one. She smiled and I pulled her toward me. Making a tent out of the sheets and losing myself in her.

Once it started, we couldn't stop. The feeling we had kept growing and growing, until I was sure that someone would guess the truth. Someone had to see the way we looked at each other. Someone had to know my secret thoughts. I came to despise my wife. I wanted to divorce her, as Monique wanted to divorce Clive, but we both knew that in so doing the forbidden love that we shared would be exposed.

It felt forbidden because I'd always been like a second father to her. Now I was making love to her with a passion and depth that I'd never felt for anyone else. We had to make a decision. But at the moment when the obvious decision seemed imminent, just do the right thing, get the divorces and stop spending our lives sneaking around in hotel rooms and deserted beaches, it was all snatched from us as rudely as it began. And I had only my own ambition to blame.

The first time I saw my face on the poster, I knew that I couldn't throw it all away. Not for Monique or for anyone. VOTE FOR THE

MAN WITH THE PLAN JOHN LANIER FOR LIEUTENANT GOVERNOR. When they asked me to run, I didn't hesitate for a moment. After all that's what my whole career had been engineered for. My law practice, all of the political contacts carefully massaged through the years. The aborted congressional campaign ten years ago, nursing my wounded pride, but always keeping at the back of my mind the hope that someday I could get back out there in the political fray. And now was the day and I wasn't giving it up. No, I could not throw away my kingdom for the woman I loved. I guess I wasn't English enough for that type of drama.

The night that her husband was killed, we had met in the cottage that I rented in a deserted corner of Montauk. We'd started going there because we could come and go quietly without anyone knowing or caring.

"So you're definitely going to run?"

I avoided her eyes. I couldn't look at the hurt. "Yes."

"So then I guess that means that it's just to hell with our plans. Isn't that what you're saying John? Because heaven forbid if the press got a hold of this juicy morsel—John Lanier, respected attorney and candidate for Lieutenant Governor, in a love tryst with married woman, daughter of best friend…"

"Monique…I can't walk away from this. You know how much I want it. I mean, damn it! My whole life I've wanted this, and now I'm just supposed to throw it all away!?"

She looked at me with disgust, and then grabbed her coat, spitting the words out, "You're just like Clive. You're no different from him!" She slammed the door behind her. I remember looking at the clock—exactly midnight. I remember because I thought of the symbolism of it all. A moment before the beginning of a new day, and the moment I turned my back on the only real love I'd ever had.

"John! Are you listening to me?!"

I jolted back to reality. My wife was leaning in my face shouting. "Did you hear what I said????"

"No…No…I guess I'm in shock about Monique."

She slammed down her coffee cup, eyeing me suspiciously. "Well, I'm not. I always knew she'd end up to no good. Even as a little girl, she had a nasty temper. I'm not surprised at all."

My wife continued to talk, but I blocked out her words. I continued reading the article. *God, what am I going to do?* She was with *me* when Clive was killed. The coroner listed the time of death as between 11:30 and twelve midnight. I was her alibi. Her only alibi, and I saw my career shredding like a million pieces of gaudy confetti being blown away by the wind.

Desperate thoughts overwhelmed me. Maybe I didn't have to say anything. I could deny it if she told the truth. No one else saw us. No one else could prove that we were together. Maybe I could just say nothing.

CHAPTER THIRTY-EIGHT

Monique

Numb. The things that happened to me in the past forty-eight hours hadn't really happened to me but to someone else. I was merely a casual observer. Perhaps that's the only way that I could cope.

My bail hearing was slated for tomorrow. The look on my parents' face when they came down to the station will forever haunt me. As if all the hopes and dreams they'd had for me, their only child, had ended up as some cruel joke. A meaningless statistic. I wondered what they'd set bail at. My lawyer said it may go as high as a million dollars because it was a murder case, and they thought that I'd hop on a plane and disappear forever on some obscure South Sea island.

They wouldn't let me see my child, they decided it was better if she didn't know exactly where I was yet. Clive's mother had insisted on moving back in the apartment and caring for her. I wanted my parents to take her, but the psychologist thought it would be better for Ariel if she stayed in familiar surroundings. She'd grown so attached to Clive's mother during the time that she stayed with us after his death that everyone decided it was better for Ariel to be with her. Except for me. I didn't want his mother living in my apartment, sleeping in my bed, but my opinion didn't seem to matter these days.

I lay on the cot, staring at the cracked cement ceiling. My world had become a 10 X 12 holding cell. A cot, a toilet and my thoughts whirling around in my head. I'd called John when it happened. He was out of town and hadn't called me back. He knew the truth. But would he tell? Would I tell? What was worse, the humiliation of being charged with a crime that you didn't commit or exposure for one that you did? Which one would hurt my parents more? Which one would hurt my child more, murder or adultery with my father's best friend? Perhaps

John would lie. No one else saw us there. It was his word against mine. And with his career on the line, would he consider my life a necessary cost of doing business? I don't know. I thought I knew him, but now I wonder if I even know myself.

Sleep had started to invade my thoughts. I didn't fight it. I had no reason to stay awake. My world was more palatable in the dark anyway. I drifted into a dream but it all seemed so real. I was home in my apartment. It was the night that Clive was killed. But earlier. He was rushing off to some cocktail party. For once he came in to say goodbye. He must have wanted to talk about something. I didn't want to talk to him. My evening later with John, in the cottage, the place that had become my sanctuary, was the only thing on my mind.

Clive intruded on my thoughts. "Monique, I need to talk to you." I glanced his way, thinking what now.

"It won't take long."

"All right, so what is it?"

"I'm liquidating my business."

"I know you told me already…and?"

"And I'm not going to start another firm like I told you. I'm taking the money and I'm getting out of the business. I'm leaving New York."

I sat down stunned. "And what about Ariel and me? Does this mean that you'll finally agree to a divorce without fighting me every step of the way?

He was silent for a moment. "I don't know."

"What do you mean you don't know? You tell me you're going to pack up and move to God knows where, but you don't know what you want to do about our marriage and our child?" I stood in front of him, shaking with anger. And for the first time that I could remember he looked broken and weak. I shouted at him. "What is all this about anyway?"

"It's about trying to make some sense out of my life."

"Yes, at everyone else's expense as usual!"

"Monique…please…"

"What is it really, Clive? Are you finally going to go away for good with that woman?" I turned my back on him. "I hope you didn't think that I didn't know."

"No...I'm not leaving with her. I had planned to, and then I decided that I needed to be alone. I haven't told her yet. I can't be with anyone."

"Oh then there must be someone new. You've dumped both of us for some third woman."

"Monique, it's not about some woman. For Christ's sake, will you just listen to me for a minute!"

I pursed my lips, saying nothing.

"I've been doing a lot of thinking about my life lately, and everything I've always wanted for it...I don't know where it is or what it is anymore. I just need some time to sort it all out."

"So in the meantime, we're all just supposed to cool our heels until you come back from this spiritual retreat to wherever that you're going to...is that it?"

He walked over to me and took my hands. "I know I've been a bastard these past seven years. But will you try, could you try and...forgive me...just try?"

I looked at him, and I felt triumphant. For once Clive January was begging me for something, but I wasn't going to give him the satisfaction of getting his way. Not this time. I shook my head slowly, remembering the tears that I'd cried, the baby I'd lost, the humiliation of everyone knowing that your husband was playing you for a fool with another woman. "No. No, I will not forgive you. Ever. Never."

Clive turned and walked out of the room. And through the dream I remembered that that was the last time that I saw him alive. Except for now. Because the dream had ended, and now it's present time and we're talking.

I asked him, "Clive why did you marry me?"

He didn't hesitate, saying, "Because I thought I loved you and because you reminded me of someone that I had loved, like a mother.

She had loved my father, and he'd loved her. But I was jealous, and I wished that something would happen to break them apart."

"And it did?"

"Yes it did. My father was killed, so I got my wish. They were never together, but I lost my father, the only person who had ever loved me unconditionally without asking anything of me. So I married you thinking that maybe if I could make you happy, it would make up for the pain and sadness that I had caused my father and this woman. Instead, I only caused you more pain and sadness."

I wanted to go over to him and comfort him, but I couldn't. I was still too angry with him. I couldn't let myself release the anger. It felt like a cancer eating away at my flesh, but I wouldn't let it go.

"Do you know why I wanted to leave New York?" he asked.

"No."

"Because I was running."

"From what?"

"From her. My mother. She had found me, and I knew that she would torment me like she had when I was a child. So I had to get away. Until I could figure out how to get away from her for good in my head, so that even if she found me again, I wouldn't care.

"Every day I wondered if she'd come back to the apartment. If she'd try and ruin everything for me, like she'd tried before. So I figured that I'd close everything down before she could somehow snatch it away from me. I'd get away and figure out what to do with my life and figure out why I was still running from a woman whose only power was in my head. But I was afraid to take you or Ariel, because it seemed as if everyone that I'd ever loved had died because of me: my father, Red. And I didn't want that to happen to you."

I injected softly. "Or to that other woman."

"Or to her."

"That's why you were leaving alone."

"Yes…that's why."

"And where are you now?"

"I don't know. But I'm not free. I'm trapped somewhere, and I want so much to get out. But I can't. Something is holding me back, pushing me further and further into this darkness where I am."

Suddenly, I felt sorry for Clive, and I wasn't angry anymore. Because I saw him as he was, not the distant, arrogant man who'd been my husband, but a soul struggling to come to terms with his past.

"Did you ever love me, Monique?"

"Yes. You know I did."

Then I don't know why, but something pushed the words from deep inside of me. "I forgive you, Clive. I forgive you for everything." The minute I said it, I felt as if I had been absolved and purified from all of the anger and hatred I'd felt for him. And now *I* was being reborn and cleansed. And I wasn't afraid anymore. Looking around me, I saw that the place where I'd been was covered in a warm pink light that seemed to rotate around me. For a moment I saw Clive's eyes flash in front of me and I heard them say, "Thank you."

John

I bolted awake. I'd been dreaming about Monique, hearing her say—I forgive you. I had this wrenching feeling in my stomach, knowing I didn't deserve her forgiveness. Knowing that I had planned to walk away from her for my own ambition. Feeling this putrid sickness rising up in my mouth, I ran into the bathroom and vomited into the toilet. Hating myself.

I don't know how long I sat there on the cold tile floor. Long enough to pass over my life and examine painfully what it had become. My marriage had begun with the best of intentions. I did love my wife when I married her. The only problem was that I was so young that I don't really think that I knew what love was. And when I found out, I realized that I was married to the wrong person.

I stayed out of duty, out of obligation to my children and probably most importantly because I refused to admit failure. So I stayed. And stayed. Well past the time of boredom into the season of contempt. For that is what I felt for my wife now, contempt: for her pettiness, and meanness and her hardness of heart. For the fact that she didn't love me either but still she stayed, for her own reasons.My career. An auspicious start, Harvard Law School, the best firm, then my own practice, well respected, turning away business I had so much. A roller coaster of success that wouldn't end. Until my ambition, my ego, my need to prove that I could be more, that I could have it all, money and power, knocked me into the ditch. A disastrous Congressional campaign, forced withdrawal. But not a failure, I would not admit failure. I'd run again. They'd want me again. And they did, the Lieutenant Governor's race was just the beginning. They had plans for me, bigger than the ones I imagined for myself. So no, I could not turn my back on it. It was the right thing to do. To hell with everyone and everything else.

So then why did I feel like I could never look at myself in the mirror again? Why did I have this sour feeling in my stomach ever since my wife shoved the paper in my face, crowing triumphantly over my lover's fate? As if she secretly knew the truth. Why did I dream of Monique every night? And why couldn't I live with myself another minute?

Is it worth it? I'd never squarely asked myself that question. But now I had to. *Is it worth it? Is losing any goodness that I have left in my soul worth it?* A Faustian dilemma if ever there was one. I always knew the answer, even without asking. I just had to hear her say "I forgive you" to push me into the inevitability of what I must do. Not just for her. But for me so that I could live again. And live with myself.

CHAPTER THIRTY-NINE

Detective Bob & Clive

Cameras flashing. A parade of lights and reporters. I was watching it all, seeing the reporter shove the microphone in John Lanier's face as he held tightly to Monique January's hand. "Mr. Lanier why didn't you come forward as soon as Mrs. January was charged? Why did you wait until now to tell the police that she was with you?"

"Mr. Lanier, are you going to withdraw from the race for Lieutenant Governor?"

"Mr. Lanier, what was your wife's reaction? Are you and Mrs. January going to marry?"

"Mr. Lanier, we need a statement!" Lanier and Monique January ducked their heads, trying to skirt away from the knot of photographers following them out of the station.

I just stood there thinking. *Shit. What the hell just happened?*

It had all started yesterday. Lanier had come in to give a statement. He admitted that Monique January had been with him that night and that between the hours of 11 and midnight, they were in some cottage that he rented. He gave the statement under oath. It turned out that someone else had seen her pull up to the place. A kid riding around, lived in the area, he identified Monique's car and remembered seeing it pull up around ten. When the kid rode past there around midnight, he said the car was still there.

My head was spinning, but what about the gun? It was the murder weapon. It checked out with ballistics. I'd even had them run the test again. How had it gotten there? I was thinking all of that as Monique January and Lanier ducked into a waiting car. Driving away to freedom.

Snatches of things were stacking up in front of me. The Japanese connection, Haven and Simmons—the gun. Laurel Davenport—the gun. The gun. I couldn't get away from the gun. I knew it was the murder weapon. I'd stake my whole fuckin' career on it. How did it get there? Dolly. No...Maybe...who else...who else...And then I started running, 'cause I knew this time.

She opened the door, and I looked into the eyes of Clive's murderer. "You did it, didn't you?"

"What you talkin' 'bout?"

"You killed your son, and then planted the gun in Monique's closet to make it seem like she did it! Didn't you!"

She laughed—a cruel, hard-edged laugh, not scared, not defensive. "Yeah...and so what of it? Who's gonna send an old woman to jai? I'll be dead 'fore the trial begins anyway." She slumped down into a chair, her thin, bony face looking more gaunt and pained than I remembered.

"Naaana..." Ariel wandered in the room, clutching her blanket. She climbed into Clive's mother's lap. She stroked Ariel's hair tenderly, kissing her on the top of the head and saying gently, "You go on upstairs and play for a bit...Nana'll be right up."

Ariel gave her grandmother the sweetest smile. "O...kay." She skipped out of the room, humming to herself.

Clive's mother turned to me and all the gentleness was gone. "That's why I did it...'cause of her...my grandbaby. He was gonna take her away from me. He wouldn't let me be with her."

With an intensity that looked like it would burn through me, she sat up. "That boy took everything from me, everything. I tried to send him away when he was young, so I could get some life of my own, but 'stead he took my husband from me. Like I said, he took everything from me, and he wasn't taking her, too. I wasn't gonna spend the last days of my life alone 'cause of him. And that chile is all I got."

She sank back in the seat, closing her eyes. "I got cancer. I don't have much time, so what did I have to lose? Nothin. Nothin at 'tall. So I went out there. I knew he'd be goin' out to that place of his, and when his girlfriend left, I shot him. In the back. And then I left." She squared herself off and gazed into my eyes. "And I ain't sorry."

I was trying to shout out something, but I was frozen. In front of me I saw a darkness blotting out the lamp in the corner of the room, suddenly coming up through the floor, surrounding Clive's mother. I could barely see her through the darkness. Then I saw Clive. Anger and disbelief were on his face, as if for the first time he understood who had done this to him.

He shouted, "I hate you! I hate you. I've always hated you!" Clive's voice cracked with all the pain he must've held in since he was a kid. "You were always the one who spoiled everything for me!" I could see tears on Clive's face. "You could never just let me be happy!"

His mother turned and hissed back at him, "You didn't deserve happiness. You ain't never been nothing but trouble for everybody you ever been around, yo wife, yo girlfriend, you brung nothin' but pain to everybody!"

"You're the one! Not me! That's why Daddy left you. That's why he took me with him and left you." The darkness around Clive was getting thicker as he shouted. "I wished you'd died instead of Daddy!"

"Yo Daddy, yo precious Daddy, always yo Daddy." His mother laughed cruelly and then stopped herself, almost like she'd wanted to say something for years, but then didn't.

I got this sick feeling in the pit of my stomach. My hand was shaking hard. My whole body was vibrating. The darkness had taken shape. I could clearly see that it was apart of Clive. Its face was distorted with hatred, ugly and twisted with anger. I wanted to shout out—Clive stop, don't say anymore. Can't you see what's happening—but I couldn't. My voice was frozen. This ugly part of Clive was getting stronger and was shouting out, "Why couldn't you've died instead of Daddy? Daddy loved me. My life would've been so different if he'd still been here. Why were you the one who lived, instead of Daddy?!"

His mother pulled herself out of her chair and hurled words at Clive, "He wasn't yo daddy! I don't know who yo daddy was! Four of 'em raped me! You ain't got no daddy!"

For a minute it was quiet, like something had been yanked out of Clive. I could see his eyes through the darkness, tears clotting his throat as the words tumbled out of him, "I already know everything! Daddy told me the truth. He wrote me a letter. He told me what had happened, and he told me he loved me. That I was his real son, no matter what. He didn't care what had happened. He told me he loved me!"

"He didn't love you. Nobody could love a chile like you that come in the world in shame like that. He didn't love you no mo than them that done it to me—that day—that day God punished me. I don't know why God punished me with you…"

Her voice kinda trailed off, and she stumbled over to a chair, sinking into it weakly, like even after all those years she couldn't stand to remember what they'd done to her. "Did he tell you how it happened? Did he tell you I was walking through the woods taking the shortcut Ma had told me not to take when I heard 'em? They was drunk, and then when I seen 'em I thought I was gonna be all right 'cause I knowed 'em. We'd growed up together, played together. I thought they'd leave me alone. They was like brothers to me, but they didn't. They wanted me, and they took me. All four of 'em. Even though I knowed 'em. That's why nobody believed me. 'cause I knowed 'em, they told everybody that I'd asked for it. That I was always actin' so uppity with everybody. Like I thought I was too good for the boys there. That I asked for it. They said, that'd show me tryin' to put on airs and act like I was too good for that town. And when I tried to tell 'em what really happened, nobody believed me. Nobody. Not even my own pa. Nobody believed me!"

"But it wasn't my fault!" Clive's voice sounded like he'd broken in two, cracked with the wear and tear of never being loved by your own mother. "I didn't ask to be born! All these years you've blamed me for something that wasn't my fault!"

His mother whirled around, and I could see tears on her face as she barely choked out the words, "It wasn't your fault? Well it was your fault the whole town turned on me. Sheriff wouldn't do nothin', nobody cared 'bout a sixteen year old colored girl that got raped by four sixteen year old colored boys. Nobody gave a damn 'bout me. An' then when I got real big with you, they kicked me outta high school. A pregnant colored girl couldn't finish high school.

"So all my dreams of getting out, of doing something big with my life was gone. Jus' like that. An' every time I looked at yo face, I seen the reason I spent my life in a factory sewin' on buttons 'stead of making something of myself. I seen the reason I never married the man I loved, 'cause he dropped me after I got pregnant with you, left me jus' like that. I never loved yo daddy. The man I loved left me 'cause of you!"

"That's why you stole my college applications, because you hadn't done anything with your life, you weren't gonna let me either. I hate you. I wish you'd been the one who'd died instead of Daddy. I wish you'd been the one!"

Now I could see that with every word, the dark part of Clive was taking over him, wrapping itself tighter around him. First his legs. Then twisting around his arms. And his neck. Like a hungry boa constrictor. Strangling him slowly. He was being strangled and choked by this evil twisted version of himself that he couldn't run from 'cause it was him.

A shaft of light cut through the blackness. Little pinwheels of brilliant color were shooting toward Clive. The shape of a man had started to form. I heard a voice come out from the bright light saying, "Clive...we don't want to lose you..."

Clive could barely get the words out. "Who is it? Who's out there?!" He was drowned out by screeching voices coming from the dark part of himself. Even louder than before.

Now the whole room was shaking with the cries. "Don't listen to him, remember everything that she did to you, remember!"

The light grew stronger. I saw a man step out from the brightness, walk out to Clive and put his hand on his shoulder. A tall black man, and he whispered, "You can escape. You have the power. You just have to use it."

"Daddy!" Clive tried to reach out to his father, but the darkness in him was so thick that he couldn't get through.

I could hear the twisted mocking version of Clive's voice say, "Don't listen to him. He's lying. He's not your father!"

Some part of Clive, the goodness that was resisting the hate, still knew the truth. He cried out, his voice choking with pain, "Daddy, I've been trying to come to you, ever since...I...died, but I can't. Something's holding me back...Daddy, help me, please, help me!"

His father seemed to glow with an inner light that was bigger than him, coming from some far away place. But he shook his head sadly saying, "They won't let me, Clive. You've got to do it yourself." "But, Daddy, I don't know how!"

Clive's father started getting fainter, but his words rang out clearly. "Remember the love they gave you."

"Who, Daddy, who are you talking about?"

Clive's father was getting fainter and fainter. Clive cried out desperately. "Daddy, don't leave me. Not again!"

His father's image was completely gone, and his voice was just a whisper in the room saying, "Remember the love."

Frantically, Clive tried to push the darkness in himself away, begging, "Daddy, please don't leave me here!" Before his father could answer, Clive's mother rushed over to him, blotting out the last slivers of his father's light.

"I told you he didn't love you! Nobody's ever loved you. Not him or none a them. They jus' used you, like you used them. You don't know nothin' 'bout lovin' nobody,"

"You're wrong, you're the one who could never love me or anybody, and I'm *not* like you!" Clive raised his hands to his mother's neck. The thick blackness pouring out of Clive covered them both. I could barely see anything but I could hear him, "I'm not like you!"

Clive's other voice whispered, "Kill her. Kill her. You hate her. Kill her!" Clive tightened his grasp around her neck, draining the color from her face. He was choking his mother, harder and harder, she'd stopped fighting back. Her eyes closed. She was struggling to breathe.

Coughing and choking in the blackness, he suddenly stopped himself. Looking at his mother and then down at his hands in horror. It was like he finally understood—the same darkness that had surrounded her *was* in him. And it was eating him up just as it had twisted and worked itself into her.

"I'm not like you, Ma," he said shakily.

He stumbled away from her weakly. I couldn't see his face at all because of the blackness around him. I could barely hear him say, "I'm not like you…I do know what it is to love somebody and to be loved. They loved me. Monique loved me and Laurel loved me, and I loved them. Even after everything between us, they still loved me, because they…" and then he stopped, like he knew why he was where he was and…what had *really* held him back. "They forgave me…Oh God, they forgave me."

The voices, the twisted angry part of Clive screeched louder, "It's a lie. It's all a lie. They didn't forgive you. They all hated you. They were lying." The darkness within Clive knotted itself around every part of his body.

I could see Clive gathering all of his strength to break free, screaming, "You're wrong. You're all wrong. They both forgave me. They should've hated me. They could've after everything I did, but they didn't…instead…they forgave. They forgave *me*."

He was trying to push the darkness away from him. Trembling and shaking, exhausted, but determined to pull the words out from his soul. "Now I understand what Daddy meant. He tried to get me to understand all those years ago. He asked me to forgive you, but I couldn't. I just couldn't. And that's what's been holding me back all these years. The hate I had for you and who I was, is what kept me from forgiving and moving on with my life. It kept me from getting over all the pain. It was always the hate. And Daddy was right. I had the power. I could've let go, But I didn't want to. That's why I could never get to him, 'cause Daddy only had love…like Laurel and Monique. They let go of all the pain I'd caused them, and they forgave me…I understand. I finally understand…It's so clear now."

He hesitated, then slowly and deliberately said, "I forgive you, Ma. I forgive you…I understand now and I forgive you."

Slowly the darkness started lifting. I could see tears rolling down his face as he said softly, "I forgive you, Ma. I forgive you." Little starbursts of light were starting to eat away at the dark cloud. I could tell that Clive was getting stronger and stronger each time he said, "I forgive you."

The starbursts of light ate deeper and deeper into the cloud, dissolving the anger and hatred, pushing it away until Clive was covered completely in light. His face was radiant, and the darkness was gone completely from him. For the first time since all this craziness started, Clive looked at peace.

"I don't need yo' pity," his mother screamed. "Who is you to forgive me? You is nothin' but a bastard chile that nobody loves. Nobody, so keep it and get away from me. Get away… Ariel, Ariel, come to Nana Ariel!!!"

Clive's mother started running out of the room, yelling angrily, "You ain't takin' her from me. You ain't!" Something stopped her. She was rolling on the ground, doubled over in pain. I realized it was all of the hatred inside of her that had turned itself outward. Coiling itself around her neck and her chest, squeezing tighter and tighter. Until she was screaming in pain. I heard her neck snap in two. A huge tremor went through her body. And she was still. I ran over to her, but I knew before I got there that she was dead.

The room was quiet now. Clive was gone. I don't know how much time had passed. Thoughts were swirling around in me, and I could barely lift my head. The only sound was the soft padding of small feet. I could feel someone tugging insistently at the bottom of my coat. Looking down, I could see Ariel's scared eyes as she said, "Is Nana asleep?" As I picked her up gently, I heard a key turn in the lock. I looked up and met Monique's stare.

"Mama!" Ariel jumped out of my arms and raced toward her mother. Before Monique could say anything, I brushed past her quickly, avoiding John Lanier's accusatory glance and saying, "I'll call an ambulance."

The next day I turned in my resignation. I knew that what had gone on was just for my eyes, so I didn't say anything when I gave the captain my file on the case. I implied that he might want to look into Haven and Simmons, but he just said, "I don't think so, Greene. I'm just gonna throw this one in the unsolved pile. And it's a good thing you decided to quit, 'cause after the way you fucked this one up, your career was over anyway."

Instead of being angry. I felt at peace. Because I knew that I had found out the truth. And I knew the captain was wrong, dead wrong, 'cause my career was just starting. Maybe not there, but somewhere else where I could be the kinda cop I'd always meant to be, the one who cared about the underdog and didn't give a damn if it ruffled some feathers to find out the truth, 'cause that's all that really mattered in the end. The truth.

I couldn't help remembering the reason I became a cop twenty years ago. I kept remembering my mother's voice telling me to help people, that's what our family's about, she told me as she died. And I knew that I'd kept my promise to her and to my grandfather and everybody else who'd died with their principles—'cause I'd helped Clive know the truth and escape from that place of darkness and hate and despair.

If I could keep on doin' that for other poor guys like him that the system didn't give a damn about enough to keep on digging for the truth, then my life was worth living. I didn't care if the captain or anybody else there knew or not, 'cause I knew, and Clive knew, and that's all that really mattered to me.

There was one other thing—Margie. I had a feeling that me being there at the end with Clive had been for a reason, and I couldn't put my head in the sand and pretend there was nothin' I had to do before I could be free, too. So I went to see her, 'cause that was the only way to try and make things right again.

"Well, hello…"

She opened the door, but not quite wide enough for me to come in, so I asked, "D'ya mind if I come in for a sec?"

She didn't say anything, just stood aside and let me in. I kinda plopped down on the couch. Knowing this wasn't gonna be easy, but I had to do it. I had to for me. "Margie, a lotta shit has happened the past coupla days—"

She cut me off, "I already heard. I know you resigned and I…know it's probably not a great time for you."

Normally I woulda been pissed from the pity in her voice, but it wasn't about that anymore. "That's not what I wanted to tell ya…'cause truth is, I'm glad I'm gone. I shoulda left a long time ago."

She raised one eyebrow like she didn't really believe me.

"Truth is, Margie, I came here 'cause I've been a real s.o.b to you—not just recently, but for a while. I know I was a selfish shit not to have married you when you wanted and when I could've, and I'm sorry. I know it can't bring back the lost years. But I am really sorry. And I just wondered…well if you could, maybe…just maybe…forgive me…"

I don't know what I expected her to say. I guess just something. But she didn't say nothin'. She just got up and went into the bedroom. I was sitting there wondering if she was trying to give me the ultimate brush off and whether I should try and save whatever little bit of pride I had by leaving before she kicked me out when she came back and handed me a piece of paper.

"Open it."

I opened it, and then kinda caught myself, 'cause it was a letter I'd written her when we first started dating: "Margie, I'm not much of a writer, but I wanted to let you know that you make me feel like nothin' else in the world matters except us. That nothin' else in the world could make me sad or mad as long as you're in my corner, rooting for me…Love Always, Bob."

She leaned against the wall. "I just kept hoping that the old Bob who wrote me those words would come back into my life. Instead, you kept getting farther and farther away. Then one day I realized it wasn't really about me, it was about you and your own demons."

She came over and sat on the edge of the sofa. "I can forgive you, Bob. But can you forgive yourself?"

Suddenly it all made sense, about Clive and me, and his mother and my dad…and all the anger and self-hate I'd had, and why I'd pushed Margie away. And now it was like I could hear Clive whispering to me, "You can do it, Bob…I did it…You can do it…"

And I looked at myself from the inside out, and for the first time I saw myself. I saw the man I'd always tried to be, the good and the bad. I saw my dad. As he was. The good and the bad. A frustrated man who'd never really liked himself or the lot that life had handed him. I realized that I'd been so afraid of being like him, that I had become him. And I couldn't forgive myself. I knew that was the key, forgiving myself. It wasn't going to be easy, but I had to start right now really trying to forgive me. I pulled Margie on the couch next to me and just held her saying, "Thank you."

Sitting there with her, remembering what we'd been to each other, I couldn't help wondering if this was the beginning or the end for us. "What d'ya think, can we try it again?" She looked at me, like for the first time she didn't know. So she didn't say anything, she just smiled.

"Is that a no or a yes?"

She hesitated. "It's a maybe." She musta seen the disappointment on my face. I was never good at hiding my feelings. She kissed me on my forehead the way she used to and said, "But a strong maybe." I knew the old Margie was back and life was lookin' real good. At last.

I felt like I was ready to start all over, so I packed up my shit and got ready to leave New York. Once I got settled, Margie promised to follow me, and this time we'd do it right. I planned to load up my car and head west to start a new life, finally at peace with myself. I didn't even need to bring my bottle of Jack, 'cause I'd found the answers, and they were inside of me. For the first time I felt good about myself and where I was going.

As I was putting the last things in the car, I thought about Clive. I never really got to say goodbye or thank you or anything. As I thought of him, I could feel his presence the way I used to in the beginning. And I knew he was there. But I could really see him for the first time. He walked up to me, closer and closer until, I could feel the light coming from him, covering me. I looked down at my hand, and I realized that it wasn't shaking anymore, and I felt light and at peace like it was me glowing at the same time as him. I heard him say…

"What are you going to do now?"

The words in my head said, "I don't know. I'm just happy to get myself back, to feel good about me again. It's been a long time..." I looked at him, and I could see that all his pain was gone. I realized it was gone from me, too. "I got you to thank for that..."

He nodded and smiled. "Thank *you,* Bob Greene...for not giving up on me..."

I wanted to say more, but I could see that he was starting to fade, like he was walking away but slowly. He squeezed my hand. I looked down my hand was glowing the way he'd been, and he said, "We're brothers, and we'll meet again."

I nodded yes. I knew what he meant. 'cause when you live each other's lives the way we had, part of him was in me and part of me was in him, and in the end you are family. And nothin' can ever take that away.

Clive

It's like the dream again. Except that I'm dead, so I can't be dreaming. But I feel like it because I'm floating. I see Daddy in the distance, and he's holding out his hand to me, but this time nothing's holding me back. I run to him. And he puts his arm around me.

I'm ten years old again, and Daddy says, "How's my, little Clive?"

And everything is finally okay.

ABOUT THE AUTHOR

Lisa Jones Johnson is a television executive in Los Angeles. Earlier in her career she worked as a screenwriter and originally began as a corporate attorney in New York on Wall Street. She has always been fascinated with the thin veil between this life and the next and thus the inspiration for her novel. She lives in Los Angeles with her husband and infant son. She may be reached at **adeadmanspeaks@yahoo.com** or **www.adeadmanspeaks.com**.

2006 Publication Schedule

	January	
A Lover's Legacy Veronica Parker 1-58571-167-5 $9.95	Love Lasts Forever Dominiqua Douglas 1-58571-187-X $9.95	Under the Cherry Moon Christal Jordan-Mims 1-58571-169-1 $12.95
	February	
Second Chances at Love Cheris Hodges 1-58571-188-8 $9.95	Enchanted Desire Wanda Y. Thomas 1-58571-176-4 $9.95	Caught Up Deatri King Bey 1-58571-178-0 $12.95
	March	
I'm Gonna Make You Love Me Gwyneth Bolton 1-58571-181-0 $9.95	Through the Fire Seressia Glass 1-58571-173-X $9.95	Notes When Summer Ends Beverly Lauderdale 1-58571-180-2 $12.95
	April	
Sin and Surrender J.M. Jeffries 1-58571-189-6 $9.95	Unearthing Passions Elaine Sims 1-58571-184-5 $9.95	Between Tears Pamela Ridley 1-58571-179-9 $12.95
	May	
Misty Blue Dyanne Davis 1-58571-186-1 $9.95	Ironic Pamela Leigh Starr 1-58571-168-3 $9.95	Cricket's Serenade Carolita Blythe 1-58571-183-7 $12.95
	June	
Cupid Barbara Keaton 1-58571-174-8 $9.95	Havana Sunrise Kymberly Hunt 1-58571-182-9 $9.95	

2006 Publication Schedule (continued)

July

Love Me Carefully
A.C. Arthur
1-58571-177-2
$9.95

No Ordinary Love
Angela Weaver
1-58571-198-5
$9.95

Rehoboth Road
Anita Ballard-Jones
1-58571-196-9
$12.95

August

Scent of Rain
Annetta P. Lee
158571-199-3
$9.95

Love in High Gear
Charlotte Roy
158571-185-3
$9.95

Rise of the Phoenix
Kenneth Whetstone
1-58571-197-7
$12.95

September

The Business of Love
Cheris Hodges
1-58571-193-4
$9.95

Rock Star
Rosyln Hardy Holcomb
1-58571-200-0
$9.95

A Dead Man Speaks
Lisa Jones Johnson
1-58571-203-5
$12.95

October

Rivers of the Soul-Part 1
Leslie Esdaile
1-58571-223-X
$9.95

A Dangerous Woman
J.M. Jeffries
1-58571-195-0
$9.95

Sinful Intentions
Crystal Rhodes
1-58571-201-9
$12.95

November

Only You
Crystal Hubbard
1-58571-208-6
$9.95

Ebony Eyes
Kei Swanson
1-58571-194-2
$9.95

Still Waters Run Deep – Part 2
Leslie Esdaile
1-58571-224-8
$9.95

December

Let's Get It On
Dyanne Davis
1-58571-210-8
$9.95

Nights Over Egypt
Barbara Keaton
1-58571-192-6
$9.95

A Pefect Place to Pray
I.L. Goodwin
1-58571-202-7
$12.95

Other Genesis Press, Inc. Titles

A Dangerous Deception	J.M. Jeffries	$8.95
A Dangerous Love	J.M. Jeffries	$8.95
A Dangerous Obsession	J.M. Jeffries	$8.95
A Drummer's Beat to Mend	Kei Swanson	$9.95
A Happy Life	Charlotte Harris	$9.95
A Heart's Awakening	Veronica Parker	$9.95
A Lark on the Wing	Phyliss Hamilton	$9.95
A Love of Her Own	Cheris F. Hodges	$9.95
A Love to Cherish	Beverly Clark	$8.95
A Risk of Rain	Dar Tomlinson	$8.95
A Twist of Fate	Beverly Clark	$8.95
A Will to Love	Angie Daniels	$9.95
Acquisitions	Kimberley White	$8.95
Across	Carol Payne	$12.95
After the Vows	Leslie Esdaile	$10.95
(Summer Anthology)	T.T. Henderson	
	Jacqueline Thomas	
Again My Love	Kayla Perrin	$10.95
Against the Wind	Gwynne Forster	$8.95
All I Ask	Barbara Keaton	$8.95
Ambrosia	T.T. Henderson	$8.95
An Unfinished Love Affair	Barbara Keaton	$8.95
And Then Came You	Dorothy Elizabeth Love	$8.95
Angel's Paradise	Janice Angelique	$9.95
At Last	Lisa G. Riley	$8.95
Best of Friends	Natalie Dunbar	$8.95
Beyond the Rapture	Beverly Clark	$9.95
Blaze	Barbara Keaton	$9.95
Blood Lust	J. M. Jeffries	$9.95
Bodyguard	Andrea Jackson	$9.95
Boss of Me	Diana Nyad	$8.95
Bound by Love	Beverly Clark	$8.95
Breeze	Robin Hampton Allen	$10.95

Other Genesis Press, Inc. Titles (continued)

Broken	Dar Tomlinson	$24.95
By Design	Barbara Keaton	$8.95
Cajun Heat	Charlene Berry	$8.95
Careless Whispers	Rochelle Alers	$8.95
Cats & Other Tales	Marilyn Wagner	$8.95
Caught in a Trap	Andre Michelle	$8.95
Caught Up In the Rapture	Lisa G. Riley	$9.95
Cautious Heart	Cheris F Hodges	$8.95
Chances	Pamela Leigh Starr	$8.95
Cherish the Flame	Beverly Clark	$8.95
Class Reunion	Irma Jenkins/John Brown	$12.95
Code Name: Diva	J.M. Jeffries	$9.95
Conquering Dr. Wexler's Heart	Kimberley White	$9.95
Crossing Paths, Tempting Memories	Dorothy Elizabeth Love	$9.95
Cypress Whisperings	Phyllis Hamilton	$8.95
Dark Embrace	Crystal Wilson Harris	$8.95
Dark Storm Rising	Chinelu Moore	$10.95
Daughter of the Wind	Joan Xian	$8.95
Deadly Sacrifice	Jack Kean	$22.95
Designer Passion	Dar Tomlinson	$8.95
Dreamtective	Liz Swados	$5.95
Ebony Butterfly II	Delilah Dawson	$14.95
Echoes of Yesterday	Beverly Clark	$9.95
Eden's Garden	Elizabeth Rose	$8.95
Everlastin' Love	Gay G. Gunn	$8.95
Everlasting Moments	Dorothy Elizabeth Love	$8.95
Everything and More	Sinclair Lebeau	$8.95
Everything but Love	Natalie Dunbar	$8.95
Eve's Prescription	Edwina Martin Arnold	$8.95
Falling	Natalie Dunbar	$9.95
Fate	Pamela Leigh Starr	$8.95
Finding Isabella	A.J. Garrotto	$8.95

Other Genesis Press, Inc. Titles (continued)

Forbidden Quest	Dar Tomlinson	$10.95
Forever Love	Wanda Thomas	$8.95
From the Ashes	Kathleen Suzanne Jeanne Sumerix	$8.95
Gentle Yearning	Rochelle Alers	$10.95
Glory of Love	Sinclair LeBeau	$10.95
Go Gentle into that Good Night	Malcom Boyd	$12.95
Goldengroove	Mary Beth Craft	$16.95
Groove, Bang, and Jive	Steve Cannon	$8.99
Hand in Glove	Andrea Jackson	$9.95
Hard to Love	Kimberley White	$9.95
Hart & Soul	Angie Daniels	$8.95
Heartbeat	Stephanie Bedwell-Grime	$8.95
Hearts Remember	M. Loui Quezada	$8.95
Hidden Memories	Robin Allen	$10.95
Higher Ground	Leah Latimer	$19.95
Hitler, the War, and the Pope	Ronald Rychiak	$26.95
How to Write a Romance	Kathryn Falk	$18.95
I Married a Reclining Chair	Lisa M. Fuhs	$8.95
Indigo After Dark Vol. I	Nia Dixon/Angelique	$10.95
Indigo After Dark Vol. II	Dolores Bundy/Cole Riley	$10.95
Indigo After Dark Vol. III	Montana Blue/Coco Morena	$10.95
Indigo After Dark Vol. IV	Cassandra Colt/ Diana Richeaux	$14.95
Indigo After Dark Vol. V	Delilah Dawson	$14.95
Icie	Pamela Leigh Starr	$8.95
I'll Be Your Shelter	Giselle Carmichael	$8.95
I'll Paint a Sun	A.J. Garrotto	$9.95
Illusions	Pamela Leigh Starr	$8.95
Indiscretions	Donna Hill	$8.95
Intentional Mistakes	Michele Sudler	$9.95
Interlude	Donna Hill	$8.95
Intimate Intentions	Angie Daniels	$8.95

Other Genesis Press, Inc. Titles (continued)

Jolie's Surrender	Edwina Martin-Arnold	$8.95
Kiss or Keep	Debra Phillips	$8.95
Lace	Giselle Carmichael	$9.95
Last Train to Memphis	Elsa Cook	$12.95
Lasting Valor	Ken Olsen	$24.95
Let Us Prey	Hunter Lundy	$25.95
Life Is Never As It Seems	J.J. Michael	$12.95
Lighter Shade of Brown	Vicki Andrews	$8.95
Love Always	Mildred E. Riley	$10.95
Love Doesn't Come Easy	Charlyne Dickerson	$8.95
Love Unveiled	Gloria Greene	$10.95
Love's Deception	Charlene Berry	$10.95
Love's Destiny	M. Loui Quezada	$8.95
Mae's Promise	Melody Walcott	$8.95
Magnolia Sunset	Giselle Carmichael	$8.95
Matters of Life and Death	Lesego Malepe, Ph.D.	$15.95
Meant to Be	Jeanne Sumerix	$8.95
Midnight Clear	Leslie Esdaile	$10.95
(Anthology)	Gwynne Forster	
	Carmen Green	
	Monica Jackson	
Midnight Magic	Gwynne Forster	$8.95
Midnight Peril	Vicki Andrews	$10.95
Misconceptions	Pamela Leigh Starr	$9.95
Montgomery's Children	Richard Perry	$14.95
My Buffalo Soldier	Barbara B. K. Reeves	$8.95
Naked Soul	Gwynne Forster	$8.95
Next to Last Chance	Louisa Dixon	$24.95
No Apologies	Seressia Glass	$8.95
No Commitment Required	Seressia Glass	$8.95
No Regrets	Mildred E. Riley	$8.95
Nowhere to Run	Gay G. Gunn	$10.95
O Bed! O Breakfast!	Rob Kuehnle	$14.95

Other Genesis Press, Inc. Titles (continued)

Object of His Desire	A. C. Arthur	$8.95
Office Policy	A. C. Arthur	$9.95
Once in a Blue Moon	Dorianne Cole	$9.95
One Day at a Time	Bella McFarland	$8.95
Outside Chance	Louisa Dixon	$24.95
Passion	T.T. Henderson	$10.95
Passion's Blood	Cherif Fortin	$22.95
Passion's Journey	Wanda Thomas	$8.95
Past Promises	Jahmel West	$8.95
Path of Fire	T.T. Henderson	$8.95
Path of Thorns	Annetta P. Lee	$9.95
Peace Be Still	Colette Haywood	$12.95
Picture Perfect	Reon Carter	$8.95
Playing for Keeps	Stephanie Salinas	$8.95
Pride & Joi	Gay G. Gunn	$15.95
Pride & Joi	Gay G. Gunn	$8.95
Promises to Keep	Alicia Wiggins	$8.95
Quiet Storm	Donna Hill	$10.95
Reckless Surrender	Rochelle Alers	$6.95
Red Polka Dot in a World of Plaid	Varian Johnson	$12.95
Reluctant Captive	Joyce Jackson	$8.95
Rendezvous with Fate	Jeanne Sumerix	$8.95
Revelations	Cheris F. Hodges	$8.95
Rivers of the Soul	Leslie Esdaile	$8.95
Rocky Mountain Romance	Kathleen Suzanne	$8.95
Rooms of the Heart	Donna Hill	$8.95
Rough on Rats and Tough on Cats	Chris Parker	$12.95
Secret Library Vol. 1	Nina Sheridan	$18.95
Secret Library Vol. 2	Cassandra Colt	$8.95
Shades of Brown	Denise Becker	$8.95
Shades of Desire	Monica White	$8.95

Other Genesis Press, Inc. Titles (continued)

Shadows in the Moonlight	Jeanne Sumerix	$8.95
Sin	Crystal Rhodes	$8.95
So Amazing	Sinclair LeBeau	$8.95
Somebody's Someone	Sinclair LeBeau	$8.95
Someone to Love	Alicia Wiggins	$8.95
Song in the Park	Martin Brant	$15.95
Soul Eyes	Wayne L. Wilson	$12.95
Soul to Soul	Donna Hill	$8.95
Southern Comfort	J.M. Jeffries	$8.95
Still the Storm	Sharon Robinson	$8.95
Still Waters Run Deep	Leslie Esdaile	$8.95
Stories to Excite You	Anna Forrest/Divine	$14.95
Subtle Secrets	Wanda Y. Thomas	$8.95
Suddenly You	Crystal Hubbard	$9.95
Sweet Repercussions	Kimberley White	$9.95
Sweet Tomorrows	Kimberly White	$8.95
Taken by You	Dorothy Elizabeth Love	$9.95
Tattooed Tears	T. T. Henderson	$8.95
The Color Line	Lizzette Grayson Carter	$9.95
The Color of Trouble	Dyanne Davis	$8.95
The Disappearance of Allison Jones	Kayla Perrin	$5.95
The Honey Dipper's Legacy	Pannell-Allen	$14.95
The Joker's Love Tune	Sidney Rickman	$15.95
The Little Pretender	Barbara Cartland	$10.95
The Love We Had	Natalie Dunbar	$8.95
The Man Who Could Fly	Bob & Milana Beamon	$18.95
The Missing Link	Charlyne Dickerson	$8.95
The Price of Love	Sinclair LeBeau	$8.95
The Smoking Life	Ilene Barth	$29.95
The Words of the Pitcher	Kei Swanson	$8.95
Three Wishes	Seressia Glass	$8.95
Ties That Bind	Kathleen Suzanne	$8.95
Tiger Woods	Libby Hughes	$5.95

Other Genesis Press, Inc. Titles (continued)

Time is of the Essence	Angie Daniels	$9.95
Timeless Devotion	Bella McFarland	$9.95
Tomorrow's Promise	Leslie Esdaile	$8.95
Truly Inseparable	Wanda Y. Thomas	$8.95
Unbreak My Heart	Dar Tomlinson	$8.95
Uncommon Prayer	Kenneth Swanson	$9.95
Unconditional	A.C. Arthur	$9.95
Unconditional Love	Alicia Wiggins	$8.95
Until Death Do Us Part	Susan Paul	$8.95
Vows of Passion	Bella McFarland	$9.95
Wedding Gown	Dyanne Davis	$8.95
What's Under Benjamin's Bed	Sandra Schaffer	$8.95
When Dreams Float	Dorothy Elizabeth Love	$8.95
Whispers in the Night	Dorothy Elizabeth Love	$8.95
Whispers in the Sand	LaFlorya Gauthier	$10.95
Wild Ravens	Altonya Washington	$9.95
Yesterday Is Gone	Beverly Clark	$10.95
Yesterday's Dreams, Tomorrow's Promises	Reon Laudat	$8.95
Your Precious Love	Sinclair LeBeau	$8.95

Order Form

Mail to: Genesis Press, Inc.
P.O. Box 101
Columbus, MS 39703

Name ____________________
Address ____________________
City/State ______________ Zip ________
Telephone ______________

Ship to (if different from above)
Name ____________________
Address ____________________
City/State ______________ Zip ________
Telephone ______________

Credit Card Information
Credit Card # ______________ ☐Visa ☐Mastercard
Expiration Date (mm/yy) ______________ ☐AmEx ☐Discover

Qty.	Author	Title	Price	Total

Use this order form, or call 1-888-INDIGO-1

Total for books ________
Shipping and handling:
$5 first two books,
$1 each additional book ________
Total S & H ________
Total amount enclosed ________

Mississippi residents add 7% sales tax